MAY 13th
2012

Jul
2

G000047716

FULL CREW

KARLINE SMITH

The
X
Press

Published by
The X Press
PO Box 25694
London, N17 6FP
Tel: 020 8801 2100
Fax: 020 8885 1322
E-mail: vibes@xpress.co.uk
Web site: www.xpress.co.uk

Printed by Cox & Wyman Ltd, Reading, Berkshire

Distributed in UK by Turnaround Distribution
Unit 3, Olympia Trading Estate, Coburg Road, London N22 6TZ
Tel: 020 8829 3000
Fax: 020 8881 5088

ISBN 1-902934-17-2

Acknowledgements

I'd like to thank fellow Manchester writer Peter Kalu for his support; Courttia Newland for his inspiration. Dawn Ferrario, my English teacher; and Colin Muir at Salford University who taught me how to fine-tune my writing skills on a degree course. Thanks to all those people who bugged me constantly for the sequel to 'Moss Side Massive'. Martin Glynn, thanks for your second vision; 'Stevie 4 Real' Steve Walsh; Martin Smith, (always making me think, "yeah that's good but what if?"); Black Coral Productions London; and Manchester's Culture Identity Workshop creative writers workshop members. Thanks Mum, Dad, Jennifer, Lorraine, Tracey; my true friend Sue Graham; my best friend and soul sister Sandra Smith-Brown; Marva; Janet B; Freddy C; Elliott Rashman; Iree FM; Mr B aka Brian Bennett Company Geesus; Qaisra Mohammed; Red; Amichi; Diké; Grace; Ian Levi; and Merle Levi.

A very special thanks to The Royal Literary Society for financial assistance in writing this novel.

This book is dedicated to my son and daughter (coming up MC); Isaac Hodges and Tamaiya Hodges (Destiny's Child wannabe); and to my nephews (rough DJ) Joshua Walfall, Daniel, Jordan. And to my one and only niece, (novel tester) Sharma Walfall.

To you all always remember:
Stay focussed

The New Players

WORLDERS MASSIVE
Danny Ranks
Nero
Teeko
Stukky
Pipes
Fila
Mr. Mentian
Sizzla

DODGE CREW
Easy-Love Brown
Miss Small
Hatchet
Slide
Trench
Ranger
Michigan

The Old Players

THE PIPER MILL POSSE
Fluxy — Gang leader shot dead in broad daylight. Storm Michaels still thought of as Fluxy's killer by old members of the Piper crew.

Jigsy — Second-in-command, Fluxy's younger brother. Jigsy died after a violent car chase ending in a car crash. Bluebwai, Storm's innocent brother Zukie, and Zukie's close friends Chico and Hair Oil were travelling in the same car as hostages.

Easy-Love — Ex-third-in-command, received ten years for possession of an illegal weapon, reduced to five on appeal. Prison term served.

Teeko Martial — Now Co-director of The Worlders, Ranks' second-in-command and trusted crewman.

Bluebwai — Attending London University studying Web Authoring and Computer Programming.

THE GRANGE CLOSE CREW
Storm — Gang leader gone legitimate, owns a string of successful businesses and ventures.

Lewty — Ex-second-in-command, whereabouts unknown.

Frenchie — Currently serving a fifteen-year prison sentence for possession and supplying, not expecting to be paroled for at least another five years.

Colours — One time hitman, now a small-time independent drugs hustler.

Slim — Fatally stabbed in a fight over a woman outside a dancehall session in Liverpool June 1998.

Lick-Shot — Part time college student, dancehall promoter.

Rough-Cut — Married to Pamela, the mother of his four children, converted to Christianity, now living in America and teaching at a school for troubled black youths in Queens, New York.

ABOUT THE AUTHOR

Karline Smith grew up in Moss Side, Manchester where she got
the inspiration for her first novel 'Moss Side Massive'.
A passionate crime thriller writer, Karline has become something
of an expert of the genre having spent many years working as a
librarian. She has won various writing awards and is currently
developing a TV crime series for the BBC.

'Full Crew' is the sequel to 'Moss Side Massive'.

Prologue.

SIX YEARS AGO

HOT. STICKY. THE kind of day for swimming or water fights. Not school. Eleven-year-old Danny Ray Patterson gazed far beyond the school playground, daydreaming. The other Year 6 kids were busy, concentrating on their assignment, 'What I Want To Be When I Grow Up'. In Danny's eleven-year-old mind he was an eagle, flying freely.

"Daniel!"

Mrs Miller called him twice before he gazed back at her lazily through half-squinted hazel eyes.

"Yeah Miss?"

"Have you finished?" The boy nodded. Behind him, Shayla and Karis tittered. "*Already*?" He nodded again, licking the inside of his lip. Fidgeting. The class was watching. Waiting. A chair scraped. Chalk dust danced in the sunlight where she had turned from the blackboard.

"Come to the front and read your finished essay."

"Na-hah Miss."

"My five-year-old brother can read better than he can." Shayla muttered. "Shame innit?" The rest of the class laughed. Danny's chest burned. Bitch, thought she was so smart. Soon see what smart is with a fat lip. Later.

"*Now* Daniel."

Clutching his one page assignment, the chubby light-skinned boy rose reluctantly out of his seat, trudging to the front, aware of the mocking eyes on him and the sniggering at his oversize hand-me-downs and no-brand no-name trainers. No one noticed that he was limping slightly and covered in bruises from a savage beating last night. He held the page out straight.

"What I Want To Be When I Grow Up" by Daniel Patterson. Deep breath. Looking at his classmates deadpan he began. "When I grow up I want to be a gang leader." The room took on a deadly hush. He saw the look of horror on Mrs Miller's face. "I'm gonna rule the streets with fear. Niggaz, dogs and bitches gonna respect my name and always have it on their lips. I'm gonna have any ho I want and any switch-snitch gonna get ripped up like paper. Low-life will be my yo life and any body try to cross me I'm gonna suck their brains out their heads after I done blow it apart with my 9 milly Uzi."

"That's *enough* Daniel!"

"If anyone messes with me I'm gonna burn their mother, father, aunt, uncle. I'll drag them screaming from their beds."

"I said *enough*!"

"By the time I'm twenty I'm gonna have an empire those pussy Kray boys would have shit themselves for."

"GET OUT. Report to Mr McPherson's office. Now!!"

"That's what I want to be when I grow up. A notorious mean mothafucka."

Mrs Miller's face was red. Daniel screwed his essay up and threw it to the floor. Nodding his head with satisfaction he walked slowly out of the classroom. A group of boys looked at each other and grinned, nodding their heads in admiration. Mrs Miller picked up Danny's assignment and unravelled the scrunched up paper.

Nothing. No words. Just a blank piece of paper.

FOUR YEARS AGO

THERE WASN'T MUCH traffic on the road at this time of night, but Chico noticed the headlights behind them. He first saw them in the side mirror. The lights had been sitting comfortably behind them for the last few minutes. Terrified of the situation he was now in, he didn't know whether to mention it to Jigsy or not. He was certain that there was a car trailing them. His throat was so dry he swallowed thin air. Finally he said it, stuttering nervously.

"I th… think someone is following us."

"Where?" Easy shouted, turned and squinted out the rear windscreen anxiously. This was not what he wanted at all. "Jigsy, you speeding?" he asked.

Jigsy glanced at the rear-view mirror.

"It in't no police," he said, taking out the gun from his waistband. "They woulda flashed long time and pulled us over."

He looked in the mirror again as he pushed the gas pedal down. "Let's see what kinda firepower those motherfuckers got," he said, with a chuckle.

Jigsy took a sharp right with a screech of burning rubber, and swung the car onto the open dual carriageway. He gunned the Jag up to sixty, then seventy easily. The car behind stuck to them like white on rice.

"This is a hit, Jigsy," Easy screamed, picking up the Uzi on the floor in front of him, and hitting the button for the automatic windows to slide down. Zukie's heart thudded. Everything seemed to be happening in slow motion. They say when you think you're about to die, your whole life flashes past in an instant. Things you did, things you said, people you hurt, people you love. Zukie saw all these things. On either side of him, Chico and Hair Oil were shaking with fear. Bluebwai sat paralysed.

Easy leaned out the window as far as he could and took aim. At the wheel, Jigsy still had his foot all the way down on he gas pedal and, doing ninety, it was difficult to keeping the Jag straight. Easy didn't have time to pull the trigger before the headlights from he pursuing car illuminated him in a floodlight of full beam. In the back seat of the Jag, the hostages didn't have to be told to keep their heads down. The headlights had made them a sitting target.

"Take out those fucking lights," Jigsy barked.

Easy squinted but all he could see was two blurs of blinding white light. He aimed at what he thought was the centre and let off a short burst of gunfire. But the headlights were still right behind. He squeezed the trigger again, and again and again, but nothing. Without warning the sound of pump-action shotgun fire exploded into the air, at the same time as the Jag's rear windscreen shattered in a million pieces. The pump-action blasted again and this time it tore into the back of Jigsy's head, leaving a hole the size of a fist, and covering the windscreen with bits of his brain. Jigsy slumped down over the steering wheel, triggering the horn to sound in a loud, haunting monotone.

Keeping their heads well low, the hostages in the rear seat were trapped in the crossfire. They didn't know what was happening but they knew that some things were seriously wrong, as the Jag swerved to the left and then to the right, zig zagging erratically across the carriageway. It careened across to the central reservation and struck the barrier at an angle, which flipped it over and sent it spinning on its roof. The Jag finally came to a rest in the middle of the dual carriageway. The car behind was forced to brake hard.

The two assassins got out of the car quickly and briefly surveyed the scene. Frenchie was nervous like fuck, and looked up and down the dual carriageway to see if any cars were coming. Luckily there were only a few vehicles on the other side of the reservation and none of them stopped.

"Let's go. Come on," he urged his partner. "Now, Colours. No one woulda survived."

Colours shook his head. "We've got to wrap it up. No loose ends."

"Fuck that!" Frenchie pleaded. "None of them are getting out of that alive. Let's just get the fuck out before beastbwai come."

The glare of the car's headlamp coming down the road behind them made the matter more urgent. Frenchie tugged Colours by the sleeve and they quickly climbed back in their car, speeding away with a screech of tyres.

Homecoming

"The real tragedy is that there are some ignorant brothers out here. That's why I'm not on this all-white or all-black shit. I'm on this all-real or all-fake shit with people, whatever colour you are. Because niggas will do you. I mean, there's some foul niggas out there. The same niggas that did Malcolm-X. The same niggas that did Jesus Christ. Every brother ain't a brother. They will do you. So just because it's black don't mean it's cool. And just because it's white don't mean it's evil."

Tupac "Shining Serpent" Shakur,
Poet, actor, rap singer,
1971-1996.

GRANDMA ALWAYS SAYS time has a way of catching up on you. For Easy-Love Brown, former Piper Mill gang member, this was true. It was Christmas time, Easy was lying on his back on the hard prison bunk, hands crossed behind his head, looking up at the ceiling. He knew all about serving time, first in Hindley Young Offenders' institute in Wigan then, at twenty-one, in Strangeways, an adult male prison nearer his home in Manchester.

He was allocated a cell with a greasy-haired white guy called Dave and a black schizophrenic. On Easy's first day, the schizoid stabbed himself in the throat with a sharp piece of metal. Sad fuckin' life terminated.

Early on he got weekly visits from Cassandra, who brought Mario, their three-year-old son. Then the visits stopped. It was only later that he realised that the bitch had cleaned him out: disappeared with everything he had dodged a bullet for, steamed the cash stash, his thirty grand Beamer — the lot. Every fucking thing. His possessions were one thing, but taking little Mario — that hit Easy low. The greatest thing he could offer his son — fatherhood — was gone. Like his gang status. Gone. The Piper Mill posse was no more. Teeko Martial was the last of the gang. And the last Easy heard was that Teeko was working for some off-key buccaneer called Danny Ranks.

Easy knew little Danny. At thirteen, Danny was a keen scout for the Piper Massive. And now that most of the older hustlers, like Easy, were serving time, he had fulfilled his ambition of becoming a big-timer. Easy barely remembered Ranks from back in the day; little Danny was one of any number of yout's who were only too keen to scout for the Piper. The kind of yout Easy didn't much notice — cocky, confident and force-ripe. Back then, they were all like that. All desperately yearning for their chance to become tomorrow's bad bwai gundeleros. Seventeen now and with more snap than an Uzi, word out on the street was Danny's crew, the Worlders, was the deadliest thing out there and made the Piper crew look like a bunch of Sunday school pricks. His only rival was a 31-year-old Jamaican mampie woman known as Miss Small, leader of the Dodge crew. Huge and deadly she ruled her territory like a merciless momma. But that didn't concern Easy. All he could think about was that Ranks was sitting on his throne, Worlders were controlling his turf and soon, with the return of the don, they would witness the power of street knowledge. He had plans. BIG plans.

Easy had played it cool for four years, done his time with a smile on his face. An ecstatic smile. The parole board was pleased with his progress, and were particularly impressed with the fact that he was using his time well to study accountancy and business. With the Governor's recommendation and hard work by his lawyers, Easy-Love's bid was cut in half. He had no intention of returning. Times had changed. Judges were making examples of bad bwoys who made the mistake of getting caught. Easy-Love Brown didn't intend on making that mistake again. In a few hours time he would be back on the streets. Coming back for sure. Still the same 'G' he was when he was taken off the streets. With scores to settle.

Easy-Love turned on his stomach and looked around at the bare walls. He gradually fell into a deep, dark, cavernous existence, dreaming of his dead mother telling him something, shouting his name repeatedly.

He woke up sweating. A prison officer stood by his bunk, gruffly calling his name. It was morning already. The day of his release.

LOWERING THE LEVEL on the base tube, 'Nero' Campbell reversed the blue Lexus into the gap outside the West Indian bakery and 24-hour pharmacy in the row of renovated shops along Princess Road, Moss Side. Except for the gentle breeze catching the fresh scents of freshly baked hard-dough bread and stirring up empty crisp packets and fools' gold scratch cards, this side of town was unusually quiet. Everybody was away doing last minute Christmas jugglings.

Nero was Danny Ranks' lean but mean bodyguard. He took care of Ranks, and Ranks looked after him. Nerome was an investment, an increasingly valuable asset to the crew. This was a yout' who could take care of himself and was ready to die for his ranks. Every ranks from here to Birmingham had tried to recruit him — how many other street soldiers could claim to have been war veterans at the age of seventeen?

Danny Ranks' rise to the top was equally precocious. At fifteen, Ranks was the owner of a luxury car, though not old enough to legally drive it. Two years later he now owned five, his favourite being the Lexus.

Nero got out first and glanced furtively up and down, his right hand in the side pocket of the bulky flak jacket. Again he scanned the scene quickly until he was sure that everything was cool. Ranks climbed out of the passenger side, slamming the door hard. He was agitated. Today Easy-Love Brown was going to be released. He knew Easy was going to come looking for him.

An old man on crutches stood in the doorway of the bakery, begging money. He looked pitiful. The two young men approached, Ranks taking a rapid lead in his heavy duty Cats, Nero covering his back. Ranks' face was stern. His head was clean-shaven, like his dead hero Tupac Shakur. His nose was straight, and his eyes hazel, almond-shaped, impassive. His face was oval, his complexion a lightly tanned brown.

Nero was taller, a few shades darker and very good looking. Square jawed and dimpled, he wore his hair in short dreadlocks and had a habit of licking his lips constantly, unconsciously, like he was always thirsty.

Ranks could not believe it when the old man dared to stick his open palm out to greet him. Ranks blinked in wide-eyed astonishment, one eye closing a second before the other, a dangerous fuse sparking inside.

Dipping a hand in the pocket of his Moschino's, Ranks pulled out a condom. The old man looked confused. Ranks addressed him in a low, calm voice.

"Do us all a favour, Jack, blow it up and suffocate yuself. Maybe if your mother put it on your father's dick you wouldn't be here begging in my face." With that he stepped into the bakery. His boss safely inside the bakery, Nero stood guard outside. Taking pity on the old man, he fumbled in his pockets and took out a crumpled twenty-pound note and handed it over. The old man thanked him and hobbled away hurriedly.

A few moments later, Ranks emerged from the bakery with a bun and cheese. "You gave that old lying wino-skettle some money din't ya?" he snarled. "I bet you fifty greens he's in the off-license 'round the corner."

Nero kept his jaws clenched shut. He was used to Danny's bad words. But he would allow it. Because he knew Danny needed him, his lieutenant, his right hand, now more than ever.

Yes, me friend, me deh pon street again.

IT WAS BAD luck amongst released prisoners to glance back at the place of their incarceration once released. But Easy did. He glanced back to curse the high brick walls and vow that he was never going to pass through those gates again. Ever.

He hadn't told Grandma of his early release. He wanted to surprise her. This was going to be her best Christmas in years. Easy could already see the tears on her face. Like when he got sent down. But these would be tears of joy.

Even now Grandma refused to believe that her grandson had anything to do with guns or drugs or gangs. He'd been set up, she insisted, and she would fight to clear his name. He told her to save her strength and her hard-earned savings for Sharon and Kurtis, his half-sister and half-brother.

On parole and with his belongings wrapped in a parcel under his arm, Easy walked away from Strangeways, and then simply kept on walking. Eventually he neared the city centre. The streets were full of Christmas shoppers. Seeing people buying presents like crazy was a reminder to Easy that he was coming out of prison to nothing. He who had left home at sixteen and nearly had it all at seventeen, didn't want to move back in with Grandma at twenty-three with fuck-all.

So how the fuck was he supposed to go straight? That wasn't something he had learned inside. The first thing he was going to sort was security. An Uzi and a Magnum Special preferably, but he'd take what he could get. So long as it fired good.

And another thing: Easy needed a crew. He couldn't do shit without a crew. He needed to recruit some top-notch soldiers, no amateurs.

Strength, Grandma always says, comes in numbers.

DANNY'S MOBILE PHONE began to ring *Jumpin'* — *Jumpin'* by Destiny's Child. Taking it out of his back pocket he answered, and walked into the record shop doorway. Nerome stayed close. About to take out his lighter, he saw a purple Volkswagen Golf GTI tear up Princess Parkway, scream to a stop, and then reverse full pelt in front of Ranks' Lexus.

The Volkswagen's rear bumper crunched into one of the front headlamps and side indicator. Bits of glass and orange plastic flying like rain. Swinging around, Ranks stood gaping, taking the phone slowly away from his ear.

Quickly, he inspected the damage to the front of his car. The GTI was totally unmarked. The driver of the other car casually got out. Assessing the situation, Nerome's hand went to the small at the back of his waist where his Browning lay in wait. Nerome grew hot and nervous. Tingling. He built a profile. Height, five-six, very light-skinned, clear grey eyes, late teens, maybe slightly older, goldy-brown long dreadlocks tied back. Nerome knew the faces of every single gang-member, but couldn't match this one. He kept his right hand hovering behind the small of his back, painfully remembering the inexplicable hesitance that caused the loss of the life of his friend and fellow soldier. Aston.

The other boy spoke. Shakily.

"Shit! I'll just exchange insurance and…"

He couldn't finish. Ranks gripped him by his neck, pushing him down on the bonnet of the car. Leaning on him, face close to the other boy, he trapped him beneath his body. Cars slowing down on the Parkway watched the commotion.

"Insurance? Fuck you! Yu goin' to dish the dollars for the damage to my wheels this fuckin' minute!"

"Get yuh hands off me!" The boy was raging, his peanut-coloured complexion reddening with anger. Suddenly, he stopped, his grey eyes acknowledging Ranks uncertainly.

"Wait. I *know* you don't I?" He asked, breathing slowly. Licking his lips, frowning Ranks blinked slowly.

"No." Tersely. Swallowing, Ranks unexpectedly backed off. The kid straightened himself, scratching the back of his creamy-coloured neck. His frown deepened. Like he was trying to remember. Scrutinising Danny's face.

"I know you. I definitely know you from somewhere."

Ranks dropped his eyes.

"Look! I said you don't fuckin' know me, all right?" Nerome could feel the agitation rising from Ranks like steam. Danny never walked away from anything.

The main door leading from the new recording studio and record shop opened, the hum of bass turning into a recognisable Mr Vegas tune as the sound flowed through the open door.

"Heads high kill dem with the blow—"

A tall, cinnamon-brown complexioned yout' appeared on the street. Strikingly handsome, hair cut low, a soft square chin with a dimple, he had a superior air about him that wasn't contemptuous or superficial. Totally cool and unaffected he stood and observed silently, his eyes travelling impassively from Nero to Ranks, to the dreadlocks, and back to Ranks. Keeping his eyes on Ranks he called to the dreadlocks boy.

"Yo Zukie? Wazzup?"

"I crashed into his car, innit." Zukie, the dreadlocks kid, said dismally. The tall dark yout', dressed in designer jeans and sweatshirt, lit a cigarett, his eyes still on Ranks steadily.

"What's the damage?"

Ranks cleared his throat.

"Nah, no problem, star."

"I in't your fuckin' star," the tall yout' said, dark eyes raging silently. "You see my brother has a problem with his memory. He gets frustrated easily, sometimes forgets what he's doing so if he's damaged your car, I'll fuckin' pay, all right?"

Nostrils flaring Ranks walked towards his car, kissing through his teeth. Getting into the car, he slammed the door viciously. Nerome joined him, wondering what the play was. But Ranks wasn't chattin'. The only thing he said was, "Drive."

As they pulled away Nerome looked back at the sign above the record shop. In bright letters it read,

STORM MULTIMEDIA: Vinyl, Books, CD's, Multitrack Recording Studio.

G PLATE. BATTERED LOOKING. Racing red. BMW. Tinted windows. Tyres screaming like tortured eagles in the sky. It stopped inches from his feet nearly knocking him over. He jerked back with seconds to spare. Two black yout's leaped from the car. Shouting. Screaming. He didn't recognise the faces. They aimed it straight at his face. A self-loading hand pistol. Easy's heart slammed against his chest. Looked like a Browning Hi-Power. Easy reacted instinctively, his fist catching the gunman's jaw. The head snapped back. The gun fired shots upwards.

Easy turned quickly. Screams behind him. Curses. Pursuing footsteps. Panic. Easy ran. Slamming into people. Pushing people out the way. Breathless. Eyes streaming. Throat dry. He ran down a side street. Turned into another. Blood pumped furiously through his body. Sweat poured off him in hot streams. Easy flicked and turned, hearing shots puncturing metal and slicing up brickwork. The bullets hissed close. Too close. Grazing his shoulder. Easy tripped and bounced flat on the pavement. A bullet hissed over him. Easy twisted, got up quickly then somersault-rolled behind the protection of a rubbish skip. Shots ricocheted. Against the skip Easy sat breathless, a vein in his head throbbed away. The car was close. Cruising. Easy could smell, could almost feel, the heat of the engine. The shots stopped. Easy was ready to chance it again.

He looked.

The street was a dead end.

Easy closed his eyes.

Fuck!

CLIFTON 'STORM' MICHAELS sat in his shop office, thinking. For the moment, he was happy. Things were running smooth. He was running his own business. Tight. And legal. Trying a t'ing to set himself and his people up for life. He felt positive about the way things were going. The last couple of years hadn't been easy though. Pure hard work and commitment. The Old Lady had ultimately forgiven him for his gang war that nearly cost her life. He made amends by sending her home to Jamaica for good, to recuperate in the warm climate. But if Zukie knew the truth, would he?

Storm was beginning to worry that his brother's memory and concentration seemed to be improving dramatically. Zukie had suffered traumatic memory loss as a result of the accident. He couldn't recall anything leading up to it nor the catastrophe itself. In a way, Storm was glad. If Zukie remembered his brother's role in the crash that killed his best friend Chico and left Hair Oil paralysed, he might never forgive him. He certainly didn't want Zukie reminded of painful days gone by, days when his crew, The Grange, ran the streets recklessly, not caring if innocent people got in the way.

DOORS SLAMMING. FOOTSTEPS. Feet. Hands reached down grabbing him to his shaky feet, dragging him violently towards the BMW. G plate. Battered. Tinted windows.

"Where ya think ya was doing, Mr Easy Squeezy? Training for de Olympics? Get in the bloodclaht car or we're gonna smoke you right here and now!"

Easy-Love felt that earlier fear return to him. They tossed him into the car.

"Bling, bling! Welcome home. Kickback and enjoy the ride." Easy was flanked on either side by two bad boys. They warned him not to look at them. Easy was defiant.

"I'm gonna get you," he hissed. They laughed.

"Yeah but we got you first, dickhead!!"

Easy had no time to see the baseball bat coming towards him. He felt a painful explosion inside his head. A screeching, roaring sound. Bright colours sparking behind his eyes. Then came, the deep, inviting, dark blackness.

EASY'S HEAD THUMPED. Nauseous. Bound tight. Numb. Blindfolded. Gagged. He lay horizontal on a cold, wet, linoleum floor. His hearing acute. A TV in the distance, maybe in another room. Rain against a window and from somewhere behind him, the distinct sound of water dripping loudly from a tap into a sink. At least he was alive.

His breathing quickened. His heart slowed. Time fooled him, played with his mind like a kid jumping on his shadow. Maybe minutes, maybe hours passed. Easy wanted to piss. Badly. Hunger gnawed at his stomach. Grandma, he suddenly thought, but this made the pain in his stomach unbearable. He felt eyes upon him. Then he smelled the strong scent of crack-cocaine.

A giggle. High-pitched and savage. Someone tore the gag from his mouth, removed the stuffed handkerchief.

"Yu better be glad I'm tied up, because if I was you I wouldn't be laughing. I'd be fretting," Easy spat.

Another laugh. Other voices. Whoops and yelps.

"What do you want from me?"

Footsteps shuffled towards him. A stick or some other similar object stabbed him fiercely in his ribs. Easy gasped.

"The question is, Easy Squeezy, what do you want from us?" More high-pitched giggles and whoops.

"Pussy hole me know yu?"

Easy felt the rod strike him on the lower half of his body. He cried out in pain.

"I hear your bitch Cassandra took off with one of yo' enemies while yo' bin in de big house, get what I'm sayin'?" More voices, sniggering, edging Mr Big-Lick on. "Wanna know who? Colours innit, the guy who shot yu and Jigsy off the road, your ex been livin' wid him four years now. She got two babies to him but I heard that eldest one that suppose to be his, in't his. I hear that first one looks just like you. Anyways, my man Colours and his woman, dem have dis nice lickle drum in Didsbury fulla good furniture and shit. T'ings copa fe dem."

Easy was angry, fighting hard to conceal it. How could she? Colours of all people, a dutty Grange bwai. How come Cassie never told him she was pregnant again?

"I in't coming back on no streets again." Easy said resentfully.

The stick lashed him severely across his backside. Easy bit his lip, tasted blood. A groan escaped his lips.

"Yu triflin' wit' me, glory boy. You got plans."

Easy said with forced calmness. "I just come out prison, man. I got nuttin set up on street."

The stick tore into the space between his shoulder blades.

"Big fucking ol' timer like you just going to blow off? Juss gwaan retire, potter 'round in the garden and read books an' shit? Yu t'ink we're stuhpid? Yu t'ink we don't know you got big plans, old player?"

Who were they, Dodge, or Worlders? How dare they ask him his plans? He had every right to claim back what should rightfully have been his after Fluxy's death. The streets belonged to him.

"Come on Easy lemon squeezy. Let us in on your status." The coolness in his tormentor's voice changed to an angry whine.

Easy said it.

Couldn't contain his outrage any longer.

"You'd better make me a dead status, bwai, because if I come out of this alive you're going to wish you'd never made the mistake of imposing your stupid fucking acquaintance on someone of my calibre."

Easy heard the wind as the rod swiped towards his head, feeling the first two agonising, stinging blows.

In the next second he was in that darkness again.

ZUKIE FLICKED A loose dreadlock out of his vision and placed the box of new items on the counter, absently bobbing his head to the breathtaking bass pouring from the immense wall speakers. The walls of the record shop were covered with posters of various ragga pop, hip hop, reggae, soul and R&B stars, including the late reggae king Dennis Brown. Various items were for sale, including banners, flags, caps, key rings, scarves, whistles and black interest books. The shop also had two computers for public use. Software included a stock catalogue database and net access with links to MP3 and sound system websites or the latest changes in the music industry. Next to the studio was a small café area providing refreshments and hot food, cooked by Taniesha who worked part-time.

Turning the music down on the system, Storm turned his attention to Zukie who was checking the orders against the invoice.

"That boy you crashed into, earlier on, what was he sayin' to you?"

Storm was expecting Zukie to say "what boy?" But he didn't. Instead he said.

"I think I remember him from somewhere."

Storm carefully looked at his brother, now twenty-two.

"Where?"

Zukie looked up and blinked slowly.

"His name is—" Storm saw the dangerous excitement in Zukie's clear eyes. "Danny!" He whispered, breathing hard. "Danny! And I think he was there the night I was in that car crash."

Storm felt his feet quake, felt the room move slowly, felt like his life was going to turn and spiral backwards into a bottomless pit.

"He knows something about the car crash. I just know it."

Storm wished he had never brought the subject up. But as long as Danny didn't show up around here again, things would be cool. In the meantime, he'd think of something to keep Zukie's mind off Ranks.

IT WAS CHRISTMAS Eve. Storm smiled, winking playfully at his younger brother Zukie as he put a friendly arm around Beppo Dread. Dripping in jewellery and sporting a gold front tooth, well bling, Alphonso Beppo Mackenzie was one of their best clients. He always booked the multi-track studio and rehearsal rooms for twenty-four hours. At thirty pounds an hour studio hire plus half a kilo of good weed supplied by Storm, things were looking good. Zukie smiled back at his brother and for the first time in his life felt positive about the way things were going.

Losing his best friend Chico in that car crash was the most devastating thing that had ever happened to Zukie. He and Chico had been best friends since high school. Zukie still remembered that first day when Chico, testing Zukie's badness, challenged him to a fight. As a teen Zukie had always been little and girlish-looking, the target for bullies but Chico was moderately surprised when Zukie floored him.

After emerging from his coma after the accident Zukie had wondered what had happened to Chico. The three of them had been in a shocking car crash, he was eventually told. And when they thought he was mentally strong enough they told him. Chico was dead. Beautiful, smiling, joking Chico. Why did he die? No one had any answers. Strapped in a wheelchair, Hair Oil could only stare back at him with haunted, despairing eyes. Hair Oil had suffered brain damage caused by a massive blood clot on the brain. The last time Zukie went to see him, Oil was dribbling and sunk in the chair, his limbs turned inwards due to involuntary muscle spasms. It had made Zukie sick to see Oil this way. He hadn't been back.

Zukie felt guilty. He knew someone was to blame. Maybe he was. He was thinking more and more about Chico and Oil since running into that kid Danny's car two weeks ago. Did Danny have something to do with it?

"Bepps an' me goin' in the office to chat business, Zukie. Man de shop, nuh?" Storm said, cutting into Zukie's thoughts. Zukie nodded detachedly, putting a Sanchez CD on the system. Storm and Beppo disappeared into the back.

Singer Sanchez's haunting word rang in Zukie's ears as he bellowed out a poignant tune,

"There are lots of signs of life,
Some that you may not like,
You could be living this minute,
the next minute you're gone away."

Beppo and Storm had been gone two minutes when Zukie heard the intercom buzzer sound. He looked up at the video but soon realised that it was off. Climbing off the stool near the counter Zukie switched it on. A black and white image of a shaven head yout' filled the 14-inch monitor. The yout' pressed the buzzer again. Frowning Zukie spoke into the system.

"Yes?"

"I want to buy some music for my woman, Ashanti, y'know Christmas present. Been tryna get that CD all over." The voice was familiar. Zukie glared at the screen. Suddenly he noticed the face belonged to Danny. Zukie's heart bounced, his finger hovered over the door release button shakily. His throat felt parched, his heart rammed painfully in his chest. Storm had warned him specifically about letting anyone in who wasn't a regular client. But this boy's face had prompted something that tugged at Zukie's memory. Zukie pressed the button. The buzzer screeched. He saw the yout' smile.

Once in, the yout' stood in the shop dressed casually in a pair of black jeans, a red sweatshirt, and a huge black puff parka-style jacket open all the way down. Looking around, his eyes fell on Zukie. Zukie got the tingles. Felt that he had made a mistake, a major-mega mess up. Felt it in his blood.

"HOW YU FEELING?" Grandma's voice. Her hand reaching towards his shoulder. Easy was lying down. She touched his face delicately. Her hand warm and comforting. He wasn't dreaming. Grandma was there, clapping her hands together in a mixture of relief, praise and mirth and looking upwards to God. He followed her eyes and saw Christmas decorations taped to the ceiling.

"Christmas?" Speaking was painful.

"Eve." Grandma said. "You in hospital. You been in here two weeks."

Two weeks. Unconscious. This wasn't what he planned for Grandma. Easy's throat felt sore, hurting as if a sharp stone was stuck in his gullet. He watched the old woman draw nearer, resting on her walking stick. He wondered when Grandma had become dependent on a walking stick. Seventy-three years of age and it was as if Easy was seeing her for the first time in his life. Light-brown shiny face containing freckles and age blemishes, hair almost completely white, worn in a braid down her back. Indian. She looked so fragile, as if she should be the one resting. Easy suddenly felt an immense love and respect for his grandmother.

He had not known his father. His birth certificate contained only his mother's name, Damia Brown. In place of his father's name there was a blank. That blank had haunted him for years. Eleven years ago, his mother was killed by a speeding van. After her funeral, Sharon and Kurtis's father drifted off. He used to send money for them occasionally, and take them occasionally. But then he remarried, sold the house and left them. So Grandma, Idey Mahalia Brown, was left to raise them. She came down from Coventry and slotted back into their lives, growing up her dead daughter's babies.

"Who found me? Where?"

She didn't want to talk about it. "Lord God, just thinking about what nearly happen, how me nearly lose me Grandson, how dem beat you nearly kill you and bruk up yu arms and foot and—" The old woman started to weep.

Easy spoke, his throat hurt as he forced out each word.

"You always say put your trust in the Lord, Grandma." He knew her faith was the only thing that maintained her through her harsh life. When the hurdles got higher, God was her vaulting pole. Easy learned from an early age that he could fake his belief in God, if only for *her* sake.

Grandma smiled. It was a weak smile, but he had succeeded in resurrecting her faith. He glanced at the Get Well cards next to the bowl of fruit and drinks on his bedside cupboard. There were two. Easy didn't have any friends, but he didn't give a shit. Friends were for women.

Following his gaze, Grandma glanced over at the cards. "One is from Sharon and Kurtis," she explained. She thought the second was from Cassandra, it looked like her handwriting. Easy went stiff at the mention of his ex-girlfriend's name, and his heart fluttered with a little pleasure and sadness. At least she hadn't forgotten him; maybe she still cared about him.

Easy asked about Sharon and Kurtis. He hadn't seen them much since the day he left Grandma's house, six years back. While in prison he rarely asked about them. If Grandma had talked about them he couldn't remember. All he remembered about prison was rage.

"Dem not kids anymore," Grandma commented with more than a hint of regret in her voice. "Sharon going to college in September. She doing Art and Design and seh she a go do her degree in it. She want to be a fashion designer."

Easy-Love cleared his throat and closed his eyes. He started to feel pain. "That's good. I'm proud."

Grandma agreed. Sharon was the apple of her eye.

"And Kurtis?"

Grandma dropped her eyes, fussing around him, fluffing up his pillow.

"Yu feelin' any pain? Mek me call the Doctor mek him give yu something."

Easy swallowed painfully. Something wasn't right. He knew her long enough to know Grandma was hiding something from him.

CHRISTMAS EVE. NEARLY three p.m. A cold biting wind blowing. Streets deserted. Kurtis James pedalled furiously on a mountain bike he'd liberated from a back street in Withington. He was shivering. It was freezing. More importantly he needed to score. No money to buy shit. Taking his hands off the cold handlebars, he blew into them.

Up ahead the lights changed. Green, amber, red. He didn't give a fuck. He would have jumped them if it wasn't for the yellow Porsche pulling up alongside.

The car was mint, the absolute dett. Miss Blonde Bling-Bling Money No Object sat chatting and laughing into a phone, her black handbag tossed casually on the leather passenger seat.

He moved fast. The monkey wrench was out of his puffa jacket in a flash. In the same movement, the car window shattered and the bag was gone. Kurtis furiously peddled down an alley to the sound of hysterical screaming. He didn't stop peddling until he got to the embankment, his cheeks puffed out air in short sharp gasps. A train passed, its wheels clanked noisily over the iron tracks and echoed in a nearby tunnel. He opened the bag hungrily and smiled at the huge bundle of money. He tossed his head back and laughed. Christmas was going to be splendiferous.

NEROME CAMPBELL SIGHED, ejecting the Yard sound bashment CD and replacing it with mellow tunes. Bashment was OK but some of it didn't make sense to him. Nerome liked cultural roots music, reggae that came from the heart of the ghetto streets of Jamaica, music performed by reggae greats Luciano, Sanchez, or Morgan Heritage.

Nerome looked at his watch. Been sitting in the car for ten minutes now waiting for Ranks to come out of Storm's record shop. What was he doing in there? Recording a tune?

Rain again. Nero strained to see through the shop's slanted blinds, making out Ranks browsing through the CD stacks. He was surprised he got in. Must have been the kid with the memory problem. No way would the serious-looking one let Ranks on his premises.

A rap on the car window made Nerome jump unexpectedly. Nero cursed inwardly for allowing his attention to slacken. Kurtis James' brown face was at the car's passenger window. Eating chicken and chips from a bag, grinning like a buffoon, putting greasy fingerprints on the smooth clear glass. Ranks wouldn't be pleased about prints on the window. Pressing a button the car window slid down electronically. Nero felt the cold air as the teen poked his head through.

"Yo, where's Ranks?" Well unless he's a two-inch dwarf, hidin' under the car seat it don't look like he's here does it? Nerome thought sarcastically.

"What ya want him for?" he asked.

"I need a blast man."

"Go check one of him man out on street."

"There in't none. It's Christmas Eve, innit?"

"Yeah, an' in't you got no family to be spendin' it with?"

Kurtis shrugged. Nerome noticed that the teen's breath smelt stale, his clothes ragged and dirty. Body odour hung around him like a restless spirit. His hair tangled in small raggedy dreadlocks twists. But the teen seemed sprightly pleased with himself.

"Got money to pay him, y'know all dat I owe him." The only accounts Nero was interested in was his weekly wages. Kurtis was waving his newfound riches about like it was the latest flavour for ice cream or something. Looked like he had at least two grand in his hands.

"Can I get a ride over to Stukky's?" Nerome wanted to ask Kurtis if he thought he looked like a chauffeur.

Nerome kissed his teeth. "My orders are to wait here for Ranks."

"Aw c'mon man," the teen begged.

"Where's your bike?" Nerome forced himself to stay calm.

"Punctured." Kurtis was already stepping into the rear of the car. A wise move. Three Fedz cars drove by in a row, one behind the other, close, furtively like a long venomous snake. Nerome suddenly smelt the boy's trainers contaminating the clean air-conditioned atmosphere. Ranks was definitely not going to welcome this uninvited guest.

DANNY RANKS LOOKED up at Zukie studying him. Lowering his head back down to the CD rack, Ranks smiled to himself. Finding the CD's he wanted he walked over to the counter, noticing the yout's grey eyes on him. Now was the time to test.

"Sorry, 'bout stressin' you a coupla weeks back, yu know, with the car an' that?"

"It's OK." Zukie answered, nodding, retrieving the CD's from the locked barrelled cupboards against the wall. Danny was slightly puzzled. Thought Storm said he had a memory problem.

"Your brother was OK about it?"

"Sure." Cool as steel, which was as cold as his grey eyes.

"Is he around?"

"Why? You wanna talk to him?"

"Might."

"Cos somehow I get the impression he don't wanna talk to you."

Ranks tingled, smiling warmly at Zukie. Cautiously Zukie returned the smile.

"But *you* might," Ranks said, analysing Zukie's response. The boy froze. At that moment the door leading to the office swung open abruptly. Beppo and Storm walked out, chatting, laughing. Storm stopped instantly. The dread looked too blipped to notice, or feel the change in Storm but Zukie and Ranks did.

"What is *he* doing in my shop?" he barked at Zukie.

Zukie looked slightly bewildered.

"Just settle man, I'm just buyin' some music, bringin' business." Ranks offered to justify his presence but Storm didn't allow him to finish. Flying over he gripped Ranks by the throat, slamming a fist into his face. Danny staggered backwards into the CD rack display, scattering cases around him. He landed on his backside, rubbing his jaw, blood spilling from a split lower lip. He spat out some more blood, shaking his head slowly, a string of bloody saliva slimed down his coat from his mouth. He looked up to see the Dread and Zukie restraining Storm. Storm was ranting and raving like a lunatic, looking like a clown in a circus mad at the crowd for going home.

Ranks burst out laughing, despite the pain in his jaw, and rose to his feet. Walking over to where they stood bemused, he threw his money on the counter and took his CD's. Then he focussed on Zukie, touching the yout's face slightly. Ranks felt an electric tingle shoot through his fingers from the slight touch of Zukie's distrustful face.

"I can see you're still experiencing a lot of anguish," he announced solemnly like a clairvoyant, squinting at Storm's ink-black eyes, making sure this was for Storm's benefit as much as his brother's.

"If Chico had known what was going down that night he'd never have got into that car." Wiping the blood from his lower lip with the sleeve of his puff jacket, he opened the door and left, aware of Zukie's haunting eyes on his back.

"WHAT HAPPEN?" LEANING over quickly Nerome opened the car passenger door for Danny Ranks to get in. Ranks was chuckling to himself, dabbing at his mouth with a white handkerchief which was quickly becoming red.

"That Storm's a fucking fruitcake, star,' Ranks lisped. "But if he wants cold play I'll play cold." Nerome frowned. He couldn't believe that Ranks had put himself in blatant danger like that. Ranks caught sight (and smell) of Kurtis in the back seat. His smug mood quickly altered to aggravation.

"What you doin' in my car Kurtis?" he asked calmly, his voice displaying a slight edge to it. Nerome started up the engine.

"Awww I need a blast," Kurtis groaned, holding his head.

"Fuck off out my car before dibs bwai t'ink we're loadin' drugs."

"But I got your money."

"Where?" Ranks began sarcastically. "Don't tell me, ya got a magician's black hat with fourteen hundred in it sittin' right next to da fuckin' white rabbit." Turning around he saw the notes the naive teen was waving at him. Ranks' eyes opened wide. "The whole fourteen hundred?"

"Yep." Kurtis said chirpily. "Got another six hundred to buy some rocks to smoke and maybe trade." Ranks snatched the money from the teen's hand.

"Fuck me f'real. The teen ain't ramping, Nero." Nerome smiled at the shortened version of his name Ranks often used. Ranks was laughing, a high-pitched giggle, like a squirrel chewing LSD-laced nuts, touching fists with Kurtis who joined in the mirth. Ranks stopped laughing abruptly and his tone of voice turned cold. "So Kej where's the interest?"

Kurtis' titter trailed away as he realised the joke was on him. His face crumpled into a puzzled frown.

"Interest?"

"Yeah. I charge interest on late payments and currently you owe me another fourteen hundred."

Nerome saw Kurtis's face as he did a quick mental calculation.

"I-I haven't got, I-I can't pay that." Ranks reached across and snatched Kurtis by the throat. "Well you'd better think of something quick and satisfactory." He snarled into the teen's startled face before releasing the squirming boy. Kurtis started to cough and splutter. Ranks smiled and in a calm matter-of-fact tone asked. "So tell me Kej, how's Easy?"

Kurtis leaned back, thinking carefully of the question asked of him. Ranks rarely called him Kej either, an abbreviation of his full name Kurtis Ethan James. Kurtis looked through the car's window at the passing streets.

"He's OK, I hear. Grandma's with him now."

"Tell you what," Ranks said, "forget what you owe me. Keep the money; buy some clothes, deodorant, new trainers whatever. Come over to mine. You can have as much rock as you want. Clean break yeah?" Kurtis suddenly looked contented. Too contented Nerome thought, and that was gonna be a big mistake with him.

BONES HEAL. EASY-LOVE Brown figured, in time he'd get over the pain and the inconvenience. But never was he going to get over the anger and rage that was increasing inside him day by day.

Grandma, told him, eventually, how he was found, dumped like useless meat on a waste ground in a tough district known as Longsight. A woman had made an anonymous call to the police. Back in the days when Piper Mill and Grange first started to claim the streets, people had a sort of respect for each other.

But what right did these kids have to fuck with him? To take him off the streets within minutes of him stepping back out on them? To beat him senseless and then just dash him back on the streets like some dog?

Retribution was inevitable.

Retribution against Ranks and his Worlders crew, on those he believed must be the perpetrators.

But it was odds against him winning any war without weapons, without money, without a crew. Yeah, Easy-Love Brown was a general without an army.

A DEEP, HEAVY bass-line aching roughly as the rhythm sliced through the smoky atmosphere through huge amplified tweeters. Tall speakers set against the walls of Storm's Matrix One nightclub. The crowd, young and old, black and white, totally gripped by the music Zukie was playing at the New Year's Eve party. The New Year itself was around half a minute away. Zukie was thinking about Chico. Sadly, Chico wasn't around to share this historic moment. And Hair Oil? What significance did another New Year have for his brain damaged mind?

Zukie stood around the sound system that he once owned with Chico and Hair Oil. Since the tragedy he'd sold the equipment on to MC 'Silver Fox' Wade, Selecta Anton 'Balti' Baltimore and Engineer Dwayne, all good friends from secondary school. Known as 'Nemesis' they had gained the reputation of being one of Manchester's hottest sound systems, specialising in a variety of music. With the nickname 'Light-finger', Zukie often guest mixed and from the roars of the crowd his technological mixing talent was well appreciated. It was no secret that Storm had helped them to achieve this high-ranking status by assisting them financially. Their music was one-cuts, unique renditions of dancehall ragga, garage, and jungle versions usually sung by the same artist. For the right money no one else would have the same copy of a particular track that was mixed especially for Nemesis.

MC Silver Fox began his shout outs of special requests.

"As we go down into the last music of this year nuff respect to the Birmingham, London, Manchester, Leeds and Liverpool massive. All ghetto people big up yourself. Shout outs to my brothers Lucas, Tristan, cousin Lorenzo, Malik, Wiley, Levi — ah you dis, Sonia-sugar — love ya girl to the max. Hassan and Mr Ali, me bredrin Zukie Light-finger — baby keep mixin', my baby mother Angie, manager

Storm, Donna and my daughter Shoni, Sista P, General Smiley, Soldgie, big up oonuh self inna de New Year party. Also last but not least absent friends, lost in the last coupla years — Flags, Leroy, Paul, Fabian, Carl Thomas, Ricky, Danté and Chico. We miss unuh bad, bad, bad." Zukie felt as if his heart was going to burst out of his chest as he checked his watch and remembered Chico.

Twenty seconds remaining until the New Year. A new beginning Zukie hoped, putting old ghosts to rest. With earphones on, nodding his head to the captivating bass line, he looked across at the crowd. It was time. Across the stage, he saw Storm smiling, thumbs up. Zukie stopped the track he was playing and Silver Fox Wade snatched up the microphone. His rough baritone voice reverberated through the speakers as he screamed.

"Are you ready for it people? Are you really ready for the New Year?" Wade started to sing the Fugees theme tune in his deep and melodious voice. Whoops, yells, screams. Fervour. Stomping feet. *"Ready or not here I come, I'm gonna find you and make you happy."* Zukie's stomach knotted as Wade began to chant the seconds down into the new year.

"Hold tight. Here it comes. And right now it's better than sex to rahtid! *10, 9, 8, 7, 6, 5, 4,"* the crowd joined in, screaming at the top of its voices, *"3, 2, 1…"* Silver Fox screamed into the microphone. "Happy New Year !!!!" Lights flashed on and off. Screams reached the top of the spotlit ceiling, balloons cascaded down popping rapidly, sounding like gunfire as people pinched and burst the bright colours. They beat the walls and stamped their feet like a deafening drum roll. Zukie was so hot he felt like he was going to pass out. Anton popped open a large bottle of expensive champagne and showered its contents into the frenetic crowd. Zukie suddenly found himself wondering what it was all about and what it meant to him. A time of celebration and positiveness? Yeah, if he could remember it would make a difference to him. A big difference.

Zukie saw tears and laughter in the crowd as people embraced friends, family or lovers. Zukie's eyes searched for Storm. He saw his brother watching him from the side of the stage. All around them was chaos. They stared at each other for a few seconds, smiling, until Storm walked towards Zukie, streamers and poppers landing around him delicately like pirouetting ballet dancers. They embraced gently, slowly building up the grip until Zukie could feel their hearts thumping in unison. Zukie thought Storm would never let go. As Zukie drew back from his brother's embrace he saw the tears forming at the corners of Storm's eyes.

"Four years ago, I thought — well I thought you wouldn't be here. Happy New Year."

"Yeah, you too, bro'."

Zukie left the stage and headed for the toilets, aware of his brother's eyes on him as he was swallowed into the tumultuous writhing crowd.

AS IF IT had a life of its own the crowd seemed to open up as Ranks and The Worlders crew gate-crashed Storm's party. It was like the biblical parting of the Red Sea as people made a wide corridor for the yout's to pass through. Ranks walked confidently, pulling into a corner near the toilets. The boys were heady. All had been on the pipe. Ranks didn't mind Kurtis tagging. He was staying at Danny's. Besides Danny had plans for Easy's half-wit, half-brother. Nerome stood close by.

Stukky, a short dark yout' with a round face and Fila, a black-cultured white yout' who looked like rap star Eminem, were sitting comfortably around a table as the menacing crew approached.

Nerome judged it safe for Ranks to join the others. On occasions like this, Mentian usually acted as second security, a back up bodyguard. Dressed ruggedly in a long overcoat, baggy trousers and Timberland boots, Ranks was looking for one person, a specific individual. In the next few seconds he found him, light-skinned and grey-eyed, fighting his way through the crowd. Every now and then someone would stop him, asking for a dedication, or grab him to them, lifting him high wishing him Happy New Year. Scantily dressed bashment girls who had had too much to drink forced their lips on his neck or face. Laughing, he fought off wandering hands and pinches, face flushing red. Bling!

Ranks smiled, took a gulp of his Dragon Stout, and waited. Sure enough, as Zukie swung around towards the exit leading to the toilets he saw Ranks. He paused, seemed to draw in his breath, before walking on. Ranks leaped from his seat grinning sadistically and blocked Zukie's path. Zukie attempted to side-step, but Ranks followed suit. Kurtis laughed. Zukie stepped the other way. Ranks outmanoeuvred him. The crew edged Ranks on, sniggering, whistling and laughing. Ranks could feel the fury steeping from Zukie. His face was just an inch away from Zukie's. They stared at each other indifferently. Ranks maintained his cool gaze.

"Ain't you gonna wish me a Happy New Year, Light-Finger?" Ranks asked. Zukie looked uncomfortable, nervous. "Tell you what, play a New Year dedication for me nuh? A Bob Marley, the old prophet, tune. It's called 'Running Away'. Balti must have dat in his selection box. I want you to play it for your brother, Storm." Zukie stared at Ranks for a minute. His grey eyes looked shadowy, and he blinked slowly. The crew was silent now. Zukie looked over at them, across at everyone, his eyes stopping on Nerome then back at Ranks.

"Why?" he asked, "why that tune?"

Smirking, Ranks shrugged his shoulders casually. Scratching his nose, he sat down again took a gulp of his Stout and said quirkily, "I'm afraid, star, only your brother Mr Storm knows the answer, to that one."

EVERYWHERE WAS DIFFERENT. Easy expected that after nearly five years in prison. Yet he wasn't prepared for it to be this way as he discharged himself from hospital and the taxi took him through Hulme.

All around him Easy could see changes. Gone were the disastrous architectural designs of the William Kent, John Nash, Charles Barry and Robert Adam deck access flats, also known as the bullrings. In their places were new, sleek, designer and much-desired dwellings. Easy didn't think it made much difference to the living standards of poor, unemployed people.

As the taxi pulled into the Alexandra Park housing estate, Moss Side Easy saw the whole estate had been architecturally renovated. Grange Close and Dodgington Close had retained their notorious names. The Piper Mill pub, opposite his Gran's, on Piper Mill road, had been replaced by some sort of Government Yout' Employment Project.

The whole place definitely looked different, but didn't feel different. Easy had memories of standing on cockroaches crawling inside his trainers and rats as big as rabbits sprinting across the uneven roads like gold medal-winning athletes. And once inside Grandma's the feelings of desperation and vulnerability were still the same and clung to him like his shadow.

Home again.

He let himself in with a key, trudging upstairs into the room he used to share with Kurtis, placing the bottles and pills the hospital had given him on the dresser. Easy looked around Kurtis's bedroom; the walls were covered with posters of expensive cars and old Manchester United football stars: Dwight Yorke, Andy Cole and Wesley Longsight 'ghetto-kid-done-good' Brown. Then Tupac,

Master P, DMX, Dre, Ja Rule, So Solid Crew and Snoop Dog.

In Kurtis's wardrobe he found some old clothes he had left there before his rise. Not surprisingly, they were too big for him. Jeans that had fit him snugly as a tall, healthy, sixteen-year-old now hung off his backside. Easy was unintentionally 'bussing sags', the hip style of wearing trousers halfway down your arse.

When he looked at himself in the splintered wardrobe mirror he looked like the scarecrow in The Wizard of Oz. No Calvin Klein, Armani, Levi, Wrangler, Gucci but to name a few. He had gone into the New Year badly. Things weren't exactly going his way as planned. Easy stared hard at himself in the mirror.

Grandma came in, smiling palely.

"Everyt'ing all right?" she asked, concerned, her eyes straining all over his body. Easy tried to keep a trembling sigh from fleeing the depths of his chest. He swallowed deeply. Grandma smiled bravely. "There's some dinner for you on the table downstairs."

"Thanks Grandma but I in't hungry."

"Look at you, boy, yu body need building up. You know Grandma's food is going to give your body the strength it need to heal and get better."

"Alright then, Gran." Nervous. It would be the first time that he would come directly face to face with Kurtis and Sharon in years. He made his way slowly towards the bedroom door, limping slightly, aware of how tall he stood over his grandmother. For a second he fought desperately to overcome dizziness, but steadied himself as the blood slowly moved away from his head, flowing warmly around his body.

"Welcome home!" The roar and applause went up as Easy entered the packed living room. Easy was stunned. Appalled. Embarrassed.

"Gran you shouldn't have wasted any money on me." His grandmother only smiled, blinking back tears of happiness. The table was laid with cake, drink, biscuits, various Jamaican delicacies like curried goat, rice and peas, bread, fried fish, jerk chicken and salad. An assortment of relatives Easy had not seen in years and couldn't even name individually stood around the table.

"I'm just so glad to have Daima's first-born back home where he belongs," she said, leaning on her stick. Sharon popped open a bottle of champagne. It exploded like a gunshot, almost making Easy flinch. She poured a glassful, amidst cheers.

"Welcome home Barry," she yelled in his ears, half-dragging him towards the table. "Gran says you're a changed man. No longer a sinner." She said smiling. "She's got so much faith in you, and I just know you're not going to let her down again." Easy forced a smile as Sharon handed him a glass of champagne. He said nothing as his eyes travelled sleepily over cousins and Aunts in the room. Finally his eyes rested on a pair of twitchy, cool inky irises watching him steadily.

Easy's eyes met the resolute gaze. They belonged to a tall, dark handsome yout' who looked like a mature version of a brother he last saw as a ten-year-old. Kej. His not-so-little brother who never came to see him in prison or visit him in hospital. His face looked staunch. He was wearing better clothes than Easy. Why hadn't Grandma tell him what she had planned? At least he could have been mentally if not physically prepared. Anyway, what mattered now was getting to know Kurtis again.

Easy started to walk towards the good-looking yout' that was Kurtis. It looked as if Kurtis had inherited his good looks from Momma's side of the family. He had large brown eyes and although his hair was shaved quite close it was clear that there was Indian ancestry in him by the straight texture of his hair and his rectilinear nose.

Kurtis put down his glass, looked coldly at him, turned around, and headed towards the porch. Easy shuffled forward, his cries of "Kej wait!" drowned out by music and laughter. He was barely in time to see Kurtis head through the back gate into the vast estate into oblivion. Sharon was suddenly by his side, holding his arm gently.

"Give him time," she urged. "I'm glad to see you back even if he isn't." Why didn't that last statement make him feel any better? Easy felt himself shaking slightly as a cold unexplained chill crawled up his spine like a centipede with icy feet. He looked at Sharon, then through the open door where the back gate was swinging in the wind. "Come on." Sharon said smiling reassuringly, gently tugging on his arm. "It's your party."

It's *somebody's* party, Easy thought, but it ain't mine.

STORM WASN'T SLEEPING well lately. His plan to prick Danny's conscience had failed. He wanted Danny, as the last known member of the Pipers crew, to feel remorseful about Zukie's and Oil's injuries and Chico's death. Danny was the one who gave Jigsy the information that caused Zukie to be captured and held to ransom by Jigsy. But everything had backfired.

Instead, Danny was getting closer to Zukie. Storm had seen Ranks talking to Zukie at the New Year's Eve party and now Danny was hanging around the shop all the time. The piece of shit seemed to be popping up everywhere.

After smoking a bag of weed and contemplating deeply Storm's mind was made up.

He knew what he had to do.

He was gonna find out why.

ZUKIE WOKE, GASPING for air. Felt like surfacing after being underwater for a long time. Perspiring. Shaking. Cold.

His nightmare was still vivid in his mind. He'd been plagued by the same dream since seeing Danny Ranks at the New Year party. Chico and Hair Oil. They were with him in the back of a car. The car crashing, rolling over and over. Then he'd wake up. Like now. Perspiring. Shaking. Cold.

He sat in the dark bedroom looking around. Paranoid. Aching with terror. Heart thumping in his chest. It passed. He calmed himself, breathing slowly, covering his hot face. He was full of pain, anger, and guilt. It would never go away. But he didn't understand it. He needed to comprehend why Chico died. Shit, if only he could remember. He climbed out of the mass of tangled sheets and headed towards Clifton's bedroom, but Storm's room was empty and his bed unslept in.

It was two o' clock in the morning. Storm hadn't said he was going anywhere. Maybe Zukie had forgotten, as usual. Dressed only in boxers, he shivered as the cold night air touched his bare skin. Frost formed on the windows in crisp sharp triangular shapes. The central heating was off. Picking up the telephone Zukie decided to phone Storm's mobile. The number went clear out of his head, like someone had created a hole in his mind. Then he suddenly found himself wondering what he was doing, standing with the phone in his hand, semi-naked in the middle of the living room. Couldn't remember. Panic rose. Then it came to him, he was trying to phone Storm.

His brother's mobile was switched off.

Danny's words haunted his ears as if he was in the room.

"If Chico had known what was going down that night he'd never have got into that car."

"—play a new year dedication for me nuh? A Bob Marley tune. It's called 'Running Away'. I want you to play it for your brother, Storm."

Zukie exhaled deeply. Did Storm have answers? Did the other, forgotten, Zukie have the answers? Zukie suddenly started to weep. He didn't know why. He just needed to. He needed Storm. He needed to talk about what was happening to him. Where was his brother?

24

"TOOK YA TIME, din't ya?" Ranks said with more than an air of arrogance, as Storm was led into the main large room by the white boy who had answered the door two minutes ago. The atmosphere was thick with cannabis smoke. The room was lit by an Ikea spotlight at floor level and the flickering image from a huge monitor, which faced Storm. Four yout's of varying complexions and sizes stared up at him. Ranks was playing a racing game on his PlayStation, and looked up briefly as Storm stepped onto the wooden floor. As soon as he entered, as if on cue, the yout's exited, looking him up and down with blatant scrutiny. Stukky, Pipes, Mr. Mentian, and Sizzla. No sign of the bodyguard. A huge Rotweiller dog ran up to Storm from nowhere, growling. Intimidated, Storm raised both hands defensively.

"Here Zell." The dog went to her master. "Easy, girl. Easy." Ranks patted the dog and she lay low, watching Storm suspiciously with coal black eyes.

"Feel free to have a seat." Ranks offered, sensing Storm hovering close by. Storm looked around. The set up was for work, play, and pleasure. Weights, dumbbells press benches, keyboards, an expensive Kenwood hi-fi system, a multimedia PC, a row of high-powered remote control toy cars, and a large Futon sofa bed.

"No thanks." Terse. Pausing the game Ranks walked wearily over to the Futon, placing himself down on it. The dog followed eagerly and sat next to a large antique pine coffee table. Ranks began to build a spliff, blatantly looking Storm up and down with scrutiny. Storm was self-possessed. He'd allow the piece of shit to get away with this show of haughtiness. For now.

Storm weighed up Ranks. Their clothing was opposite. Storm was dressed for the cold February weather, long coat, Armani trousers, scarf, jumper, and gloves. Except for a Nike stocking cap and jewellery, Danny was dressed casually in stretch CK boxers. For a teen his body was muscle toned, worked on well, an eagle tattooed skilfully over his left upper arm. The apartment was warm, welcoming, and furnished excellently. But Storm hadn't come here to admire, nor relax.

"Aren't you gonna ask me how I found you?" Storm asked.

"Man as smart as you could find a tiny piece of hair in the ocean." Danny remarked nonchalantly. Storm didn't know whether to be flattered or cautious. "I'm just surprised it took you so long to reach me." Ranks started skinning up, rolling the king-size Rizla paper together expertly with long-nailed fingers covered with gold signet rings, watching Storm carefully with cool hazel-coloured eyes. Storm began to feel agitated. He fiddled with the stud in his ear, and then looked at his expensive watch.

"Got more *pressing* things to do, star?" Ranks asked, lighting the zook.

"Time's all mine," Storm said with more than a hint of impatience in his voice, sniffing.

The teen sucked through the spliff as if it was life-saving oxygen, exhaling deeply. Thick intricate smoke curled into the room.

"Want a burn of dis?" Storm started to seethe inwardly but he wasn't going to let this little shit-wipe see him uneasy. Storm knew that was his ultimate desire.

"Lately," Storm began, "I keep seein' your face around my premises and family."

Ranks suddenly burst into laughter, which annoyed and puzzled Storm. Ranks was suddenly serious again Looking at the glowing end of the spliff as it burned, he blew on the end harshly. It glowed bright, grey ash scattering everywhere.

"*Family*? Yeah, you pretty tight with your little brother now, since that bad accident he remembers nuttin about. And don't give me that blood is thicker than water crap because I in't buyin".

"You say Zukie has memory problems since Jigsy's car got gunned off the road with him, Chico, Oil and Blue in it right? So, obviously, he don't *remember* your gang past. He don't *know* you as bad bwai Storm, leader, or should I say ex-gang leader? He's got no idea you give the mention to Colours and Frenchie to blast my man Jigsy off the face of the earth."

Sighing, Storm found himself scowling. He spoke through gritted teeth.

"If you'd have kept your mouth shut about who Zukie was to me Jigsy wouldn't have got sprangy."

Ranks fired back quickly.

"All I did was confirm that the kid in the back of Jigsy's car was Zukie who was your kin. I in't takin' no guilt rap for the shit that went down, star. It was *your* fuckin' show."

Storm reflected bitterly, feeling a deep painful tug at his heart. He wasn't in control of events that night. Things had flown thick and fast. He didn't know that Jigsy and Easy-Love Brown had forced Zukie and his friends into their car at gunpoint. The hit had been arranged. Things were in motion and it was too late to stop it. He had tried, but it was too late. Yeah, it was *his* show all right. A fucking horror show. Storm looked down at Ranks. Ranks was sprawled on the futon, smoking casually but watching Storm intently. Slowly he sat down next to Ranks, hands in his pockets. He looked at the polished wooden floor, looked ahead at the large TV screen then finally, he looked at Danny Ranks.

"What the fuck do you want?"

Ranks held his breath deliberately, then said slowly.

"Easy-Love. Off the streets. Permanent."

Storm was slightly perplexed.

"Easy's a Piper bwai, one of your old crew."

"Piper Mill ting done dead an' buried. Worlders crew ah run tings inna de ghetto right now," Ranks growled. "I'm in control now, runnin' tings militant."

Leaning forward Storm clasped his hands.

"So Mr Milly if tings runnin' so militant, and you in control, baby, what the hell you want *me* for?"

"Easy's an old player and you're an old player. I also thought it was a good opportunity for Storm Michaels to execute vengeance."

Storm shifted in his seat uncomfortably and laughed. He saw a spark of annoyance in Ranks' eyes but at least he had commanded the teen's full attention.

Storm got up slowly, brushing down his expensive long coat.

"I got a business to run. I'm legit now. I put all that shit behind me."

Ranks jumped to his feet irately, pushing his face into Storm's and shrieking. The dog's ears pricked up.

"All that shit? You call somebody deliberately running down your mother shit? You call somebody holdin' your brothers ransom, shit? Man yu got serious tings to care of." Kissing his teeth he waved his hand dismissively at Storm. Storm sighed, closing his eyes momentarily.

Swallowing, Ranks stared at Storm, gesticulating with his hands. "Don't you feel that salt taste in your mouth when you look at your brother struggling to remember, don't you feel it hurting in your gut when you think of how dem man tek liberties wid yu family? Don't you just want to get hold of Easy and stab that fucka right in his skull?"

"No," Storm said emphatically.

"Yeah. Yu right. You've changed. A man couldn't do dat to me. *My* family? Nah, I'd fuck him up good style."

"Danny, you ain't me. I've moved on. I've made a new life for myself, my kids, my mother and for Zukie. I've got a beautiful house.

I can forget the past."

"Like Zukie huhhhnnn? Ignorance is bliss huhhhnnn? I reckon if Zukie finds out what you really are, what you really did, how you put the mention on Jigsy and killing his best spar Chico, turning Hair Oil into a veggie roll I reckon you can just kiss Zukie bye-bye, innit?" Danny continued relentlessly. "You're living a lie, a big fuckin' Mac-whopper of a lie, Storm."

Storm couldn't hold back his anger anymore.

"You're young, Danny. Seventeen years old. You may be tough, but plenty men out there got years on you." And as Storm said this, he wondered if he really was talking to a kid of seventeen. Danny acted much older.

"I want us, me and you, runnin' tings with Easy off the big screen. Me and you fifty-fifty. You'd be making more money in a week than that studio of yours takes in a month. Think about it."

Storm smirked. "I'll see myself out." Ranks drew heavily on the spliff. "Oh and by the way, keep your distance from Zukie and my recording studio."

"Zukie wants to know the truth. I know he does. I see it in his eyes."

Storm stopped instantly. He was fuming. Ranks was like super glue. He wasn't going to let it go.

"If Zukie really has to know anything he's gonna hear it all from me." Storm was already turning to leave, his hand on the door. He paused when he heard Danny's abnormally calm voice.

"Sure he is, star. Sure."

Ranks situated himself back at the PlayStation racing game, fixing his feet on the console's pedals, his hands on the steering wheel. Storm heard Ranks' cool words continue above the roar of a virtual reality Lotus.

"You go right ahead and have dat phat heart-to-heart with your little bredrin. I know he's just waitin'. And he's just gonna appreciate it, in't he, when you tell him how you fucked up his life. How your stupid little payback killed his best friend, put his other friend in a fuckin' wheel-chair and jellied his brains. Gowan go chat wid him, star. You won't have no business, no sound engineer, no partner, and no brother.

"I personally guarantee you that."

EASY HEARD WAILING. Like a cat. Awake. Listening. Expectant. His single bed was diagonally placed next to Kurtis' empty bed.

28

Kurtis hadn't returned home since the surprise party. Four fifteen a.m. Dark shadows falling on the blind over the window. Hadn't slept at all. The wind was howling, it was pissing down rain. Easy heard the strange noise again. Soon realised the sound wasn't an animal at all. Straining his ears, lying on his back frowning. It was coming through the walls. Easy climbed out of the bed slowly, hobbling towards the door. Easing the door open he walked through, tip toeing barefoot. Light from Grandma's room. No light under Sharon's bedroom.

Grandma. She was crying again. Like she did at nights when he was a young teen living there. Easy's heart boomed painfully as the memory resurfaced. Grandma was crying.

"GRANDMA?" HE STARTLED her. As soon as he spoke, she almost jumped into the air off the bed.

She was grasping a handkerchief, her eyes red and bloodshot popped wide as he walked across and took her little body in his arms. She tried to fob him off by telling him it was nothing but Easy persisted gently.

"Come on Gran, what is it?" she dabbed her wet eyes then looked at him.

"I borrowed, I borrowed some money from a man who came to visit on the estate. He said he was a loan manager," the old woman stuttered.

"Grandma, he's a loan shark."

Grandma looked into the distance painfully.

"Yes but he mek it sound so easy." Easy-Love felt his shoulders stoop heavily. He sighed with frustration. Why didn't she go to a bank? But he knew the answer to that already. The old woman hated authority, despised doctors, and banks alike. Easy knew her desire was to go back to Jamaica. But it was a dream for her. She had no homestead to return to, and no money to purchase land or property.

As Easy watched her staring ahead emptily, he remembered that he could have used some of his money to buy Grandma a nice, big beautiful home by the sea in Negril, Jamaica. God knows if anyone deserved happiness and a good life it was Grandma, especially after taking on Kurtis and Sharon when social services had considered her too old to adopt her own grandchildren.

"How much did you borrow, Gran?" The old woman turned to look at him with weary blood-streaked eyes, twisting the handkerchief around her fingers nervously.

"I borrowed a t'ousand pounds."

"Why?"

"Kurtis needed it for college. He used his grant to buy clothes. I just wanted to see him through. But that's not the worse of it, child." She paused, shaking uncontrollably. "I was tidying his room, getting it ready for you and I found letters under his bed, letters from the college to say he's not been going there since November and them going to throw him off his A level course. He done so well with his GCSE's getting nine in all. I thought he was trying for university next year but he's lyin' all the time."

Grandma was wailing again, tears streaming down her wild face, mingling with mucus dribbling from her flaring nostrils. "All the time he's been pretending to go to college, gettin' up in the morning, packing his lunch and books. I don't know where the hell he goes. I use to think I was going soft in my head when I couldn't find my purse or there was money missin' but now I know for sure it's him. I set a trap. I put some money under my bed and sure enough he found it. Lord knows what I'm gonna do. I got behind wid my payments and now that loan man wants three thousand from me."

"Three grand? For a loan you took out only months ago? Surely that's not right?"

"He showed me the papers I signed." Easy's head was spinning like a drunk ice skater spinning out of control on a melting rink.

Kurtis was out of order. Robbing from his own blood, chippin' outta college and now sleeping out. He was contributing to the old woman's debt problem, which ironically she instigated to help him. He was also causing the old woman unnecessary pain and stress. Easy held Grandma tight to him, as if he could push all his reassurance into her. She sobbed against her grandson. Easy kissed her wrinkled forehead.

"Don't cry Grandma. I'll help you repay the debt. Don't fret."

It was time for Easy to swallow his pride. He didn't want to work in no superstore but if that's what it took.

SILENT, STORM SAT in the Mitsubishi Shogun 3.0 turbo, still parked outside Rank's yard. Engine switched off. Cold. Raining. Windows steamed. He lit the spliff he had built.

Storm felt lost. Cornered. For a long while he clung desperately to the steering wheel, groaning as if he was in deep agony. In a way he was. There were two ways out of his present situation. Eradicate Easy, or do what he wanted and pop Ranks instead. His secret would remain safe. Zukie would never know the real truth. He thought the second option would be best. Time had brought him a new enemy. He hated Ranks like he hated Easy-Love Brown. Storm put the key in the ignition, started the car, and drove off.

NEROME HAD LISTENED through the walls to the conversation between Storm and Ranks. Normally he'd wait until Ranks decided to confide in him. He was inquisitive about Storm. *The* Storm. Heard quite a lot about the notorious gang leader when he had first come out of the army and was living in a bed-sit in Leeds. How much of it was hearsay or hype, Nero didn't know. But to him Storm looked and acted in a way his name contradicted. Cool, in control and calculating. Nerome wondered just how Ranks thought he could outsmart somebody like that? Blackmail? He knew Ranks was making his job to protect his arse harder.

Nerome felt sorry for Zukie. He was messed up, and trusted his brother to be telling him the truth.

Nerome lit a spliff and his thoughts slowly trickled back to the book he was reading.

But it was no good.

He just couldn't snap back into the story again.

"YOU'RE NEEDED AT the checkouts. Packing." Easy-Love looked up. There he was, bespectacled batty bwai Bennett, suddenly in the cereal aisle hovering next to Easy like a stinky, hanging fart. Easy just couldn't stand it, being told what to do by some mothafuckin' supervisor who seemed to have been born for the sole purpose of fuckin' his head up. The cold brotha's name was Colin Bennett and he was no older than nineteen. A part-time University student, well spoken and arrogant, he was working there for the extra income to see him through college. Colin didn't like the way Easy mingled with the pretty female staff. He always seemed to be on Easy's case, giving him trolley loads of items to stack every second of the day. If Easy didn't need the job to help grandma pay off the loan shark and generally help her out, he'd have told Mr. Merciless where to get off. And the money was shit, £4.50 an hour. Ask a kid to wash a car and he wants a fiver for half an hour's work. How the hell was a man supposed to raise a family on that? No wonder he'd got into drugs in the first place.

The superstore was busy, full of mithered mothers, scrimping students, sneaky shoplifters, and price-watching pensioners alike. Voices over the intercom system either summoned members of staff for various reasons or announced today's not-to-be-missed bargains. Easy stopped unpacking the cornflakes and stared at the supervisor coolly as he repeated his order. There was no smile and no "please could you come and help at the checkout." This boy needs a quick lesson in manners and respect, Easy thought scornfully. Dutty nigger like that wouldn't survive a day out 'pon street. "What are you waitin' for?" The supervisor barked. A few shoppers turned their heads and looked. Easy's face burned with humiliation.

"Sonia told me to stack these items on these shelves."

"Sonia finished her shift half an hour ago." Mr. Merciless skinned his pretty white teeth. "I'm in charge now." Controlling his boiling temper, Easy strode over to checkout number one, glad to see Aisha on it, a beautiful dark skinned girl with a friendly smile. She was smiling as Easy limped across. Easy began to pack people's shopping as they paid for their goods. The job also required him to take the shopping to customer's vehicles if they needed the extra assistance. Easy was aware of his supervisor studying him as he worked. Easy decided there and then he was gonna sort this fucka out very soon.

Still fuming, Easy began to put the next customer's shopping in the bags when her elaborate Jamaican accent made him look up. She was fairly overweight, brown-skinned, pretty, with huge dimples, like dents in her face as she smiled. She loved her food. Easy could tell that by the huge amount of shopping she had bought. Well over two hundred pounds worth. Yeah, she'd definitely need assistance to her car or taxi. Speaking into her mobile phone, she laughed and joked and paid by credit card. It took a moment before her eyes registered Easy observing her. She stopped laughing, putting the phone away slowly. Easy smiled. He knew who this was even though he had never met or seen her in his life. Looking at her anybody would think she was an ordinary innocent housewife or mother doing the weekly shop. No one would believe she was the leader behind one of the deadliest gangs in the North-West. It was unmistakably Miss Small. She fumbled with her credit card before dropping it. Easy picked it up and handed it back to her outstretched mampie hand but not before reading her name. Veniesha Brooks.

Easy recited the stupid script. "Hello, I have been assigned as you shopper helper. May I assist you to your vehicle?" Miss Small looked lost for a second, but with this much shopping she knew she couldn't refuse the help at hand. Easy smiled. *'Caught you'*.

NEROME LOOKED IN on Ranks. Sleeping. Twelve thirty-two in the afternoon. As usual Ranks was sprawled halfway across the bed, the duvet entwined around the lower half of his body. He slept with his forearm covering his face shielding it from the bright daylight now pouring into the bedroom. The girl next to him opened her eyes as Nero cleared his throat. She was dark-skinned, very pretty, petite, with a tiny waist and huge chocolate breasts. She made no attempt to cover herself. Looking at Nero watching her body as she rose naked, swinging her hips and retrieved a pair of knickers from the floor. Smiling she stepped into them, and then left the room.

Next to the bed was a tray containing take-away food from Chicken Run, a delicious Caribbean takeaway in Moss Side. And next to the empty box was more rubbish, spliff ends, Rizla papers, empty beer bottles and a SKY satellite TV magazine.

Ranks wasn't deep asleep, Nerome knew that. His breathing was medium. Nerome cleared his throat, looking at the mobile in his hand.

"Stukky's on the phone."

"Tell him to call back later."

Says it's urgent." Ranks turned over.

"The only person I wanna talk to right now is Storm. No other fucker. Ask Stukky what he wants."

Nerome put the phone to his ear and spoke, watching Ranks yawning as he got out of the bed before scratching his balls.

"Just tell him," Stukky said, "Dodge crew slowly trying to hustle in on Raby Street." All Ranks said when this was relayed was:

"Let's go and get some food. I'm hungry."

VENIESHA MICHELLE BROOKS' BMW beeped three times as she aimed the alarm fob at it where it was parked in a far corner. From the corner of her eye she thought she saw Easy smile as he carried her excess shopping towards the car.

"So what's a nice girl like you doin' struggling with your shopping while your old man's at home probably with his feet up watchin' Man United?"

Was he pretending not to know who she was? If he was, he was a damn good actor. "Shoulda deh ah Hollywood," Veniesha thought to herself cynically. She lifted the boot of the car, ignoring him, trying to place the bulky shopping into the large interior herself. A cold breeze curled round her neck.

"Here, let me get it." In a flash he was helping her to put the things in the car. Miss Small watched him carefully. She shoulda have her man them eradicate him when they had the chance.

Easy was grunting slightly, wooing and panting exaggeratedly.

"No woman of mine, especially one as beautiful as you, would be doing this. No way, I'd be shopping for her, carrying her t'ings, driving her." For a second she was taken aback then flattered. It was a long time since anybody had paid her any compliments. However she wasn't going to let him think he'd won her over that easily.

"Y'ever hear bout woman's liberation? Ooman nuh need man fe do tings for we no more. We almost at the top inna everyt'ing now," Veniesha said seriously, hoping to throw him off her with her severity. Easy laughed.

"Yeah nuff respect. I love independent, strong women, know what I mean? I love women who know what they want and how to get it. What's your name?" He asked boldly.

Miss Small hesitated.

What the hell was she gonna say to him?

My name is Miss Small and I was the one who got my crew to beat you up when you stepped outta prison only you don't know that.

"Come on, tell me your name."

VENIESHA BROOKS KNEW she couldn't lie to Easy-Love Brown standing waiting expectantly before her. Besides there was every chance he might have seen her name on the credit card when it fell. She couldn't understand why her mind wouldn't switch off from him and her feet take her into her vehicle. Easy-Love Brown was beautiful, cocoa brown cool complexioned, naturally textured hair showing in his dreads, deep brown eyes, twinkling mischievously, and an absolutely breath-taking smile. Veniesha hated herself for allowing herself to be hypnotised by him.

"Veniesha." She finally answered. "That's my name." Easy

outstretched his palm. She took it and shook it.

"Barrington."

"I know." She said. He frowned slightly then smiled as he caught on.

"Yeah. I said it before, didn't I?"

"Yes, you did." Easy began to pack away the rest of Veniesha's shopping. Veniesha's heart was racing. Now what? What the hell was she doing, fraternising with the enemy? She didn't want to converse with Easy-Love, never mind get mixed up with him. Yet he couldn't possibly know who she was and that it was she who organised his beating. No one except her close crew knew her.

After Easy had finished he stood around expectantly. Veniesha fixed her handbag on her shoulder.

"I hope yu not waitin' for a tip."

"Yes, but not the money kind." Veniesha smiled. "Your smile's so beautiful I got to see it again."

Suddenly, Colin the supervisor was in the car park. Veniesha saw him marching across and clocked Easy's frustrated face as he saw his boss striding across.

"How about your phone number?" Easy said quickly.

"What for?"

"So I can cook you a good back-a-yard dinner. Or take you out for a meal." Again Veniesha found herself smiling. Obstinate. But no one ever got anywhere by not being. Reaching inside her bag she pulled out a card, handing it to him. Easy's boss was suddenly right up to them.

"Get back on the shop floor," the yout' barked. Veniesha was disgusted. But if this was the Easy she thought it was, she knew he could handle it. Turning to her Easy said, bowing: "Veniesha please excuse me." Then he turned to his supervisor, kneed him in the groin, and said. "Fuck you. And you can stick the whole superstore up your tight little batty." Veniesha put the car into reverse, and drove off laughing. Well he had certainly made an impression on her.

"THAT DANNY WAS there wasn't he, on the night of the accident?" Zukie fixed his questioning grey eyes on his elder brother. Storm put his pen down sighing heartily. They were in the studio taking a break from mixing. Storm had been going over the accounts, getting them ready for Tariq next week.

"Yes," he answered cautiously, lowering his dark eyes.

Zukie felt elated. He couldn't remember Blue being there. All the other details were patchy but he remembered Danny's face and remembered Danny's name. He smiled before realising Storm didn't seem to be sharing his joy.

Zukie rubbed the back of his neck. "Cliff, are you hidin' something from me?"

Storm sighed. Licking his lips he said. "Chico was shiftin' brown and crack, Zukie. He got caught up with the wrong crowd. Danny was, still is a part of that crowd. He was involved in some bad things. You, you were forced into the car they were travelling in." Zukie felt weak as if all the strength had been sapped from his body. For a second he was confused. He remembered suddenly. A handgun. The feeling of fear combined with anger. The leather seats of a car. The unseen faces. His heart thumped viciously.

"What? But I thought you said we were just accepting a lift from Chico's cousin. Why would someone I didn't know force me into a car?"

Storm cleared his throat. "I'm sorry Zukie. I didn't want to destroy that good image you had of your friend. If it's any consolation to you Chico died trying to protect you. Danny can't give you any answers, only lies. You gotta stay away from him, believe me, blood, he's no good."

Zukie was bewildered.

"I don't understand. I do remember that it was against everything we stood for. Chico hated hard drugs, hated what it was doing to our community. Why would he do that?"

"There's a lot you don't know, wouldn't want to know, trust me. But things are all right now. You got to look to the future. We've got a business to run. Chico's dead. He can't help you now. It's just me and you and no bad bwais from now on, little bro. OK?" Zukie looked at Storm. It didn't feel OK. Just final. Like he was sayin' this was the way it is, accept it. The pieces of the puzzle were more far apart than ever. Storm's eyes seemed like they were almost pleading. Zukie felt himself frowning. He couldn't, for one single second, imagine Chico and Hair Oil drug dealing. Something wasn't quite right. His heart beat strongly. Storm began to write again, leaving Zukie to conclude that the topic was no longer open to further discussion.

"I don't believe you." Zukie suddenly announced, watching his bother's reaction carefully.

"What?" Storm swung around almost dropping the accounts book. It seemed to slip through his fingers. He fumbled to retrieve it.

"I said I don't believe you."

STORM STARED BACK at Zukie totally stunned. His eyes wide, watery, mouth opening wide.

"I don't believe you. I think you're talking a whole heap of crap. Chico never, never defended drugs, I know dat for a fact. And, and this Danny, seems to be hinting at you knowing something more about Chico, every time I see him."

Storm closed his accounts book, closing his eyes momentarily. Zukie looked at Storm sternly.

"I want the fuckin' truth, Storm. Don't you see I need to know?" His voice was breaking.

Storm dropped his eyes then seemed to gather his composure; his voice was low and tremulous. "OK" Zukie saw Storm's hands shaking slightly. Zukie's throat suddenly went dry.

"You're right. I haven't been truthful." Storm sighed, looking beyond at the glass that partitioned off the empty studio. "The truth is, the truth is Danny is a threat to you. A serious threat. I lied about there not being any bad bwais around but that's not true. Danny will kill you if he gets half the chance because he thinks you can implicate him in Chico's death."

Zukie was quick on the draw.

"Implicate him to who?"

"Dibs."

Zukie frowned. It was painful.

"He was part of a posse that made you get into the car that crashed." So that part was real. It had happened.

Zukie shook his head fiercely. "I don't understand. If he wanted to kill me, wouldn't he have tried to by now?" Storm stood up pulling Zukie's arm, indicating to follow. Silently Zukie walked after his brother to the back of the shop, down into the basement where they kept surplus stock and equipment. The musty smell climbed into Zukie's lungs, making him wheeze slightly.

"Get the light, nuh?" Zukie did as he was asked, flicking on the light, watching Storm remove a couple of boxes. He retrieved something wrapped in a patterned cloth. Storm stood next to Zukie and unravelled the mystery object. Metallic. Tubular. Short. Shining under the dim stockroom light. Storm put it into Zukie's hot hand. Zukie's breath left his body in a jolt. It felt cold, so cold the touch of it almost shocked him into stillness. He felt the food he'd had earlier rise to the top of his throat and stall there.

"Believe me, Zukie. Danny is lethal. They call him Ranks. You need security twenty-four seven. When you're with me you're safe.

He knows that. You need to be protected at all times. Keep it close to you. Here." Trembling, Zukie not only felt the weight but felt the terrifying power of it. He shook as he caressed the smooth alloy grip, his heart thumping violently. Whop, whop, whop!

"Where, where did you get this, Storm? Why?" Breathless.

"I got to protect me and mines. Know this… I've never used it, believe. But no man's gonna walk in here an' try and tek what I work hard to achieve, not without a fight, anyway." Zukie watched as his brother handled the gun like a professional, snapping the magazine into the chamber. "Nothing points or handles like a Hi-Power, believe. Fits your hand comfortably like a natural extension of your body. Comes with magazine safety. This means that when the magazine is withdrawn, the gun won't fire." Zukie watched in awe as his brother released the clip on the left hand-side of the gun, wondering where his brother had acquired this gun knowledge. Where did he get this gun and what was it doing hidden in the storeroom? "Lift it up and aim where you want to take out any bad bwai."

"What?" Zukie was alarmed.

"Like dis." Storm stood behind Zukie, raising the awkward arm holding the gun, swivelling Zukie around to face a floor-standing mirror. "Its sights align quickly and naturally. It's just like pointing your finger. Its trigger system is rugged, yet gives you the precise break of a single-action trigger." Zukie saw their reflections. He saw himself pointing the gun at himself. Sweat on his face. But, in the dark misty mirror it altered from his petrified face to the laughing, mocking face of Danny. Danny Ranks. Zukie's finger hovered on the trigger. A surge of electric fear and excitement seemed to pass through his body.

Danny Ranks was a dead man if he ever, ever tried to cross his path again.

DANNY RANKS WITHDREW the wooden padlocked box from under his bed, unlocked it, and emptied its contents. These were the things closest to his heart, comics, bullets, birthday cards and newspaper cuttings. and a huge pile of letters tied in a black ribbon. Smoking a cigarette, Ranks lay across the bed and untied the ribbon. This was all that remained to him of his mother. She'd started to write to him two days before his second birthday. Danny picked out the first letter. Blowing smoke ahead of him he squinted in the light that poured from a bedroom lamp. Outside his room he could hear music and laughter. Danny began to read the letter he'd read so many times before.

"Dear Daniel,
This is the first of many leters than I'm going to write to you. Forgive my speling but I never did too well at scool. I supposse when you are old enouf you will unnerstan why I did what I did. If I have cause you hurt or shame I am so sorry. I give you up because at just fourteen I knew I couldn't really look after you. I wanted you very much. Don't think you were a misstake but I just couldn't keep you. I know my sister Celia will make a good job of looking after you. I think it's better that you and me dont meet. It's selfish of me I know because I would want to take you home and I don't have nothing for you. I'm sorry but love alone can't take care of you. But if you don't mind we can write to each other. I'll know how you getting on because Celia will always tell me but it will be nice to get letters from you, if you want. I preffer it if you didn't try to contact me but things may change when you get older. Take care my love, your always in my thoughts, you're mother,
Veniesha Michelle Patterson."

Danny didn't know where Veniesha lived. Her full identity and exact locale were a mystery to him. All his letters to her went through Aunt Celia who had taken care of him until he left home at fifteen. He hadn't written to his mother for about six months. A couple of years ago Aunt Celia had told him that her sister had started a new life and a new family and that's all she knew. She'd gone abroad to live in Jamaica. Danny didn't know her new second name or whether she was still in Jamaica but in a strange way he didn't think she was far from him.

Danny took out a piece of A4 paper and a pen. Using the box for support and taking out a pen he started to write.

"Dear Veniesha," he crossed her name out then wrote Dear Mother. But somehow it felt phoney so he screwed it up and started again. Ranks' spelling wasn't much better than his mother's. "How are you? Hope fine and well. It's been a while since I wrote but here I am. I am doing fine. I have just finished my GCSE's and got ten grade A's. I'm going to college to study. I want to be a doctor." Ranks put the pen down. He sighed. He wanted her to be proud of him. "Anyway, I really want to meet you at last. I think you owe me that after all these years. Aunt Celia said you are married. Why can't you just tell me where you live so I can come and visit? Are you ashamed of me becos you had me so young? I really want to see you. I know you don't really know me but I want you to know that I love you and don't hate you for what you did. Please say you'll meet me.

Your son Danny Raymond P."

After he had written it Ranks stared at the letter. A stubborn tear fell from his eye. He wiped it away quickly. He screwed it up and threw it across the room. He was suddenly angry and hurt. The bitch, she had betrayed him.

If she really wanted to know him, all she had to do was call around to see him when he was a kid.

That's all.

"IT'S GOOD STUFF innit?" Kurtis James lit the crack pipe, sucked and passed it to the eager Stukky on the right of him. Smiling as the wave of crack rippled through his body, his senses heightened, his thinking cleared.

Suddenly the door leading to the large living room burst open and Ranks stormed in, glaring at Kurtis.

"Ain't you got no home to go to? Ya been here for weeks."

"But you said-"

"What? What the fuck did I say? You got the keys to my Bimma? I warned you, never take me for granted. And by the way you owe me for that supply you've smoked-"

"My money's done."

"That's *your* problem Kurtis. I've got accounts to maintain and suppliers to pay. Don't fucking come back here until you can find five ton to make up for my loss-"

Kurtis felt everybody's eyes on him, sat in a semi-circle on the wooden floor. TV was on turned down low, music was playing in the background, tough bad bwai ragga lyrics.

"-some bwai diss me de other day,
and swear seh dem get away,
me nuh play wid fool like dose,
de whole ah dem ah get spray."

Kurtis's eyes moved from Pipes, to Fila, Mr. Mentian, Sizzla, and Stukky but all they did was look away when his eyes met theirs. No one rose to his defence. A minute ago they were laughing with him, telling jokes and smoking Ranks' crack. Before Ranks went into his room ten minutes ago he was OK with him smoking, being part of the posse. He even gave Kurtis a small room in his apartment. Now he was sour and sullen and Kurtis didn't know what he had done.

Didn't have the guts to ask him. Ranks suddenly hurled his clothes at him. Jeans, sweatshirts, socks, underpants, and trainers fell on top of him in a huge, degrading heap. Kurtis bundled them up in his arms quickly, peppery tears scorching the corners of his eyes.

Kurtis got up slowly. He really liked Ranks and waited to be close friends with him.

"What am I gonna do about my rocks and runnings?" asked Kurtis.

He was surprised by the mellowness of Ranks' reply. Ranks sighed and appeared calm. "Get my five and maybe we'll talk about how we can solve your problem." His tone switched again. "If you can't get it, yu gonna dead fe wants, star." Ranks spoke so coldly Kurtis felt himself shiver. Putting on his jacket he stepped out of Ranks apartment.

Closing the door.

A tear fell from his eye.

Then another.

KURTIS TRUDGED AROUND aimlessly on the Alex Park Estate for nearly two hours, watching kids revving around on a stolen motorbike. Kurtis decided, reluctantly, to go home. Found no one at home. Sunday. Sunday lunch was still in the oven. Grandma was probably at prayer meeting with Sharon. And Easy? Kurtis couldn't care less where he was. Walking into his bedroom, Kurtis was stunned to find some of his posters removed from the walls. Bedroom furniture had been moved around. Wasn't his room no more. His bastard of a brother, Grandma's favourite grandson, had reclaimed his kingdom. A strange sort of hot darkness swept over Kurtis. A loud voice reverberated in his head. You gotta destroy everything Easy has contaminated!

Kurtis attacked his room with a fury.

Smashing things that could be broken with his feet. Tearing the remaining posters off the wall.

Taking a black marker pen from a bedside drawer he began to write on the walls muttering to himself incessantly.

He that desecrates the house of Ramah shall die.

EASY-LOVE BROWN was the last person Teeko Martial expected to see, when he answered the knock at his front door. Nevertheless the tall figure of Easy stood smiling, leaning on his front doorpost casually dressed in a superstore uniform. Teeko glared in astonishment at the former Piper Mill second-in-command soldier, remembering days when he used to take orders from him and Jigsy. It was raining outside and Easy was blocking the light from the streetlight.

"So wassup blood?" Easy asked. "Yuh in't got nuttin to say to me?"

Teeko swallowed nervously.

"Whahhzup bad bwai?" Instinctively Teeko Martial walked towards Easy. Laughing, they embraced each other warmly.

"Cool, star."

"How'd you find me, dread?" Teeko asked, flexing his muscles.

"How many red jeeps are there in Moss Side with the private registration TEEK 01?"

"Yeah, you know how much I like my Suzuki's. Come, come on in."

Teeko looked up and down the street as he let Easy into his home. Content no one was watching, he closed the front door firmly, feeling Easy's long frame close behind him as they headed towards the luxurious living room. The room was well furnished and tasteful. African ornaments adorned the walls and floors. Also there were assorted trophies and awards for various martial arts. Soft soul music was playing. Teeko saw how Easy noticed the blown up photographs of Teeko's twin sons Remi and Ramone who were about the same age as Easy's son Mario now.

Teeko told Easy to take a seat on the sofa, handing him a spliff he'd built earlier. Easy sunk into the comfort of the sofa readily, watching Teeko steadily.

"So what's happening T?" Easy asked. Teeko started to build a spliff as he sat down next to Easy. He handed Easy a lighter to light his spliff.

"Well, you – know– t'ings cool."

"True. True."

"And *you*?"

Easy half-laughed, rubbing his hands as if he was cold. "Stepped outta prison one minute, the next I was waking up in ward 6 at the Royal Infirmary." Teeko nodded slowly. He was listening.

"Yeah, I'm sorry. I heard all about that shit."

"But you never once came to visit me, blood? Prison nor hospital." Teeko knew this was coming. The spliff took the edge off his unease.

"No," he said. "No, I was busy."

"Hustling for Ranks?"

"Yeah, man haffi eat yuh know and support family an' ting, spar. What's the problem anyway? Danny was a Piper Mill. He was always one of us."

"*Who* said I had a problem with Danny? Or has Ranks got a problem with *me*?" Teeko cleared his throat. He remained quiet. "Oh! I see. Well, if Ranks has got a problem with me then you must have. Explains the lack of visits." Easy rose to his feet. "Well, it was good seeing you an' all T, and I was hoping we'd catch up on ol' times but that in't gonna happen is it? You know what Teeko? I never took you for a man that would settle for less. I mean Ranks was under us. He use to scout for us. Twenty pound a week to spy on the Grange or pick up soundings on the street. Or maybe he'd get fifty for shifting brown now and then.

"We were the big players. Me, you, Jigsy, and even that shithead Bluebwai. How the fuck did a seventeen year-old kid rise above you? Never mind. I just thought, thought you had the calibre to be runnin' t'ings wid me in prison and Fluxy then Jigsy shot dead by that pussyclaht Storm." Easy was walking towards the door. "Looks like I was wrong." Teeko felt himself growing cold. He got up quickly.

"Easy, wait up, hol' up a minute, star."

Easy looked down at Teeko's hand on the arm of his shirt. "Come back in and sit down wid me, man." Easy did as he was asked. Teeko sat down, pulling heavily on the spliff. Felt himself shaking slightly. Easy was looking at him expectantly. Teeko sighed. Looked at his friend. He looked thin, tired. Dreadlocks ragged, clothes rough. Teeko felt sorry for him.

"Ranks had nothing to do with you getting beaten up. Yes, he's got a thing about you coming out back pon street but I would never have let them beat you up like that." He paused deliberately, sighing. "I hear it was Small and Dodge man dem." Easy looked a little taken aback. "That was dirty, mean and underhanded. I mean all's fair in love and war innit, Easy? But only if man have the means fe defend himself, know what I'm sayin'?"

Easy smiled, cocking his handsome face toward one side, he extended his hand. Teeko took it slowly and laughed. They crossed palms, clenched hands, shook, then twisted their hands around the other's in a wrap of solidarity.

"Hey T, remember back in the day when we'd catch up at Jigsy's all night smokin' and watching your Bruce Lee movies on that big screen TV?" Teeko felt a warmth rise in his stomach, smiling as the picture and sounds played in his mind like a DVD movie.

Teeko's voice was low and mellow. "Yeah and remember when

Fluxy brought dat gyal back to the flat cos he was in love with her long hair."

"Yeah and when he woke up in the morning her hair was on the pillow."

"The bitch was a phoney." Teeko leaned back in the sofa, laughing along with Easy.

Easy leaned forward. "Remember when Jigsy got that Grange bwai with his Rottweilers? What was his name?"

Teeko became serious. Cleared his throat. The memory came hurtling back.

"Lewty." He leaned back. "That was gross. All that blood an' shit."

"Gross? It was da lick! Yeah Jigsy, maximum respect wherever you are. Life goes on. I think we owe it to the Ellis brothers to resurrect the Piper Massive." Teeko was quiet.

"So what are you sayin' T? Yuh fancy settin' up wit' me or what? Huh, yu lookin' at me like I in't got fuckall to be doin' shit but I'm tellin' yu, it in't over 'til the fat bitch sings."

"You want me to leave Ranks? He'd probably try to 'radicate me."

"Don't worry about that. Where we're goin' no one's gonna touch us. Trust me."

After a pause Teeko asked. "What's the game plan?"

"Well, that's where you come in." Teeko frowned. "I need a borrows." He almost sighed with relief. Thought Easy was going to ask him to spy on Ranks. Teeko was no traitor. He'd rather leave The Worlders than betray his own.

"What for and how much? If I'm gonna go in with you I don't want you holding out on me."

"OK. I need about five ton because I'm taking a fat VIP on an important date. I'm low on cash, yuh know, wanna look good and flush wid the readies." Easy's previous words suddenly had meaning — *it in't over 'til the fat bitch sings* — and Teeko saw in his mind which way Easy was heading. He understood who Easy's VIP was. Teeko knew of her deadly reputation but thought Easy could take care of himself. He laughed as Easy did. Easy hadn't changed. Still cunning and smart. Teeko shifted his stocky body and withdrew some money from under the sofa. Holding the spliff in his mouth, and half-closing his eyes as the acrid smoke assailed them, he handed the lot to Easy.

"You don't have to count it, Easy. There's two grand." Teeko took a notebook out of a drawer next to him, wrote something down, then tearing the paper from the notebook he handed it to Easy. Easy frowned at the mobile number with the name Chris written next to it. "Chris does a good deal on firepower. Anyt'ing you want. Big or little." Smiling, Easy got to his feet, putting the money and the note in his pocket.

"I knew I could depend on you, blood," Easy said. 'I'll be in touch."

Teeko suddenly realised Easy didn't have his mobile or pager number. "How will you find me?"

"My sixth sense will guide me." With that he left. Leaving Teeko wondering how he was going to deal with Ranks.

"DIRTY! CONNIVING, LYING bastard." Kurtis James yelled at the wall. He was lying on his broken bed, breathing hard, hurting like a woman betrayed by her man. Suddenly the bedroom door swung open and Grandma was standing there wearing a furious look on her face.

"Kurtis Ethan James what have you done to your room?"

"I live here. I can do what I want. This is my room."

"Since when? Yu left here and been gone nearly six weeks without a word."

Kurtis jumped up suddenly. "*I've* been gone? What about Easy? He's been gone eight fucking years without a word."

"Don't you swear at me and don't speak about Barry like that."

"Why not? He's nothing but a bad bwai."

"Who tell you that Kurtis? It nuh true. The police frame him. Barry would never get mix up with those kinda people. Barry is a good boy. I want you to be just like Barry." Kurtis bellowed with hoarse laughter.

"Be like Barry? Sure. He walked out on us when we needed him. Years ago. He never once called back to see how we were doing. Yes, there was a time I really wanted to be like my big brother. I adored him, looked up to him but he left us, Gran."

"The Lord says we must learn to forgive and forget."

"Yeah, yeah, yeah we're all God's children and all that shit."

Grandma looked mortified. The disgust echoed in her voice. "Kurtis! I won't have you blaspheming in my house."

"Barrington is the devil. He's Satan. He's the beast." Kurtis was screaming. Grandma had that frightened look in her eyes. Kurtis wanted to shake some sense into her but instead he took his fury out on his furniture.

"It's you that's got the devil in you. You, Kurtis, you."

VOICES. HIGH-PITCHED. HYSTERICAL. Sharon James heard them as she entered the house in total darkness. So far as she knew no one was at home. Kurtis was living away, and she had left Grandma at church to continue with the prayer meeting with the other church sisters. Sharon had returned home because she was feeling unwell and thought she'd be better off at home in bed with a hot-water bottle. But as she mounted the stairs the pain in her stomach seemed to ebb away as fear filled her guts instead. Sharon treaded the stairs with mounting trepidation. The voices grew louder as if two people were arguing. Sharon pushed the door to Kurtis' room open wide and the sight that met her eyes made her Sunday dinner rise to the tip of her throat.

Kurtis was dressed as Grandma. Her best church dress was too tight on his body; her tights were laddered and pulled closely over muscled calves, huge feet crushed themselves into her petite size fours. Kurtis was oblivious to Sharon's presence. He was playing two parts, shrieking as he pretended to be the hunched up figure of Kurtis under a duvet in the bed. His voice altered from delight to fear as he spontaneously switched from grandmother to teenager expertly. Glancing around quickly Sharon saw various crucifixes on the walls turned upside down. Also there were many five pointed stars in a circle drawn on various half-torn posters of football stars. There were about a dozen or so lit candles. Slowly, Sharon walked into the room.

"Kurtis?" He swung around quickly. The wig was lopsided and was falling down his face. Long looped earrings dangled like Christmas decorations. He looked like a badly made-up drag queen. His mascara was exorbitant, the rouge on his cheeks crude and his lips painted a grotesque bright red. It was a shocking, horrific sight.

"Kurtis, baby, what are you doing in Grandma's clothes? What's the matter with you?" His response was to push her out of his room and slam the door against her. He locked it. Sharon pounded on the door, turning the locked handle. Sharon was terrified. She called his name but there was only silence on the other side. This was serious. Something terrible was happening to Kurtis. He was ill.

How long had he been like this?

And Easy?

Where was he now they really needed him?

IT STOOD OUT a mile. The huge moving advertising bill showing a shiny yellow 3-litre injection Toyota Supra, three door, boot spoiler, alloy wheels. It stood against a stark grey sky, against a row of dilapidated shops on Rochdale Road near to Factory Lane on the busy northern side of the city. Easy stood in the entrance of the shop which was severely burned out, perhaps by extortionists or the owner himself. Easy was pretending to read a newspaper so that Chris, the gun and ammo supplier could mark him out.

Stubbing his cigarette, Easy looked at his watch. Fucking Chris was fucking late and Easy needed his tings speedily. There was no way he was gonna meet Small unprepared, especially now that he knew her and her crew, The Dodge, were responsible for beating him up. He was sure of that.

Throwing the newspaper aside, Easy jammed his hands in his pockets, hunching his shoulders against the wind, which swirled around him in the shop's doorway like a mini-hurricane. It was viciously cold, threatening to rain. He just knew it. Chris wasn't going to show. How could Teeko recommend somebody unreliable? Kissing his teeth savagely, Easy started to walk off when a silver Ford Galaxy car drew up close. In the back of the car, in one of the car's seats, was a sleeping baby. Easy didn't know if it was a boy or a girl. Easy didn't care. In the front, a dark-haired pretty woman with clear white skin held the steering wheel. Leaning over towards Easy she smiled. The passenger window came down automatically.

"I'm Christine — Chris. Get in." she spoke with an Irish accent.

"What?"

"Jesus! What are you waitin' for?" She spoke again, only this time Easy heard a little bit of impatience in that soothing Irish lilt. "Teeko said you needed…"

Easy smiled cautiously. He had thought, expected, Chris to be some roughneck white boy from Openshaw not this porcelain-skinned brunette beauty who smiled ravenously as Easy climbed into the car.

"THE SHOTGUN. HOW much?" Easy picked up the pump-action, snapped it down and checked the mechanism.

"Five ton with ammo thrown in." Chris said. Easy put it down, his eyes surveying the collection of weaponry now unravelled from beneath a huge blanket on the floor of the Galaxy. They were parked in a deserted car park outside a pub called The Dog and Bone in Reddish Lane in Stockport. The weather had carried out its surly threat of rain. The car was backed up next to some bushes. Easy surveyed the guns hungrily, his eyes drawn to the shiny 9 mm Uzi.

"You like it don't you?" She said. He glanced at her, noticing that she was diminutive but trim, hair worn short, pretty full lips. When she smiled her blue eyes danced provocatively. Easy swallowed. Licking his dry lips, he picked up the Uzi. He snapped out the magazine and checked the chamber. Easy knew this was his piece. It felt right, like love at first sight.

"Teeko mentioned that you'd just come out of prison." Chris said.

Easy said nothing. He was caressing the Uzi. He felt Chris near him. She touched his arm, her sultry breath on his neck.

"Have you been with a woman since you came out?" Her question was direct. Easy felt her small lithe body massaging against his. He felt himself willingly growing stiff. "D'y'know, your boy Teeko, never mentioned how good-lookin' you were. Such a good, strong body."

"How much is it?" Easy asked clearing his throat.

"More money than the blaster." She murmured, allowing her voice to trail out in a seductive drawl. Easy turned towards her, smiling, pointing the gun in her face.

"Guess what?" Easy said. "I'll take it." She slapped the gun away. In one violent movement, Easy snatched her up and threw her down on the floor of the Galaxy, simultaneously making a space between the guns. She looked surprised but excited. In that instant Easy knew women like Christine weren't loyal to any political movements. She just loved danger, excitement. Her lips were suddenly on his, pulling him down on her, breathing heavily. She wanted it rough. Pulling her legs apart, he shoved his hand inside her jeans, inside her underwear, thrusting his fingers deep inside. She gasped loudly, laughing like a wild jackal screeching against a desert sky. Hoisting her hips upward, she wriggled out of her jeans.

"Yeah-" Easy said in between sharp breaths. "I'll definitely take it."

"YOU'RE LATE." LALAH Morris declared sharply, opening the door wide for Storm to walk in. Five minutes late. That was all. But not all to meticulous Lalah, who was recalling how he'd turned up late for his daughter Tia's birth five years back. But then, he hadn't really been late had he? Tia had simply decided to come into the world four weeks early.

Storm could hear Tia laughing. He walked into the living room, its floor full of toys. Lalah looked as if she was getting ready to go out, probably with her new man, Marcus, some light-skinned church brotha. Storm wasn't sure how he felt about his ex, whether he still loved her or was simply reluctant to let her get on with her new life and new man.

Lalah was uniquely beautiful, petite and redskin. He watched her as she bent over, dressed in a tight pair of figure-hugging trousers. She wore her hair with shoulder-length braided extensions. As she turned around, putting her hand to her face, he saw it. Third finger on her left hand. A huge diamond engagement ring. The rock glinted in a ray of sunlight that bounced through the glass over the front door.

Storm couldn't believe it. Not so long ago they had been planning a future, but all that changed when she realised he had lied to her. He was still a gang leader. He was still dealing in death and destruction. He had tried hard to prove to her and his other woman Jasmine that the bad days were well and truly over, but neither wanted to know. The club, his business, the recording studio and shop meant nothing to them.

"Daddy!" Little Tia ran from the kitchen straight to Storm. Storm picked her up, swinging her around.

"Whappen my little princess? Mmm?" He kissed her neck and she giggled. Storm suddenly noticed that Lalah was watching the two of them. Her hard frown had disappeared and a warm smile had replaced it. "I'll have her back in by three." Putting on his daughter's coat and taking her towards the jeep where nine-year-old Lee — his son by Jasmine — sat waiting, Storm realised that although he was with neither woman, he was still lucky. He had his children. And nothing and nobody could take that away from him. They were now looking forward to quality time together, a Walt Disney movie at the new multi-complex, a MacDonald's meal and a quick walk in the park.

LIVING CLEAN AND livin' large is good Storm thought as he pushed his five-year-old daughter Tia higher on the swing. The child screamed with delight.

"Higher Daddy. I want to touch the sky."

"You can have the sky, princess. You can have anything." Times like these, Storm treasured. Precious. Peaceful. He took his children whenever he could. Now that Lee was getting older he realised how crucial it was for a father to be with his son and to guide him away from the life he once lived. Storm watched Lee waving to him on the seesaw. Storm loved Lee. Their bond was exceptional. They talked about football, girls, computer games, Grandma, everything.

The park was almost deserted. It was fairly cold too, frosty for spring and Easter just around the corner. All Storm wanted to do was to protect his family. There was no way he was going to allow his son to get mixed up in badness. He didn't want Lee to be exposed and vulnerable, to think that the only way forward was through drugs or guns. Like he had. Ironically, that's why Storm had done it, to set his family up. He wasn't going to go back down that road again. Not for Ranks, not for Easy not for no one. And that's why he regretted showing Zukie the gun.

Storm looked at his watch. It was later than he thought. He'd have to get the kids back to their mums, then get back to the shop to make sure Zukie and everything else was OK.

"YOU LOOKED AS if you were a million miles away." Taniesha Kanes, Storm's part time assistant, placed the cup down on the counter loudly breaking Zukie from his trance. She laughed as he jumped slightly.

Blinking hard, Zukie smiled, as the beautiful image of Taniesha captured him. Slim, large dark brown eyes, dark-skinned, hair in long braids cascading down her back. She had full lips but wore no lipstick, in fact very little make-up. It was no secret that she attracted a lot of attention and that was a good thing. It meant business boomed because of her. Storm would deny such a sexist reflection, preferring to think it was their excellent choice of stock and good reputation. Zukie had to admit to himself that he felt a stab of painful jealousy whenever male customers chatted her up. Yet as far as he knew, Taniesha Kanes was young, free and single.

She had made them both hot drinks, herbal mint tea for him and coffee for herself. She sat down at the counter next to him, sipping her coffee. Zukie could smell the scent of her perfume. His cock stirred to life. He had finished cashing up and was preparing to lock up the studio. Business had been unusually quiet today. Maybe because of the rain, Zukie didn't know. But all day long his mind had been preoccupied by Ranks.

Twice, Zukie thought he saw Danny Ranks drive past in his car on Princess Road outside the shop. In fact Zukie was pretty sure it was him. The way the Lexus slowed down, paused and then pulled off. Storm was right. Ranks was watching, waiting, and he meant no good. Zukie thought about the gun that Storm had given him. He couldn't get the sight of it out of his mind.

"I was wondering if you was going to Leeds for the Mister Vegas show?" Taniesha asked suddenly breaking into his erratic thoughts.

"What?"

"Vegas in Leeds." She was hopeful, hinting, but Zukie heard nothing.

"Oh yeah. I'm going with my brother. We got courtesy tickets."

"Oh," Taniesha said. Zukie failed to hear the dejection in her voice. He was too busy looking out of the window watching all the cars drive past. Storm was late, but he had phoned to say he was delayed.

"Do you go everywhere with Storm?"

"Mmmm. More or less." Zukie said abstractedly. Taniesha shifted in her seat. She sipped her coffee. Then Zukie understood. "Why?" he suddenly asked.

"Nothing." She answered coyly. Zukie frowned. He knew she was sussing something out but his mind couldn't concentrate. He started to think about the gun. If he saw Ranks again he'd make sure he had the gun. Zukie kept thinking and thinking about what Storm said to him. It didn't make him scared. Just angry. Chico was dead, Hair Oil was in a residential care home, and Ranks had something to do with it. Zukie felt a cold shiver wrap itself around his shaking body.

"Zukie? I was wondering if you might like a drink after work, maybe we could go to the Little Apple."

"I can't I'm meeting Storm." Zukie began to feel hot and irritated. He felt eager to do something. It was a strange nagging feeling, like the feeling you get when you've left the house, you're halfway to your destination and you think you've left something cooking on the stove. It hit Zukie head on: Ranks. Ranks was out there and it bugged him.

"Do you always do everything your brother says?" Zukie began to lock cupboards. He stopped. He looked at her. Really looked at her this time. "I mean you two seem to do everything, go everywhere together. Don't you have any friends?" Zukie thought about Chico and Hair Oil.

"He's always looked after me, y'know, since the crash. That's all. He's a bit protective. Maybe."

"A bit protective?" Taniesha almost squealed in amazement. She rolled her eyes and moved her head back a little. Her eyes travelled over the posters of various soul and reggae stars on the walls. "It seems — I don't know."

"What?" Zukie urged gently.

"Unhealthy for you both to be in each other's pockets. You live together, work together and go out together, like Storm doesn't want to let you out of sight for a second." Taniesha sighed. She seemed to be struggling with the right words. "Don't, don't you have a special woman in your life?" Zukie began to think. He smiled. Paradise. Once there had been a girl called Paradise but they had drifted apart quickly, mainly because he did not remember loving her. That was sad but it was a fact.

Zukie looked at Taniesha. He liked her. Zukie shook his head slowly still smiling. He was close to her. Words drifted into his head slowly. *Am I my brother's keeper*? Slowly Taniesha reached out and touched Zukie's face. Her touch was soft, yet strong, soothing yet vibrant. Like healing. Zukie knew that experience — like a long forgotten dream. It seemed to melt away his fears, ease his trepidation, and unleash his burden. He moved his face slowly towards hers. She took his face in his hands and kissed him.

Zukie placed his forehead against hers, smiling. He was so lost in her he didn't hear the car pull up. Nor did he hear the sound of the shop's door buzzer as it sounded sharply, causing them both to look towards the door. It was early closing time on Fridays. Zukie's heart pounded. He was in no doubt as to who it was. Danny again. Haunting him like some dark spectre.

Zukie knew he had no time to get the gun Storm had given him for protection. But before he had a chance to consider an alternative plan Taniesha had pressed the buzzer allowing the shadowy figure behind the shop's glass front door to enter the shop.

The figure was that of a woman. She was wearing jeans, boots and a long leather coat. She stepped into the shop, slowly glancing up then back behind her. She seemed to beckoning someone little into the shop.

"I'm sorry. We're just about to close." Taniesha said.

"Is Zukie here?" she said in a soft-spoken voice. She was wearing a scarf to protect her from the harsh rain and cold outside, but it hid half of her face. Zukie frowned. A strange sensation filled him as he watched the young woman take the hand of a small child, a little girl. The young woman removed her scarf slowly, stepping forward and directly under the light. She had shoulder length dreadlocks, full red lips, oriental eyes, and a stud in her straight nose. Zukie held his breath, and then let it out slowly.

"Paradise?"

TABLES. CHAIRS, SOFT reggae music. Dim lights. Wine. Laughter. Exquisite Jamaican cuisine. Miss Walla — Walla's Crazy Dutch Pot was a renowned Caribbean restaurant situated in the cosmopolitan area of Chorlton, Manchester, on the main high street that crossed through Chorlton's village of shops, banks, businesses, wine bars and restaurants. It had won many prestigious culinary awards for its authentic Jamaican dishes and also for its impressive array of unique exotic beverages and cocktails. The owner also had a partnership with Miss Small. She supplied the protection and they paid her their monthly insurance fees. She also used the restaurant to entertain guests. Easy had done his homework and knew this. He knew the entire set of exit points should things run hot. They were seated in a far corner of the semi-packed smoky Caribbean restaurant. Feeling brave and confident but not cocky, Easy poured Miss Small another glass of wine.

"What yuh ah try fe do? Get me drunk?" She said smiling. Easy shook his head slowly. She was dressed in a loose blue sequinned dress, which made her look slimmer. She had gold rings on her chubby fingers and several gold chains hung around her neck. Her make up was light, her hair tied up in a style that showed off her pretty cocoa complexioned face. Easy thought she had beautiful brown eyes, large and crystalline like brown marble.

Looking around Easy noticed that the restaurant wasn't really half-packed. Slowly he began to notice her men, the Dodge crew, placed strategically on tables close by on surveillance. Slide, Trench, Ranger, and the two Palmer brothers Hatchet and Michigan. One of them, in particular, watched him coldly. Easy knew this was Small's 'co-director' and 'security-consultant' Trench, a.k.a. Terrence Michael Garvey, a mean motha who had once served eighteen months for robbery and GBH. He possessed a one-inch thick scar that crossed over his right eye. Easy gave brief eye contact, smiling inwardly.

Missy Small's men stuck out like cacti in a bed of roses. Hard-faced and bandit looking compared to the smooth designer suited Easy, with his funki-dreadlocks tied back off his face. The suit cost him nine hundred pounds and the shoes one hundred pounds. He was putting a lot of investment in Miss Small, which he hoped would pay off.

They had nothing in common apart from a shared interest in gangs and drugs, but conversation came effortlessly. Easy-Love lit a cigarette. He told her about Mario whom he had not seen for nearly five years. She talked about a grown-up son that she knew only through photographs and letters, carefully reminding him that she wasn't an unfit mother, it was just circumstances. She spoke stiltedly, keeping her emotions intact. He nodded and sympathised. They talked about music and her love of Jamaica. They talked and laughed until the minutes and hours ticked away. Looking up to where scarface was, Easy saw that he had left his position. The table where he and the others were seated was deserted.

She smiled broadly. They fell silent as a waiter cleared their table. Easy asked for the bill.

"I think we should cut the games, Easy."

It could all backfire any second now.

"You know who I am."

Easy smiled.

"Who's playing games, Veniesha?" Easy was looking at her steadily. He really wanted to ask, and did you play fairly when you had your man dem tear me up, beat me senseless and dash me on wasteland like yesterday's rubbish?

"I find you attractive," he said, without lying. Miss Small laughed. "You've got this beautiful smile and such an intriguing personality."

The waiter came with the bill. Easy settled, throwing four crisp twenty pound notes on a plate. By the expression on her face he concluded that she thought he was flush. Easy took another twenty from his wallet and said to the waiter.

"Here's your tip. Bring us a bottle of your best table wine." He turned his attention back to Miss Small who was now leaning across, her chin resting on the back of her hands, elbows on the table. She was glowing.

"I could have you shot dead, the minute you step outta this restaurant. You took a big risk, Easy." Easy smiled. She knew who he was from day one and knew he knew who she was.

"The risk I took is that somewhere deep inside of you there is a chance that you might like me and my style, the things I can do for you and the crew. As my Grandma says experience teaches wisdom." Veniesha bawled out a merciless laugh. Easy took a drink of his wine, aware of the restaurant's staff watching the odd couple. Veniesha was silent. He refilled her glass. "Besides: one, if you had really wanted me out of action you woulda done it when you had the chance weeks ago, but you spared my life for some strange reason; and two, how do you know that I don't have some protection on me — the minute you give your man dem the mention to shoot me outside I'd pop them all?"

Miss Small's large body rocked with laughter like an exploding volcano.

Easy kept cool, looking her dead in the eye.

"Me and you are going to merge, Veniesha, one way or another," he said slowly. "So let's drink to you, me, the new year and the start of our unique relationship."

"You hope," she said. Easy raised his glass.

"I *know*," Easy said, and clinked his glass against hers.

"HELLO ZUKIE." SCRATCHING the back of his neck where it suddenly began to prickle and burn, Zukie was wondering what Paradise Browne was doing at the studio. He knew she had visited him in hospital shortly after the car crash but after when he discovered he had no memory of their relationship she simply stopped coming. Yes he remembered, knew who she was, but only that she was Paradise, Pastor Browne's daughter who sang in the choir at The Old Lady's church on Sundays and who also claimed to heal people.

Taniesha cleared her throat loudly, waking Zukie to her presence. She clearly felt as if she was intruding.

"I'll just get my coat." Tossing her long plaits over her shoulder, Taniesha strode away, disappearing into the back of the shop and leaving Zukie and Paradise alone. Zukie felt a strange wave of emotion pass over him. He felt a wariness rise in his soul.

Zukie stared at Paradise. Her beauty was breath taking. Her skin was brown, neither dark nor light. Drop pearl earrings dangled daintily from her ears. Her eyes studied him cautiously. He hadn't seen or heard anything about her in three years. It could have been more; Zukie wasn't exactly sure. He gazed at the small child who seemed to be fascinated by the CD jewel cases in the swivel kiosk stands. She swirled them with her tiny fingertips. He looked back up at Paradise.

He was thinking if they'd had such a fantastic relationship like she told him when he was recovering from his injuries, then why did she just disappear? The child, who was spinning the kiosks and laughing, suddenly demanded Paradise's attention.

"No, Kyesha don't do that. They'll break. Mummy won't be pleased." This revelation that the child belonged to Paradise stunned Zukie slightly. The little girl ignored her mother. "She's so stubborn," Paradise offered feebly, "and damn fast!"

Kyesha was wearing a navy hat and below her pretty head were long golden-brown plaits. She looked at Zukie with mischievous large grey-blue eyes. Zukie's heart boomed as he suppressed a gasp.

At that moment Taniesha re-entered the reception area of the shop. She stood and stared at Zukie and from the shocked expression on her face, Zukie saw that she was reaching the same conclusion as he.

He had a daughter he did not know he had.

'NAH! NO FUCKING way!' Trench bawled, bringing his fist down on the table firmly. Calling the crew back into Miss Walla-Walla's restaurant, Miss Small had explained that she was giving Easy one month's trial in the crew providing he could pay an initiation sub of five grand. Trench stood up and swept the items off the restaurant table irately. Glasses and bottles fell to the floor and smashed. The restaurant's staff looked frightened and concerned. Miss Small glared at Trench.

"No way! If he comes in with us, I'll kill him myself." Easy sat across looking at the table twisting his lips, slouching. He recognised the nasal drawl of the guy who had took pleasure in beating him only months ago. Easy smirked. Rising slowly, he put his hands up in pretend surrender.

"Look if it's going to cause a problem I'll leave until you two to sort-"

Trench snatched Easy's expensive jacket, threw him down violently on to the table. Easy felt something hard and metallic pressing in the space between his eyes. He heard the deadly click of a safety-clip being released. Even from its business end, Easy could see clearly that it was a Colt. 45, its nose fat and its barrel stubby. Everyone, including Miss Small, sprang from the table.

Easy scowled inwardly. He tried to rise up but Trench pushed him back down.

"Trench put the gun away. *Now!*" Miss Small ordered. Ignoring her, straightening his arm, Trench levelled the gun right between Easy's eyes again. "Terrence-me seh puddown de gun. W'happen to ya?" Easy could feel Trench's well-built body shaking against him. Half-kneeling on the table, half-standing on the floor. He was heavy. Easy took in his features quickly. A scar spoilt his baby-faced good looks. It was only an inch-long, starting just above his right eyebrow and ending on the lid. The eye itself was twitching ferociously, like the finger against the trigger. He had huge dark-brown and blood-shot eyes. His face was clean-shaven, with small lips. There was a gold looped earring in his right ear. Although Trench held Easy in a submissive position Easy knew he was going to win. Besides Trench was going to learn a massive lesson tonight.

The lesson of his stupid arse-hole life.

And that lesson was never, never to fuck with Easy-Love Brown. With a grunt, Easy brought his right knee up swiftly in that vulnerable spot at the top of Trench's legs. Hard and brutal he shoved everything into Trench's groin. The scream seemed to reverberate around the restaurant's high ceiling as Trench jerked backwards crashing onto the table behind him. Easy was on him in a flicker, snatching the small handgun from Trench's loose right hand. Easy replaced the catch before putting the gun in the back of his trouser waistband. Trench was writhing in pain. A blue satin tablecloth wrapped itself around him like a burial shroud. Easy grabbed either side of Trench's head holding it steady. He bounced Trench's head four times viciously against the table.

"You listenin' pussylicka?" Easy put his face low and close to Trench's hot face. Trench refused to answer. "Yu ah hear me?" Easy smashed the back of Trench's head against the table so hard something sounded like it had cracked.

"Huuuuuhhhhhn. Yeah. Yeah." Trench drawled. Blood trickled from his nose.

"Who am I?" Easy felt the others drawing near. He knew one of them could pull on him any second, but not while there was a tray of cutlery nearby. Easy reached out and snatched a huge carving knife. "I said who am I?"

Trench's eyes looked glazed.

"Easy." Trench eventually answered breathlessly.

"My full name!"

"Easy-Love Brown."

"Just so you don't forget," Easy said gritting his teeth savagely. "Here's something to remind you." Easy raised the knife, turned Trench's face, grabbed Trench's left ear and sliced the knife through the lobe. Blood spurted over Easy's shirt. Easy raised himself off Trench. Screaming in pain, Trench instinctively put his hands over his ear, bringing his knees up and falling off the table. Turning towards Miss Small, Easy raised the piece of bloody ear like some barbaric triumphant ritual.

Miss Small smiled.

SHE WAS HIS. He just *knew*. Zukie paid Ricky for their order, then sat down watching Kyesha as she ate. Kyesha had the most beautiful smile he had ever seen.

As he sat opposite in the dingy café on Claremont Road Zukie began to notice Paradise's bling-bling appearance. The Lexus outside which he had mistaken for Ranks' belonged to her. She was wearing copious jewellery, and a long leather fur-collared coat — designer label. Zukie noticed that the child too was wearing expensive clothes.

Zukie asked the question.

"She's mine, in't she?"

Paradise nodded, looking relieved.

"Yes, Kyesha's your daughter."

She took a cigarette from a packet and lit it with a gold lighter. Zukie sighed and smiled, his eyes darting down to the rings on her fingers and to the chains around her neck. In a second, an image planted himself in his mind. Chico and Hair Oil. They were adorned with expensive gold chains and signet rings. It was a dark blues party. Someone was pointing at him. Someone he didn't know. A face he couldn't see. Asking Chico questions about him.

"Are you OK?"

"Just thinking. Remembering something," Zukie mumbled.

"What?" Paradise asked.

"Nothing. It in't important as knowing I have a child." He paused, watching the little girl as she ate her burger. Zukie looked down at the vegetable burger on his plate which he didn't have the stomach for.

"I see you're still a vegetarian," she said.

Zukie smiled. It was weird. You don't remember creating a child but you remember being a vegetarian.

"What's her name? Her full name I mean?"

Paradise looked at Zukie intently before exhaling deeply, blowing smoke ahead. "Kyesha Amehra Browne."

"Hello Kyesha Amehra Browne." Zukie said, leaning forward. The first thing he was going to do was change her last name to Michaels.

"What's your name?" Kyesha asked in a sweet angelic voice.

"Zukie."

The child laughed. She obviously thought Zukie's name was funny.

"You look good." Zukie said to Paradise. He was about to go on to say that she looked different to how he remembered her but she spoke first.

"Oh, I manage. I sing and that." Another memory surfaced quickly. Paradise on a sofa, building a spliff, singing to him. It faded as quickly.

"On CD?"

"Of course." Paradise frowned. "Your brother's record company manages me." If Zukie had not been sitting on a firm seat, he would have fallen over. It was as if someone had hit him with a cricket bat. She was studying him. Zukie dropped his eyes to Kyesha. Kyesha was deliberately spilling her drink on the table. Paradise took the drink away.

"I've been in America backing people for the last two years. Wyclef, Mya, Foxy Brown. I couldn't have managed it without your brother. He's been good to us. I found out I was pregnant with Ky just after you were in that car crash. I thought you was going to die. I told you I was pregnant while you were on life support, hoping it would bring you round."

The emotion started to swell in her. Her voice was tremulous. Zukie saw the tears in her eyes. He swallowed deeply.

"I couldn't manage without you. I had no choice but to go back home. Only when my dad found out I was pregnant he threw me out. Storm saw me through, paid the bills, bought us clothes. He stood by me when my parents didn't want to know. And still don't want to know their grandchild or me. They've never seen Kyesha. I saw my mum once, on Stockport Road, in Longsight, near the market, and she crossed over to the other side like she never even knew me."

"I'm sorry," Zukie said sincerely.

Paradise stared into the distance tearfully.

"Don't be. It's nobody's fault." She regained her composure swiftly. "Storm was good. He was the one who encouraged me to sing professionally." Paradise sighed, dropped her eyes, and knocked ash from her cigarette into an ashtray on the table. "I've never forgotten about you, even though you did — unintentionally. I've waited for the day when you'd be strong enough to know about Kyesha." Kyesha started to wail, rubbing her eyes simultaneously. She was obviously tired.

"Will she come to me?" Zukie asked. Paradise shrugged her shoulders. Zukie opened his arms. "Kyesha come." Kyesha rushed off her seat and straight onto Zukie's lap. Paradise raised her eyebrows in surprise but smiled, inhaling smoke. Kyesha nestled herself in Zukie's arms, closing her eyes slowly.

"I saw you through the shop window with that girl…"

"Taniesha."

"She looks like she really likes you."

"It's very early days yet. She's a nice girl." Zukie said, stroking Kyesha's golden-brown plaits.

Paradise dropped her eyes again, nervously. "I don't want anything from you Zukie. I don't need child support or anything."

"No you don't," Zukie said resentfully. "My brother has seen to that."

"Does that bother you?"

"Yes. She's my daughter."

"Yes," Paradise said. "And now you know." Zukie looked down at Kyesha. She was peacefully asleep in his arms, breathing gently.

"WOULD YOU LIKE some coffee?" Storm tried to hide his surprise as his ex-woman invited him in, unexpectedly. This was rare. He usually collected Lee on the doorstep or at Jasmine's mother's house. Initially, after she found out he was still with Lalah and still gang leader for the Grange, Jasmine went through a stage of deep hatred. She left the home they shared and went into hiding, taking his son with her. It took him a year to find them and it took her a while to agree to Lee seeing him. Storm glanced at his watch. Taking his leather gloves off, he wiped his feet on the mat at the front door. Lee was talking excitedly about the plans he and Storm had made for the coming weekend. Jasmine ushered him upstairs to have his bedtime bath. Even though she was not his woman anymore he still felt as though she was. After all, they were childhood sweethearts. He was proud of her achievements. She was at teacher training college and doing well.

Storm followed Jasmine into the warm kitchen. She invited him to sit down at the kitchen table.

"How's Zukie?" Jasmine asked, taking two cups from the pine mug stand.

"Fine. Remembering a little."

There was silence except for the sound of the kettle humming.

"Sugar?"

Storm smiled to himself.

"I still take two sugars, Jazz."

She handed the cup of black coffee to him. Thanking her, he took a cautious sip. Jasmine leaned against the sink, twisting a corkscrew curl around her forefinger. Long red nails. Storm noticed that she was shaking slightly.

"Lee was—"

"I wanted to—"

They both began to talk at the same time. Jasmine laughed, then her face became serious.

"You first." Storm said.

"I wanted to tell you something," she said. "I didn't want you to

60

hear it out on street."

Storm felt himself growing hot and it wasn't the heat in the kitchen.

"Lee is going to have another brother or sister." She said it quickly, her chest heaving with relief after she'd got it out. Storm looked at Jasmine. He had noticed she was putting on weight. Storm's throat became dry. Jasmine looked nervous. "Well, say something, nuh?"

What did she expect him to say? Why did she tell him? Maybe he had thought, foolishly, there was still a chance. Now where was his chance? Storm put his hot cup of coffee down on the table slowly.

"I gotta chip," he said solemnly. "It's late. I have to lock up the studio and ting." He rose to his unsteady feet, keeping the painful groan deep within the pit of his stomach. Jasmine touched his shoulder gently. Shaking his head, Storm shrugged her away.

He heard her sigh. "Clifton."

Turning to face her slowly, Storm forced a smile.

"Anyway, congratulations. I'm happy for you and Dalton."

"Carlton," she corrected.

"Whatever," Storm muttered.

"We've moved on Storm, haven't we? We're different people doing different things."

"If you say so, Jazz." Storm was walking hurriedly towards the front door, feeling insipid and foolish. He needed a cigarette. No, he needed a massive spliff. What the fuck was the point? Circumstances had forced him to change his lifestyle, to put up the gun for good. He tried to persuade her that he had changed for the better. No drugs, no gangs, no guns. He wanted them — Jasmine, himself and Lee — to live in peace and safety. He was running several successful businesses now but she still didn't believe in him.

Hell, if she had no faith in him then he might as well join Ranks now and take his revenge on Easy. Yeah, Easy along with Jigsy had fucked up his life, destroyed his chance with his women. Maybe Easy did deserve to be wiped outta the picture. Lee suddenly ran downstairs, dressed in his pyjamas. The sight of his son quickly brought everything back into clear perspective.

"Dad. I thought you were staying longer. I wanted us to play Tekken." Storm felt his heart hammering away. He didn't want Lee to see the hurt on his face.

"I can't stop, son. Another time. The weekend yeah?"

"I'm sorry Cliff. I forgot to tell you Carlton and I are going to The Lakes. We've rented a cottage."

What next? Storm thought resentfully, a white horse with the two of them on it galloping off into a distant sunset? Another man was raising his child and sexing his woman. Storm cut her off. "Come Lee. Give Dad a kiss goodbye then." Lee jumped into Storm's arms. Storm picked Lee up, swung him around and kissed his child's laughing face. Lee was getting too big to pick up now. Lee was turning into a little man. Storm felt that Lee was somehow slipping away from him. Like his mom. Storm wasn't going to let it happen.

RANKS COULD FEEL it. Something was gonna happen. He felt it in his blood. Felt it in his urine. He didn't like it but he knew it was inevitable. He had just completed lifting weights and was starting on the dumbbells. Sweat dripped off his compact body like a small river. He was pushing beyond. He always took the exercise regime that Teeko had taught him to extreme limits, pushing his mind and body. He had been chubby as a youngster, and got teased by his classmates. It was a memory that stayed with him. Danny took a long drink of his chocolate flavoured Power Up health supplement drink. Savouring the taste, he wiped his mouth with the back of his hand.

But he was still thirsty.

Tough gangster rap music tore through his speakers. Master P inna fine style.

Things were quiet. Too quiet. The calm before the storm before the battle. But Ranks was preparing himself for imminent strife. The Dodge Crew were trying to take liberties, and he wasn't ramping with Easy-Love Brown.

THE LAST TIME Storm had felt this lost was years ago when the odds were stacked steeply against him. Storm walked into the living room, keys jangling, still thinking about the bombshell Jasmine had dropped on him when a strange sight greeted him.

Zukie was up, half-slouched on the settee dressed only in white stretch boxers. The living room was filled with weed smoke as if Zukie had been bunning spliff since evening. It was highly unlikely that he'd been entertaining guests. Zukie had no friends, and since the accident never went anywhere without Storm.

"I'm sorry I wasn't there to lock up. I got delayed." Storm cast his eyes around the living room. The whole place was a mess. Zukie was usually meticulous. Instantly Storm felt a tense vibe. He realised Zukie was looking at the TV but not watching it. The radio was on, but Zukie didn't seem to be enjoying the revival selection Bagga Don and Barry Dread were playing. Suddenly Storm felt his heart pounding.

"What's going on?" Storm asked, placing himself on the arm of the leather sofa. He twiddled with the gold stud in his left ear.

"Why didn't you tell me Clifton?" Zukie asked without turning his head. Storm swallowed. What the hell was up? Was this the moment he was dreading? Storm pinched his nostrils. In the next few seconds Zukie sprang to his feet, suddenly. He was in Storm's face spitting his words out angrily.

"Why didn't you fuckin' tell me?" Storm stood up, amazed by his brother's ferocity, backing up two steps. Zukie's grey irises were wrapped around red bloodshot streaks. It almost looked, too, as if he might have shed some tears. Storm wasn't used to this. For the past four years Zukie had been calm, unchallenging, almost subservient. The perfect brother. Before the crash Zukie hated his guts. Zukie would never have dreamt of setting up in business with him, never mind living with him.

"What should I have told you Zukie?" Storm asked quietly.

"Where shall I start? How about you are managing my ex-woman? Or how about I have a daughter who doesn't know who I am?"

Storm held the sigh of relief in his chest. Zukie was pushing his face into Storm's. Storm could smell alcohol and cannabis.

"I did tell you."

"Wha — What?"

"I told you ages ago. I told you when you were in hospital. I told you all about the baby and everything."

"Well how come I don't—"

"Remember?" Storm saw the despair in his younger brother's eyes and it hurt him. Zukie's face crumbled. "Your memory was so poor back then we didn't push it. We took photos and videos of you with her when she was born.

"I can show you them."

"No. It in't the same thing is it?"

"I'm sorry Zukie." Storm walked towards him.

"What are you sorry for?" Zukie asked. "You had nothing to do with me getting in a car filled with gang bangers. I was there. Me. It happened to me. You know maybe I was one of them. If Chico and Oil were dealers who's to say I wasn't?" Storm felt helpless. Zukie was torturing himself. He wasn't sure what he should do next. He had never seen Zukie look so broken. Zukie looked up at his brother.

"I'm going to bed," Zukie announced, quietly striding towards the living room door. Long after he had gone, Storm sat alone. Zukie had started to call him Clifton. Since the accident he'd readily accepted Storm's street name.

Now, he was calling him Clifton.

NEROME CAMPBELL DROVE his boss over to Teeko's place, a redbrick terraced house on Roseberry Street. Ranks hadn't been able to sleep because of the doubt playing on his mind. Lately, Teeko hadn't returned any of his calls. He hadn't seen him in a long time. In this game, you had to be a sniffer. If trouble was coming, you could smell it a mile away.

If he had just come out of prison like Easy-Love Brown, he'd be recruiting soldiers, building a sure-fire posse. And if Easy was recruiting, he'd start with soldiers he knew and trusted. Soldiers like Teeko Martial.

There were no lights on at Teeko's but his new red jeep was parked up. It didn't really mean anything. Teeko could easily have been over at his woman Shanieka's where he stayed sometimes. Ranks knocked on the front door heavily. He just knew Teeko was in.

Bending down, Danny peered through Teeko's letterbox into the hall. A child's bike. A football. Laminated wood flooring.

"You're wasting your time," Nero said, lighting a cigarette. "He in't home." Sighing and kissing his teeth Ranks headed back to the car. He then changed his mind. Maybe he was being presumptuous. Maybe he should give Teeko the benefit of the doubt. After all, he'd taken Teeko on when the Pipers de-crewed after Jigsy's death. He'd made Teeko one of his front-runners. Teeko should be eternally grateful to him, right? Taking a pen and piece of paper from the glove compartment he wrote. "Call me. D."

Just then from the corner of his eye he caught a tiny movement from an upstairs bedroom window. A flicker of a curtain. A dark shadow half-hidden behind it. Teeko was in all right but it looked like he had nuttin' to say to Ranks. With a subtle nod of his head, Ranks motioned to Nero to walk over to him. They both walked back to the black sports Vauxhall Nova GTE. Ranks ordered Nero to open the car boot. Inside the boot was a can half-filled with petrol, rope, a chisel and a spare tyre. Taking the can Ranks walked over to the house.

"What are you doing?" Nero asked, slightly alarmed. Placing the can on Teeko's doorstep Ranks lit a cigarette coolly.

"His kids or woman might be in there."

"Int nobody at home you said." Ranks said tersely, picking the can of petrol up. He unscrewed the top. "Or is there?" He started to pour petrol through the letterbox.

"Ranks you can't do this-"

"Nigga, Ah just done it." Ranks took his mobile out of his pocket and rang Teeko's number. From outside they could clearly hear the phone ringing in Teeko's house. Teeko answered almost immediately. "How do you like your steak Teeko? Medium, rare or well done?" Ranks cut the call and put the phone back in his pocket. He looked at Nero who was watching him impassively. Ranks turned, lifted the letterbox and flicked his lighted cigarette inside. There was a muted explosion, a whumph kind of sound. Ranks walked calmly towards the car, as if he was out for a leisurely stroll on a summer's day. Nero followed, got in, and started the car.

"Wait!" Ranks ordered. He took another cigarette out of his pocket and looked towards the house. The front room was already in flames, turning the dark reflections of the car's windows bright orange. Ranks lit his cigarette. He smiled. "Drive."

Nero shoved the gear stick in first, put his foot down and the car tore away.

TEEKO HAD WAITED for Ranks' car to drive off so that he could retrieve the twenty-five grand hidden under the floorboards and then do a disappearing act, but it had cost him precious minutes. The money was in the front room and the fire had started at the front door. Hot flames prevented him from going anywhere downstairs.

Thank God the twins and their mum Shanieka were at her sister's.

Teeko had gone to bed naked and was struggling to find clothes in the dark. Thick black smoke was everywhere. He felt blindly for his mobile phone on the floor of his bedroom. Choking. Finding it he tried to dial 999. Beep. Fuckin' battery was dead. Panic. Flames licking high. Intense heat. Choking, he retreating to the top of the stairs. He was trapped. Eyes watering, streaming from the smoke, he quickly became disorientated. The heat seemed to be sapping all his strength. Slowly, his eyes began to close.

Shit! I don't wanna fuckin' die this way.

Teeko forced his eyes open. Saw nobody. Got up quickly, gaining consciousness with every movement. That familiar urgent voice had roused him. Teeko crawled under the smoke towards the back bedroom, coughing and spluttering violently. He had to get out. He had to! Teeko headed to where he thought the window was. The window was black with smoke. He grabbed Ramone's computer chair. He hurled it. The window exploded.

Fresh cold air filled the room. Teeko stuck his head out, gasping. The hole wasn't big enough. Teeko felt for the duvet on the twins' bottom bunk bed. Snatching it off, using it to break the remaining glass. He saw dark sky. He saw bright stars. He saw the flat kitchen roof extension several feet below. Teeko wasn't sure he was gonna make it. He closed his eyes firmly. He thought of Shanieka, and his twin sons. Sirens screamed loudly in the night time sky like frantic seagulls.

Teeko jumped.

The smell of smoke was in his goatee beard, skin, and clothes. He had to reach safety. *Watching*. He couldn't go to Shanieka's. He couldn't put her or the kids in any danger. Ranks could still be out there. *Waiting*.

He saw the telephone box and ran to it. Fighting dizziness Teeko tried to think. He couldn't call any of the Worlders Crew. It was obvious that Ranks had sussed him. The only person he could think of was Easy. But he had no contact number for Easy. He hadn't made up his mind to work for Easy but after tonight Ranks was fucked. Teeko tried to calm his breathing. His chest was wheezing dreadfully and it hurt.

Teeko thought of one person he could call right now.

Hands shuddering, he dialled the number.

STORM DIALLED HIS Nokia mobile phone, alone, long after Zukie had gone to bed upset. The leather sofa armchair offered him no comfort, might as well be sitting on a bed of nails. The ashtray was full of spliff ends. Storm put the spliff to his mouth and inhaled. He listened. Waited. The voice answered after the fifth ring sleepily.

"Why did you do it?" He asked quietly.

"What?" The voice became more alert. "Are you sick? It's five in the morning."

"Why do it to him? Why turn up at the studio like that?"

"He has a right to know."

"We had a deal. I give you money. You stay away. He wasn't ready."

"Money doesn't buy everything, Storm. It can't buy love. And I love Zukie. That's all you need to know."

The line clicked.

It went dead.

Storm listened to the silence.

The silence screamed at him.

First Ranks. Jasmine pregnant. Now this. Paradise, screwing up his brother's head.

MISS SMALL THOUGHT that Easy was just being practical, that he was working on the theory that if he couldn't beat 'em, he'd join 'em. And she liked Easy. She knew Trench wasn't happy, but she wasn't going to be a fool for love.

After several dates, she bought him to her abode, a top floor apartment at Salford's trendy Trinity Riverside Bluestone developments. She shared her salubrious, well sought after habitat with the likes of businessmen, lawyers, doctors, and the nouveau riche. She kept herself to herself greeting her neighbors with only a quick hello as they passed in the hall or lobby

Three lines of cocaine later, Miss Small closed the bedroom door, never taking her eyes off of Easy. He was lying across her huge circular bed, amongst the huge cushions and pillows, propped up sideways, finishing the last of the two bottles of wine they'd had. Miss Small undressed slowly. The lights were on bright. He would see every inch of her huge body. And if his expression altered even slightly, if there was even the slightest hint of repugnance she would have him popped. She offered him a line of coke set out on a metal try next to the bed.

"No offence, but I want a natural high." He said. Miss Small smiled. "No offence taken but I never dine alone," she said. Easy sold thestuff but had never taken shit. No way. He'd seen what it had done to Jigsy's brain. He had never even tried it. Miss Small was shoving the line towards him. He had to take it. Sycophancy alone wasn't going to win her over. One line. That was all he'd snort.

Shakily, Easy took the rolled up bit of cardboard and sucked the line up his nose. Instantly it scorched his nostril, gagging him, watering his eyes. She laughed at his virginity. Easy shook his head and laughed too. At first, he wondered why the hell people took the stuff. Then, out of nowhere, he suddenly felt as if a fierce electrical bolt had passed through him. He felt the horniest sensation as if he had climaxed and was ready to come again. His heart beat venomously.

Miss Small stripped down to her purple and black-striped velvet Basque, fishnet stockings and suspender belt. Easy leapt off the bed and walked towards her, clasping his fingers through hers. He looked deep into her eyes and smiled, caressing her face brushing his fingertips across her heaving breasts. Easy took Miss Small by the waist gently. He rocked her slightly until she realised he was dancing with her. Slowly he manoeuvred her around the carpeted bedroom to music only she could hear. Gently he started to kiss her on the neck, nuzzling down to her huge bosom. He brought her to the circular bed and lay down on her slowly.

"Thank you." He whispered. He started to kiss her neck softly, circling his tongue on her trembling flesh. She closed her eyes and sighed. "I won't let you down." He murmured, removing his jacket while still kissing her. "I'm going to make your heart and your profits rise. Trust me Veniesha."

CHRISTINE BERNADETTE MCDERMID, wrapped hands poised, dressed in a sports bra, tracksuit bottoms swung her body around and jump-kicked the heavy bag suspended from the ceiling, remembering the training techniques she'd learned at the martial academy back in Belfast. The techniques which would devastate an opponent in competition or on the street.

The heavy bag was a great tool for increasing power, endurance and stamina. This was one of her favourite routines. It was important to establish right away that the bag was more than an object to punch and kick. Instead, she formed a mental picture that the bag was an opponent. Therefore, she reacted to the bag as though it was to be defeated. Her strategy was to never let the bag touch her body. If it did, it was like a clean hit. As the bag came towards her, she would side step it and throw combinations to possible openings. Although sometimes this could be very difficult, with extra practice, she acquired more balance and technique. She kept her gaze on the movement of the bag — 'eye conditioning' — remembering the old adage of never taking your eyes off your opponent.

Although it was late and she wasn't competing internationally in major female kick-boxing championships any more she still trained, usually late at night. The spare room was no more than a box-room but there was enough space. Sweat poured off her fit, well-toned body. She levelled the bag with her eyes and gave it a succession of swift punches. The phone started to ring. She delivered a couple of blows to the bag but couldn't continue. The ringing was intrusive, putting her off. Suppose it was a call from Easy, whom she hadn't heard from for a couple days now? Running into the bedroom, Chris snatched up the receiver.

"Hello?"

There was the sound of someone coughing. Then:

"It's Teeko. I need your help."

ZUKIE WAS RUNNING breathlessly. He knew he shouldn't look back because IT was chasing him. Everywhere was dark. Zukie took a quick glimpse over his bare shoulder and saw the mechanical eagle swooping out of the sky towards him. Its metallic wingspan was enormous. Its iron claws looked like sharp knives. Petrified, Zukie closed his eyes.

He wasn't running any more. He was in the back of somebody's car. Chico and Hair Oil and his half-brother Eugene also known as Bluebwai were on either other side of him. The eagle had converted into a car, which seemed to be pursuing them.

Bluebwai was grinning. "You better duck down low." He said. "It's gonna get us." Zukie, Chico, Blue, and Oil all doubled over on the back seat of the car. They were sounds like huge fireworks. The back window imploded showering glass over them. The eagle tore into the car and savaged the back of the driver's head. We're going to crash, Zukie thought. We're all fucking dead. In one sudden violent movement the car seemed to wrench to one side. Somebody screamed. Then they were turning over and over. Zukie was squashed, panicking, kicking, crying, screaming, trying to get out of the car. But he was trapped.

"Zukes, stop hitting me man."

Zukie woke up shaking brutally, drenched in sweat. Thank God, he was safe, at home in his bedroom. Storm must have come in. He was holding him tightly.

Breathing hard, barely able to form words, Zukie stared into Storm's concerned brown eyes.

"This huge eagle was tryin' to get me." He stammered clinging to Storm, as if his brother had just saved him from falling over a cliff. Tears streamed effortlessly down his face.

"It was just a dream, Zukes. No one's gonna get you. I promise." Zukie was groaning as if in pain. Storm wrapped himself around his brother more tightly, rocking him gently. "I promise."

DANNY LIT A spliff, unconsciously rubbing the tattoo of the powerful-looking eagle over his left shoulder. He sighed. It was too bad about Teeko, but shit, in't that the way life goes down? Play with fire and you're gonna get bu'n up, for real, in't ya? Ranks lay back on his bed. Contemplating. He was now one soldier down and he desperately needed to recoup. What he needed now was expertise, planning, fortitude and experience. Storm Michaels was all of these. He needed Storm.

Ranks was very used to getting anything he wanted.

"HERE, A TENNER oughta cover it." Chris paid the edgy-looking Asian taxi driver double as Teeko Martial got out, looking exhausted and in a terrible state. They said nothing to each other as Teeko wearily climbed the stairs, crippled up them, to her flat on Broom Lane Levenshulme, a nondescript built up area on the city's Southside.

Christine's flat was cramped, filled mainly with junk, superfluous rugs on the walls, lit candles, multiple kickboxing trophies and medals, and beaded curtains that rattled in every open doorway. There was a strong aroma of coconut oil.

In the kitchen Teeko virtually collapsed in the chair by the kitchen window, his head in his hands.

"Teeko. Here." She handed him a cigarette and a glass of brandy. The hand that held the glass shook like a rocket on take off. He drank it all in one gulp looking around at the various lit candles in the flat. Even the slightest flame seemed to make Teeko Martial sweat.

"So-what happened?" She asked, smoking, leaning against the sink in the dark kitchen.

"Someone mistook me for Guy Fawkes," he said, sniffing, wiping spilt alcohol from his mouth with the back of his hand.

"That's not funny," she said, attending to the gash on his arm with a cloth and some antiseptic. "Guy Fawkes would have been our hero if he'd pulled it off. Besides, you could have been killed." Teeko was a well-built guy. Like her, he exercised frequently. His fitness had helped him to survive.

She'd met Teeko two years ago at a gym in town. She was circuit training for a kickboxing title defence, which she went on to retain. Teeko's wound required stitching. Chris knew enough to know that Teeko couldn't visit any hospital emergency rooms. He'd have to stay low for a couple of days. He needed somewhere to stay.

After a quick freshen up, she had changed into a cropped Nike T-shirt, and Lycra shorts. Hugging her trim waist, she studied Teeko's downcast face.

"Need to contact anyone?" She asked, stroking her short brunette hair.

"Only Easy," Teeko said wearily, raising his wide brown eyes up at her. "But I don't have a number for him." Chris smiled.

"I have." She said turning around and putting the kettle on to boil. "He should be back here any day now. He's just away on business." She said slowly. She took a roll of cotton from a kitchen drawer, removing a sewing needle from it.

"Roll up your sleeve."

CHERUBS AND ANGELS. Kurtis couldn't understand why he didn't have any praying around his hospital bed like the other guy opposite. Instead Kurtis had elves with fangs and diamond-shaped red eyes that glowed in the dark like electric lights. The little bastards stank too, dressed like nurses injecting poison into his blood.

Sometimes they spoke to him through the TV. Sometimes they pretended to be his friend, only to get near him and hit him on the head, giving him terrible headaches. And people were fools believing the millennium bug was gone. The millennium bug was in everyone's fucking brains.

Kurtis had to leave this place. It wasn't a psychiatric hospital. It was a spaceship and the aliens were holding him prisoner.

Grandma and Sharon had to rescue him.

But not Easy.

Easy was one of them.

EASY-LOVE BROWN eased out of Veniesha Brooks' bed carefully.He had spent two whole days with Small. Veniesha was sleeping soundly. He dressed hushed, constantly watching Small for wakefulness. After he had finished, Easy wrote the number of the new mobile phone Chris had bought him on a piece of paper and left it on the empty pillow next to Veniesha. All the time wondering how he was going to get the five grand initiation sub. Putting on his designer jacket, he suddenly felt the weight of his small mobile banging in his pocket against his hip. Taking it out Easy turned it on. A text message from Chris was waiting, wanting to see him urgently.

Bending down Easy kissed Miss Small on her warm forehead. He turned to go.

"Wait a minute." Easy frowned as Veniesha woke up, reaching down underneath the mattress. She threw a set of keys to him. Catching them Easy looked down. He saw the BMW emblem.

"I didn't wanna wake you. Veniesha are yu sure?"

"I notice you have no wheels. You can borrow it but do, nuh crash it."

"I'll be back."

"Yeah," she said. "I know you will."

Throwing her a kiss, Easy stood up and left.

STORM AND TANIESHA looked up as Zukie entered the shop. Both were surprised to see him; he should have been in class. Zukie was dressed in a hooded sweatshirt and jeans. Storm frowned as Zukie walked towards the counter. The studio was booked and the café was brimming with the members of a soul band eating fried dumplings, fried chicken and rice. Zukie smiled at Taniesha. She returned the smile warmly.

"You OK?" Storm asked. "Why aren't you in class?"

"I've put it on hold." Storm looked at Zukie flabbergasted. "I wanna talk to you." Storm followed Zukie into the back into the office. They were both aware of Taniesha's dark inquiring eyes on their backs. Closing the door firmly Storm was wondering what the hell was going on.

"Zukie what's wrong with you? That course is costing the company four grand a year."

"I want my life back."

"What?"

Zukie cocked his head sideways.

"You know those tickets for the Mr Vegas show? Well I want them. I'm gonna take Taniesha." The telephone began to ring.

"Zukie, I don't think you should go anywhere without—"

"You? Why not? I'm a big boy now." The telephone seemed to be ringing more pressingly. Storm looked at it.

"What about what I told you?"

"I in't afraid of something I don't remember no more."

Taniesha suddenly popped her head around the office door.

"I'm sorry to disturb you, but there's someone on the phone who wants to speak to you." Storm was a little bewildered, distracted. Zukie was already walking towards the door, leaving Storm confused.

"Zukie hole up a sec." Zukie was gone. Taniesha looked embarrassed. "Storm? Someone's on the phone wanting to speak with you urgently." Storm eyed her from head to toe. She was dressed in a short skirt and a tight-fitting top. He came to the realisation that Zukie's change in personality had to do with a sudden interest in one woman and the reappearance of another.

"Who the hell is it?" he snapped. Taniesha looked startled.

"I don't know," Taniesha stammered. "He didn't say."

"In future always make sure you get the person's name. It's good business practice." Taniesha dropped her huge brown eyes hurtfully.

Storm snatched up the phone in his office, all the while staring at the flustered-looking and angry Taniesha.

"Storm Records and Studio. Clifton Michaels, manager speaking. Can I help you?"

"Hello Clifton Michaels, manager."

A very familiar deep voice said. "You can help me very much indeed." Storm looked up to make sure the girl had gone and the door was closed.

"Who tell you to phone my shop?"

"Had any conversations with your brother yet?" Storm was about to rant down the line, to tell Ranks to fight his own battles, when he realised Danny had hung up.

"W'HAPPEN?" EASY ASKED, his head still banging, his throat raw and sore from his two days with Miss Small. All this time he had had no idea his brother Kurtis had been in psychiatric care and he felt guilty for Grandma withstanding the worst of it all without him. But she, at least, was forgiving. Sharon, however, was not so forgiving. He was glad he had gone over to Grandma's first, instead of going over to Chris's as her text message demanded. Kurtis had been released from care and was now being looked after at home, a community psychiatrist due to visit fortnightly. Easy entered Kurtis' bedroom. Kurtis was sitting in bed listening to music. Easy sat down next to his brother.

"I'm gonna stick around." Easy said.

"Hey," Kurtis began sarcastically, "you don't have to do that on our behalf. We've managed many crises before without you. Y'know like when Gran couldn't pay the 'lectric and you'd gone bout your business. Or like the time when the cooker broke down and Gran had no money to buy a new one."

"Kurtis I was just trying to hustle money back then."

"Everyday I thought you'd come home and take care of us. I wanted Gran to be safe and for everything to go back the way it was." Kurtis sighed. He lay back on the bed. Easy looked at him.

"This time I'm gonna stick around, make sure you get better." The image of the kid stabbing himself in the neck in prison flashed in

Easy's mind. He didn't want Kurtis to suffer a similar fate because of his mental illness.

"Then you can start college again. Finish your computing course. Get a good job." Easy's mobile began to ring. He answered it; it was Chris wanting to know where the hell he was. Easy rose.

He had to go.

Time was getting on. He walked towards the door. He didn't look back at Kurtis.

If he had, he would have seen Kurtis crying.

"IT INT MUCH but it can help pay something towards the loan." Easy handed over five hundred pounds to Grandma. Sharon kept her gaze on the large screen of the rented TV.

Rising out of her chair, resting on her stick, Grandma looked at him.

"No is all right. I already pay him off. Me nuh owe him nuttin." Easy was puzzled. "I cash in a few insurance policies and some other things matured. I was saving them for my funeral expenses."

"Funeral expenses? Don't talk like that-"

"Anyhow, you keep yu money."

"No Gran, I want you to take the money. Look, put it away safe and then first thing tomorrow put it into the bank OK for a rainy day or sumtin." Grandma smiled.

Easy wrote down his mobile telephone on a piece of paper and gave it to Grandma.

"If you need anything, *anything* juss call me on this number right? I'll be here in no time. Now, ya sure everything is OK?"

"Yes, dahlin' everyting is fine." Smiling, tipping on her toes, Grandma flung her arms around him and kissed him on the cheeks. Sharon looked at them both, shaking her head wearily. She then got up and went into the kitchen, leaving Easy and Idey alone.

"I know I won't see you for a while. God go with you, my grandson."

"I love you Gran. You know that don't you?"

Grandma nodded, smiling, tears shining in the corner of her eyes like miniature diamonds.

KURTIS HEARD THE conversation between his elder brother and grandmother outside the living room door. See, so much for checking to make sure Kurtis was taking his medication. He wasn't gonna stick around. Easy couldn't even stick to treacle toffee. Easy had no loyalties. He only cared about himself.

Later when Grandma and Sharon had gone to bed, Kurtis packed a bag, sneaked into the living room and helped himself to the money Easy had given Grandma. He left through the back door, throwing his tablets in the back garden.

THE BLACK MITSIBUSHI colt drove slowly over the traffic-calming humps, music pumping through expensive tweeters.

"Bad man nuh wait fe night fe come down,
Anything gwine happen mek it happen and done-"

Ranks, Stukky, Fila, Mr. Mentian and Sizzla sat quietly, listening to the ragga CD. The car drew up near Teeko's burned out house, or rather, what remained of it. Five-O had cordoned off the area. Danny noticed that Teeko's jeep had gone.

Ranks saw Shanieka. Pretty and thin, dressed in designer attire, she was standing not far from her blue Saab Convertible. Not bad for a council care worker on £3.80 per hour or some shit like that. Hands flailing, shouting, Shanieka stared in disbelief at their belongings, now blackened remains in a heap on the pavement. Ranks lit a cigarette casually.

She walked over and peered anxiously into the car.

"Where is he? Is he hurt? He hasn't phoned me. Why hasn't he phoned me?" Sassy, loud, dominant. Bitch talking to Ranks like he was her man or dog or some shit like that.

Ranks was as cool as ice water. "He's laying low, babes. Don't worry. He'll be in touch. You up for protection?"

Shanieka nodded, hugging her body. Ranks dashed cigarette ash outside the car. Shanieka walked back over to her convertible followed by Stukky and Sizzla.

Ranks smiled.

"THAT'S IT! WE'RE gonna get that fucka." Easy paced up and down in the small space of Chris's living room, listening to Teeko's close call at the hands of Teeko's former employer, Danny Ranks.

"What if you had the twins stayin' over-" Teeko closed his eyes and swallowed. Obviously, it didn't bear thinking about; the thought had tortured him enough during the past couple of days and nights. He was dressed in fresh clothes Chris had bought him. Chris had retrieved Teeko's jeep and it was parked up outside on the lane.

Easy's funki-dreads bobbed wildly, his face screwed into a ball of hate and fury. Teeko shook his head. His shirt was open revealing a smooth muscled chest with a strong washboard abdomen. Teeko rubbed his hand over his shiny bald head. Easy noticed the bandaged arm.

"No one can touch him," Teeko said.

"They say Jesus Christ was the Son of God but he still got crucified," Easy stated. "He in't invincible yu know. Every wall's got a crack in it somewhere."

Teeko looked like he was in Outer Mongolia. "I still han't contacted Shanieka," he said sorrowfully. "She must be going mad with worry."

"Women are tougher than you think." Easy said. Chris looked at him. Easy smiled at her. He liked Chris. She was on the level. She smiled back, taking herself and baby into the kitchen.

"We can do it. We can take him on." Easy knew he was trying to convince Teeko. But he was wondering what had happened to the tough, strong Teeko he used to know. The same guy who would karate up a man if he stepped out of line. As if he had read Easy's mind Teeko said. "I'm getting tired of this madness, Easy. We can't take Ranks on. For a start we in't got no crew."

Teeko sounded like a trueborn defeatist. Easy looked towards the kitchen and lowered his voice so that Chris wouldn't hear. It sounded like she was talking baby talk to Tyrone who was now cooing back to her.

"I'm checking Small."

"What?"

"She's my woman now."

Teeko sighed. "If Chris finds out you're out on your arse bwai. Nobody fucks with Chris."

"I can handle women. Second nature, baby," Easy boasted. "But what I want to know right now is how I can mash down Ranks' resistance. You know him. You know his ways, his deals." Teeko looked towards the wall vacantly. "I don't believe it! The guy tried to bu'n you like firewood and you still don't want to—"

Teeko stood up and shouted.

"It can't be done! Anybody who has ever tangled wid Danny has got dussed. He's got Nero as his security. It's going to be even worse if he gets Storm to work for him. He's after Storm bad."

"Storm?" Easy shook his head, half-smiling half-frowning. "That eediyat? You know what my Grandma says Tee? She says everyday bucket go ah well, one day the bottom must drop out." Teeko stayed quiet, jumped when Easy hit the coffee table. "Now *tell* me. I want to know everything he's got planned." Teeko looked at the floor.

"He's got a big pay off going down." He mumbled. Easy sat down on a nearby stool, fighting hard to contain his exhilaration.

"Where? Who? When? What's the retail?"

"Kadeem Hussein. The old baths in Longsight. Three weeks on Tuesday. Big dunsi. Enough to make Danny the main don of Manchester."

Easy smiled. "Is that so?"

MISS SMALL LOOKED at the huge bouquet of flowers admiringly. The card attached to it simply said. "Missing you loads. See you later. Easy." She sat with the crew who were counting out money on a table in her apartment. Ranger weighing cocaine, placing them in small wraps. Slide and Hatchet smoking a couple of crack joints, smiling and laughing as the high kicked in.

Trench, wearing a huge white cotton dressing on his left ear, suddenly kissed his teeth savagely.

"He's fucking using you and you can't see it. Where's he been for days, heh? Days yu in't even seen him." Trench drawled, gazing out the window at the dockside. Far into the distance, he could see Manchester United Football Club's huge North stand. Despite the warm weather, he was wearing a woolly hat, a scruffy black coat, and dirty boots. Looks just like a mad dub poet from New York, Miss Small thought contemptuously.

"Be careful Trench. You don't know who ah use who."

"You be careful. He's just biding his time. Waiting for the right moment." Trench mumbled on resentfully, touching the bandage over his sliced ear. Hatchet, Slide and Ranger stopped counting, tuning in to the conversation. One look from Miss Small convinced them to continue with their task.

"What is your problem Trench?"

"That bwai Easy. Him ah go squeeze you and you can't see it."

"I'm in charge of this yah crew. I always was and I always will be. I took my chances when I took the kilo I was carrying inside me for Anthon's crew from yard and ran at the airport. All now dem still ah look for me. Is *my* runnings dis and no one gwine tek it from me. Same way me lick out Tanga, Morris and One Foot Fletcha me will out dissa bwai candle if him fuck with me."

She was fourteen years of age when she arrived in England. Her Jamaican mother sent for her not knowing she was pregnant and carrying a kilo of cocaine in her intestines. She was meant to meet up with Yardie gang associates in Harlesden but never showed up, keeping the coke for a year before establishing a buyer. She chose her 'career' before motherhood, giving her son to her sister to raise while she built herself up as a tough-dealing gangster woman.

"He's already fucked with you." Trench muttered. "Look like yu liked it too." Trench was jealous, he felt threatened. But if he didn't ease off, she would smash another bottle over his head like she did last time, scarring the other side of his face.

"Easy is now a part of this crew and yuh just gwine haff to ackcept it. If you nuh like how me run tings, see de door deh. But 'member seh any how yu do dat yuh gravestone already mark, yah hear me?"

Trench shook his head, slowly walking into the bedroom. More like *your* gravestone's marked, he thought, in Easy-Love's handwriting. Here lies Miss Small duped by a smart hustler. She wouldn't listen to him but Trench was sworn to protect her. From now on he was going to scrutinize Easy-Love Brown's every move.

He slammed the living room door.

"MMMM. T'NGS AH look stush." Thinking aloud Ranks was checking his stocks and shares on the FT website, pleased with himself. He then logged onto his on-line bank account to check his finances. Everything was cool. Kadeem was cutting him in on a big deal. Stukky and Sizzla were at Teeko's woman's house waiting for him to show. And if Easy thought he was gonna get a piece of the action using Teeko, Ranks would deal with that too. Ranks continued to smile. Just then, the doorbell rang vigorously. Danny wasn't expecting anyone. Nero walked into the bedroom first. Tall and slim, he looked tired.

"It's Kej. Says he's got sumtin' fe yu." Danny frowned. Nero left and Kurtis walked in sheepishly. Danny noticed that Kurtis looked well, he was shaven, and the raggedy twists that were forming in his hair weeks ago were shaven off. Kurtis smiled. With his huge round eyes, he always reminded Danny of Richard Blackwood, the TV presenter, rapper and comedian. He hadn't seen Kurtis since Kurtis smoked his crack, and Ranks had chased him out of his apartment weeks ago.

"Got the money you owe me for my rocks?" Ranks asked.

"Yup."

Kurtis handed over five hundred pounds.

"Where yu get this from? Yu rob a church or what?" Kurtis laughed in that way that reminded Danny of Easy when he used to run the Pipers crew. Back in the day Easy didn't even know who the fuck he was.

"I gotta proposition fe you." Kurtis said.

Danny sat down on his bed.

"Yeah? Waddat den star?"

"If you let me come in with the crew I'll tell you all my brother's moves." Kurtis said. Danny laughed broadly, his light skin glowing like honey under the low Ikea lamp. Ranks looked at Kurtis carefully. Though in different classes, he and Kurtis had been in the same year and form class at Godfrey Paul's High School on Lloyd Street South in Fallowfield. Kurtis was in the top sets for every subject. He remembered Kurtis as a computer nerd with no friends. A gawky, big glasses, no dick freak who always seemed to want to hang around with Danny and his crew on the days when Danny decided to show up at school and before he finally got expelled for possession of an A class drug.

"Got a few t'ings I in't comfortable wid," Ranks said. "One, he's your beloved brother, ain't he? And two, why would I trust a bonehead like you?"

Kurtis's face soured.

"He ain't no brother of mine. If you want my services just tell me cos right now Easy's lookin' bling. My Gran's suddenly got money, Easy's driving around in a BMW with a fat woman as his passenger. So what does that say?" Ranks stared hard at Kurtis and saw that the other teen was deadly serious.

So, it looked like Easy was hooked up with the fat bitch, despite the fact that she had him beaten up. Interesting. What game plan was this? Ranks definitely needed to know.

"How yu gonna tab Easy's every move?"

"I'll be working with him before the week's out. Trust me."

"And what do *you* get out of this?" Ranks asked lighting another ready-rolled spliff with an immaculate gold lighter.

"The best white powder you got in the house on the house when I want."

"OK."

"And I stay here occasionally."

"OK, nigga, yu got yuself a deal. Welcome to the Worlders Massive." Ranks said wrap-shaking Kurtis's hand firmly. Kurtis smiled. "Step this way, sir, my homeboy Nerome will show you to your room."

RANKS' VOICE SOUNDED eerily real, as if he was right there in the room with Teeko Martial. The voice was cold, threatening, relayed from a day's old voicemail message on the other mobile Teeko had left in the glove compartment of his jeep.

"One hundred and thirty-five Old King's Road, Old Trafford, right? Blue door, white gates, wooden blinds in the front room window. Shanieka's got good taste in furniture style innit? But pine burns like firewood Teeko." Teeko's heart pounded severely as he sat on the mattress in the spare room of Chris's flat staring up at the ceiling, smoking. He was in a no-hope situation. If he walked out on Easy, Easy would come after him. As it was Ranks was hot for his blood. How was he going to get Easy to back off? He thought he could simply say he'd heard the payoff was off. But Teeko thought Easy was way smarter than that. He'd suss it.

Teeko conceded the only other choice he had was to take his woman and kids and leave Manchester. He ruled this course of action out quickly when he realised Ranks might be watching Shanieka's house in Old Trafford. Watching and waiting for her to leave and meet him at a rendezvous. He could not risk it yet he could not risk Easy going through with ripping off Ranks' payoff. Ranks knew Teeko was in hiding.

What the hell was he gonna do now?

TEEKO COULDN'T PUT it off any longer. He punched in Shanieka's number. She answered on the first ring.

"Shani?"

She screamed down on the phone at him.

"Teeko! Thank God, you're OK. I've been phoning you for days and when your two mobiles were switched off, I thought the worst. Where the hell are you? Why didn't you phone? I really thought they had got to you in the fire."

Poor Shanieka. She obviously thought it was Miss Small's crew Dodge who were responsible for the fire. She had no idea it was his own crew. But she also had no idea that by burning him out Danny had left him no alternative but to work for Easy.

"I'm all right. I'm sorry for not phoning but I had my reasons. But listen to me good, cos I don't have much time. Is the house being watched?"

Shanieka laughed.

"Everything's safe," she began earnestly. "Ranks put Sizzla and Stukky with us for our protection." Teeko swallowed hard as if it could stop his heart pounding, or still the tremor in his soul. Sweat was boiling on his skin. He sat up. Slowly.

"What?"

"They've been guarding us twenty-four seven. In fact, Sizzla's great with the boys. He keeps lettin' them win him on the PlayStation. Ranks said to let them know the minute you called." Teeko stood frozen still. He felt his body sway. "Tee? Tee, baby, are you there?"

Teeko lowered his voice. "Yeah. Shanieka I want you to listen to me. Listen to me good. Take the boys to Anthea's in London."

"Why?"

"Just do it. Don't tell Stukky what you're doing. Tell them that your mother's sick and you have to go. Just do it, now."

Shanieka's blithe female voice was replaced quickly by the stern rough edged voice of Phillip Kensington otherwise known as Stukky.

"Hello stranger. I have a message for you. Danny says if you come in you've got nuttin' to worry about. Shanieka and the kids'll be safe." Teeko heard Remi and Ramone laughing in the background.

"Leave my woman and kids out of this," he snarled.

"You knew the risks Tee, when you became a part of the crew. Fuck with Ranks and not even your distant cousins in Alabama are safe. Turn yuself in. Don't mek we haffi come after you."

"I wanna talk to Shanieka."

"Shanieka can't talk right now. She's what they say in the movies — otherwise engaged."

Teeko heard a click and the line buzzed a dead tone.

"SHE'S GONNA BE the brand new international lick, boom style in't she?"

Taniesha Kanes didn't agree or disagree. Paradise had a rare voice quality that was very similar to the Grammy and MOBO award winning R&B star Lauryn Hill.

Dressed in jeans, a purple vest top and her dreads tied up in a high ponytail, a band was backing her from Leeds.

Both Storm and Zukie were mixing her vocals. She sang, closing her eyes, losing herself in her music, slim body moving like a magical river.

Paradise stopped singing. Hugging the top-set headphones, she smiled and said into the microphone huskily.

"This song is dedicated to someone I used to know and love a long time ago. Unfortunately, I had to say goodbye to him because he didn't remember our love. But I kept the memory of our love inside of me." Taniesha's heart slammed painfully against her ribs. Turning towards Zukie, Taniesha saw him swallow. She saw the slight frown on his troubled face. Paradise broke into a strong ballad. A reggae version of the Bee Gee's and Celine Dion's Immortal. The song came from the depths of her tormented soul. There was only a glass partition separating her new lover Zukie from his old lover Paradise.

And like everyone else, Zukie sat totally transfixed. Taniesha looked back over at Paradise singing. She was electric, focussing her attention on Zukie, and Zukie alone.

They were swarming around Paradise in the crowded studio, like she was some sort of Goddess, or queen. Taniesha observed jealously. Paradise was revelling in the attention and adulation, laughing, and throwing her head back, making her long wavy dreadlocks bounce over her shoulders. However, it didn't take long before the others moved away leaving Zukie and Paradise alone. Zukie complimented her singing.

"I was wondering if, well, do you fancy going for a quick drink later? We could talk about when I could come and see Kyesha." Zukie asked clumsily, awkwardly, nervous, looked like he was blushing.

"You could see her tonight if you like, Zukie. Yeah. And it's yes to the drink." Paradise said, readily agreeing to the invitation. "Kyesha was asking about you a few days back."

"Yeah?" Zukie asked, excitement creeping into his voice. "Do you fancy a quick one at the Queen Alec?" She nodded, smiling. Zukie smiled deeply, touched. Taniesha watched the couple. There was no denying it. Sensuality oozed between them like a sexual aura. She was nothing to someone who had missing history and was now rediscovering himself. Taniesha put on her coat, smiling. It hurt, but she knew she was already forgotten in Zukie's mind.

STILL HOLDING THE letter from Celia in her hand, Miss Small sat in the darkness of her large living room apartment, contemplating. Celia always wrote. Even though she had Veniesha's number, Celia never phoned. The only time she telephoned was to say Pappa had died in Jamaica. Otherwise, she wrote. Celia's letters were always detailed about the boy, her nephew, though she treated Daniel like one of her own children.

Miss Small knew this day was coming. It was inevitable. The boy wanted to meet her. Miss Small sighed deeply. She lit the spliff and inhaled. Maybe the time was right. Now that she had just discovered she was carrying Easy's baby. Easy didn't know yet. The thought of the baby warmed her soul. She would never lose this baby like she did Daniel. After a few more deals, Miss Small planned to settle down and bring her daughter up in security and peace. No more drugs, no guns, no bad life for her little baby girl. Veniesha was so convinced she was carrying a little girl she even had a name for her. Cara.

Miss Small planned to go to Jamaica for a couple weeks, just to tie up a few business deals and land interests. She was thinking of whom to leave in charge during her absence. She trusted and loved Easy, that she couldn't deny. Hadn't he, alongside Jigsy and Fluxy made a success of the Piper Mill Massive? He had good business sense. He knew how to do things tight. She knew that from the first time she saw Easy-Love eight years ago that she liked him. That's why she didn't want Trench to kill him outright. If she was going to step down after her baby was born, Miss Small needed a successor. Trench was far too hot headed and had no business logic whatsoever.

The door to her apartment opened. Easy walked in holding the spare keys she had given him. Smiling he walked over to her. Holding her from behind, he kissed her neck.

"W'happen baby?" he asked, holding her tightly. Miss Small wrapped her arms around his.

"I'm all right."

"Well I've got a surprise for you soon."

"Yeah?"

"Yeah but first I'm gonna take you out for a meal."

Miss Small laughed. But she had great belief in Easy, and she knew once the initiation sub was paid Easy would soon become second in charge.

IT WAS ONLY a matter of time wasn't it? Watching Zukie with Paradise today Storm knew. The truth was going to come out somehow. Storm was resting in his bedroom. Thinking.

Zukie was becoming more independent of him lately. When Zukie first came out of the hospital, he was totally dependent on Storm, even to do basic things like getting dressed. Every month Storm escorted him to the clinic at the Royal Infirmary where he worked on his memory skills. Storm was there to calm the violent tantrums and to comfort him through his nightmares, and for a whole year they stayed in the same room, Zukie refusing to sleep in complete darkness or alone. Now it seemed the violent nightmares had returned.

Storm was truly concerned for his little brother's safety, and mental state. The truth would be so devastating for him it might send him completely over the edge. Yet Zukie was out there and Storm had no control over who he was seeing or talking to. No control. He'd lost it the day Zukie bumped into Ranks. Storm had a feeling that things were going to get worse. Much worse. The phone rang. It was Angie, Hair Oil's sister. He knew the news was going to be bad. He hadn't spoken to Angie for a long time.

Not since the night Chico got killed.

NINETY DEGREES. THE Queen Alexandra pub in the middle of the Alexandra Park Estate. Outside like a mini carnival. Full car park. Yout's on mountain bikes hungrily watching girls as young as thirteen in body hugging flesh-revealing clothes, acting like big women. Sports, high performance convertibles, tops down, new registration cars. Music booming from powerful stereo systems, ghetto voices of Eminem, Dr Dre, Cobra and Buju Banton fighting for dominance.

Inside, Deejay Diggy D was taking requests from the dancers on the floor of the main dance room. The pub was a well-known haunt for certain drug-dealers and even midweek it was rammed. Easy felt comfortable in the pub. Miss Small had a stake in the takings. He sat at the table in the corner with Teeko, and Chris. A couple of very pretty girls walked past them giggling, pausing to look at Teeko and Easy. From the corner of his eye Easy saw Chris give them an obnoxious look. The two girls, one blonde-haired and white, one black with a huge weave kept their eyes on Easy lustily as they swayed over to the bar. The words of a reggae tune came through loud and clear.

"Log on and step pon chi-chi man."

Dressed in a purple suit, black shirt, and expensive shoes, with jewellery Miss Small had given him, Easy knew he was looking copa. Chris downed the bottle of beer quickly, and started on another bottle. Easy cleared his throat and looked at Teeko but Teeko looked like he was in the clouds, hand-gliding in Honolulu.

Hard core, rough bashment rhythms bounced off the walls of the smoky sweaty pub walls. The overpowering smell of cannabis was evident.

Faintly, against the background of bashment music, Easy's mobile phone began to ring. Picking it up he glimpsed Veniesha's number in the caller display. She'd gone to Jamaica, leaving him in charge. He answered, turning away from Chris.

"Yo."

"Where yu deh?" Miss Small asked.

"Can't hear ya." Easy shouted exaggeratedly. "The reception's bad. I'll call you back later, yeah?" He switched the mobile off. Chris was quick.

"Who was that?"

Easy shifted in his seat, but looked Chris straight in the eye.

"Sharon." Chris folded her arms, looking disconcerted. Easy looked at Teeko who now looked as if the sky had opened and a massive meteorite was about to drop on him. "What the fuck is wrong wid everyone here? We're suppose to be celebratin' our teamwork."

"I gotta talk to you about sumtin," Teeko said, looking worried. Easy looked at him. Like John The Baptist, he had no time for doubters. Standing up, Easy said.

"Let me get some more drinks in first." Ignoring Teeko's crestfallen face Easy hurried through the crowds to get the drinks.

He was served quickly, aware of a few curious small-time dealers' eyes on him. Grabbing the six bottles of Pils quickly, he turned. The sight of the grey-eyed dreadlocks yout' immediately seized his attention. It was like seeing a ghost. He had heard that Storm's brother had been badly injured in the crash. Easy watched as the yout' bought drinks. Obviously, he was entertaining some gyal. He smiled across at her, fawningly, dribbling. Easy's eyes followed Zukie's across the crowded pub seeking out Zukie's pretty female companion. He laughed. Paradise. The preacher man's daughter. Just then, sensing that someone had him in their sights, Zukie's eyes met Easy's temporarily. But his eyes held no recognition. They flitted over Easy's face before moving away quickly back to the girl. He had looked through Easy like he had never seen him before in his life. As if Easy had never held him at gunpoint, run over his mother, threatened his life and forced him to stay in Jigsy's car. Zukie and his companion got up and left. And by the looks on their faces, sex was definitely on the cards tonight, Easy could tell.

Easy made his way back to their little corner, aware of his female admirers still studying him. One of them called over to him, much to

Chris's fury.

She stood up as Easy sat down, placing the bottles of Pils on the table.

"Siddown Chris. Ah no nuttin. Relax. Sit down." She stood, ignoring him, resolutely glaring at the girls. The black girl kissed through her teeth. The white girl laughed. They looked no older than eighteen.

"Chris." Chris sat down slowly biting her lower lip. Teeko grabbed a bottle of Pils and started to drink it quickly.

"I gotta talk to you, Easy."

"Yeah but first, look over at the door, the red dread leaving. In't that Storm's brother. The one that looks like Bluebwai?"

"Who?" Teeko looked confused. He pulled on a spliff eagerly.

"Over there." Teeko raised his body and looked over. His expression was of pure disinterest.

"Yeah, yeah, yeah."

"He don't remember me."

"He's got memory problems or sumtin. Anyway, I gotta talk to you."

"What yu mean memory problems? Don't he know who the fuck he is?"

"Fuck him, man, I got real problems, Easy," Teeko muttered.

"His brother is responsible for Jigsy's death, or have you got memory problems? I ended up in prison cos of Storm's brazen recklessness."

Teeko raised his voice, his face contorted with bitterness. "YU IN'T FUCKIN' LISSENIN' TO ME, ARE YU EASY?" Teeko stood up, drinking the last of his beer grabbing his jacket. Easy was perplexed. Calling Teeko's name softly, he pulled him down to the seat at the table.

"Yo, wassup with you, star?" Teeko was shaking his shiny baldhead slowly, swallowing. For the first time since evening, Easy noticed the look of desolation on Teeko's face.

Teeko sighed hollowly. "Ranks got two of him man dem hol'ing up Shanieka and my yout's at dem yard."

"When? How long?"

"A week now."

"What? Why didn't yu tell me?"

"I'm tellin' you now. And I can't go through wid anything wid yu cos he'll do sumtin to dem. I know dat."

Easy laughed. Teeko looked mystified. Easy took a slow drink. Chris was already starting on another bottle, stroking her hand through her wavy brunette hair.

"That ain't no problem. I'll go in there, buss inna de house, take his fool-fool bwai dem out-"

"Naw! That's fuckin' obvious, innit? I mean, a man like Ranks would just be expectin' you to pull a mad move like dat, wouldn't he?" On second thoughts, Easy was inclined to agree.

"OK. I'll think of something. Chris do you want another drink? Chris? Chris?"

DJ Diggy D had pulled up a tune and was playing a special request by the two girls, dedicated to Easy and Teeko. Chris's eyes were firmly on the scantily dressed black girl who was staring at Chris with provoking looks.

"Grab on pon dem.
Hold on pon dem.
Grab on pon dem ah next gyal man get tek weh."

Suddenly Chris leapt over the table in a flying leap straight towards the black girl. In an instant, she had smashed the empty beer bottle over her head. Fortunately, the brunt of the blow was cushioned by the huge weave she was wearing. Both women were screaming obscenities at each other. The black girl grabbed Chris's hair with two hands. Chris knocked her forehead against the girl's forehead. Screaming, Chris's assailant reeled backwards against the bar, knocking glasses and bottles over. People moved out of the way lazily. Almost an everyday occurrence in the pub, women tearing themselves apart over men. Easy was on his feet in a second, tearing across the pub to pull his lover away.

"Whore! Slag! Bitch! You fuckin' keep your eyes off my man!" Chris was screaming. Easy had to get her away. He didn't want this getting back to Miss Small. He dragged her out, screaming and spitting, ignoring the jeers and whistles. Once outside he shook her violently. She calmed instantly. Easy was so furious he could barely talk. Opening the door of Miss Small's BMW, he shoved Chris inside.

On the way back to Chris's apartment, the car was silent.

"GIVE DADDY A goodnight kiss, Ky." Giggling, Kyesha gave Zukie a kiss and then ran away laughing.

It isn't every day that you get told that you have fathered a child. But for Zukie it was the most wonderful shock he had received during the last few years. If anything joyful had come out of this senseless tragedy, it was the knowledge that he was a father to this beautiful little girl before him. She was running about and laughing, dressed in the little pink silk pyjamas Zukie had bought her. She thought it was a game, refusing to go to bed. Pretending to be fed up, sucking through her teeth, Paradise scooped the little girl up and carried her screaming up the stairs. Zukie laughed.

As they disappeared up the wooden spiral staircase Zukie focussed his attention on the TV. Paradise's home was comfortable. Her furniture was top quality. She had framed photographs of Kyesha everywhere. Zukie took another drink of his Red Stripe beer. The TV was showing a wildlife documentary on birds of prey. Eagles. Finding the remote control quickly, Zukie switched it off. He realised he was sweating. Running a shaking hand over his sandy brown dreadlocks, he sighed. Those damn nightmares! He took another drink. It was then he saw it, just under the coffee table. A large photo album.

Leaning forward off the large sofa, he retrieved it. Flipped the pages. Photographs of himself and Paradise, images that contained no memory or stirred any emotion. Paradise alone with a swelling stomach. Paradise holding a newborn baby. Zukie turned the pages, totally unprepared for the images he saw next.

There he was, strapped to machines and wires in a hospital. Beside him was Paradise holding his hand, smiling bravely. Zukie cast his eyes over similar photographs until eventually he was without machinery, sitting up, looking serious. He saw photographs of himself with Clifton, the Old Lady and his other brother Bluebwai. After a few photographs, he was holding baby Kyesha. So, Storm was right. In another photograph Zukie was standing up holding on to a set of bars; underneath someone had written the date and, "Zukie walking!" *Zukie walking*. Zukie could barely find the strength to continue with the cataloguing of the missing period in his life but he knew he had to.

How could he remember his father's funeral? How could he remember his half-brother Bluebwai? How could he remember being a roots man but not remember being in love or recovering from the accident, or even having the accident? Zukie found looking at the album too painful. He felt resentful. He wanted to remember things the way they were.

Footsteps on the wooden staircase alerted him to the present. Fighting back the tears and hurt burning inside, Zukie slammed the album shut. Suddenly Paradise was in the living room taking up toys and generally tidying the area, oblivious to his suffering. She was wearing a short mini-skirt, a tight red t-shirt with no bra, and her dreads were tied up in a high ponytail. She was beautiful.

"I had to sing to her to get her to sleep."

"Sing to me," Zukie said softly.

Paradise stopped and stared at Zukie. He saw her oriental shaped eyes travel over to the photo album resting on the sofa next to him. "What do you want me to sing?" she offered quietly.

Zukie felt his chest heave.

"I remember — I think — you were singing." He wasn't sure if this was a reality, a dream, or merely his imagination.

Paradise smiled and frowned at the same time.

"I was singing a gospel tune." He smiled. His memory was slowly reforming like a patchwork quilt.

"Sing it now for me." He said.

She began to sing. It came to him in a rush as he closed his eyes. Zukie found himself seeing the images in his mind like a montage. Her parents, Pastor Browne and Mona, were out. She invited him in. They were bunning weed and drinking. They had sex and he stayed the night. The next morning he awoke to the wrath of Pastor Brown roughing him up. Then he saw nothing. He felt nothing. Just a deep, painful ache in his soul. When he opened his eyes, he saw Paradise walking towards him on the sofa. She held out her hand to him.

Trembling, he took it. Her touch was gentle soft and warm. She gave a tug and pulled him up to his feet.

"Stay. Stay with me Zukie."

CHRISTINE WAS VEXED. Well and truly. In the short time that he had gotten to know her, Easy had never seen her this way before. She was in a dreadful state, throwing things, screaming and hitting him. Moreover, his ego was at stake at here. Teeko was in the bedroom directly next to theirs and Teeko could hear everything. So could the whole neighbourhood. What would Teeko think of him, unable to keep his woman under manners?

"What the hell's wrong with you? Why yuh ah dark pon me so?" Easy hissed. She aimed an open-handed slap at his face and missed. He grabbed her by both wrists, holding onto her firmly. She was breathless and ragged, her hair in her face, make-up ruined.

"I gave you money Easy. I gave you firepower and ammo. I set you up. I saw you eyeing those bitches in the pub tonight!"

"You're just stressin' yuself up over nuttin'," Easy muttered.

Chris continued relentlessly. "I don't see you for days sometimes.

You've got another woman haven't you?"

She'd been drinking and smoking weed for the rest of the night, stewing and brewing, while Teeko and Easy had been surveying Shanieka's house in preparation for early tomorrow morning. Easy's head was spinning. He was hungry and tired and she was getting off on one.

Broken ornaments, and pictures in the bedroom, which contained Tyrone's cot, surrounded them. The baby, thankfully, was at her mother's. Easy let Chris go. She seemed to crumble forwards, holding her stomach as if in pain.

"I love you," she bawled repeatedly, "I love you." She now knew the meaning of Easy-Love's alias. Women fell for him quickly. Schoolmates had crowned him Easy-Love. He was easy to love and in his earlier yout', he had many women on the go but had soon given them up for Cassie.

Suddenly, catching him off guard, Chris punched him. Easy staggered backwards, tripping and falling on to the bed. She sprang on him like a tiger, raining blows to his face. They started to fight, rolling on the bed, wrestling, each trying to force the other to submit. Soon Easy's strength was no match for Chris's inebriated state. He gained control, sitting astride her. She was snarling and biting, thrashing her head from side to side like a savage. He felt her kicking beneath him.

"Get off me you bastard. I hate you. I hate you."

Easy smiled, manipulating her legs apart.

"No you don't."

"I hate you."

"And I love you."

"No you don't," she screamed.

"I want you to have my daughter, Christine. I don't want no other woman to have my little girl. Just you. Cos I love you."

"Bastard!" Chris screamed, writhing wildly beneath him like a maniac. "Liar!" Easy's shirt was open. He felt himself harden. He tore at Chris' blouse, exposing a pair of round breasts with their nipples cocked. Still holding her down, Easy bent forward and started to kiss her. She was moaning eagerly. Her writhing changed to a deeper more meaningful kind of frenzy. Chris began to call his name repeatedly.

"I love you. Nobody else. Believe." he muttered. She struggled to release her hands, grabbing his dreads until she heard him gasp in pain.

"Just remember that Easy, no one else." With that, they began to twist and gyrate, both fighting for sexual dominance, staring intently into the other's eyes, shedding each other's clothes. With a violent thrust, Easy was inside her. Chris screamed with pain and pleasure as Easy forced her legs further apart and pushed himself further and further inside. The bed was banging like an elephant stampeding against the wall. Easy was sweating, he held off climaxing. Chris screamed his name, begging, crying, coaxing. He was making her know that he was the one running tings.

That's right baby, nobody else.

KURTIS CLIMBED INTO the tattooist's booth in the back streets of Manchester's Piccadilly. Nearby was Piccadilly train station, and not far away was the newly rebuilt Arndale Shopping Centre, shattered after the IRA bomb of '97, now a re-modernised structure standing erect and proud in the face of bloody terrorism.

The tattooist, a tall, lanky greying Scotsman in his late thirties, sniffed as he showed Kurtis a book of 'exclusive' designs. Kurtis saw what he wanted quickly.

Kurtis chose the eagle. He smiled. It was huge, its wings wide, ready to swoop. It was exactly what he wanted. Identical to Danny's.

"WHERE YOU BEEN man? I've been worried about you. Where's your mobile? Is it switched off?" Zukie said hi to Tariq sitting quietly in a corner. In his ecstatic mood, Zukie failed to see the sombre look on Tariq's dark face. He passed Storm at the counter, eating an apple.

"You know where I've been," Zukie answered. "Where's Taniesha?" Looking at the computer monitor, Zukie studied the studio bookings nonchalantly, ignoring his brother's anxiety.

"I dunno. She didn't come in for her shift this morning. Didn't phone in either. Zukie, I need to talk to you." Glancing at the clock, Zukie saw that it was three in the afternoon. He hadn't meant to stay the night or most or the following day either. But he had enjoyed every moment with Paradise and Kyesha so much. He had a joyous feeling clinging to his soul that life from now on for Zukie Michaels, could only get better. He was falling in love with Paradise all over again. The thought of her flesh on his, alone, made him tingle. With her and his daughter, nothing else mattered. He could put what he remembered of the past behind him and look forward to the future.

"I know," Zukie began, scrolling down the list of names on the computer for studio bookings. "I treated her bad didn't I? I'm gonna level with her soon about me and Paradise. I'm back with Paradise, Cliff, ain't you gonna say something?"

Zukie suddenly noticed a strange silence in the shop. He felt Storm staring at him. He looked up at his brother. He noticed Storm's eyes filling up.

"Cliff? Cliff what's wrong?" Storm sighed, dropping his eyes, looked into the far corner of the shop then back at Zukie. Zukie noticed that Storm looked aged. A feeling of sheer trepidation crawled into Zukie from the feet upwards, seizing his body motionless, and resting under the base of his skull, throbbing there excruciatingly. "Cliff, you're scaring the shit out of me. What is it?"

"I got some bad news last night, bro."

"Is it the Old Lady?"

"No. No. Mum's fine."

"What? Shit, what is it?" Storm remained quiet, swallowing, shaking his head gently. He dropped his eyes, not knowing how he was going to tell Zukie.

STUKKY, HAIR IN trademark thin cane-rows, like tram lines on the top of his head, peered around Shanieka Jennings's front door, a cigarette dangling from the corner of his chapped lips. Moments before, someone had pressed the doorbell. Stroking his goatee beard and moustache, he frowned at the spectacled cropped-hair brunette woman standing on the doorstep. Dressed in a loose-fitting grey trouser suit, she stood holding a sturdy brown leather briefcase. Stukky didn't like the look of her. She looked too official. Official meant problems.

"Yeah?"

"Mr. Gardiner?" She sounded Irish.

"Who?"

"Are you Remi and Ramone Gardiner's father?" Stukky frowned, thinking, now what the fuck does this bitch want now?

The woman flashed an I.D. badge in his face then whipped it away quickly before he could study it.

"I'm the school welfare officer. I've come to find out why the boys haven't been at school."

Stukky had to think quickly. "They're on holiday. Canada. With their mum."

He wasn't the only one thinking quickly.

"Oh?" The young woman peered down the glasses, looking past the slightly open door. "Well, I need to fill in some papers about that."

She started to push her way inside.

"Oi, bitch, you can't juss push your way into—" He didn't finish his sentence. His mouth encountered the sole of Chris's shoe. Followed quickly with two swift turn-kicks to the jaw. Disturbed by the noise and commotion, Sizzla flew down the stairs brandishing a semi-auto that Chris knew could take her life out in an instant. She froze immediately, watching as Sizzla smiled, eyes roving all over her body, levelling the gun at her head, between the blue eyes that watched him steadily.

"WHO THE RAAS are you?" Sizzla asked sarcastically, "Jean-Claude Van Damme's bitch sister?" Chris didn't reply to the cynicism. She lowered her gaze onto the unwavering gun for a second before eye conditioning her opponent. Stukky was moaning on the tiled hall floor, slowly coming to. Right then, aroused by the sound of crashing Sizzla swung around to the direction of the back living room. In the next instant, Chris jump-kicked him, sending him flying. The gun fired a round of shots upwards as Sizzla squeezed the trigger reflexively. Hearing screams from above, Chris leapt up the stairs. Easy soon entered the house, quickly followed by Teeko who came in through the front. Easy was swift to level his handgun at Sizzla. Teeko took out all his rage and frustration on Stukky, kicking him repeatedly, aiming vicious blows at the yout's head.

"No Tee." Easy shouted. "Let him live to pass on their failure." Breathing heavily, Teeko backed off. He was met at the bottom of the stairs by Shanieka who was weeping. Close behind her, Chris was carrying one of the boys. The other followed sleepily. Easy took the loaded semi from the unconscious Sizzla. Blood was pouring from a head wound. Easy admired the gun and placed it under his arm.

"Let's get outta here before the police get here." Chris said.

Easy smiled at her.

She had done a wicked job.

ZUKIE'S CLEAR GREY eyes searched his brother's face desperately. Storm hung his head.

"Come on Cliff. Tell me what's going on."

"It's Carl. He, he died yesterday."

"Hair Oil? Dead? What? How? How come?" Zukie sat down slowly on the stool near the counter. Mouth dry like a desert. Eyes ached. Heart felt like it was amplified through his ears. Dizzy.

"Angela phoned last night. He developed an infection."

Feeling the shop dip and swirl, like he was on a boat in a stormy sea, Zukie lunged towards the studio in the back, hearing Storm call after him. He couldn't answer. There was this big hole in his throat that had sucked out his words like a vacuum cleaner. He staggered into the studio and switched on the equipment, quickly finding the track with Paradise's voice on it. Her voice poured powerfully through the huge speakers into the soundproofed room. Five minutes later, he was aware of Storm in the studio, leaning in the doorway.

"Can I come in?" Zukie didn't reply. "What are you doing?"

"One of the tracks lacked something."

"What?"

"I in't sure 'til I hear it."

"The funeral's the day after tomorrow. I told Angela we'd be going."

"I'll be busy." Zukie said.

The astonishment was evident in Storm's voice.

"Doing what?"

"Remixing Paradise's album."

"There's nothing wrong with the mix. And you know it," Storm said gently. Zukie could feel Storm near him, breathing, too close. "He's getting buried next to Chico. Angela and the other sisters are gonna expect us, especially you, to be there paying your last respects." Zukie rose out of his seat. He paused to look at Storm.

"Why the hell can't you juss keep outta my business? I don't want you in my business, ya hear me? Get out my face. And here. Tek this." Pulling out Storm's hand, he placed his mobile phone into his brother's outstretched palm. "You can stop taggin' me now." He looked at Storm coldly before walking out of the shop, leaving his brother perplexed.

ZUKIE SAT WITH the curtains drawn in his bedroom, shutting out the daylight, as if he could shut out the live nightmare in his life. He held his head in hands. Music played, coming out of the stereo in the corner. Zukie began to rock backwards and forwards. He wanted Chico and Hair Oil back. He wanted to rewind to the weeks and months before the accident.

You just don't lose your life like that.

Somebody had to know why this happened.

Somebody was to blame.

And that person had to be Danny Ranks.

Like his brother said.

DANNY RANKS JUST missed potting the black, the news had completely put him off his stroke. Or maybe it was the sight of the Smith and Wesson .38 Special lying on the pool table, next to the pocket, its dark, polished handle gleaming under the light above like a star. Everyone surrounding Ranks was pretending not to notice. But it wasn't like Ranks. Ranks never lost at pool. And he wasn't about to lose now. The pool and snooker club belonged to the crew along with the pub that was run alongside it. Stukky stood shakily, still caked in blood, awaiting directions from Danny. He stuttered when he was nervous, the words getting stuck on his tongue, hence the name Stukky.

"Wha-wha-what do you want me to do?"

"I want you to shoot yourself in the foot," Ranks said.

"Wh-wha-what?"

"You know that expression shoot yourself in the foot, nigga, that's what I want you to do — literally. You mek some scrawny little gyal come in dere and kick yu up like Jackie Chan's bitch. Yu let dem tek Shanieka from under your nose. Yu don't deserve to be in my crew."

"But the g-g-gyal was good."

Ranks stopped playing immediately, leaning on the cue stick. Nerome drew close.

"So was you, Stukky. Now I don't believe you let some pussy just walk in and take Shanieka."

"No, Danny, believe I — Teeko was there. He's in wid Easy."

"Don't tell me what I know already fool. Cos no pussy could get ever, ever anyt'ing over any of my man, seen?"

"Juss let me explain."

"Take the gun Stukky and shoot yourself in the foot."

"No— please."

"Fucking do it or I'll do it for you." Ranks screamed.

Tearfully Stukky looked at the pool table. Ranks took a cigarette out and put it to his lips. Nero gave him a light. Stukky grabbed up the gun.

He levelled it at his foot.

Then he squeezed the trigger.

His scream reverberated around the large poolroom.

Thankfully, he soon passed out.

BOARDED UP WINDOW. Smoke stained. Teeko Martial began to chip away at the back downstairs window of his burned out home. Eventually he managed to get in, working his way around to the front room. Mentally, he wasn't prepared for this amount of devastation. Every room was either destroyed or gutted by fire. He'd left a stunned and weakened Shanieka with Chris, but the place was getting over-crowded. What Shanieka needed was money to move to London with the boys.

Teeko stepped over debris in the front room. The floorboards were still intact although blackened. Teeko loosened the floorboard near the window. It opened. Reaching down, he felt blindly for the bundles of money. It was wet down there, probably from the fire crew's water hoses. Teeko was fishing, hoping and praying it was still there. It was. Teeko's outstretched fingers met three wet bundles of hundreds. He retrieved the money, dusting ash off his Levi's.

Now he could do what he had to do and not worry. He'd give Easy the money Easy needed. He and Easy would take on Ranks with the help of Miss Small. Nothing or no one could stop them now.

"COME TRENCH SIDDOWN."

Trench purposely stood apart from the others seated around the table, outside on the huge balcony, leaning against the wall, folding his arms. The day was hot. Beautiful. Bright. Far into the distance the water of Salford Quays sparkled, and a cool breeze blew off it.

"Naw thanks Vee. I prefer to stand. Yuh have a good holiday?"

The Dodge Crew — Easy, Miss Small, Hatchet and his younger brother Michigan, Slide, Trench, and Ranger — convened at Small's apartment for a meeting after her return from Jamaica. Despite the barbecue and beer for later, there was a strained atmosphere. Easy thought it had a lot to do with the fact that Miss Small had asked him to pick her up from the airport instead of Trench. On the way from the airport Easy told her everything about Teeko and the deal Kadeem had with Ranks. He explained his cut lip. It got cut rescuing Teeko's woman from the house. It was a lie, but he obviously could not tell her he'd been fighting with his other woman.

"Yes baby. Coco-B senn him love and the All Bright Crew downa Jungle. Maxi seh fe senn him tings. Him Reebok trainer and Manchester United football shirt whey yu seh yu gwine get him last year."

Trench laughed. Easy felt ill at ease with the familiar exchange going on between the two founder members of the Dodge Crew, reminding him that he was an outsider who thought he was well and truly in.

"Yeah man, me nuh forget him. Respect fe dat."

"I made a few decisions while I been away. Some adjustments to the crew." Easy held his breath, hoping she hadn't had second thoughts about him.

"Like gettin' rid of Mr Easy, lemon squeezy." Trench sneered.

She continued, ignoring him, taking out a piece of paper, flapping in the breeze out on the balcony. Placing a pair of reading glasses on her face, she began to read from her list. "Michigan and Ranger are still in Sales and Debt Recovery. Hatchet and Slide are Security. Trench, I want you to be the crew's main Security Consultant and Easy I waan you to be Co-director with myself as Company Director until I decide to evaluate certain positions in de near future."

There was a ripple of discontentment. Easy sighed inwardly with relief. Trench stared at him coldly.

"Co-director? Why now?"

"Easy seh he has a plan-to set us on top."

Trench kissed through his teeth.

"What plan?" he asked contemptuously, his coal black eyes boring viciously into Easy's spine.

"Listen up. He'll tell you." Miss Small squinted in the sun.

Easy told them about the plan to hi-jack's Rank's money while Miss Small scattered some coke offering some to her boys.

"No way," Trench said. "You can't rob a next man of his pay. War will break out."

"Are you prepared for battle Trench?"

"Ranks is gonna be more than prepared especially after what went down today at Teeko's woman's house. Can't you see he's settin' you up, Veniesha? And where's his fuckin' initiation sub?"

Miss Small jumped to her feet quickly.

"I have it right here." Taking the bundle of money out of her pocket Miss Small threw it down on the table. Easy smiled at Trench gloatingly. "Look Trench, yu either with us or you're with dem. Mek yu choice."

"Ohhh I'm in all right," Trench declared boldly. 'I'll be in until the day I die, baby."

"Well I want you to shake Easy's hand and forget dis shit yu got goin' on with him."

Trench stared disbelievingly at Veniesha. He saw that she was serious. Easy stood up and outstretched his palm. Swallowing Trench walked over and took it. Easy wrapped his palm around Trench's.

Trench held on solidly.

"And another thing. Nobody must touch Danny, y'hear? Nobody nuh shoot him. Not yet. Me want him to live to see everything around him mash up," Miss Small said.

"So when are we going to do this ting?" Trench asked.

"Tomorrow night." Trench looked surprised that it was so soon. "Tomorrow is when it's going down. Are you still in this till the day you die?"

Trench smiled.

ZUKIE SWEATED, WAITING impatiently, sucking on his cigarette like his life depended on its smoky breath. He was in Old Trafford outside the two pool houses he'd heard Ranks and his bad boys frequented. Zukie had been waiting for an hour, waiting for Ranks to show his gutless face. Huddled in the doorway of the funeral directors next door. Since hearing about Hair Oil's death, he hadn't been able to think about anything else. He shivered, but he was not cold because the weather was humid. It was gone ten in the evening and turning dark after a long hot summer's day. The streets surrounding Ayres road were silent and empty. Only a dog, nearby, barked angrily.

Zukie lit another cigarette, shakily. Bright vibrant laughter stabbed his senses. He dashed the cigarette to the kerb. Someone was laughing exaggeratedly. Peering around, Zukie saw Ranks exiting the pool house, talking into a mobile phone, swinging a beer bottle held by a handkerchief. *Déjà vu.*

Zukie's heart flipped painfully. Ranks was either intoxicated or blipped. He was talking into a mobile phone, fast, loud, in great spirits. Zukie waited for Ranks and his companion to cross over the road to the large BMW parked on the other side, next to the row of self-contained apartments. It faced the opposite direction. Tall and athletic with brooding features, Nero, his bodyguard, climbed into the driver's side.

Zukie sprang, like a rat, out of the inkiness of the doorway and into the bright streetlight towards the BMW. Ranks' bloodshot eyes met Zukie's almost immediately.

"Nero, look yah now, its Goldilocks, where's the three bears?" Ranks joked, putting his mobile away. Nero slowly started to get out of the car. "Cool yo Nero. It's only Storm's wimpy little bro." Ranks was exuberant. From the inside of his hooded Pod jacket, Zukie pulled out the Browning hi-power Storm had given him. He levelled it, hands swaying, at Ranks. The triumphant smile evaporated like steam into the atmosphere.

"Hey! What ya think ya doing star?" Danny asked coolly.

"Killing you for killing Hair Oil and Chico."

Zukie stood wide, aiming the gun at Ranks shakily.

"Hair Oil's finally dead is he? Dat don't have nuttin to do wid me, star," Ranks shrugged his shoulders indifferently. "Nigga gone to gangsta heaven to join his G-boys." Hot rage started to bubble like paprika soup inside Zukie. All day long, he'd been smoking and drinking, thinking about how he was going to blow Danny's head off. Now the time had come. A terrible, incommunicable fear was seeping into his blood weakening his resolve. Quakingly, Zukie's finger hovered over the trigger. Zukie could feel Nerome stealthily rising out of the car on the other side.

"Get back into the car or I'll waste him right here and now." Zukie said.

Danny became contemptuous. Screwing his eyes shut he began to shout and gesticulate wildly.

"Waste me? You couldn't waste a hamburger on a barbecue. Look at you. Yu hands are shaking like yu got some brain disease."

"Shut up," Zukie screamed, eyes wide. "Or I'll fuckin' duss you like yu did Chico."

"Star, tell me how I did dat? I was thirteen years old. I had no reason to brown off Chico and Hair Oil." Ranks stared at Zukie. Zukie saw a slight hint of fear.

"Dread, put the gun down. It ain't you."

Zukie was trembling uncontrollably, but his voice was unnaturally steady.

"Get out the car," he ordered.

Danny sighed heartily, looking disdainfully at Zukie.

"Move!"

Zukie never saw Ranks coming. Ranks swivelled his compact body around quickly, kicking both feet towards the half open car door. The door flew open, sending Zukie spiralling backwards, against the side of a passing car. Zukie pressed the trigger and the bullet ripped from the gun into the air. There was a crunching thud. Nero got out of the car. The other car braked hard, a few yards up the road.

Ranks and Nero stared at Zukie lying still, sprawled in the road.

"HE'S LATE." SIZZLA said. "He in't usually this late."

Mr Mentian, wearing a blue Nike baseball cap lowered over his malt-brown face, checked his watch in the darkness of the car and looked at Sizzla next to him. The music in the car was low. Sizzla was nodding his head and tapping his finger to the beat. Although it had been raining it was warm and sticky. The night was just getting dark. No one was thinking about Stukky.

The car's interior was filled with ganga smoke. A few people walked past paying no attention to the three young men who, despite the clammy heat, were dressed in parkas and bubble jackets. Fila was seated in the back seat, the illumination from a streetlamp lighting up his white face .

"My belly's starvin', man," Fila said. Mentian looked into Fila's large blue eyes.

"Yu can get all the patty and dumplin' yu want when we collect."

Fila grinned. He slouched against the leather seat, staring vacantly through the window. They were parked on a very public road in Longsight, armed and dangerous. The car they were in belonged to Mentian's sister. Mentian felt strange and couldn't understand why. Maybe it was because Stukky had messed up and the burden was on him tonight to carry things through professionally and expertly. Ranks couldn't and wouldn't tolerate anything screwing up. A lot of money was at stake here. Mentian tried to shake the negative feeling. Fila sniffed.

Mentian turned around. It was then that he saw it. Kadeem's new Black and Silver Mitsubishi Shogun slowly coming towards them on the opposite side of Hathersage Road. The four-wheel drive's headlights flashed twice briefly.

Mentian started the car's engine.

"He's here." Fila sat up alertly, swallowing. "Let's go."

WORRIED. SMOKING HIS fourth spliff, Storm stared out onto the cul-de-sac in the upmarket East Didsbury area, where he lived with his brother in a four bedroom semi-detached house worth about 250K. It was late. For the last five hours, he hadn't seen nor heard from Zukie. Phoning Zukie's mobile was fruitless. The phone was still in Storm's leather jacket pocket. Storm had phoned Paradise but she said she hadn't seen him, though she could have been lying.

It had stopped raining and the night was warm. Storm's black funeral suit hung on the wardrobe door. If every truth were known, Storm would rather not attend. But having avoided Chico's funeral, Storm felt he had a duty to represent the Michaels' family at Hair

Oil's. If he didn't see Zukie by tomorrow, he'd leave a note in the hall by the phone asking Zukie to meet him at the church.

NERO LEANT OVER Zukie cautiously. His heart quickening, he was expecting the worst. Zukie was moaning gently. The driver of the other car ran towards them. Other members of the Worlders crew exited the pool house and rushed over. The driver was staring at the gun beside Zukie on the wet road. Pipes picked it up, examining it curiously before placing it in the waistband at the small of his back.

Looking up at the crew of boys staring at him menacingly, the middle-aged driver quickly retreated, got into his car, and screeched away. Nero pulled Zukie upright gently, using his own body as support. Zukie's breath was punctuated with gasps of pain. A massive bruised lump rose from his forehead. Zukie's left arm hung limply, Nero knew it was busted. Pulling Zukie further upright Nero said encouragingly.

"Get up, star."

Zukie attempted to move but the effort was obviously too much for him. He grunted sharply with pain.

"Leave him," Danny ordered indignantly.

Nero placed his arm under Zukie's knees, under his back and picked him up, walking sturdily towards the car. He could feel Zukie shaking violently, probably from shock. Ranks ran in front of Nero, stopping him in his tracks. He screamed at Zukie.

"Rudebwai want to come shoot me now? Think yu ah bad man? See what yu get when you mess with Ranks. Lucky yu neveh dead tonight. Lucky yu neveh go join yu dead spar dem, Mr dead Chico and Mr dead Hair Oil." Nero walked around Danny. "He in't going in my car Nero. Where the fuck are you takin' him?"

Danny howled with laughter.

"Fool!" He screamed into the night air, laughing. "Fool tried to kill me! Me! No one can kill Ranks. I'm the man ya see. I'm the Don. No one can test yah! No fuckin' bwai." Nero kept on walking with Zukie, knowing that Ranks was following him and despite his anger, he would get into the car.

SITTING IN THE black VW Golf VR6 outside the old baths on Hathersage Road, Trench, Easy, Hatchet and Slide waited silently, patiently. Easy held the driver's wheel, a pump-action shotgun resting over his lap. His mobile phone rang. Teeko's number flashed up on the small LCD screen. Easy answered.

"They're going in."

"I see them." Easy acknowledged coolly.

"We steppin' in?"

"I in't got no quarrel with Kadeem and I don't like the look of his men. We wait."

KADEEM HUSSEIN WAS Moroccan. He had Dusky skin and dancing dark eyes. His expression was never serious. Life for him was a ball. He was rich but his money was mainly tied up in investments and property so he required additional income. His family had been smuggling cocaine and heroin for years. He was a rotund man with a double chin, and he never went anywhere without his four minders.

The dilapidated baths were a perfect meeting place for criminals. Rats were their only observers. Mildew. The faint smell of chlorine. Kadeem grinned, looking at the three yout's. He liked Danny's crew. They made their payments and they made them on time. He particularly liked Danny. Very astute, meticulous and extremely ambitious. The boy was destined for big things.

"How is Danny?" Kadeem asked, handing over the brown bag containing the pay off to the dark, handsome but mistrustful Mr Mentian. It was hard to know what Mentian was thinking. He was as cool as ice with good looks and good bone structure. He had a fit, lean, tall body. His features were dark and moody and his eyes darted about like a lizard.

"Fine." Mentian looked up under his baseball cap and smiled slowly. Kadeem knew each one of them was armed.

"Here's a little extra for Danny. By way of thanks for good business." Kadeem threw a brown parcel over. Mentian caught it expertly. He handed it straight over to Fila who put it under his jacket. Kadeem noticed how Sizzla was studying his huge minders.

"Tell Danny I'll be in touch." Kadeem turned and left. The boys always allowed him to exit before them. They usually followed a few minutes later.

EASY WATCHED KADEEM'S Shogun tearing from back of the derelict swimming baths. He smiled. He didn't care what Miss Small said about not touching Danny. He was gonna out his light tonight.

"Come. Mek we go deal wid dis ting yah."

Snapping the pump-action, he got out of the car, climbed into the passenger seat and gave the steering wheel to Trench. Trench turned the key in the ignition. The car roared to life. Trench slammed his foot on the accelerator pedal and tore towards the unlit rear of the old swimming baths.

THE TWO CARS came squealing from nowhere, totally blocking their exit. Fila was the first to leap from the car. Instinct. Teeko leapt from his car in hot pursuit.

Mentian pulled his gun from his inside pocket, stuffing the money from Kadeem under the seat. A shot cut through the windscreen showering glass fragments over him and onto the front seats of the car. Mentian lay low, panting heavily and cursing as a volley of shots was fired in quick succession over his head.

SIZZLA WAS ALREADY out of the car, using the passenger door as a shield amd firing into bright headlights. Bullets hit the car door, passing through, pock, pock, pock! Sizzla aimed and fired. He only had a handgun and by the sounds of it he was being shot at by a high-powered automatic, possibly an Uzi. The door was being shot to pieces. Sizzla heard the lyrics of a certain reggae song in his head as he rolled across the hard ground, still firing shots. The world turned helter-skelter as he twisted his body and ran towards the wall opposite.

"Jah-Jah city Jah-Jah town dem a turn it inna cowboy town yah.
Bloody city bloody city them ah tun it inna rudebwai town."

RUNNING. TEEKO POUNDED his powerful body in a sprint after Fila running towards the housing estate on the other side of Plymouth Grove in Longsight. Teeko knew he had to get him before the estate swallowed him up. He was yards behind the short blonde-haired kid. With a roar, Teeko leapt into a flying tackle and brought Fila down. Fila struggled and swore beneath him. Teeko took out his gun and levelled it at Fila's head. The sight of the gun stilled Fila instantly. Teeko released the safety catch.

Teeko was mad. They had burned him out of his home, threatened his woman and kids. Somebody deserved a bullet. Fila looked at him, panting heavily.

But not Fila.

Teeko stared back at his former friend. Fila's blue eyes were emotionless. They stared back at Teeko emptily. Teeko got up off Fila, slowly, holding his gun on him. Fila rose to his feet slowly, staring, saying nothing. He turned and ran, not looking back once. Closing his eyes, dusting himself Teeko swallowed and cursed.

Teeko was going to tell Easy he had lost him.

It was as simple as that. Fila got away.

SIZZLA GOT HALFWAY across the yard. A bullet caught him in the shoulder. Felt like fire. He went down screaming. The shots stopped. Sizzla groaned

MENTIAN URGED SIZZLA to stay down. He heard the sound of a car engine running. Heard the sound of slow footsteps walking towards the car. Mentian cocked the hammer on his gun. The gun felt slippery. He rose quickly. Another gun was already in his cheek, pressed firmly against his teeth.

"Give it up, Mentian. Don't be a dead fool." Mentian swallowed deeply. "Y'hear whah me seh?" Mentian nodded slowly. "Where's Ranks?"

"He didn't come with us."

"Too bad. I had a bullet waiting in my gun for him. Guess he must be wiser than I t'ink." Mentian grunted. "I want all of it. All the money. Now." Reaching down beneath the seat, Mentian retrieved the bag and handed it though the open window. Mentian heard a laugh.

"Sizzla's gonna tell Ranks that Easy will be seeing him real soon. In the meantime, Mr Mentian, you *are* the weakest link... goodbye." Mentian closed his eyes tightly and waited for the bullet to tear into him.

He waited.

Waited until he realised he was alone and the wind was cold on his face.

NERO DECIDED HE couldn't leave Zukie, Danny's would-be-assassinator, alone and confused in Casualty. He wasn't quite sure why; after all Zukie had tried to out Danny. Leaving Danny drunkenly asleep in the BMW in the car park, Nero stayed while they treated Zukie's fractured left arm, and observed him; he had suffered a concussion. Ranks soon woke up and wandering into casualty semi-drunk searching for Nero. He created a scene. Security requested the police. Nero decided to leave, taking Zukie with them. Danny had passed out in the back of the car. Zukie, drowsy due to painkillers and sedatives, was unable to tell Nero where he lived. He was unconscious in no time leaving Nero no alternative but to take him to Ranks' apartment. Nero half-carried Ranks in, then Zukie. With the help of Pipes, Nero undressed them both, putting Ranks in his room. He decided to place Zukie in Kurtis' room.

Kurtis' door was locked. Unusual. Retrieving the spare key from Ranks' room Nero unlocked it. Switching on the light he realised there was no light bulb in the light fitting. Nero got a table-lamp from the living room and plugged it in. Straightaway Nero saw a collection of photographs, all with Danny in them. Nero frowned. As he pulled back the duvet on Kurtis's bed he saw a large pile of women's clothes on the floor next to the bed. Nero wasn't aware of Kurtis bringing any women in. Perhaps he was sneaking them in after everybody had gone or when he was alone in the apartment. Nerome picked up the clothing, flimsy underwear, short nighties, lacy bras, and dresses. Looking closely Nero realised some of them still had their price tags on them.

Nero decided that Ranks would have to deal with this shit himself in the morning. He put Zukie in the bed. Shattered, he stretched out on the opposite end, closed his eyes and was soon deep asleep.

TRUST AND RESPECT. Trench had neither for Easy. The way Trench saw it Easy was like a carbon monoxide poison leak. Silent and deadly. Nobody was gonna know he was causing damage until it was too fuckin' late.

He watched as Easy shook the expensive bottle of champagne vigorously before opening it. It sprayed over Miss Small's apartment living room floor. Miss Small whooped and yelped like a teenage school kid. Slide ran over with the glasses just in time, and Easy poured the bubbling drink into them.

The money was in piles on the huge coffee table. They had counted out an incredible five hundred thousand pounds in used notes, much more than they had expected.

"See, Veniesha. Big tings ah gawaan. In time I'll have treble, quadruple this amount of greens." Trench stood back watching. Easy beckoned him over. "But I can't take all the credit. Trench did his bit along with Teeko." Trench forced a smile

"Veniesha, I was thinking of adding someone else to the crew. I hope you don't mind." Easy said.

Veniesha smiled.

"Who?"

"My kid brother Kurtis."

"Him on the level bout things?"

"Kurtis is sound and keen. He'll be no trouble I promise."

"Whey him deh? Bring him mek me see him, mek me check him out." Trench felt the sigh building up in his chest, threatening to hurl out into angry words. He watched as Easy got his mobile out and made a call. Sixty seconds later there was a knock on the door and Kurtis appeared. It was a set up, obviously Easy had planned this and had his kid brother waiting downstairs. He had taken a diversion earlier after the raid. He must have picked him up. As Kurtis walked in, a strong feeling of familiarity assailed Trench. The teen's features were familiar. He stood taller than Easy but was awkward and lanky. An uneasy feeling clung to Trench like sticky-tape. Trench knew he had seen Kurtis somewhere before, but couldn't place it.

"Yes. He will do. Three month probation. Him fuck up and him out, y'hear?"

Easy was joyous but it seemed to fade quickly as Kurtis suddenly announced that he had to go. Trench was thinking. What the hell was that all about?

TANKS. A HELMET. Boots. The convoy came to a sudden halt. Nerome heard yelling. Then he saw them. Iraqi soldiers holding white flags. Aston was way out to his right. Suddenly, there was some confusion. Shots. A trick. The Iraqis weren't surrendering at all. It was an attack. Nero saw an Iraqi soldier screaming something at him shouting something about Allah. He then turned and aimed his gun at Aston. Nero should have took the Iraqi out but he was rooted to the spot, gripped by an awesome fear. All he saw was Aston, his best friend, falling into the wet sand. And Nero heard banging and shouting all around him.

Nero woke up sweating and in a panic. The shouting and banging was for real, no longer pulling at the edges of his consciousness. He sat up quickly and assessed his surroundings, realising that he was not in the Gulf War. The Gulf War was over. He was in his late twenties living at a drug-dealer's house, protecting his ass.

Sighing, heart still racing, Nerome crawled over Zukie's legs. His head was buzzing. Walking into the living room, he found Ranks seated on the edge of his sofa, screaming at Mentian. "I expected that. I expected ya to take care of it not give him my fuckin' money. What is it me have here? A bunch of gyal?" Mr Mentian was standing over him, his face stern but sad.

"What? What is it? What's going on?"

Mentian looked at Nero.

"Easy jumped us. He gave them all the money." Ranks said.

"Where's Fila, Sizzla?" Nero was already putting on his jacket. He could see Ranks' left temple pulsing angrily. Ranks got up and threw his mobile phone across the room. It hit the wall and smashed. Nerome didn't think it was a good time to tell him Zukie was sleeping in Kurtis's room.

He sat down again and lit a pre-rolled spliff, rubbing his head. Agitated. Sober.

"Wesley?" Nero called Mr Mentian by his proper name. Mentian lifted his head slowly. Nero saw the bloody nose. "Where are the others?" Mentian shrugged his shoulders. "Sizzla's probably at the hospital. I called an ambulance and fucked off outta there. I don't know what happen to Fila."

Nero's mobile rang. He answered. Fila came onto the line.

"Look like yu gonna live long star." Ranks' eyes widened. Mentian looked concerned.

"Tell Ranks," Fila began. "I still got some stuff and tell him seh I'm here, coming up the lift." Sighing, Nero slammed the phone shut, conveying the good news. Mentian looked put out. Fila was the hero of the day but he would live with that. He gave as good as he could.

STORM MICHAELS STOOD alone in a corner by the closed bar, silently observing Hair Oil's mother Amelia. She looked forlorn as she sat at the family table staring emptily into the corner. Carl Jones was her only son. Her companion Dotty, who was Chico's mother, was holding her hand to comfort her. Storm remembered them both from childhood church days. Hair Oil's father, Brother Jones, sat on the other side, a solemn look inscribed upon his leathery brown face. The funeral reception was being held at Carmoor Road West Indian Centre in the heart of Longsight. It was a good turn out, friends from school and church attended. Hair Oil, dead, four and a half years after the shooting. Brushing down his Armani suit, Storm nervously approached the family to pay his condolences.

"I'm so sorry," Storm offered sincerely. They had no idea Storm was behind the shooting.

"De Lord mek no mistake," Sister Anthony exclaimed. "He knew dat boy was suffering. He takes him to be with Him. God rest him soul." Sister Anthony patted her friend's back gently, before walking away. Angela, Hair Oil's eldest sister, joined them holding her two-year-old son Marcus.

"Hi Clifton. How is your Mum?"

"She's O.K. Lapping up the good Jamaica sunshine." Angela smiled, though her eyes were sad.

"Thanks for helping out with the funeral costs. The family appreciated it."

Storm cleared his throat, looking down at the glass of brandy he was holding in his hand.

"No problem. Carl was a decent kid. Zukie talks about him all the time."

Angela looked around. "Does he? Where is Zuchael?"

Storm sighed.

"He's ill," Storm lied. "Another relapse."

"Oh. I'm sorry."

"No, Angie. I'm the one that's sorry."

Angie frowned slightly then kissed him on the cheek.

"Thanks for coming. Say hello to Zukie for me."

Suddenly Storm felt that if he didn't leave the room he would suffocate. This feeling wasn't new; he had felt this turmoil and vulnerability before. It was as if there was a giant puppet master in the sky cutting the strings to his body.

Storm walked out of the West Indian Centre, glad to leave the sadness and burning guilt of Carl Jones' funeral reception behind. He crossed Carmoor Road towards his Mitsubishi Shogun jeep. Police had cordoned off half of the road. Some shooting last night. He pressed his alarm fob, deactivating the car alarm and releasing the central locking system. About to open the driver's door, he sensed a presence behind him. Glancing in the car door's window he saw three figures reflected in the glass.

Storm swung around quickly.

NEWLY PROMOTED DETECTIVE Inspector, Colin Edwards knew this place like the back of his hand. In his early thirties, tall, handsome, and athletically built, he knew the furrow-like corridors like a mole knows its tunnels. Visiting Manchester Royal infirmary was getting to be a habit. He'd been informed of last night's shooting at the old baths on Hathersage Road and he was here to interview a one Julian Thomas, street-name Sizzla. He found the private room off Ward 6 upstairs quickly. A uniformed officer was guarding the door.

The yout' was sitting up in bed watching a portable TV. His shoulder was heavily bandaged and although he might have been in a considerable amount of pain he, like others before, held it well.

"Hi." Colin held out his hand. "I'm DI Edwards."

Sizzla looked at him from head to toe and subtly kissed through his teeth. Ignoring him, Edwards pulled up a seat next to the yout's hospital bedside. A drip poured saline into Sizzla's arm.

"Two bullets from a fast-firing semi-auto, probably an Uzi, tearing straight through your muscle and ligaments. Must be pretty painful."

Sizzla turned up the volume on the TV with the remote.

"Any further to the left and you would be in the morgue freezer downstairs." Edwards continued, raising his voice above the noise of a fast car commercial.

"What do you want?" Sizzla asked contemptuously.

"Answers."

"Tried the internet? Or a fucking encyclopaedia?"

Edwards laughed lowly. He sniffed.

"You're lucky to be alive, Julian. Surely that counts for something? Surely that means something to your mother, your family and kids?"

Sizzla grunted.

"Names. I want names."

"Gonna want then, DI Coconut. I in't got no names to give you. It was dark. I saw nuttin. I was alone. Don't know why they chose me to practise target shootin'."

"You've got previous for possession and drugs, Julian."

"Yep and I don't do it no more. I'm clean. You got nuttin on me."

"Well, right now we have bullets found at the scene. All we have to do is match them with the gun you were firing and we're combing the area."

"I take it you in't found no gun then?"

"No because we suspect the person with you took it before he called the ambulance. I'm just trying to help you Julian, or do you prefer to be called Jules?"

"Julian," Sizzla snorted, leaning back on the pillow, looking as if he was in pain.

"Right, Julian. As I was saying, just trying to help you. I could offer protection." It was Sizzla's turn to laugh scornfully. He laughed until he coughed and the pain tore into him. "You're not helping yourself. Next time they might complete their mission and kill you."

Sizzla looked at Edwards frostily, his eyes bloodshot and livid. Edwards had seen that look before over and over again.

"Not before I get the bastards first." He had also heard these vengeful words before. Edwards rose to his feet. He had gained nothing from this interview; he had known he wouldn't. Five years back he had worked on the shooting of gang leader Fluxy and the war that followed. Easy-Love Brown had been implicated in the shooting, but Easy had escaped real justice. There was only one thing Edwards was sure of: things had been relatively quiet on the streets until Easy-Love's reappearance from prison six months ago. He knew before long there would be another gang war but if no one was prepared to give evidence or a proper statement, King Easy-Love was going to reign supreme.

SMILING, KURTIS JAMES walked casually into Ranks' apartment. Putting the front door key in his pocket, he was about to tell Ranks the good news. He'd been accepted into Small's gang. He could tag his stupid brother now. The apartment was quiet. No sounds. No TV or music. No computer games. No smell of cannabis. No one at home. The first place he checked was Danny's room. Danny's duvet was flung across the bed. The room was in semi-darkness. Kurtis sniffed. He threw himself on Ranks's large bed and smiled. Here he felt close to Danny. His best friend. He decided to snort a line of coke, celebrate his homecoming and initiative. One line became two. He pinched his nostrils and lay back waiting for the hit.

He suddenly noticed the envelope half-sticking from under the pillow. Kurtis felt no qualms picking it up and reading it.

Dear Daniel,
I am glad that you have agreed to meet me. Celia says that you want us to meet up at hers. She was thinking around five o clock, next Saturday, if that OK with you. If not we can meet sumwere else. I look foward to meeting with you and hope that we can establishe a good relayshunship if not as mother and son, the least we can be is very good friends.
Love Veniesha.

Suddenly a door somewhere slammed. Kurtis put the letter back under the pillow and hurried out of Ranks' room.

"GET IN." DANNY ordered gruffly, standing aside and sliding open the rear door of the large seven-seater vehicle. They were leaning against it, Nero, the white boy Fila, Mentian and Ranks. Ranks lit a cigarette. A crowd of mourners left the West Indian centre watching Storm and the group of yout's curiously as they made their way to their cars.

"Excuse me?" Storm asked.

"I said get in." Danny repeated angrily.

The wind picked up, swirling around Storm's feet. It was going to rain, hopefully breaking up the unbearable heat of the last two weeks.

"I in't goin' nowhere with you and your crew, Danny." Storm looked at them, surveying each of them carefully.

Ranks sniffed and inhaled his cigarette. He was under severe pressure what with Easy jackin' his money, his estranged mother wanting to see him sooner than he planned, and that fool Zukie trying to shoot him. He had one soldier in hospital, probably won't ever be able to lift his hand and fire again, and another soldier crippled because of his own stupidity. He wasn't in the mood to take no crap from Storm. He swaggered over to Storm.

"I believe I have something that belongs to you." Ranks spoke slowly, taking out something wrapped up in newspaper. Storm frowned as Ranks unravelled the newspaper, revealing a Browning Hi-Power gun.

"Are you stupid, showing me a gun in bright daylight and outside a funeral reception? Put it away."

Ranks thrust the weapon at him. "Star, it's yours. You put it away." Storm held his hand up backing away slightly.

"It's nothing to do with me."

"Right, right, right. My man Storm doesn't do guns or gangs no more. He doesn't try to kill people. That's why he's at the funeral of a man he helped to kill."

"That's history."

"Once a G boy, always a G boy." Storm was looking around self-consciously afraid that Hair Oil's relatives would hear the conversation. "Or have you passed on your gangster skills to Zukie?"

Storm found his forehead burrowing painfully. His throat felt dry. His heart flipped like a metal spring. Looking at the gun, he suddenly recognised it as the one he'd given to Zukie. He snatched it and put it into his suit pocket.

"Yeah, you thought if you messed with Zukie's head," Danny tapped the side of his forehead, "he'd mess me up din't ya?"

Storm lowered his voice leaning towards Danny's ear. "Everything was OK until you starting messing with me and mines."

"Last night he tried to boom me with the gun you're denying, outside Potter's, I was gettin' in my car with Nero and had to kick him out the way. Unfortunately for him, he landed against a car that was passing. You're fucking lucky Nerome decided to take him to hospital. The way I felt I woulda left that wanna-be Terminator in the fuckin' road." Storm closed his eyes as the realisation hit him. That's why Zukie hadn't come home.

"Where is he? Is he in hospital?"

"Step in the car and let's negotiate how you're gonna help me get Easy-Love off the streets-permanently."

"Where's my brother?"

"Our deal comes first."

Storm's desperation was mounting. It was evident in his voice.

"Where's my fucking brother you piece of shit?" Ranks stared at him with narrow hazel eyes, deliberately lengthening the agony for Storm. He spat aside on the pavement. Gritting his teeth, Storm suddenly lunged at Ranks, snatching the collar of his leather jacket he swung him around and pushed him up against the side of his jeep. The others were onto him quickly, trying to pull him off. Storm's temper and strength were intense.

Finally, Nero succeeded in pulling Storm off. Storm straightened himself but kept his eyes on Ranks steadily.

"Do you know how much I hate your stinkin' guts right now?" Storm asked slowly.

"I in't the one you should be hating. You should be hating Easy-Love cos he and Jigsy made sure your brother got in that car that night. They knew you would probably send some man after them — not me, they used your brother as insurance, not me star." Storm was breathing heavily, his eyes wide and staring. He forced himself to calm down.

"Just take me to Zukie."

"Not so star. I reckon you owe me. Are you gonna work with me? Tell me now."

A SCREEN, A pine chest of drawers, large framed photographs of fresh naked black girls. Fast cars on the walls. Half-conscious Zukie Michaels realised he was in a strange environment. The room smelled of perfume. His heart slammed furiously.

"What are you doing in my room? This is my room. It was locked. How did you get in here?" The dark shadow in the doorway was talking to him. Zukie felt hot. Tired. His throat hurt. Everywhere hurt.

He rose laboriously, his left arm heavy and throbbing. Looking down at it he realised it was in plaster. Zukie gasped.

"What happened-to me? Where's Chico and Carl? They were with me in the car last night-they were just here. We were in the car when it crashed. Shit… My mum, somebody ran her over."

"I don't know what you're talking about," Kurtis said.

Zukie hauled himself out of the bed painfully. Even his bones seemed to ache. He saw the other yout' watching his sore and bruised body.

"I have to go home, see if my mum's OK. I need – to – get dressed. Where are my clothes?" Zukie saw his clothes on the back of a chair, muddy and ripped. "Help me get some clothes please? I need to go home."

The yout' disappeared and returned with a pair of Levi's and a blue sweat-shirt. Zukie's ribs felt sore but he was able to get dressed. Touching the side of his head he winced. There was a huge, tender bump.

"Jigsy did this to me," Zukie mumbled, all the time aware of the other yout' looking at him suspiciously. "Where am I?"

"You're in my room."

Zukie snapped back.

"I fucking know that cos you keep telling me. Who are you?"

"Kurtis."

Zukie swung his legs over the side of the bed gingerly. "Where am I?"

"Danny's yard."

Zukie swallowed and frowned. They were going to Quinney Crescent blues on the Alexandra Estate last night. He, Chico and Hair Oil, laughing and joking. Hair Oil and Chico got into a car that had just pulled up next to them. A large blue Jaguar car. Jigsy's car. Zukie knew the car was full of gang bangers. They offered a lift. Zukie didn't want to accept the lift. The memory faded. Another picture came into play. He was now in the back of that car but not willingly. He couldn't understand what his newly discovered half-brother Bluebwai was doing in the car. In a flash he remembered. Blue was working for Jigsy and his crew selling drugs. Jigsy had pulled out a gun forcing him into the car — for a reason. Danny had told Jigsy something, and Jigsy seemed pleased. He'd been taunting Zukie. Something about his mother walking in front of his car. Zukie felt nauseous. Danny? The kid who told Jigsy who he was? He was only about twelve or thirteen. How come he was at a thirteen year-old boy's house?

"You mean Danny's parents' house?"

Kurtis was staring at him like he was from another planet.

"Danny's parents? This is Danny's flat in Salford."

Zukie's head ached. Salford.

"I live in Hulme. Can't stay here. I need to go home to see if my mum's OK. Got to go home."

Confused and irritated, Kurtis watched Zukie put his jacket on, limping towards the bedroom door.

"SOON. WE'RE GONNA be moving from here very soon," Easy said, throwing Teeko a can of beer. "Very soon." Teeko caught the can expertly. It bubbled and sprayed when he opened it. Chris looked on, frowning.

"Why? It's my home. I like it here," Chris said tersely. The atmosphere was thick with cannabis smoke. They were seated in front of a glass coffee table, containing mobile phones, and a huge pile of banknotes. Ragga music was playing in the background. The heavy beat of a bass line thumping like a giant's heavy footsteps.

Easy was changing. Moving away from her. Deep inside, Chris could feel it. And it terrified her.

He avoided eye contact, preferring to focus his attention on smoking a big spliff. "We can't stay here. For one it's too small. We need somewhere bigger, better furniture."

"What?"

"Classier stuff. New clothes. Here." Easy handed Chris a bundle of notes. He'd outdone Miss Small. He had only given her three quarters of the money. He'd kept over a hundred grand for himself and Teeko. "Go and pamper yourself. Do your hair, buy some clothes, jewellery whatever you need. In fact get some feminine clothes, show off those curves." He was taking over, telling her what to do and now what to wear. But Chris loved him. She took the money and pushed it into her pocket.

"We need to move because people notice too much things going on. I've already got somewhere in mind."

"Where?"

Easy smiled.

"Trust me, Chris. You'll like it." He took a quick drink of his beer. Chris's heart was racing. Her palms felt sweaty. He had a way of not answering her questions. In the next room Tyrone, who had woken up from his sleep, started to cry.

"He needs a little sister." Easy was watching her with his beautiful

115

dark eyes, watching her body seductively. "I think we need to work on that tonight." Chris sighed inwardly. She had just finished her period. They weren't using contraceptives and she couldn't get pregnant. Before Tyrone was born, she had miscarried two babies. A third pregnancy resulted in a baby girl that died two hours after being born. Chris needed her little girl back.

She wanted Easy's baby. She was desperate to have his baby. Maybe if she had his baby he would settle down, forget these dangerous games, and stay at home with her.

Easy took her hand and lead her to the bedroom. Chris gasped. The room was filled with candles. The bed was covered in a sheet made out of ten and twenty pound banknotes.

"Lie down Chris. I want us to make a baby in our money bed."

KURTIS WAS IN the main living room when they entered, on the settee, iced out of his skull. Ranks tore into Kurtis's room, where Nero had placed Zukie, his bargaining monopoly on Storm. Zukie wasn't there. He looked into his own room and found no one.

"Where's the kid?" Ranks yelled frantically. "Zukie? Where is he?"

"He's gone." Kej said blankly. Danny felt something pass through him like a bolt of lightening. He snatched Kurtis by his neck.

"You let him go?"

"I'm sorry. I didn't know I had to keep him here–"

"Like you fucking didn't know your brother was gonna rob me, you shit."

Ranks eyes bulged dangerously. He gripped Kurtis' neck tightly. Kurtis gasped and coughed, trying to pull Danny's hands away.

"I swear-I swear to you — Danny — I never knew. Danny please, please stop." Ranks pushed all his anger into Kurtis and shoved him across the room. He fell on to a glass coffee table shattering it. Kurtis was choking, almost crying. Nero, Fila and Mentian watching him unsympathetically. No one had noticed Storm walking in, breathless, his forehead knitting at the scene. Fila shook his head slowly. Kurtis suddenly rose, staring at Storm, hurt. For a few seconds their eyes met before Kurtis ran to his room and slammed the door.

"Where's Zukie?" Storm's eyes held Nero in a cool stare. Nero dropped his eyes. It was Ranks who answered.

"In't here. He took off." He said abruptly.

Storm frowned.

"Is this some sort of joke?"

"Took a taxi to Hulme." Ranks said sitting down.

Storm's head began to pound. "Are you playing games with me? You stopped me at Carl's funeral with a gun, led me here and now

117

you're telling me he's gone?"

"Kurtis, the guy who was here when he left, said Zukie said he was gonna see if your mum was OK," Ranks said, sounding tired.

Storm swallowed deeply but the hole in his throat was too wide. He stared at Ranks, his eyes widening. "My mother's in Jamaica. She's been there for a year and a half."

"He took a knock on the head last night," Nero said in a gentle voice, his expression concerned, guilty.

Ranks sighed, "We'll help you look for him."

"No thanks," Storm said firmly turning to leave. "You've done enough."

"What do you mean, I've done enough?" Ranks was incensed. "You're the one who fucked his head up not me."

Storm swung back around. "He was OK until he ran into you."

"He was OK until *you* gave him a gun which he pointed in *my* direction."

"I in't arguing with *you*," Storm said scowling, face to face with Ranks, eye-level. Nero and Fila looked on.

"Cos yu got *nothing* to say, star. Cos you *know* you're wrong. Now I'm offering you my help cos your brother is wandering out there trapped in Wonderland. Yu don't know what the fuck is going down in his head right now. I'd say you're fucking *lucky* that I'm offering my help."

"I don't *need* your help."

Ranks shook his head slowly, scornfully. He leaned into Storm. So close they could feel each other's breath.

"I feel sorry for Zukie. Sorry he's related to a mothafucka like you."

"You know what *your* problem is Danny? You leave yourself too open. If I can find you here, any fucka can."

"And you know what your problem is Storm? You're a mothafuckin' *liar* and I wanna be there when Zukie finds you out. And despite the fact that the kid tried to kill me, I like him, I don't wanna see nuttin happen to him. So if you want us to help we're here. Whatever you have to tell him and when you tell him is your business. But he'll keep coming *back* to me Storm. He'll keep reaching out to me, time and time again. He knows I *know* the truth."

Storm stared at Ranks. He closed his eyes momentarily. Turning he walked on.

"OK," he said. "*OK*."

MISS SMALL STOOD sideways, looking at herself in the full length pine mirror, smiling. She was showing a slight bump. She'd been for an ultrasound scan test at the hospital on Thursday, they confirmed that she was nearly four months pregnant and that the baby was definitely a girl. They had given her a special photo of the baby, which she kept in her purse. Things were looking up. She couldn't wait to share the good news with Easy and she was also looking forward to meeting her estranged son Daniel. The crew was doing well now they had a massive injection of capital. Easy and Teeko had proved their worth. She had had no qualms about Easy eventually taking over.

Suddenly her bedroom door swung wide open, catching her by complete surprise.

"Trench?" Miss Small adjusted herself quickly. "You don't how to knock?"

"Sorry. I need to talk to you."

Miss Small took in Trench's anxious features. He looked peaky, harassed. There was a good cure for that.

"Want a line?" Opening a bedside drawer Miss Small took out some coke. Then she remembered she'd have to cut back a little because of the baby.

"No, thanks. I need to talk to you Vee." Veniesha sat down on the bed, lighting a cigarette. She noticed the time. It was getting late. She needed to phone Easy, find out where he was at. Today he might be at the factory checking production or collecting taxes.

Trench stood before her awkwardly. The doctors at the infirmary had made a good job of stitching his ear back on. Trench was good-looking but he was no match for Easy, thought Vaniesha.

"Whah ya waan talk to me 'bout, Trench?"

I want to talk to you about Easy," Trench drawled, watching Miss Small's reaction carefully. She didn't flinch. Leaning back on her bed, she closed her eyes.

"I think you should rethink his position in the crew."

She laughed.

"I thought we did dun this conversation."

"Something in't right. I in't sure what it is."

"Easy brought a whole heap of money our way. I think everything is right, right now, wouldn't you say?"

"He was in a crew that seen two leaders shot dead. I mean, is that bad luck or what?"

"What yu tryin' to say?"

"I in't sure." Miss Small kissed through her teeth savagely, like he was wasting her time. Maybe he was, Trench thought, because there was nothing concrete he could offer her. Trouble was around the corner for them because they had hijacked Danny's payroll. Why couldn't she see that? Why couldn't she see that Ranks was going to come after them for what rightfully belonged to him? Did she really believe a crow like Easy would protect her when they came full force, as Trench knew they would? Why couldn't she see?

"Let me get dis straight, Trench. You waan talk to me about Easy but yu don't sure what it is yu waan talk about?" Trench realised how foolish he looked and sounded. Miss Small shook her head, laughed and said. "When yu go out of my bedroom, make sure yu shut the door and if yu waan to come in again mek sure yu knock twice then I will know it is you and I will just ignore it. Mek haste gwaan. I need some shut eye." Trench stared at Miss Small, lying on her back on the huge bed.

She was already snoring.

She seemed to be doing a lot of sleeping lately.

ZUKIE KNEW HE was in Hulme, the area where he was born. But it looked strange, no longer run-down. Where he expected to see the dilapidated flats of John Nash, Robert Adam and William Kent Crescents he saw there were new skylines, slick new buildings where there shouldn't have been. He suddenly felt dizzy and sick.

Images, some vague some frighteningly familiar rushed through his mind, playing quickly like a video recorder on fast-forward. He felt strange and alone, fighting the hot panic rising in his chest. He walked unsteadily over New Birley Street towards a housing complex that he felt shouldn't be there, but knew had existed for as long as he could remember. He understood that beyond the housing complex was his street, Newberry Street, where he lived with his mother. Limping towards the Nia Centre Arts and Culture building he saw that it looked as if it had been closed down for months, if not years. Zukie was confused. Hadn't he been there a couple of weeks ago with Chico at a Buju Banton show? As Zukie turned the corner, he suddenly felt a cold breeze envelope him. The street where he lived with his mother was a green area, a park.

He felt more than confusion. Where the hell was he? What had happened to his house? Where was the Old Lady?

Think, Zukie. Remember.

Zukie's legs weakened.

This isn't where you live anymore.

Chico and Hair Oil are dead.
Last night you tried to kill Danny Ranks.

GRANDMA WAS IN the kitchen when she felt the first pain. It seemed to come from nowhere. The pain seemed to gather in her chest, strong, like severe indigestion. She held onto the kitchen worktop in an effort to steady herself. The room was warm. Grandma could see that it was still light. She heard the ticking of the clock and the food on the stove. Sharon's favourite, boiled dumplings, cassava, bananas, yams and potato with chicken pieces. The second pain made her scream out in agony, clutching her chest. She closed her eyes. In a moment Sharon would be here with her boyfriend, whom she had invited for dinner. Grandma thought she couldn't allow them to see her this way. As the kitchen floor seemed to rise up to meet her, all she could think of was her grandson, Barrington, also known as Easy.

"GRANDMA?" SHARON KISSED her boyfriend joyfully as she opened the front door, and holding his hand led him into the house looking forward to granma meeting him. The first thing she noticed was the smell of burned food. She heard the loud sound of hissing coming from the kitchen. "Gran. Where are you?" Fear and trepidation started to build with each choking breath. Her boyfriend of just three months, Neville, whom she had met at church, followed behind her. There was no answer from Grandma. Sharon and Neville walked into the kitchen. They found Grandma lying on the lino floor, still, lifeless, but clutching the cross on a chain around her neck. Sharon reached down to her grandmother screaming and crying hysterically.
"Grandma! No! No! Noooooooo!"

THEY MUST HAVE spent an hour driving around the changing face of Hulme looking for any signs of Zukie. Storm had allowed Nero to take the controls of his jeep. The vehicle cruised along clean, new streets while Storm scanned the area looking for his brother. Storm had decided to cover the North Area of Hulme, where they used to live. Nero couldn't believe the area could be so big with so many new developments and new streets. Personally, Nero thought it was hopeless. The kid could be anywhere. Could be miles away.
Ranks was with Mentian covering South Hulme and had phoned

several times checking progress. Still nothing. No sightings of Zukie anywhere.

"Pull over," Storm suddenly said, his voice wavering with strained emotion. "I need a cigarette." Nero pulled over, watching Storm struggle to light the cigarette with shaking hands. "Shit!"

"He's gonna be OK."

"How would *you* know?" Storm asked quietly.

"I just know — Ranks coulda damaged him for what he tried to do to. Nobody points a gun at Ranks and lives. I've seen what Danny can do to people who fuck with him. Ranks likes Zukie, and liking is rare for Danny. I mean he has other important things he should be doing right now."

"Like getting back the money Easy took last night."

Nero stared at Storm. Storm blew smoke ahead of him. Storm looked back at Nero and smiled. "I know everything. And I know that Ranks is switching tactics. He thinks that he don't need to blackmail me into revenge but that if he helps me I'll help him with Easy."

"I don't know about that," Nerome sniffed. It felt cold in the car and it begun to rain heavily again. The sky was dark and heavy. If the kid was out there, he'd be drenched through to the bone.

Silence.

"You're my age, right?"

"Twenty-seven."

"OK. A coupla years older. How much does he pay you to watch his back?"

"Ahhhh, that's my business."

Storm snorted and smiled. "Got any kids?"

"One. A boy of five. He lives with his mother."

Storm inhaled deeply and sighed. He looked straight ahead. A couple of kids rode by hurriedly on mountain bikes. Nerome took the photo of his son and showed it to Storm. A small, fair-skinned boy smiled back at him. Reminded him of Lee.

"Nice kid."

"He looks like his mother." Nero paused purposefully. He sighed. "I see him when I can. Every penny I make goes back to Candice. She thinks I work in legit security."

Storm handed the photo back.

He said nothing.

"EASY THIS IS ridiculous. I can't bloody see!"

Easy led Chris from the car, blindfolded. He was sure she would be pleased with the new apartment. She stepped out gingerly.

She felt him sweep her up in his arms. Chris screamed with delight. She giggled uncontrollably as she felt him putting her down.

"Can I look now?"

He removed the blindfold. Chris opened her eyes. Time stopped. She was in the most stunning town house she had ever seen.

"Oh my God, Easy. It's beautiful." It was huge, spacious, light and full of modern furniture. There were lamps, a cream suite, polished floorboards and an enormous marble fireplace on which stood framed photographs of Tyrone. Chris felt a tear at the corner of her eye.

"Let's check out the bedroom," Easy said, smiling. He picked her up and flung her over his shoulder. She was screaming protests feebly, but deep down was looking forward to this particular part of exploring the house.

"ALRIGHT, HOLD ON. I'm with ya." Paradise had just put Kyesha down for her nap when she heard the doorbell of her Stretford home chime urgently, as if someone was keeping their finger on the button. Humming to herself, she ran down the wooden stairs and opened the door. Zukie stood on her doorstep. His eyes looked haunted. He was absolutely soaked through. A massive bruise shone on his forehead. Paradise saw the arm in plaster. She also saw his broken soul.

"Zukie. My God. What happened to you?"

He tried to talk but swallowed, lowered his eyes slowly and dropped his head to his chest.

Paradise pulled Zukie inside, straight upstairs. He sat down silently when she manoeuvred him towards the bed. His eyes stared at nothing. Paradise thought he might be in deep shock or trauma. She felt a deep wrenching pain in the pit of her stomach. He wouldn't answer any of her questions. Slowly, she began to remove his wet garments, gasping as her eyes saw bruises and cuts covering his torso. He winced as she pulled and tugged, lay back and covered his eyes.

"Wanna talk about it, baby?" Paradise lay on the bed next to him. He was naked only for a pair of boxers.

"I tried to shoot somebody. Last night," Zukie explained in a low, breaking voice. "I wanted, really wanted to waste him. I was out my mind Paradise. Later, I realise he done nuttin to hurt me, ever. All he did was tell Jigsy who I was. I know that now." Paradise was stunned.

She didn't believe Zukie had in it him to hurt anybody, never mind try to kill someone. She could see this bothered him. She was also shocked that he had remembered. He was anguished at what he could have done. The thing that made her really shiver was the fact that he might have been killed. She was also concerned about the reasons he tried to do it. Guns and wasting people wasn't Zukie's style, unless someone had put him up to it. Storm.

STORM'S BELLY WAS aching not from hunger but for his brother, aching for Zukie to be OK. He thought of the promise he had made to The Old Lady to look after Zukie after she had gone to Jamaica for good a year ago now. Storm was desperate, and that desperation, that unknowing was eating away at him, like acid in his soul, burning. Deep down, he said a little prayer. If he found Zukie, he would end this. No matter what, he would tell him everything. So long as Zukie was alive. Even if Zukie never wanted to see him again because he inadvertently killed his two best friends and then lied to him to protect himself, he would take it.

Storm's mobile phone rang piercingly, cutting into his weary thoughts. He answered, aware of Nero's cool dark eyes studying him curiously.

"It's Paradise," The voice said firmly. "Zukie turned up at mine fifteen minutes ago." Storm felt his heart thumping rapidly, making his head beat. It was like seeing his winning lottery numbers flash up.

"How is he?"

"He's sleeping."

"I'm coming over."

"No. Don't. He's bruised and tired. I think you should stay away from him for a day or two."

Oh My God. Storm's voice was shrieking inside his head. He knows! He's remembered.

Paradise cut the call. Storm listened to a dead tone. Nero was watching him expectantly.

"He's OK," Storm said, reading Nero's mind. He closed his eyes slightly.

"I'll drop yu by Danny's." Storm said, before starting the engine and turning the Shogun around to face the opposite direction. Nero remained silent. Staring through the window. "I want to thank you, anyway, for the help you gave my brother, you know not leaving him and taking him to hospital."

"It was nothing." Nero said, still watching Storm and thinking. "I did what any other decent guy woulda." In a lot of ways, he believed Storm and Danny were alike. There was a part inside them where there was a sign saying, "No Entry."

"YOU FUCKED UP," Ranks declared calmly, breathing hard and pointing a stern accusatory finger at Kurtis. "You let him go and you didn't tell me what Easy was plannin'."

Everyone sat silently, looking away or into the distance pretending to be unconcerned. Furniture lay upturned or broken. Ranks' Rottweiler barked furiously, sensitive to her master's aggravated mood. Kurtis sat shaking, afraid.

"I told you before, Dans, I didn't know," Kurtis stammered, totally terrified.

"And if I find out you're pissin' about with me you're a dead mothafucka-"

"I'm not Danny. I swear. I swear to God I never knew." Ranks could see the sweat on Kurtis's face. He was burning for another hit. He needed some rock badly. "I'll do better next time. I swear. I really will. Please don't end our partnership. Please."

"I need information. I want his next move. I wanna fuck him up for fuckin' wid me. Y'hear me?"

"Yes."

"I coulda had Storm working wid me. I was this fuckin' close." Ranks demonstrated with his forefinger and thumb, a tiny fraction of a space in between them. "All ya had to do was keep his brother here."

"I'm sorry. I didn't know. Didn't know he was Storm's brother." Kurtis hung his head. He wasn't even sure what he was sorry about. All he knew was that he needed some crack so bad his hand was twitching violently.

"Don't know shit but crack or coke, do ya? Get your crackhead backside out there and give me something solid on Easy." Kurtis stood up, visibly shaking, looking irritated and scared. "Know what I mean?"

"Danny, he can't go out like that." Nero said quickly defending Kurtis. Danny stared at Nerome coolly before turning his attention back to Kurtis.

Ranks snapped his fingers at Fila. Fila left the room, came back seconds later, carrying a brown bag. He handed it over to Ranks. Ranks threw the bag over to Kurtis. Smiling ingratiatingly and thanking Ranks endlessly, Kurtis sat down and took out his instruments. He was popping his pipe in no time, sucking and blowing like it was his last breath. He made groaning noises as the high kicked in like a mule. Gradually the sweat evaporated from his face. Nero didn't want to watch the freak show. It was obvious that Kurtis was a hard-core crack-addict. Nero looked away, preferring to think about Candice and the strange way he felt at ease with Storm, enough at ease to talk to him about Jake.

It didn't take long for the alertness to return to Kurtis. He felt and looked supremely confident.

DANNY LAY ON his bed, naked, wide-awake while the others slept, thinking. He was hot, but his hotness wasn't caused by the sultry night. Already, Zukie trying to shoot him was at the back of his mind. He could deal with that, seeing as the kid's head was fucked up. But Easy? Easy was playing with fire. Danny's armpits boiled, his light-brown body poured sweat. He was hot for vengeance but he wasn't going to jump. It was too easy. He felt that Easy-Love was baiting him into a trap, and he wasn't going to fall for it. Not one bit. He wasn't going to go for Small, hijacking a next man's pay wasn't her style at all. This was a new play. Easy's play. Danny unconsciously played with the thick gold chain around his neck. He wondered if Small had any kids. He pictured some plum kid at home eating a pile of doughnuts while his fat mommy played gangsta bitch. Ranks chuckled.

He was going to get Easy. He was gonna get Storm to work with him.

He was gonna get Easy good fucking style.

But for the moment he would put Easy on the back burner. Temporarily. Tomorrow was the day he was going to meet his mother.

CHRIS LAY AGAINST Easy's brown chest, serene, happy and asleep in their new home. The evening was hot and humid and their naked bodies were practically glued together with sweat. They had made love practically all day in the new house. Outside a dog barked and Easy could hear kids playing. Easy stroked Chris's soft brunette hair. She muttered in her sleep. He kissed her damp forehead gently. All the time he was thinking, rehearsing ways of keeping ahead, expanding, increasing his reputation. Shops and businesses in the area, all due a cold call.

He had expected Ranks to come after him straightaway and he

was prepared for that. But Ranks didn't show his face. At first he was puzzled but then he understood. He knew Danny was no fool. He also knew time was moving on and things had to move swiftly. He didn't expect Ranks to come directly after Miss Small but he knew Miss Small's crew would expect that, wouldn't they? He no longer needed Miss Small; he wasn't sure how he would get rid of her, but he knew things had a way of working out for him.

As Grandma always says, where there's a will there's a mothafuckin' way.

GRANDMA WAS CONNECTED to tubes and wires in the intensive care ward. Her breathing was assisted, her eyes closed. Sharon and Neville sat by her bedside. Neville held Sharon's hand, giving her spiritual strength and composure. Grandma looked at peace. Sharon watched her grandmother's face. She was a strong woman. She had made Sharon who she was. Sharon loved her and didn't want her to die. She needed to contact Easy. If Easy came to see her it might mean the difference between life and death.

AS STORM PRESSED the playback button, voices poured from the answerphone. The weather had changed again, the humid climate of the last two weeks had returned. Storm started to strip out of his suit, preparing to have a long cool shower. Tariq reminded Storm of a mentoring event for which he was to go into their old secondary school to talk about his change from bad bwai gangster to successful black businessman. Naked, opening the side cabinet, he poured himself a glass of brandy. The other message took him completely by surprise, jarring his senses entirely like an electric shock.

"Hello Clifton, it's me." It was the Old Lady, calling from Mandeville, Jamaica where she was settled. 'Look like Ah call when you out. I cyaan remember yu mobile phone number. I hope everything all right and yu looking after Zukie an' yuself. How Jasmine and Lee? I hope all right. De sun hot out here and I am keepin' good health. Anyway, me don't like talking too long into a machine, feel like I'm talking to myself. I miss you and love you both. I will talk to yu soon and maybe I can come over for a visit."

Drinking his short glass of brandy quickly, Storm poured another, then another. Thank God he'd been out when she'd called. What the hell would he have said when she had asked to talk to her youngest, Zukie? Zukie had been knocked down while trying to shoot somebody. Zukie hadn't been home for at nearly a week; the longest Zukie had been away since they moved in two and a half years ago.

Storm was afraid.

Something was happening beyond his control.

Something was happening to Zukie.

ZUKIE WAS REMEMBERING. Little things at first. Hazy. Patchy. His favourite colour? Purple. His mother was in Jamaica. Jigsy ran her over in his car and she got sick and she went to Jamaica. His girlfriend was called Paradise. Jigsy was talking to Storm in the car the night Chico got killed. Storm sold jewellery, rocks, before he set up business. No, not the jewel kind of rocks I saw in his bedroom. He lied to the Old Lady, I knew he wasn't making that huge amount of money selling jewellery.

Zukie lay awake, unsure if the scenes flooding his brain were in actual fact scenes from his life or painful half-remembered nightmares. Did these things really happen? Sighing he turned towards Paradise next to him. At least this part was real. He knew he had loved her and he knew he loved her now. Paradise turned to face him. They lay face to face. She put her arm around him. The next thing he felt was his daughter Kyesha, beating his sore face, waking him up.

It was morning. Another haunting day lay ahead.

PEOPLE WHO KNEW them said there wasn't much difference between Celia and her sister Veniesha, same height and weight, hazelnut-coloured skin and the same outgoing personalities. The difference was one of age: Celia was thirteen years older and she was a mother first, and a part time adult education teacher. Veniesha, unknown to Celia, was a big time drug dealer, racketeer and the leader behind one of the most infamous gangs in Manchester. All Celia knew of her sister was what she told her: she was a successful retail director and her products were crystals. Business must be going well, too, because Veniesha was wearing loads of gold jewellery and had turned up in a brand new black Mercedes convertible.

"Where yu plan to meet him?" Celia asked her sister, pouring more tea into the bone china mug. Veniesha looked around the well decorated semi-detached house in Withington, Manchester. Celia's home was nice, very prim and proper. But Daniel had said he would meet her not far from the park. Miss Small was in agreement. Where they met should be neutral. They would meet by the park up the road, go to a MacDonald's restaurant and then — whatever. Celia explained that she and Daniel hadn't seen each other in about two years.

"He's like his mother," Celia said, smiling. "Secretive."

"Independent." Miss Small said, quick to defend a son she hardly knew. Celia had never forgiven her for staying away from the family, for keeping her affairs to herself. Miss Small felt like a stranger in her sister's home. Uncomfortable in the front room that was practically a shrine for her son, Daniel. There were framed photographs of him everywhere. It was evident that Daniel had been loved and cherished like Celia's own children, and being the youngest he was probably spoilt. Veniesha thought about her unborn child, wondering if she would resemble her big brother. Miss Small drank the last of her tea, and gathered up her handbag. She sighed and looked at her watch. She felt awkward and nervous, it was an unusual feeling. She was going to meet Daniel at last. And he would know.

The sun was high. A burning ball of bright yellowy-orange. Miss Small crossed over the road opposite the park, wearing dark designer shades, a long loose sleeveless white dress and sandals. Her long brown hair was freshly relaxed by a top hair designer in Chorlton and it was styled off her face, bringing out her even features. Gold earrings dangled from her ears, and the jewellery around her neck, fingers and wrists glinted in the afternoon sun. It was such a beautiful day. Today was going to be the first day of the rest of her life. She could feel it. She was so positive and happy. Everything was going to change.

She watched as children swung on tyre swings, screaming and laughing. Some were stripped down to their shorts or swimsuits as they shot each other with turbo gun soakers. Others rode through the park on BMX bikes, silver scooters or roller blades. It occurred to her that Daniel was raised here and that he, too, would have played in this park. Veniesha stopped to look at them. If things had been different she'd have shared moments like this with Daniel. But it wasn't too late. They could still share something, especially now she was carrying another child.

After today, if things started OK with Daniel, she would give it all up. She'd give up the gang to Easy, give up her flat, give up the drugs, buy a house in Cheshire somewhere and live the rest of her life in anonymity. Her and her daughter, alone. A thought came to her suddenly. The park had two entrances and she hadn't been specific to Daniel about which entrance to use. It was obvious he wasn't near this side of the road. She'd been waiting ten minutes or so. Miss Small decided to stroll through the park and see if Daniel was waiting on the other side.

Turning around she came face to face with a hooded figure on a mountain bike. Wearing dark clothes, dark gloves and a black balaclava, it stared coldly, lips curled in an evil smirk. A gun held waist high glinted in the sunlight. It looked like it had a makeshift silencer attached to the nozzle.

"You!" Miss Small exclaimed.

PARADISE WAS WONDERING. Why was Zukie punishing himself like this? He had insisted on going to find Hair Oil's grave. He came out with it suddenly. They dropped Ky off to nursery and then headed down Princess Parkway towards the south side of the city, to Southern Cemetery. At the gate he bought a bouquet of flowers from a lone florist operating from the back of a car. The day was hot but Zukie didn't seem to notice. Hair Oil had been buried next to his best friend Chico. Zukie placed his flowers down on the grave and looked back at Paradise. He swallowed. She saw the desperation in his clear grey eyes. His anguish was gut wrenching. Why had he insisted on coming here? Still, she let him stand, swaying slightly, staring at Chico's grave for a long time, until she pulled his arm gently. In a second he was in her arms, holding her tightly, trembling against her.

RANKS WAITED, HIS eyes looking for any signs of the woman who had said she was his mother. Nero was just around the corner in the car, waiting. Ranks was dressed in a pair of light combat trousers, string vest and a shirt open wide at the front. No guns, no vest, no danger, no need. He waited, sucking on an ice cold strawberry-flavoured slush drink. He had been waiting half an hour. Ranks never waited more than ten minutes for anyone. But he wanted to see her. Curious. He had things he wanted to say to her, questions that needed answering.

Where the hell was she? Didn't she say meet him at this park? He used to play here with what he thought were his older brothers and sisters, but later discovered were his cousins. And the woman he thought was his mother was his Aunt. She said it shouldn't have made any difference because she loved him like her own. Maybe he could have accepted that if his older step-cousin Theo hadn't taunted him repeatedly about being dumped like dirty washing on to Aunt

Celia. Theo dedicated his life to tormenting Danny, to stripping him of his self-confidence and ultimately his dignity. Ranks hadn't thought about Theo in years. Until now.

Danny also remembered the park had more than one entrance. Maybe she was waiting on the other side. And maybe the bitch had bailed out and simply didn't want to show. Ranks couldn't believe it. He had other important things to take care of, like figuring how he was going to make Easy pay for dissin' him.

She'd wasted his time.

Ranks drank some more of the slush, savouring the ice coldness as it chilled his warm throat. That's it. Chance gone. He was fucking off outta there.

From the corner of his eye he caught sight of it. A fedz helicopter. It was getting nearer to where he was standing, circling over the park and the surrounding area. He heard sirens. A police car sped towards him. Danny felt fear rise in his gut. It passed as the car sped past, followed by two more. Ranks turned. Something was kicking off. He hurried back towards where Nero was waiting, trying not to run. Nero was already steering the car towards him. Throwing the slush to the kerbside, Danny climbed in.

"Fucking Dibbles everywhere, innit star, like ants on a dead cockroach."

"What 'appen to your mother?"

Ranks shook his head.

"Musta decided I wasn't worth knowin'. Must have better t'ings to do or sumtin."

Danny lit a cigarette and opened the sunroof, letting cool air into the car. The sky was dark. After three weeks of burning sunshine, it was going to rain again.

MISS SMALL LAY on her side against the green park railings, shaking and clutching her large chest. Blood covered her white dress and pumped from her wound like a red fountain. Clearly in pain and shock she was panting, trying to claim her breath. Blood bubbled out of her mouth as she gasped. Her gaze was fixed. She was unaware of the police and people surrounding her.

'My son — I was going to — I didn't get to see him."

The emergency paramedics team were trying to make her comfortable, because that was all they could do. The blood loss was extensive. The blood from her mouth indicated that she was haemorrhaging internally. The fact that she was still alive after such a terrible gunshot was probably down to her huge size. But they knew they were losing her. Her pupils were large. She was perspiring heavily, still clutching a mobile phone. "Easy, my baby, my baby."

They tried to get her not to talk. She was wasting precious energy. A female paramedic held her other hand. She held on tightly. Upset mothers in the park steered their curious children away. Older children stared until the police moved them on. Word got round that she'd been shot. The cops tried to dispel the mounting speculation. Someone uttered that it was a damn disgrace, especially as it was so near to a public park and children could have been killed. Police were trying to gather witnesses and evidence. Neither was forthcoming until one child, visibly shaken, tearful, spoke of what he'd seen. Someone on a bike, he said. The police suggested he take a ride with them to the police station. The kid turned on his heels and tore away across the park into oblivion.

The female paramedic holding Veniesha's hand realised she was no longer gripping firmly.

The chubby hand loosened.

Her eyes stayed wide open.

Miss Small had slipped away.

BY THE TIME DI Edwards arrived, the ambulance had started to pull away. No lights flashing, no urgency, for its patient was definitely dead and heading for the mortuary. The time of death was given at 2.55 pm. A single shot to the chest. She'd held on to life for a staggering and impressive fifteen minutes.

A crowd had gathered. Edwards observed the hostile, frightened faces. Many of them were residents, angry that the shooting was in their neighborhood. Already somebody had laid a bouquet of flowers on the blood-soaked pavement.

This was not a random robbery. Her jewellery and handbag were intact. This was a stylised execution. Somebody had wanted her dead. And they had taken a big risk — broad daylight, in front of small witnesses. Gunned down mercilessly, she had no chance.

As usual no one was coming forward with statements. A news crew pushed a microphone into his face, asking him to comment on the appalling incident. Already they were hindering his investigations. Edwards cut them off with a smile, promising them further details when they arrived. He was keen to hear what, if anything, her dying words were.

EASY-LOVE SHOWERED briefly, washing the sweat off his lean, coco-brown body. He dried himself and changed into fresh clothes. Walking into the bedroom from the Ensuite bathroom, he sat on the bed. He sighed, running his hand through his dreadlocks. He looked at the time. It was three pm. Easy fastened his expensive wristwatch, picked up his car keys and left to go to the hospital. Thank God it was only five minutes drive away.

"HELLO, ME GRANDSON." Grandma Idey's eyes fluttered open slowly, her voice was low and croaky. Sharon was overjoyed. She knew having Easy would make a difference. But he looked strained, agitated, uneasy. Easy started crying openly. Sharon had never seen him upset before let alone this distraught. He sat by her hospital bedside, next to the huge bouquet of flowers he'd bought her. Months ago the situation was reversed. He was the one lying in a hospital bed, beaten to an inch of his life and she was praying for his survival. Now it was she, paralysed by a stroke, lying motionless. He kissed her limp hand, then raised over her to kiss her face.

"Don't die on me, Gran."

"Die? Wheh me waan fe die for, bwai? De Lord nuh ready for me yet." Grandma Idey whispered into his face. "Yuh lookin' after Kurtis?"

"Don't worry about Kurtis. He's fine. He's with me. Just concentrate on getting better for me."

Closing her eyes, Grandma nodded and went back to sleep. Easy stayed with her, holding her hand, burying his face in the bed. His body racked with sobs. Between the sobs Sharon heard his words. "Forgive me. Forgive me. I didn't mean to do it, Gran. Forgive me."

KURTIS SLASHED HIS bedding frenziedly with the knife, trying to get the spirit of the grey-eyed kid out of his bed. Zukie. With each thrust he bawled out Zukie's name.

"Zukie! Zukie! Zukie!"

"ZUKIE?" STORM WAS stunned. He scratched the back of his neck awkwardly. Zukie turned around slowly and stared at his brother with exhausted eyes.

"W'happen, star?" Storm chanced a smile, but stopped when he saw Zukie's left arm in plaster, and his brother's bruised face.

"You look like you've been through hell and back. Are you OK? I was looking for you. Why did just you go off like that? Come here, let me look at you."

Zukie dropped his eyes, sighed then looked back up to his brother. "I'm cool. I'll survive. Who's Kadeem Hussein?" The question was like a punch from a heavyweight boxer's right glove. "I went through the drawers at home. I went on the home computer, his name is everywhere. I also found cheques from him paid to you."

Why? Why had he done that? What was he searching for? Storm walked over and examined Zukie's face, shaking his head. He felt Zukie's eyes studying him.

"He's what they call a sleeping partner. He's the director of my music business," Storm responded.

"What am I then?"

"My business partner."

"I've never heard of him. Why the secrets?"

"Because you never really needed to know. Why don't you go home and rest? You look tired."

"We're not gonna talk about me tryna kill Ranks then?"

Zukie smiled but Storm noticed that his eyes looked cold. Storm's heart boomed viciously, he knew that look. He wondered if Zukie was back from wherever it was that he had been for the last four years.

"I in't going home," Zukie said turning around. "I'd rather keep busy here, that way I don't have to think."

"Well at least, at least let me get Dr. Stephens to look at you."

"Stop fussing, Cliff, I'm fine. I'm a survivor." With that he gave his brother a smile but Storm wasn't convinced. He wasn't convinced about a lot of things.

IN THE EVIDENCE room of the Central Manchester Police station, Edwards examined the contents of Miss Small's handbag. Fifteen hundred pounds in cash, a bunch of keys, an expensive bottle of designer perfume, two driving licences, and various credit cards made out in different names. They knew she was involved in a big way with drugs. They knew she had links with Yardie gangs abroad and in the UK. They also knew that she had plenty of enemies. He concluded that they had finally traced the elusive Miss Small. Veniesha Michelle Brooks. Aged thirty-one, the force behind many vicious beatings and killings. She had married twice and had lived in

Miami and Kingston.

Why had she been so careless when she knew she was a marked woman?

Something inside Colin Edwards sank deeply.

Her Nokia mobile phone revealed a list of recently dialled numbers. The first in the list was the call she tried to make just after she was shot.

Edwards redialled.

WAITING FOR HIS order of chicken and rice, Trench stood near the counter of the Caribbean takeaway. His eyes were wide, circling. After the shooting the other night outside the derelict swimming baths, he knew he had to be vigilant. There was no doubt that Danny would come after his money. And maybe Danny didn't care who he took out.

The day was hot and sticky. Trench looked up at Michigan through the shop's window. He, too, was watchful, sitting in the passenger side of an open top car looking around uneasily. Things were fine until Easy joined the crew Trench thought. If he'd had his way he would have beat the fucka to death when he stepped outta prison like they planned, but Miss Small had said no. OK, they'd had disputes with the Worlders crew before, but no one had dared to snatch Danny's money from under his nose. That was deliberately asking for trouble.

Michigan pointed to his watch. Trench nodded. Michi was impatient, edgy and hungry. The cook was taking his time. A Yard sound dancehall tape played in the kitchen. Suddenly his mobile phone rang. Trench was tempted to ignore it. He answered the call, it was from Miss Small.

"Yeah?"

"This number was nearly dialled from a dying woman today." The male voice said, throwing him completely. Who the hell was this on Miss Small's phone? For a second, Trench was puzzled until the significance of the words sneaked up on him.

"What? Who is this? Is this some kind of joke?"

"Did you know a Mrs. Veniesha Brooks?"

Trench's heart knocked dreadfully in his chest, like a pendulum. The reply felt like it was snatched from his throat.

"Who the fuck are you?"

Why did he ask? He knew the sound of a beast bwai and he sounded like a black man. He switched off his mobile, staring at the tiled floor of the shop. He didn't hear the assistant asking him for payment. He didn't see the puzzled look on the assistant's face either, when he turned and left, leaving the food behind.

"Did you know a Mrs. Veniesha Brooks?"

Did you??

Past tense.

Did.

Meant dead.

"GET ME A bitch." Danny said gruffly. "Any bitch. I want her here. Now." Nero looked at Ranks slumped in his green Habitat armchair, shirt open, legs wide. Ranks currently had a vast choice of women, girls who came and went, who asked no questions but enjoyed it when he gave them money or bought them gifts. Of course he had special girls. Girls who sometimes stayed and played for three or four days until he got bored with them or thought they were getting too close to him. Sighing, Nerome narrowed the selection down to Kelly, Jamilia, and the beautiful long-haired Anglo-Indian girl, Meeta.

"Kelly, Jamilia or Meeta?"

"Don't givva shit. Toss a rahs coin. Heads whoever is out. Tails I get to sex her." Nero stared at Ranks. He hated women being disrespected this way, but he didn't want to anger Danny further. Danny lit a spliff, and opened a can of beer, stroking his chestnut coloured stomach, moving his hand slowly down to his crotch. "Tell you what. Get them all over here. Shares or swaps with you." Nero dialled each girl's number, expecting them to decline Danny's sexual invitation. No one did. They were young, naive, and all loved Danny.

Nero politely declined Danny's double bun and triple cheese invitation, leaving Ranks to enjoy himself with the girls when they arrived. After a while two of them left, one shortly after the other, leaving Meeta alone with Danny.

Erykah Badu played softly in the background as Ranks thrust himself deeply inside her, gradually building up his pace. Meeta ran her fingers over his smooth tattooed shoulders and body. His hands caressed her gently. He nuzzled her neck. She threw her head back, enjoying his tickling bites. Slowly, he nibbled his way to her breast, biting harder.

"Danny. Please, careful, you're hurting me." She gave short gasps of pain but he continued to bite even harder. Suddenly the pain was unbearable. He bit hard, sinking his teeth into her breast. Meeta screamed loudly before pushing Danny off her. He looked at her with narrow remote eyes.

"Danny, that really hurt." Looking down at her left breast. Meeta could already see the bluish circular bruise forming on her creamy-white skin. The teeth marks could be seen clearly. Ranks rolled over onto his side.

"Danny?" She called his name but he didn't respond. She felt the bed shaking slightly. Danny sighed, caught his breath, and sniffed. It sounded as if he was crying. Meeta was stunned. Danny was crying. Meeta leaned over and it was then that he lost it.

"Get out me face!" he screamed repeatedly. 'Fuck off! Gwaan!! Tek your clothes and go." Disturbed and frightened Meeta swiftly gathered her clothes.

Nero stood up, placing his book face down as Meeta ran semi-naked into the living room looking petrified and humiliated. She looked at Nero with moistened eyes. Danny was still yelling at her to get out. She put on the rest of her clothes quickly.

"What's going on?"

Meeta left, shaking her head, crying, slamming the front door.

THIS IN'T REAL. Can't be fuckin' happening.

Trench and Michigan drove past slowly, silently, stunned. It wasn't hard to find where she had fallen. It was already on the local news. The road next to Sycamore Green Park was cordoned off, crawling with the fedz.

It was raging through his head. Somebody must have known where she was going. Somebody must have known, followed her, shot her dead. And her last phone call was to him. Trench tried to picture her, lying on the road bleeding, trying to call him instead of emergency services. Or her beloved Easy. Why?

The car halted. Trench and Michigan sat completely in awe. It hurt. It pained somewhere deep in his stomach. The tears flew freely from Trench's eyes. Michigan's lower lip trembled. Trench felt like he was being chopped up into pieces. Angrily, Michigan started the car, spun it around furiously and headed away.

"It could only be that bastard Ranks." Michigan stated coldly. "We're gonna get him for this."

Trench looked ahead into the distance but saw nothing.

He felt sure this had nothing to do with Danny Ranks.

Nothing whatsoever.

CELIA FELT ICE-COLD numb after identifying her sister's executed body. Even after seeing Veniesha lying on the slab she still didn't understand it. She'd discovered the fate of her sister when the police came to look at the Mercedes Convertible, parked not far from the house. She had come out to find loads of police vans and vehicles, the helicopter hovering, and the area cordoned off.

The black detective had asked her endless questions, questions she did not know the answers to. He sat in her parlour room, in the same seat where she had entertained her youngest sister earlier that day. All Celia wanted to do was to see her sister again.

One minute they were sitting down, having tea, talking about Daniel, the next minute Vee goes twenty-five yards up the road and is shot dead. Hours later the place is crawling with police asking questions, press and all sorts. And then the police tell her all about her sister's double life. Yardie godmother. It sounded so ridiculous she had laughed initially. But soon she realised it was the truth.

The black detective said he wanted to talk to Daniel about his rendezvous with his mother. Obviously he was under suspicion. Celia said she didn't have a number for him because he changed his mobile phone number regularly. She didn't know why but she felt she had to protect Daniel.

Celia didn't like the way the police looked at her as if she too was involved in the dark life that eventually swallowed up her sister. After all, this was the second tragedy to hit the family under similar circumstances. A shooting. Her step-son Theo was shot and killed inside the park, nearly five years ago. He was found behind some bushes, naked, shot in the groin, surrounded by women's clothes. His killer was never found.

After the police had gone, Celia dialled Daniel three times but his mobile was switched off.

Celia wrung her hands nervously. What the hell was going on? Was she dreaming this bad nightmare? Suddenly looking down at her feet, Celia realised she was wearing odd shoes, one red the other blue. She'd probably been wearing them all day, at the morgue, on the street, and while the police were interviewing her.

Celia burst out laughing. The laughing reached a high hysterical pitch, until her voice cracked and Celia doubled in pain, crying out her dead sister's name.

"DAN?" NERO STOOD in Ranks' bedroom doorway. The bed was roughly made up. Danny was half-dressed, white shorts, open shirt, revealing a tattoo of a dagger over his well-toned left pec. Nero felt awkward, felt like he was intruding. He was also quite shocked. He had never seen tears from Ranks' eyes.

"Why did she do it? Why did she tell me to show like that when she knew she wasn't interested?"

For a second Nero thought he was talking about Meeta, then he understood. Nero took a deep breath and walked into the room. He sat down on the bed next to Ranks.

"Maybe she had a good reason."

"Like what? Forgetting I exist?" Danny ranted, letting his rage rise to a crescendo. "What was I to her? The product of a one-night stand? Heh? Then she just forced me outta her legs and left me in that madhouse." He hit the bed angrily. "Why did she do it? Theo was right. Always said I was Nuttin to her. Theo was right."

Nero felt like his heart was sprinting out of his chest. He knew something ominous was lurking within the crevices of Ranks' memories.

"Level with me, Dee. Come on."

Danny composed himself. Then after a while, he said.

"If you tell anybody I'll kill you."

"Looks like whatever it is, it's killing you. You know you can trust me Dan."

Ranks' eyes were swollen but the wariness in his bloodshot eyes soon eased as he began in a low breaking voice.

"Theo was jealous of me, Aunt Celia loved me you know, treated me like I was special and better than Theo." Danny stopped, stared into the distance. "You know what his speciality was? His fetish? Dressing in tight women's underclothes, tying me up and biting me all over. I begged, screamed but he just did it more. After that, it got to be his habit. And I used to think I deserved it because I mussta done something wrong. It took me a while to figure out my step-cousin was just a cold fuckin' freak." Danny sniffed. He was calming down. Feeling relieved that he was finally releasing his burden. But the story numbed Nero. He froze, not knowing what to say or do at first. He knew there was more to come.

"One night he took me to the park. I think he had some idea he was gonna share me with the other freaks he fucked at nights in there. I had started to scout for Jigsy and I sorta borrowed a revolver I found at Fluxy's yard." Danny suddenly started to laugh. "This was one time I couldn't wait for him to take his clothes off. The moon was beautiful that night, Nero, you shoulda seen it, clear, like a silver ball. It gave me a beautiful image of his face as I pointed the gun at him. I pointed it right between his legs. I let him beg and bawl for mercy like I did. But I was young, I only wanted to frighten him, to make him sorry for what he'd done. Then I pulled the trigger — *boom* — one paedo sucking the dust of the earth."

Nero cleared his throat. Danny was laughing, shaking his head.

"He deserved it," Nero said, "but you have to live with it." Nero had known what it was like to kill at seventeen and live with it, but to kill at thirteen and then to carry on with your life as if nothing happened?

"Live with it? I'm Ranks now. That scared yout' is done dead and buried with Theo Holder."

"Yeah, so about giving your mom a second chance?"

Danny looked at Nero.

"No." He said firmly.

"Phone your Aunt. Your mom deserves a second chance."

Ranks was purposely quiet.

"Danny?"

"I don't know. I'll think about it."

"And one more thing Danny, you still haven't beaten me wid Nascar." The frown on Danny's face wilted quickly and was replaced with a huge smile.

HOLDING A BOUQUET of flowers and chocolates, Easy arrived at Miss Small's apartment, to find Trench and the others packing her things into boxes. Trench didn't even look up.

"What's going on? Where's Veniesha?"

Trench lowered his eyes to the flowers Easy was holding.

"Where have you been today, Easy? I tried to call you on your mobile."

"I don't have to give an account to you. Miss Small made me co-director of this crew," Easy spat back.

"Miss Small's fucking dead." Trench dropped it down raw. Slide, Hatchet and Michigan looked on sorrowfully. Easy swallowed.

"What?"

"Yu mean to seh yu don't know?" Trench studied Easy carefully.

"No. My Gran had a stroke. She's in the Infirmary. Yu have to switch yu mobile phone off in hospital, radio interference and all that."

"Oh." Trench said hollowly. Then he said, his voice wavering slightly. "It's all over the news. I don't know what she was doing there or why, why she decided to flex on her own. Here, I bought a copy of the late edition of The Evening News. It's by the window." Easy walked over and snatched the newspaper up. He read the article quickly. It set out more of the usual sensationalism. An execution in cold blood by a lone gunman on a mountain bike. The cops had no leads as yet.

"Some higher beast phoned me on my mobile. They'll probably be going through her phone, getting numbers, so expect a call. It won't be long before they track her to here. That's why we're moving."

"Wait a minute. Wait a minute. Who said you could do this? Miss Small left me in charge-"

"You wasn't here. I couldn't find you."

"I can't believe — who coulda done that — it could only be Ranks' crew."

"Well it was your idea to clean out Ranks.

"She knew and accepted the risks." Easy said firmly. A tear fell from his eye. He wiped it away quickly. "Look, put back her things," Easy said.

"What?" Trench looked stunned.

"I said put it all back. For a start moving in the night's gonna draw unwanted attention to us, d'y'get me? We leave everything apart from personal papers and her computer. I'm in full command now and everyone does as I say."

MADNESS. STORM TOOK in the late evening news, shaking his head slowly. Small. Slaughtered in broad daylight, in a park full of kids playing. Not far from where Lee and his mother lived.

Storm put out the spliff he was smoking. The time was now. He was going to have the long overdue talk with Zukie. But walking into Zukie's room he found his brother crouched up against the wall. Shaking.

"Zukie?" Zukie's hands were over his ears. He hunched himself in tighter. Storm rushed down to Zukie's level. His brother had suffered another terrible nightmare. Storm put his arms around his brother. He swallowed. That's what you do before you tell a lie. "It's going to get better. I promise you." Storm had no right to make promises he couldn't keep. Ranks' voice was in his head. *"Whatever you have to tell him and when you tell him is your business. He knows I know."*
He couldn't tell him anything now, could he?

WORKING LATE, DI Colin Edwards examined the photograph of the boy. He had taken it from the house earlier. Looking around at the photographs on the walls there, he was adamant that he knew the face. He ran it through the computer criminal database. The photo recognition software matched the image almost 98.5% to a fourteen-year-old named Daniel Raymond Patterson who had been expelled from school for possession of a small amount of heroin. He'd been given a stern warning to keep away from drugs and his aggressive attitude had been noted.

Danny's name had cropped up in many police interviews of shootings and attacks since but statements had been withdrawn. It was rumoured that he was a fearsome gang leader, but he hadn't been charged with any offence so there was nothing substantial on him. He had a vicious and violent reputation. In one alleged incident he had thrown a gang rival off a multi-story car park roof in town. The kid survived with two broken legs. As usual the victim withdrew his statement and then left Manchester shortly after.

Edwards laughed aloud when he considered the connection between Miss Small and Ranks. Could it be? Surely not. Veniesha Brooks, the leader of the Dodge Crew, was the mother of an estranged son who was the leader of her arch rival gang The Worlders Posse. Edwards wondered where the hell this was leading.

"MISS SMALL!" EASY raised his can. The others followed suit, crashing their cans together.

"Yeah, to Miss Small. The best soldier in the world."

"For real." There was beer, music, and food aplenty because that's what she would have wanted. The Dodge Crew were having their own wake in honour of Miss Small. Late into the night and early morning they played her favourite reggae artist Don Campbell. They drank to her era, to her life and achievements. Blunts passing back and forth. The atmosphere was far from sullen at first. Hatchet soon became agitated, stoned, drunk, growling, swearing violently. Easy was aware of Trench drinking his can of beer but watching him surreptitiously. Easy drank slowly, wasn't going to allow himself to get drunk and let his tongue slip. Slide jumped up suddenly, fired by drink and cannabis.

"We're gonna get them-every friggin' one of them."

"Yeeeeaaaahhh! One by one, Danny's crew gwine drop like flies," Michigan joined in.

"Starting with Ranks." Easy said.

"Too fuckin' right." Slide uttered. Trench's eyes butterflied around the room, from one angry face to another, declaring vengeful intentions.

"First chance I get I'm gonna blast his heart out," Hatchet said.

"He in't got no heart, star." Michigan muttered.

"I'll out everyone associated with him. His mother, his sister, his yout's. Anyone."

"I'll cold blood him like he did Miss Small."

"Yes dread," Easy enthused, taking his gun out and laying it on the coffee table, right next to the bouquet of flowers he had bought Veniesha as a surprise. The others followed suit, declaring their arms ready for some serious war. "Everyone's ready fe action. What do you say Trench? When we gonna cold-blood that fucka?"

Trench gulped down his drink, took his coat and left, ignoring Easy calling after him.

NERO AND DANNY, surrounded by empty lager cans, CD games, and ashtrays filled with spliff ends, decided to call it a night. It was four fifteen in the morning. Secretly Nero had allowed Ranks to win at Nascar Racing leaving Danny elated, his trip back down memory lane forgotten. Ranks was none the wiser thinking he finally had one up on Nero. Nero yawned and stretched as Ranks switched off the huge TV. He was more than ready for bed.

"If you give me half an hour more I woulda lick yu," Nero said.

"Bold words, Nero but yu in't as good as you use to be. Bwai, yu standards are slippin'," Nero laughed. Danny's mobile rang. He picked it up, noticing he had voicemail. Danny answered his phone.

"Congratulations," the caller said emphatically. Ranks recognised the deep bass voice of Stukky. Ranks hadn't heard or seen from him since he got a bullet in the foot.

"For what Stukky?"

"Aahhh!!!! Ya bein' modest now, star."

"Congratulations for what?"

Nero was looking at Danny curiously.

"For eliminating the competition, star."

"Whah yu ah talk bout?"

"Miss Small. Yesterday."

Ranks frowned. He handed the phone to Nero.

"Talk to this fool-fool bwai because I don't understand what he's sayin'."

"What yu chattin' bout Stukky?" Nero asked, his eyes locking into Ranks".

"Word on the down-low is that Ranks total eclipsed Small

yesterday." Nero's initial reaction was to laugh.

"Ranks suppose' to out Small? Yesterday?"

Grasping what was being said Ranks beckoned the phone off Nero.

"Small's dead?" Ranks sat down slowly. He knew nobody would have eradicated Small without his say-so or knowledge.

"Word goin' down, Ranks is you and the crew dussed her. Simply." Nero was staring at Ranks. Suddenly part of yesterday's events made sense. The copter. The police. She must have been shot not far from where he was going to meet his mother. Maybe his mother had witnessed it all and couldn't honour the rendezvous. She hadn't abandoned him a second time after all. Danny's heart raced furiously, like a mouse on a wheel peddling away madly. "Ranks?"

"What?"

"Can I come back to the crew? I promise I won't let yu down again. Besides, after this, yu gonna need all the man you can get because the Dodge crew will be after ya blood."

TRENCH FELT AS if he'd lost an arm or a leg. He sat, alone, in the darkness of his basement flat in Whalley Range, rocking, wishing he could stay there forever.

He tried to warn her. He groaned inwardly as he recalled their last conversation.

"I think you should rethink Easy's position in the crew."

"What yu tryin' to say?"

"I in't sure. Something in't right."

"Easy brought a whole heap of money our way. I think everything is right, right now, wouldn't you say?"

She was dead. He was never going to hear her bubbly laughter again. She was never going to call them my boys and cook some beautiful good food for them, especially on a Sunday. Her place was theirs. They slept, ate and washed there, like a family. The Dodge boys were her boys and she didn't deserve to die this way.

The cop had said she was trying to make a call to him, maybe warn him about something. Did she die with his name on her lips, calling him? Why did she call him? Why not Easy?

A cold feeling filled his soul.

He swore he would get Miss Small's killer.

He would cut that fucka up and burn his body.

And he would smoke the ashes in a spliff.

PART TWO

Four of Diamonds

Then Allah sent a raven, who scratched the ground, to show him how to hide the shame of his brother. "Woe is me!" said he. "Was I not even able to be as this raven, and to hide the shame of my brother?" Then he became full of regrets
The Holy Quran 5.31

THE WEATHERMAN SAID it was going to be another scorching day, well into the nineties. Sneaking out of the bed, Storm left Zukie asleep, the light cover tossed aside with a floor-standing electric chrome-black fan blowing over him. After the traumatic week's events Storm figured Zukie badly needed to rest. He'd suffered another violent nightmare last night and so he'd slept close to Storm, eventually settling down. Trying hard not to wake Zukie, Storm put on a pair of khaki shorts, tee shirt and designer shades. He'd drive the convertible roadster today.

He drove to the street where Miss Small was killed; earlier he had bought a bouquet at the petrol station. There was less police activity but a mobile unit had been set up nearby. A sole policeman was guarding the spot. He allowed Storm to lay his bouquet near the rest. There were plenty, from family and friends. Storm felt his chest heave. The scene brought back disturbing memories. Taking his time Storm read each tribute. He saw they were some from her crew using their gang names initials. T for Trench S for Slide, R for Ranger, H for Hatchet, M for Michigan and EZ-L — a new member had been added to the crew: Easy-Love.

CELIA SUDDENLY REMEMBERED. A couple of years ago, Veniesha had given her a suitcase to look after. Struggling out of the bed Celia headed for the loft. Afraid of heights, she wasn't sure how the loft stairs would take her weight but she had to retrieve it. Maybe in there she would find the answer to this craziness. She still hadn't managed to contact Daniel since Veniesha's death yesterday. The police didn't believe her when she said she didn't know where her own nephew lived. But it was the truth. They only communicated every now and then, usually via his mobile and he changed that number often. He sent her letters and she replied via a friend's address. For some unknown reason Danny had chosen never to come back or associate himself with the home he had lived in. She didn't understand why. It hurt her, but after Theo died Danny changed. He soon started to get into trouble and by the time he was fourteen he was missing school and staying away regularly.

Huffing and puffing Celia made it to the loft. She sat down carefully, catching her breath. She really had to lose weight, especially if they were going to have more summers like this. From the corner of her eye, Celia spied the red suitcase. Reaching over she pulled it onto her lap. Veniesha had asked her to look after it but requested that she never opened it.

Celia's heart quickened as she found the key next to it. Blowing dust off the top, Celia opened both padlocks with the same key. The passports didn't puzzle her. They fit in with the police's story of her sister living out other lives. Yet it was strange to see Veniesha in various guises, wearing wigs. In some photos there was a visible loss of weight, so much that she looked gaunt. Next Celia went through the piles of documents. There was Danny's birth certificate. This made Celia weep.

After regaining her composure Celia went through the other documents. She found the deeds to various properties, here and in Jamaica. There were land registry documents. There was a bankbook with a hundred thousand pounds in it. Celia gasped. She found a collection of letters and photographs Celia had originally sent to her sister about little Danny. The next few items threw her completely. Newspaper cuttings, mainly about Miss Small's gang activities. Other cuttings about another gang leader, mentioned in trials, questioned by the police but released usually through lack of evidence and withdrawn statements. His name was Daniel Raymond Patterson. Veniesha had kept track of her little boy's other progress via newspaper cuttings. Like mother like son. Then Celia noticed it. An envelope bearing her name. Celia tore it open. It was a letter.

Dear Celia,

If you are reading this I'm probably gone. You now know what kinda life I lived and as a consequence of this I am dead. Don't cry for me. I enjoyed my life. The only regret I may have is not letting Daniel know me. Sorry for any pain I have caused you and the shame and disgrace I brought on the family. I know Poppa's heart broke because of me. Anyway, everything in this suitcase belongs to you. I have left the bankbook for Danny and the land titles in Jamaica for you. Sell them as you wish. God bless. Your sister, V.

Celia's head swum viciously. She needed air. Struggling downstairs, Celia found herself in the living room. She still hadn't opened her curtains out of respect for her dead sister but the room needed light and air. Celia drew back the curtains. She was stunned to see two unmarked police cars parked outside her home. What were they trying to do to her? Did they think she had something to do with her sister's killing? Did they think she was in partnership with her? Or maybe they worked as a family team like a Yardie Mafia. She was a respectable teacher for God's sake! Fuming, still dressed in her house-robe, Celia sprinted towards the front door. It took four of her neighbours to pull her off the first police car, but not until she had poured all her anger and distress into the vehicle, kicking the bodywork.

"HI. WHAT ARE you doing here?" Jasmine had just returned from dropping Lee at school. Storm caught her as she opened the front gate. She looked surprised when she turned around and saw him waiting.

"Lee's at school," she said.

He took off his shades, looked at her directly.

"I know. I, er, came to see you." Storm wanted to say "I need to see you" instead but he wasn't quite sure how she would take it. He wasn't even sure if he should be here; after all she had a new man and she was expecting his baby and things.

"Forget it. This was a mistake. I'll go."

She grabbed his arm as he tried to turn.

"No wait. It's OK Cliff. I know you by now. I know something's troubling you."

"EVERYTHING'S FALLING APART Jasmine," Storm said slowly, hanging his head. They were seated on the patio, drinking coffee and tea. Early morning birds sang as if they had no care in the world. Storm wished he was like one of them. Singer Macy Gray's unique voice poured softly through the speakers in the living room. It was early.

The recent shootings and death had brought back bad memories for both of them.

"I know," Jasmine said quietly, turning a finger around a corkscrew curl. "I never wanted it this way," she said shaking her head lightly, a pained look etched upon her beautiful features. "But it happened. You have to take the shit life throws at you."

"Shit? You got the best of it Jazzy, you got a new life, a new man, a little one on the way."

"We can still be friends."

Storm laughed.

"You're blessed with good friends, Jasmine. What do you need me for?" Jasmine was silent, drinking her tea.

Finally she said. "You're right. Besides I couldn't stay friends with somebody I'm still in love with."

Storm almost choked on the coffee. It spurted out of his mouth. Wiping his mouth with the back of his hand he gawped at her. Smiling she stared back at him.

"I've never stopped loving you but I couldn't go back to looking over my shoulder, to turning a blind eye to your dealing and the shootings."

"But I showed you I had changed. I put that all behind me," Storm said calmly.

"Only after you nearly lost Zukie." Storm squinted at the sun. His armpits scorched as if they were on fire. If only she knew. Storm shook his head. It was still going on. He was just lucky that Ranks hadn't decided to eradicate Zukie for pulling a gun on him. Thank God he'd had the understanding to know Zukie had been mentally unstable. Anyway, that was losing importance beside what Jasmine had just said.

"But tell me. If you still love me what are you doing with Carlton?" Jasmine smiled.

"You've been picking Lee up for weeks. When was the last time you actually saw Carlton?"

"But you're pregnant?"

Jasmine smiled. Her brown eyes twinkled. "I said that to see your reaction. And from your reaction I concluded you had the same feelings I have for you."

Storm felt the emotion welling up in his gut. He had waited five years for her to forgive him and to say she loved him.

"I realised that you've really turned your back on the bad life. I'm prepared to give you the second chance you deserve."

Was he really hearing these words? "I'll take you back-but if I ever see you with a gun or even get a sniff of you dealing or moving in a gang, we're finished for life."

"TEE, YOU KNOW what my Grandma always says?" Easy asked, deliberately keeping Teeko waiting before giving his answer. "Fool no go ah market bad ways don't sell." Teeko was slouched in the new leather sofa, smoking a spliff leisurely. "Ranks did us all a big, big favour, star, by dussing Small."

Teeko grinned, rubbing his smooth head. He passed the spliff to Kurtis who took it eagerly. "I'm in control now. The crew's mine. I've finally got it. A full crew." Teeko laughed. The sun was streaming through the blinds, highlighting the mess in the living room. Clothes were strewn everywhere. Easy wasn't sure if they were dirty, clean or just for ironing. All he knew was the place was a mess. Tyrone's toys covered the floor. The sink was full of unwashed dishes. Chris hadn't even got up yet.

"Chris!" Easy yelled, towards the living room door. "Get the place clean up." Turning towards Teeko, Easy muttered. "I don't think she knows what a Hoover's for." Teeko laughed. "Chris! Get up I said. Get this shit cleaned up."

A few seconds later Chris exploded into the living room, wearing only a short vest and knickers, holding Tyrone who was crying, against her hip. Teeko began to build another spliff. Kurtis's wide eyes were on Christine's slender legs.

"Look what you done with yer shoutin'. You fucking woke him," she screamed at Easy, thrusting Tyrone into Easy's hands. Easy was disgusted.

"Wha' — wha' yu ah do? He's wet through."

"You look after him then." With that Chris headed towards the kitchen. Easy realised he was quickly losing respect in front of his brother, partner and best mate Teeko. If he was the new leader of the Dodge he needed credibility. Poor Tyrone was screaming his little head off. Placing the baby on the settee Easy stormed off after Chris. The kitchen was in a worse state than he first thought, with a pungent smell coming from the overfull bin and the sink just as full. She was smoking a cigarette.

"What are you dealin' wid? Look at the place how it stay dirty and nasty. What do you do all day?"

"You wouldn't know seeing as you're never here." Chris crossed her arms, but put her face directly in his.

"I don't need to be here to know you're lazy. All you do is smoke and drink and neglect Tyrone."

Something inside Chris snapped. How dare he criticize her mothering skills? Turning quickly, she slapped his face hard. He retaliated quickly, slapping her back hard. She turned and grabbed a dirty plate from the sink. Easy knew what was coming and ducked. The plate crashed against the wall.

"Here, see the dishes clean now," Chris taunted as she threw another and another. Each time Easy ducked until there were no more. In the living room Teeko and Kurtis exchanged uneasy glances.

"Chris hold it down before you make me do something I don't want to do." He grabbed her by the wrists and slapped her again. Screaming she lunged at him, fists flying wildly. She bit, screamed and kicked. Easy fought back, slapping her firmly.

Running into the kitchen, Teeko intervened, pulling Chris off Easy. She continued to spit, kick and swear. Teeko carried her towards the bedroom. Kicking the door open he flung her unto the bed. The baby had not stopped crying. Breathlessly Teeko slammed the door shut and Easy turned the key in the lock. His mouth bleeding, his face scratched.

"Fuckin' stay in there until yu cool down. Den when yu cool down yu better clean up the place. I'm taking Ty to your mum's. Yu in't fit to be his mother. Yu in't fit to be anyone's mother!"

STORM FELT ELATED now that he and Jasmine were reunited. He felt even better when he got back to the shop and saw Zukie laughing and joking with Rastaman Beppo Dread, looking refreshed after his morning's sleep. Gone was that anguished tortured expression. He was merry and relaxed, humming a rhydim Beppo was trying to capture for one of his tracks in the recording studio for later. Zukie looked up as Storm entered the shop, giving his brother a brief smile. Storm walked up to the counter.

"W'happen blood?"

"Iree." Zukie said, holding his fist for his brother to touch. "I'm going up to Leeds later." Storm frowned. He had forgotten all about the Mr Vegas show in Leeds. It looked like Zukie was taking Paradise instead of Taniesha as he had originally planned weeks ago. Taniesha had given in her notice and simply disappeared, hurt by Zukie. Storm suddenly felt nervous. After the very recent shootings he didn't think going to Leeds was a wise move. He didn't want Zukie caught up in anything like that again. If there was anything Storm had learned it was that after the shooting of a gang leader bloody retribution usually followed. Swiftly.

"I'll come with you."

Zukie snapped.

"No thanks. Look what happened the last time you offered me your help."

"Zukie I'm sorry. I didn't realise you were so distressed. I should never give yu— I was going to Leeds myself anyway."

"Go where you like, only not near or with me."

Sighing, Storm raised both hands in mock surrender, avoiding Beppo's eyes. Deep down he was hurt.

"I hear what you're saying, bro'. Just, just stay safe."

HOLDING HIS BREATH Trench pressed the buzzer to the record shop and studio. They let him in when he said he was a musician from out of town who wanted to book the studio for a recording session. Once he was in, Storm recognised him straightaway. There was no doubt about that. Storm was standing near the counter and turned around as Trench entered the shop casually. His expression was one of shock, then distrust, which eased into repugnance as he saw Dodge bwai Trench. His brother, who stood a head smaller, noticed that Storm was staring and also observed Trench suspiciously.

"You've got the wrong shop, Dodge bwai. I don't have no gangsta boys in here," Storm uttered, screwing his eyes coldly at Trench.

Clearing his throat Trench said. "I haven't come for no trouble. I wanted to talk to you about something. Something that might concern you." He'd heard so much about Storm and respected and admired the former Grange gang leader.

Storm's expression was one of sheer hatred. "Me? Nah! You in't got nuttin to talk about wid me that concerns me."

Trench understood. Naturally Storm was distrustful of his intentions. Trench's gang leader, Miss Small had been shot dead and now one of her main men was standing in his shop. Why?

"Well, if you can't help me I need to talk to Bluebwai."

Storm stared at him with cold dark eyes. Kissing his teeth, he took a step towards Trench.

"Get outta my shop."

"It's a matter of life and death, Storm, please. If you don't help me, my blood might be on your hands. I need to talk to Blue about Easy."

Storm stared at him again.

"What about Easy?"

"I think, I think he outted Miss Small."

"What's that got to do with me and Blue?"

"Fluxy?"

Frowning, Storm looked at Zukie. Zukie was looking at him that way again.

"OK. Take off your coat." The day was hot. Trench was wearing a thick black overcoat, jeans and black boots.

"Why? I in't tooled up."

"And I ain't taking no chances."

"Lose the coat then come follow me into the back. Zukie, you hold all calls and don't let nobody else into the shop."

Storm watched Trench with mounting irritation, as he walked around the office blasé, looking at the framed photographs of Storm accompanied by prestigious reggae and MC celebrities. Each one held him affectionately or touched fists with him, while he smiled proudly. "Say what yu come fe seh. I'm busy you know. I got things to do, contracts to sign."

"People to see." Trench added mockingly. He turned and looked at Storm with tired eyes. "Not so long ago the people who you were dealin' wid was people like me — like yuself. The dealin' yu did had nuttin to do with music deals."

Storm felt a hot tide rising within him but he forced himself to stay cool.

"Would you like to sit down, Trench, before you drop down?"

Trench took up the invitation, sitting down, keeping his eyes on Storm.

"Did you kill Fluxy?"

Storm frowned slightly. "No. Fluxy and me were cool. He had me and no worries."

"You killed Jigsy, though?"

Storm looked towards the door quickly. Getting up, he walked over, opened it to make sure there was nobody outside listening. He walked back over to Trench, threw him a cigarette and lit one for himself.

"Yes. He was on my case night and day cos he thought I blew his brother. But if it was only me he was after that was fine. Instead he came after my family and I wasn't standing for that."

"I understand."

"I know all about your crew hijackin' Ranks so I in't surprised to hear he took Small's life for it."

"How would Danny Ranks know Miss Small's every move? No one knew where she was going yesterday. There were things she kept to herself. Private. Lately there was only one person who got really close to her."

"Easy?"

Trench nodded. He seemed to shiver.

"You saying Easy's finger was on the trigger?"

"It in't so ridiculous is it?"

"No," Storm agreed, folding his arms and listening. After all if the prize was a crew complete with arms and reputation Storm could see

154

the reason.

"And it in't ridiculous to consider that maybe, maybe Easy was the only person to know where Fluxy was gonna be and he outted him too. Blue could confirm that."

"Blue moved to London doing good for himself Trench, and he don't like to talk about the past. But either way it don't matter to me now. I'm getting on with my life."

Trench shook his head slowly. He rose to his feet, feeling the stiffness in his joints.

"You in't taking me seriously. This guy might have messed up your life and family and you taking it lightly."

"See you around Trench," Storm was annoyed. This was the second person who wanted him to exact vengeance on Easy for their own personal vindications. Trench smiled but his smile was sorrowful.

"You won't see me again," Trench said dolefully. "You're looking at a dead man. Then you'll know. That's the only way you're gonna know."

DANNY DIDN'T KNOW he was dreaming. He was dozing, feeling the warmth of the sun on his young body. Then Danny felt a cold shadow pass over him, waking him. Stirring lightly, he saw them circling in the sky. Hundreds and hundreds of eagles. Then they all turned and started to descend on him, savaging him. Cursing and screaming hysterically, he tried vainly to fend them off. They started to pick at his face and limbs, making a God-awful noise. Danny woke up totally wet with sweat and fighting himself. Ranks lay back down; his heart thumping like a little boxer was in his chest, punching away. He interpreted the dream. Something bad was happening. It was threatening the very core of his existence.

Danny knew he had to do two things. One was to get it across to the Dodge and all other breezes that he had nothing to do with Small's death and the other was to phone Aunt Celia, who had left a couple of voicemail messages. He wasn't sad that Small was dead. It meant less competition. If he had wanted her dead he woulda sought her out years ago, but he had no real reason to. Until her posse rolled his crew.

Nothing was gonna stop him from seeing Mr Vegas tonight in Leeds. Why should it? He had nothing to hide.

A cool draught blew from an open window. He was listening to garage music on a low level, lying on his back. As much as he didn't want to, he had to return Celia's call out of respect. The woman had raised him.

She answered on the third ring. Ranks knew there was something wrong. Normally her voice was joyous at hearing from him. This time it sounded low, nervous.

"Oh Daniel. I been trying to call you since yesterday."

"Sorry. I bin busy," Ranks lied. He turned over on his stomach and retrieved the lighted spliff from the ashtray. He took a deep, long drag. Celia started to cry. Ranks sat up quickly.

"Aunt Celia. What's wrong? What is it?"

"I can't talk to you over the phone."

"Why not?"

"It's too dangerous." Ranks' brain began to tingle. His mouth was suddenly dry. Dangerous? What the fuck was she talking about? He didn't like the sound of this one bit.

"Auntie, I'm coming round right now."

Her voice was full of panic.

"No Dan. Don't. The house is being watched by the police."

Ranks was stunned. It looked like five-o had linked him up through his aunt and were trying to bust him for drugs.

"Auntie, I don't get it. Why are the police watching your yard?"

More bawling. Uncontrolled, feverish then composed.

"I can't say Dan. Remember that place I use to take you every Sunday morning?"

"Yeah."

"Meet me there."

"I'll be there in fifteen minutes, Auntie. If you don't see me, wait I'll be there. And another thing, Auntie, don't let the police follow you there. Try to lose them."

EASY WAS AT the private nursing home where he had placed Grandma, talking to and reading to her. He told her all about how well Kurtis was doing now that he was with him. He spent a total of two hours with her, admired by the nursing staff who thought it was terrific, the way he attended to her with loving care and dedication. Already, she seemed to be improving.

FOR THE LAST ten minutes an unmarked police car had been trailing Celia Holder's maroon Rover GTI. It pulled in the Hulme supermarket car park behind her as she drew up and parked. She stepped out of her car and walked into the superstore, glancing in a nearby jeep's wing mirror. It was as she thought: one of them stayed in the car while the other followed her into the crowded superstore.

Humming to herself, Celia took a shopping trolley and moved around quickly inside the huge store. From the corner of her eye she could see the plain clothes cop straining to keep up with her. But people were in his way, elderly people and unruly kids and perhaps being a man not used to large superstores, he was quickly becoming disorientated. Celia switched between aisles speedily. This was the place to lose anybody on a hectic Saturday afternoon. She had been let off with a warning after the police vehicle-battering incident They understood she was under stress, but they had refused to withdraw the undercover operation. She knew that they were watching the house not for her protection, but to lay in wait for Daniel. Celia moved faster. She had a feeling that the plain-clothes policeman would eventually suss out her plan and then wait for her at the exit/entrance. Dumping the trolley Celia exited the store, without looking over her shoulder. Immediately beyond the doors was a long queue of black taxis waited. Celia rapidly entered the first one.

"The Odeon, town," she said.

As the taxi drove out of the huge car park, Celia couldn't help laughing as she saw the plain clothes cop come out of the store, raising his hands to his colleague in the car. They had lost her. It was the first time Celia had laughed in days. The taxi driver's eyes watched her in the rear view mirror curiously.

Celia stopped laughing.

She wondered how she was going to tell the bad news to Veniesha's son.

"FIVE MINUTES," RANKS said to Mentian. Nero was visiting his woman in Leeds and wasn't accompanying Danny. Ranks didn't mind. Mentian was as good as Nero when it came to body guarding. Mentian nodded from behind his blue wrap shades. The sun was going down, the wind building up.

Ranks crossed over busy Oxford Road, answering yet another mobile phone call from yet another person convinced that he had outed Small yesterday. He was getting tired of people giving him credit for something he didn't do. Nearby a MetroLink tram scuttled past, horn blowing, warning folks away from the tracks. Putting his phone away, Ranks saw her. Aunt Celia was waiting anxiously outside the Odeon on the other side of the road wearing a long flared skirt, a v-neck short sleeved blue top and white plimsolls. Wringing her hands nervously, she looked around suspiciously. Danny crossed straight into her arms. She held him tightly, gasping.

"Oh Daniel. My baby. Thank God. Thank God."

"Auntie what's wrong?"

Pulling back, Celia looked into her nephew's hazel eyes. She wiped her tears away quickly. Danny stared at her curiously.

"You were supposed to meet your mother yesterday,"

Ranks frowned.

"Yeah? She didn't show, tho'. So I left."

"She did. She was waiting for you by the park."

Ranks tried to hide his agitation.

"I waited there. She didn't show. Did she tell you why?"

"She's dead, Daniel."

Ranks was confused.

"What do you mean, she's dead? How can she be — when did she die?"

"She died waiting to meet you outside the park." She paused, caught her breath. "Haven't you seen it on the news Daniel? The woman shot yesterday, that was your mother."

Danny's breath seemed to stop in his body. His head seemed to swell to twice its normal size. His ears thumped a frenzied pulse and the blood in his veins seemed to thicken. The world shrunk around him. People seemed to fade into the distance.

"The woman shot yesterday — that was your mother". It didn't make any sense. He knew that the woman who was shot outside the park yesterday, apparently just yards from him, was Miss Small. They never said who she was on the TV or radio.

No. Somebody was lying. She couldn't possibly be his mother.

Then Danny took a slow, long look at Aunt Celia. She was a large, robust woman. So was Miss Small, hence her ironic street name.

"She died waiting to meet you outside the park."

"Haven't you seen it on the news Daniel?"

"The woman shot yesterday, that was your mother."

CHRIS TIDIED UP. She was sorry. She had to learn to control her rage. She would make it up to Easy. She looked proudly at the table she had prepared. A vase of flowers. Candles. Dinner plates and cutlery set for two. Teeko was away, gone down to London to see Shanieka and the twins. As far as she knew they weren't expecting Kurtis. It was going to be only her and Easy. Chris poured wine into the two glasses. Champagne for later. R&B music played in the background. Chris was happy, confident that Easy would forgive her for her temper tantrum. Her body was scented, her hair had been done and she was wearing a beautiful shiny silver dress that showed off her petite figure. She was ready and waiting. The food was cooking on a low setting.

Chris phoned Easy. His phone rang but he didn't answer. She left him a voicemail message telling him she had a wonderful surprise for him and she was expecting him around eight. An hour and fifteen ignored calls later, Chris was still waiting.

Chris felt that boiling rage again, a red mist. The next thing she knew, everything on the table was flying. The plates hit the floor; the wine bottle smashed and spilt its contents over the new kitchen tiles. Her feet hardly touched the floor as she ran screaming like a warrior into the bedroom, tearing open the closet doors. Designer suits, trousers, jeans, shirts. Taking her nail scissors from the dressing table Chris began cutting away. But after she had finished she still didn't feel content. She headed for his CD collection.

One by one, she took out his music. She jumped repeatedly on his favourite reggae discs, screwing her heels into them. Still not satisfied, she decided she needed to know. She needed to be sure. Chris walked back into the bedroom. She took up his suits, his jeans, or what was left of them. Her hands dug deep into his pockets. She found various bits of paper, cards. She examined them carefully, like she'd checked the text messages on his mobile. Always from the same person, Vee, or Veniesha. There were also fragments of messages that seem to be declarations of love, but not for Christine.

I miss you. I love you. To my babes, Veniesha xxxx.

DI COLIN EDWARDS looked curiously at the black balaclava and black clothing worn by Veniesha Brooks' assassin. The police found it clumsily concealed behind some overgrown bushes in the huge park. But the most stirring find for the Serious Crime Division was the mountain bike, covered by undergrowth and broken branches. The bike was fairly old, yet it had been painted black recently. It could have been anybody's bike, and a search for a postcode stamped on the underside of the carriage came up with nothing. It was dusted for prints but it had been thoroughly polished by the killer. So the only thing the police had to go on was killer's dark clothing.

Edwards was in his office briefing his colleague, DC Steve Davidson, a white blonde haired guy, in his late twenties, originally from B division. A call came through from Forensics.

"I think you're going to find this interesting, Colin," said Monica Watson, head of Forensics.

"What?" Edwards was eager to know. Davidson's aquatic blue eyes observed him hungrily, awaiting the news.

"Come down and I'll show you." Putting his phone down, Edwards nodded at Davidson. Grabbing their jackets they left to go across town.

EDWARDS KNOCKED ON the office door briskly but didn't wait for a reply. Monica, an attractive black woman in her early thirties with cropped hair, looked up as he walked in. She was sat her desk writing up her report on a notebook computer. Davidson sat down next to her. It was pretty clear that he fancied his chances with her. Edwards smiled wryly.

"Come on Monica, let us in on your findings."

"You don't like beating around the bush do you?" Monica teased, looking sideways at Davidson. "Unlike some people." Davidson's face coloured slightly.

"No I like to get straight to the point." Davidson cleared his throat, used to the little joke they shared between the three of them.

Monica looked Edwards straight in the eye.

"Veniesha Brooks' probable killer was European, possibly white."

"What?" Edwards was completely blown away. He was expecting her to identify her killer as black, probably male. "Hair samples?"

Monica nodded, walking over to a file and retrieving it. Davidson and Edwards huddled closer to her. Monica presented a plastic bag showing a few samples of short dark hair.

Edwards hugged his chest while he thought. This directly ruled out Danny Patterson and Easy-Love Brown, although both might have a motive to kill her. And Easy? Edwards already knew why Easy could have gone after his previous gang-leader. Edwards suspected Miss Small and her crew of beating Easy when he came out of prison. If Easy was going to get anybody first, it would be her and he would do it with stealth, planning and cunning. Edwards didn't rule out that either gang might have ordered the hit. He didn't know Danny Patterson well, but he had read statements stating that Danny Patterson usually did his own dirty work, unlike Easy. Edwards was placing his bet on Easy. He wasn't sure, but it wouldn't take him long to find out.

"WHAT WAS THAT little meeting about? You and the scruff from the hood?" Zukie demanded, closing the door behind him gently, and flicking a long dreadlock out of his face. It looked as if he had caught Storm off guard. Storm jumped slightly, putting the phone in his hand down. "And who is that yu talking to?"

Storm sighed. He could barely look his brother in the eye. His brother whom he wanted to protect so much from the truth.

"I was trying to phone Blue but his mobile must be off."

"About what? About what that guy before was talkin' about?" Storm got up and walked around his desk. He looked through the side window, his back to Zukie.

"Trench? Trench doesn't know what he's talking about. Talking crap. Ah whole heap of nonsense."

"Didn't look that way to me. He looked shit-scared."

Storm turned around and looked at Zukie.

RANKS STARED, UNSEEING, from the window of the fast food restaurant. Mentian sat opposite, watching the large woman with his coal-black irises. Celia sat in front of a huge pile of burgers and fries that were now stone cold. They had been sitting this way for ten whole minutes, silent. Mentian didn't know what to say or what to do, apart from eating his quarter pounder and fries. All he knew was that time was moving on, and Leeds was waiting.

Ranks looked ill, his face taut. He wouldn't talk, wouldn't say what the matter was and Mentian knew the younger boy well enough to know something was bugging him deeply. Every now and then Ranks shook his head slowly as if in denial. Sometimes he would laugh, then become serious again. Mentian wasn't sure how much of this he could stand. The large woman broke the mood.

"Dan." She touched Ranks' arm. He pulled away slightly. She looked offended. Mentian felt embarrassed. What the hell was going on? Mentian needed a cigarette. They had important things to be getting on with, not sitting playing Simple Simon says sit in MacDonald's and be quiet for half an hour.

"Dan, promise me that you will stop doing what it is you're doing. Don't go the same way as your mother."

Swallowing, Ranks turned and looked at her. Celia's eyes were wide. Ranks rose to his feet, got out his mobile and dialled.

"Nero, be with me in two hours. Chapletown, Club Planetarium." Snapping his phone shut, Ranks replaced it into his back pocket.

Mentian was puzzled. Did Nero know what the fuck was going on? Mentian looked at Celia, who was growing more distressed, running her chubby hand through her processed hair.

Danny lit a cigarette, avoiding Mentian's inquisitive eyes. Then Ranks stared at Mentian, taking in the cool dark brown colouring of his number two minder, a man who swore to protect him, die for him even.

"Mentian, I learnt today the answer to one of the mysteries of my life and that was who my mother was. And Mentian I want you to meet Miss Small's sister, my Aunt, Aunt Celia. Miss Small had a son called Danny, a son she gave to her sister to bring up. Me."

"Whah?"

"Auntie, this is one of my top, bona fide men. Mentian."

"You're Small's son?" Ranks nodded. Mentian felt as if someone had kicked him in the groin. He knew Ranks never knew his mother. At one stage Ranks declared war on all women, or bitches, as he called them. Nobody had really known Miss Small. Only the Dodge Crew knew her. She kept herself away from the public eye. Occasionally they caught glimpses of her, but she was one hard woman to track down. Which was just as well because if they had, Ranks himself could have eliminated her from the programme. His own mother. Mentian shook his head slowly. No wonder Ranks looked like he had just been sick.

Danny stared down at his aunt whose eyes were round and pleading. Bending down, he kissed her forehead. She held on to his hand.

"Come and say goodbye to her."

Ranks looked up towards the restaurant's ceiling, then away into the distance.

"I love and respect you for raisin' me like your own Aunt Celia. But don't ask me to come to her funeral."

"Dan, please. I'm begging you. Do what is right and proper."

"For her? No," Ranks said solemnly shaking his head, walking towards the restaurant's door. "No way."

"Do it for me."

Ranks said nothing. He kept walking towards the exit, followed by Mentian.

CHRIS SHOULD KNOW him better than that by now. When he was on a mission he didn't mix business with pleasure. Kissing his teeth frustratingly, Easy switched off his new phone. He had replaced it because he didn't want the police tracing his number through Miss Small's phone. He had advised the others to do the same.

Easy thought about Miss Small. He couldn't go to her funeral, scheduled for a few days time, because he knew the cops would be there mingling with the mourners in a bid to tag the gang. Easy was having none of that shit. Besides, he had privately said his goodbye to Miss Small the day he initiated the plan to rob Danny. As Grandma says, there's more than one way of killing a hen than slitting its throat.

It was growing dark. They were seated in the car, Hatchet and his younger brother Michigan, Slide, and Easy. Ranger stayed back because his woman was having a baby. There was no Trench. Teeko was in London with Shanieka.

The car's interior was thick with the smell of crack and cannabis smoke. Michigan was at the wheel, driving the car effortlessly and nodding his head in time to the hypnotic beat that rumbled through the phat speakers like an earthquake. The other two sat silently, smoking pipes, hyping themselves up for any showdown with the Worlders crew. Easy didn't know where Kurtis was. He had told him to stay at home; he didn't want Kurtis involved if anything kicked off.

Easy looked at the dark motorway ahead.

A sign in the distance read: North. Leeds 25 miles.

In half an hour or so Danny Ranks would know who was the king of the fucking Arena.

"LOOK KURTIS, I in't interested in yu granny, arright? Yu granny in't livin' in my house rent-free or smoking my rocks for nuttin. I couldn't care less if yu granny was a spotted-green and red Martian from outta space," Ranks shouted, still reeling from shock about the discovery earlier that Small was his mother. Still, he wasn't going to let it sour his mood. He was going to Leeds, regardless. He put on a blue silk shirt, smoothing cream over his face. He took in his lean features. Kurtis had just told him that Easy had spent yesterday visiting their grandma. Kurtis beside him was looking rough again. His hair was turning into those raggedy twists, his clothes looked a bit baggy and he was sniffing repeatedly like he had a cold.

"Yeah. Yeah. Yeah. Right. I need some smokes Danny, need some rock," Kurtis said in a monotonous tone. Ranks stared coldly at Kurtis. Obviously, Kurtis wasn't going to talk until he had his things. Ranks pulled out a drawer and gave Kurtis a bag. Kurtis tore the bag open.

"He's ambushing you tonight for Small." Danny laughed, but his heart bumped painfully at the mention of her name. "He's also going to get Kadeem to work only with him and block you out." This almost blew Ranks sideways.

"What?"

"And he's planning to tax all the businesses on Prinney Road, including Storm's."

"OK Kurtis. Tonight you get a bonus. I got some more rock in that drawer. Enjoy yourself and I will see you later. And by the way, the bathroom is the room on right. In there you'll find soap, a razor, aftershave do y'get me star? You got a nice face Kurtis an' ting, get the women bawling over you face boy, sein?"

Kurtis didn't even reply. He was too busy sucking unto his pipe, his cheeks hollow, his nostrils smoking like a dragon's. Danny shook his head slowly, and left the room, leaving Kurtis alone.

Outside they loaded up the seven-seater. A couple of handguns, rope, not to mention booze, weed and a selection of CD's and tapes to play on the way down. Mentian, Fila, Pipes, Stukky and Ranks climbed into the vehicle. They were to meet Nero in Leeds, where he had been staying at his woman's.

If it was a war Easy-Love wanted he was going to get it.

ZUKIE KNEW HE had done the right thing as he escorted Paradise into the Planetarium Nightclub. Straightaway he recognised faces he hadn't seen for years, people he knew on the music and sound system circuit when he used to play with Chico and Hair Oil.

Naturally, people were glad to see him, touching him and saying hello. His broken arm still felt strange, heavy and cumbersome in the plaster, but at least it was slingless and loose. Zukie smiled confidently, feeling proud to be with Paradise and happy that he had made a decision without his brother's involvement.

The music was kicking. Resnick Hi-Fi, Leeds' number one Sound System, was positively mashing up the place with cut after cut. Plantain, Resnick's mixer even invited Zukie to guest mix. Smiling, Zukie declined modestly, holding Paradise's hand. She looked too beautiful tonight to leave alone. Zukie was aware of the attention she was getting. He wasn't going to let her go.

EASY WAITED, WATCHING people arrive through the door, looking for Ranks and his crew. It was late, but he knew Ranks would arrive. Vegas was the hottest Jamaican artist at the moment, and if you missed a live performance by him you hadn't lived. Currently he was doing a tour across the UK and it was rumoured that he was to do a repeat performance with Beenie Man. Easy stood with his crew opposite the door. There was no sign of Ranks.

But as Grandma says, *patient man ride donkey*.

IN HIS MIND Easy heard Grandma whisper, chicken merry, hawk deh near. He laughed to himself as Ranks and his crew positioned themselves at a table near the sound system. Mentian sat to the right of him, Nero to the left. A strategic manoeuvre. A small crowd surrounded him which included Storm's brother, his woman Paradise and a heavily pregnant girl. Paradise seemed to be enjoying the music. Her pretty boyfriend was drinking from a bottle. It wasn't long before his eyes met Ranks'. Easy watched the strange interplay between Danny and Zukie. Watched with interest as the two stared at each other blatantly. Easy was annoyed. Why wasn't Ranks concentrating on him? What was this thing between Ranks and Storm's brother? Easy suddenly noticed the arrival of two Leeds bad boy crews, Spangler and Teddington.

Easy had heard much about them. Normally they were in opposition, but had recently agreed a truce. Spangler was directly from Chapletown and their leader was a rough-looking yout' of twenty-one known as Pigeon Eye. The other leader was called Playboy; hair bleached blonde, expensive clothes hanging loosely, he looked like the R&B singer Sisqo. Both crews walked in boldly. Easy felt his heart skip a beat as he realised that they were heading straight towards Ranks. Playboy winked at Danny. Ranks stood up and touched fists with both Pigeon Eye and Playboy. Turning around they faced Easy.

Dem come yah fe drink milk, dem nuh come yah fe count cow.

Easy's throat suddenly felt dry. Mentally he counted the number of men across the room. There were twenty-three men to his three. Danny was more than prepared. Someone had tipped him off. There was no contest.

Danny knew that too.

Sitting down slowly, he pointed his two fingers at Easy and shot him with an imaginary gun. Easy saw him form the word boom, laugh, and then blow his smoking gun. Easy stared him out. It wasn't long before Danny's eyes travelled back over to Zukie. Zukie looked across at Easy, stared, then looked back over at Ranks. In that second Easy knew that Zukie knew who he was. There was no mistaking it. His eyes burned with anger. Easy looked back at Ranks. The bold mothafucka was grinning, the way you do when your favourite dish is on the table and you're mighty hungry. OK, Easy thought to himself, OK Ranks.

De more yu look, de less yu will see.

KURTIS STIRRED LIGHTLY. The buzz had gone. He smelt himself. Suddenly Ranks' voice entered his head.

"By the way the bathroom is the room on right. In there you'll find soap, a razor, aftershave do y'get me star? You got a nice face Kurtis an' ting, get the women bawling over you face boy, seen?"

Kurtis got up. He was on the floor where he had fallen in a drugged heap. Looking down at himself he saw his dirty ripped jeans. How did he get like this? Kurtis walked into the bathroom and stared hard in the tiled bathroom mirror. His reflection scared him. His face was bearded, his hair uncombed. His eyes looked on wildly. What was happening to him? What had happened to the handsome Kurtis he used to know?

Wearily Kurtis walked into his bedroom. Reaching under the bed he retrieved his box of clothing and make up. Kurtis showered, soaping his lean body frenziedly. He cleaned and cut his nails, brushed his teeth, sprayed himself then shaved his face and hair. After he put lipstick on, a beautiful glossy black wig and his favourite long red dress. Kurtis looked hard at himself. At least Danny cared enough to tell him to look after himself. Danny still thought he was attractive didn't he?

Attractive enough for girls to want him.

Yeah, the time was now.

Give up the shit, get his life on the right track.

"WE'RE BUBBLING, BUBBLING, bubbling, we're bubbling like this — make some noise!" Whistles screamed loudly but unusually, there was a large hole on the dance floor of Club Planetarium. People stuck to the outside, to the walls watching, hanging back. It wasn't hard to see why. The Worlders Crew had just walked in and everyone who knew what bad bwai looked like knew that the place was crawling with them tonight.

Ranks knew what Easy was doing as Easy stood on the opposite side with his crew the Dodge, no longer Small's crew, his mother's crew. Easy watched him skinning up leisurely. Ranks watched Easy sneer then whisper in Slide's ear.

Slide glared at Ranks coldly.

STORM LOADED THE boot of his car, checking his watch. By now the Vegas dance would be well under way. Trouble was going to be there tonight. Storm could feel it.

About to drive off, he remembered the promise he had made to Jasmine. Cursing, Storm cut the engine and got out of his car. Opening the boot and reaching under its carpet he out took the gun from where it lay next to the spare wheel. Digging a hole in the front garden with his bare hands he buried it.

He got back into his car and sighed. Felt exposed. But he had promised Jasmine, hadn't he?

RAIN BATTERED THE car, hard, like spiked rods. The slip road leading off the M62 motorway *was* had lights but because of the vicious onslaught of rain Storm could barely make out the red tail lights of the car way ahead of him, shining like two unwavering devil eyes. Storm's stomach churned. It felt as if he had spent the whole of yesterday exercising, and his muscles were still in knots. He was fifteen minutes away from Leeds.

Suddenly Storm heard a loud explosion. A car overtaking him had crashed into another on the opposite side. The cars were somersaulting towards him. Storm yanked the steering wheel towards the left. No time to curse. Storm had been driving very fast, trying to make up lost time, touching seventy, eighty on the speedometer, dropping down to forty-five on the slip road. Death was whispering in his ear, life passing by in flick stills. Storm couldn't believe his bad luck. He'd spent years dodging bullets and now he was going to die on some lonely dark stretch of road in a car wreck caused by some fool.

STORM STAMPED HARD on the brakes, yet the car seemed to have a mind of its own. It snaked along the wet road. He was using super human strength. Storm wrestled with the steering wheel, feeling the skin of his palms burn as the wheel seemed to spin through his hands. Yet Storm would not give up as the car slewed into deep undergrowth, smashing into hedges, which helped to slow the vehicle down. The ABS system kicked in. The car stopped brutally. The air bag ejected from the steering wheel and engulfed Storm abruptly. Breathless, stunned, and sweating it was at least another five minutes before he shakily made his way out of the car. There was wing damage but the car was still driveable. All he was concerned with was that he had lost precious time.

WHEN A LEAF lands on water, it doesn't go down straight away. It floats, maybe circles, then slowly, very slowly, it sinks, Grandma told him. Watching Ranks, Easy knew the meaning of this wise proverb. Looking around him Easy saw Slide and Hatchet in a corner, passing a pipe between them. Michigan was nowhere to be seen. What exactly had he inherited from Miss Small? Easy wondered. It looked like the Dodge Crew was slipping away, the way they were going at it with the pipe. Easy wasn't sure if they were mentally fit for soldiering. They seemed to be nothing, nothing but a bunch of fucking cokeheads.

A fire started to swell up inside Easy, starting from the pit of his stomach, rising upwards where it seized him by the throat. If he could get Danny to simply step out of that protective circle. He needed something to draw him out. As it was Ranks was sitting tight, laughing at him with his gyal eyes. Easy was getting frantic trying to figure out how he was going to suck Danny away, like the way someone brave might suck out poison from a venomous bite.

Paradise left to go to the toilets. It didn't take Easy long to figure it out. Zukie and Ranks. Their silent interaction. Ranks raised his head and motioned discreetly with it for Zukie to join him. Ranks handed him a large spliff. Bending down, Easy pretended to tie his bootlace. Slowly his fingers travelled up to his ankle, his fingertips coming into contact with the small Colt .45 he'd heisted off Trench at Miss Walla-Walla's restaurant. It was secured to his ankle by a strap and neatly concealed under his jeans leg.

VEGAS WASN'T A reggae super star whose lyrics ostracized gangs or violence. His lyrics were born strictly out of the dog-eat-dog world, ghetto-heart streets of Kingston Jamaica. To poor afflicted yout' he was a super-cult hero. And so his renowned single Heads High brought a rapturous response. Ranks and his crew were situated not far from the stage. But neither Zukie nor Ranks' crew were taking in any of Vegas. Nero and Mentian kept their eyes on the tense crowd, diligently looking for any signs of bad play.

Smoke billowed around Zukie and Ranks like a veil that gelled the start of a strange new alliance. Silently they accepted that each had done the other wrong, but all that was behind them now. After a few minutes Zukie realised Paradise hadn't returned from the toilets. He went to look for her, walking across the wide dancehall floor, where people hung back from the stage as if it was contaminated.

He didn't realise he was giving Easy-Love Brown a clear view of him as he walked across.

EASY OBSERVED RANKS watching Zukie walk over. It was just what he suspected. Zukie Michaels was Ranks' little spar and tonight that was gonna be his downfall. Zukie, dressed in a dapper white Levi jeans suit, walked slowly, staring straight ahead. Easy switched his eyes swiftly to Ranks, who was now watching Easy curiously.

Yu cyan ketch Quaku, yu ketch him shirt.

Sensing unfamiliar eyes on him, Zukie turned as Easy, gritting his teeth, yanked him close.

"There's nuttin' *wrong* with your fuckin' memory. I saw yu studyin' me before. You *know* what your brotha done to me, ya lickle faggot. You *know* he shot Fluxy and got some of his man dem to shoot Jigsy and me off the road."

"Get off me."

Zukie squirmed. Easy's face twisted as he pulled Zukie up, threw him against a tall speaker box. A startled woman screamed. Bottles, glasses crashed to the floor. As Zukie tried to steady himself Easy pinned his body against him, trapping him. People moved away quickly.

"Want to hear the nasty part, Mr Cuteness?" Easy glanced to his left, saw Ranks rising out of his seat. Nero was holding him back, holding on to one arm as Ranks strained forward, like a dog on a lead. Playboy and Pigeon Eye looked on. Easy saw Paradise emerging from outside where she'd been talking to some friends, her face filled with horror as she realised Easy had produced a gun. "The nasty part was, despite the fact that yo' bro knew you was in the car with yu friends an' all he still went ahead with the hit."

"I don't believe you." Zukie snarled.

Easy was merciless. "Your brother didn't care. He was prepared to sacrifice you to get me and Jigsy out the picture." This ripped Zukie up.

"You liar."

"He killed Chico."

"No."

"Ya fuckin' brotha's a *murderer*!"

Reaching out for a bottle sitting on the speaker, Zukie slammed it first against the wall, then into the side of Easy's face. The bottle tore open the flesh on Easy's lower jaw. Easy screamed as blood spurted out from a small gash. Holding his face, Easy stumbled but kept his grip on the handgun. Alerted by the fracas, security started moving in swiftly. Breathing heavily, Zukie staggered hastily away across the dance floor, angry, dizzy, clenching and unclenching his fists. Vegas had started to sing his hot defiant song Bad Man Nuh Flee. Paradise stood in the centre of the club screaming at Zukie.

"Zukie please let's leave. It isn't like he said. Storm told me."

He turned around slowly, his eyes wide with disbelief. She knew. All this time. Paradise tried to act indifferently, but knew the damage had been done and that resentment was overtaking commonsense in Zukie. "Zukie, please, let's go. I'll explain in the car. Please." Zukie turned away.

Heart pounding, his mouth opened wide as he saw the 'pregnant' woman next to the sound system remove her huge stomach. Zukie stood staring, as the 'stomach' became a bag that had been attached to her body. She handed it to Ranks. Ranks quickly unzipped it, withdrawing several small handguns, which he handed to Pipes, Fila, Mentian, Nero, Pigeon Eye and Playboy.

Suddenly the sound of wild gunfire filled the hall. Vegas immediately stopped singing as the Club's resident MC grabbed his microphone, asking clubbers to remain calm. Sensing disaster, people began to look for the way out. The mass of bodies hurrying towards emergency exits turned into a frenzied flood. The waves of panic reached mountainous heights, with people screaming and shouting. Instantly Zukie thought of Paradise. Turning around to look, he saw her being swallowed up by the throng forcing its way out. She screamed Zukie's name repeatedly.

HATCHET KEPT THE club's security at bay with the loaded revolver. One of them was already on his radio calling for assistance. Hatchet fired two shots and the two-way radio fell from the security officer's palm. The officer backed away as blood poured from his hand. His face blanching like vanilla ice-cream. Smiling at Hatchet's play, Easy used this opportunity to jump to his feet, throwing people out of his way.

ZUKIE FROZE, SEVERAL feet away from Ranks' crew. The stage was deserted, musical instruments abandoned like toys in a nursery play area. A solitary soundman guarded Resnick's sound equipment, stunned by the events. Zukie suddenly saw the unease etched on Ranks' face as Ranks beckoned frantically.

Suddenly, Zukie felt a burning pain in the back of his head. His head jerked backwards violently. Instinctively he lifted his hands, but his head was wrenched back further. Zukie fell to his knees, his hands trying to prise the fingers that snatched his dreadlocks viciously. The hand gripping his hair pulled him back up again. Panting in an effort to cool the scorching sensation in his scalp Zukie rose slowly, screwing his eyes shut. The hand loosened on his dreads and snaked around his neck tightly. Zukie spluttered and choked for breath, as the forearm coiled tighter around his neck.

Easy's searing breath was in his ear.

"Yu in't goin' nowhere!"

Zukie wriggled and the grip tightened. Felt something cold press against the side of his head and knew it was a gun. Zukie put both hands on Easy's arm in a vain effort to pull him off. Easy shook him until he loosened them. Zukie heard a click. Knew it was the gun's safety catch being released. He felt drained, fighting the nausea and dizziness rising up. It was useless trying to fight.

A wall of blackness filled up the club and came crashing towards him.

APPROACHING THE ENTRANCE to Club Planetarium's car park, Storm found his way blocked. Cars jammed inside the entrance unable to get out. In the middle of the car park a seven-seater vehicle burned brightly, lighting up the whole area like a huge firework display. Horns beeped anxiously. Storm's heart plunged low. Couldn't reverse or move forward. Trapped, Storm cut the engine and stepped out of his car. A black man driving an Audi beeped angrily at Storm's apparent thoughtlessness.

Storm leapt onto the Audi's bonnet, ignoring protests as he leapt off the roof onto the other side.

"Hoi, whah de raas! How yu ah gwaan so?" Storm continued, climbing over car bonnets and car roofs, smoke climbing into his lungs, until finally he reached the entrance to the club.

A bouncer stood holding his bleeding hand while his colleague tried to stem the red tide pouring from his wrist. Hatchet stood guard with a revolver, legs astride, shouting orders; his back foolishly turned towards Storm and the entrance. Storm took a deep breath. Two other club bouncers stood staring at him. It wouldn't take Hatchet long to figure out they had company. Raising his right hand high, Storm brought his elbow down hard and fast into the back of Hatchet's head. Hatchet fell straight to the floor unconscious, his legs creasing beneath him. Storm snatched the revolver from his loose fingers. For a second he looked at it, remembering Jasmine's words.

"I'll take you back, but if I ever see you with a gun or even get a sniff of you dealing or moving in a gang, we're finished. For life."

Storm sighed. He saw the anxiety in the security officers' faces, as he snapped back the safety catch like a professional. Keeping his expression unreadable, Storm asked.

"Where are the light switches?"

They all looked confused. One answered.

"By the main door as you walk in."

Storm turned and headed towards the dancehall. Bottles, tissue, paper cups, and spilt drink came into view. Fresh blood was everywhere. The club was eerily silent. Slowly he heard a cool, deep arrogant voice. A voice he hadn't heard or confronted in five years. A voice that suddenly brought back feelings of repulsion, anger, and then ultimate despair. It was as if time had not passed. As if he was still leader of the Grange Close crew, with a gun in his hand, confronting his enemy: Easy-Love Brown.

"SO MR. DANNY Ranks? What's it gonna be? Me and you. One on one. Or what if I just shoot your pretty spar here for Miss Small. That would make us evens," Easy-Love drawled with pleasure.

Zukie forced his eyes to open. Saw dark shadows. Saw no one. Then Ranks emerged from behind a tall speaker box, brandishing a gun.

"Evens? Shoot him," Ranks said, raising his eyebrows casually. "He in't nuthin' to me."

"That in't the impression I get. I get the impression yu and him are good pals."

STORM HAD NO time for trepidation although his heart beat twice its normal rate as he walked in and saw Easy holding his brother hostage. He forced his spirit to be calm as he took in the scene and assessed the situation. Easy was up against too many men and knew it. Storm saw them in their positions behind sound system speakers standing as tall and as wide as wardrobes. Storm saw Ranks clock him. His eyes flitted over Storm but didn't linger in case Easy sussed he was there. Storm didn't know what the play was. Ranks was openly encouraging Easy to blast his brother!

"Shoot the fucka. You'd be doing me a big favour." Danny continued, holding his gun out steadily with one hand. He turned aside briefly and spat venomously on the ground.

He got the angle. Ranks was playing for time. Looking at Ranks again, Storm got his attention for five seconds. Using the gun, Storm pointed to the lights. He showed Ranks a three second countdown. Danny discreetly touched the side of his nose in acknowledgement.

"How's that?" Easy asked suspiciously.

"He tried to take me out."

Easy laughed. His body jerked and he loosened his grip on Zukie's neck. Zukie's vision began to clear. He saw Ranks' face clearly.

There was no decipherable expression.

He simply stared coldly.

STORM RAISED ONE finger. Then two. On the last count Storm flicked the light switches. Darkness. Easy cursed.

"What the fuck?!"

Using all his strength Zukie jerked his plaster-cast arm back into Easy's forehead. The lights flicked back on. Disorientated Easy involuntarily released Zukie, holding his head, dropping the gun. Ranks sprang forward as Zukie ran towards him, half-dragging him towards one of the open emergency exits. Easy picked up the gun. Mentian ran towards his boss, getting behind Zukie and Ranks protectively. Irate, Easy swivelled around and aimed two shots at Storm. Anticipating Easy's reaction Storm was already out of the way. Easy swung himself around lifted his arm. A scream of denial exited Storm's lips as he saw the scene unfolding in triple-beat slow motion.

Easy squeezed the trigger in quick-fire succession. He got one shot before realising he was out of ammunition. He got lucky with the one shot. Storm saw Mentian's head jerk back. Then his body catapulted forward as if he had tripped up over an unseen wire concealed across his way. He ploughed into Ranks and Zukie. They fell like a small row of dominoes. With a grunt Ranks rolled away. Mentian toppled fully on Zukie.

Shoving his gun under his waistband, Ranks tried to pull Zukie to his feet before Easy reloaded. Zukie was stuck under Mentian's heavy frame. Nero ran over. Pulling Mentian over, Nero saw that Mentian was gone, his flak jacket no use to him as the bullet had simply passed through his neck. Blood pumped from him like water from a broken hosepipe.

Slide and Michigan emerged behind Easy, tossing Easy another small gun. Nero and Ranks yanked Zukie to his feet, rushing towards one of the exits. Michigan shouted.

"They in't going nowhere. I took care of their car outside." Coldly it dawned on Storm why there was a vehicle burning in the car park. Firepower popped in the atmosphere as Slide and Easy let off a few rounds before ducking behind some speakers. Slide and Hatchet rose in pursuit but Easy stopped them.

There was retaliatory gunfire, chipping the woodwork and ricocheting around the walls like steel spray. Pigeon Eye and Playboy kept Easy and the rest of the Dodge boys at bay, covering for Nero and his crew as they fled the club. Storm took his exit and ran out of the club's entrance.

NERO'S HEART RAMMED in his chest. Back then he knew he had fucked up, fucked up big style, standing back watching everything happening like it had nothing to do with him, but he doubted Danny had noticed. Should have been him rushing forward to protect Danny instead of Mr. Mentian but instead he had frozen; his body seized up like an old engine. Turning Mentian over, all he saw was his dead friend Aston's face.

They ran towards where they had parked the seven-seater only to find it burning. Danny was stunned. Behind them they could still hear the cracking of gunfire. Nero looked at Zukie, skin pallid, looking as if he was trying hard not to throw up, his white denim suit soaked in crimson. He was rubbing his bruised neck, breathing hard, blinking wide-eyed.

Nero couldn't see any trace of the others behind him, but everybody knew their roles. If anything went down, the priority was to get Danny out of danger. That the van was on fire was no coincidence. Easy's plan. And any second now Dodge would catch them in the jammed car park. No escape. Nero heard the sound of police sirens. Sighing Nero snatched Zukie's loose arm, tugging him along with him. Ranks followed trusting Nero's intuition.

"STORM! THANK GOD!" Storm flew straight into Paradise, almost knocking her over in the entrance. They recovered quickly, breathlessly holding onto each other.

"Paradise, what the hell are you doing back here?"

"I didn't want to leave without Zukie." She started to walk towards the club's entrance. "Where is he? Is he all right? Is he in there?"

"Paradise, you can't go in there. It's not pretty."

Her eyes were wild, streaked with red veins. She gave him a repugnant look and started to stride towards the club's entrance. Storm pulled her arm, holding on to her.

"I wanna see him!"

"Listen, Zukie's fine."

"Then why won't you let me go in?"

Storm forced her to face him. He gripped her forearms. "There's a guy dead in there Paradise. Believe me, Zukie's fine. He isn't in there. He's gone."

She began to weep.

"He knows about you. Easy told him. He just walked away from me. Just looked through me like glass."

Storm saw the blue police strobes as sirens screamed towards them. In a few minutes he knew the area would be sealed off. He pulled her to him, stroking the curve of her neck.

"Paradise. I want you to find your car. Get in it and drive home. Try and stay calm. Drive slowly. Don't think of anything but getting home." She was in a state. Trembling.

She looked at him, her eyes wide with trust, like when she had trusted him to look after her when she fell pregnant with Kyesha. Sighing, Paradise turned. She walked in to the mass of cars. She didn't look back.

NERO LED ZUKIE and Ranks towards the rear of the club where Resnick Hi-Fi had left their sound system transport, a huge high top rental box van. The van's engine was running. Two boys stood smoking cigarettes and discussing what was going down. Nero sneaked in the driver's side of the van, leaned across, and opened the passenger door.

Ranks pulled Zukie towards the van. Nero leaned across, snatched Zukie's jacket and hauled him in fully. Ranks climbed up quickly. Nerome roared the engine. Zukie suddenly yanked a gold chain from his neck and threw it to the ground.

The two sound boys spun around.

"Hey!!!"

Nerome slammed the van in gear. The clutch spun and whirred, grinding as Nerome mis-clutched. Nerome cursed. The boys started to run towards the cab, getting within inches of the door handle. But the van was already picking up speed.

The van sped away.

WHERE WOULD YOU go if your vehicle was burning, the police were coming, the car park was jammed, and a whole heap of bad man with guns were after you? Storm thought furiously. The club was surrounded by a few roads. He suddenly remembered another entrance he'd used several months ago when he'd come here to see reggae superstar, Capleton. Storm jumped and ran towards the rear of the club. He saw the van as it exited, tearing away kicking up dust. Two boys were cursing as the Hurst Van Hire vehicle tore away.

"There goes the fuckin' deposit." One of them cursed.

They began to argue about whose fault it was.

"What happened?" Storm asked. Both boys looked at him as if he had just crash-landed from a high performance space ship right in front of them. Then recognition burned in their eyes.

"Fucking Worlders bwai tief the van."

They walked away, leaving Storm alone.

A police helicopter hovered above filling the area with light. A voice above, like God in the sky, ordered people to stay where they were and not to move. In the bright light that shone like an unnatural sun, Storm saw something glint on the ground. Bending down he retrieved it. It was a thick gold chain. Like the chain he had bought for Zukie's Christmas present last year.

Storm sighed heartily. His blood ran hot, then cold.

HOLDING A PIECE of cloth to his face-wound, Easy ran with Slide and Michigan towards the road where they had parked their vehicle. Easy had no idea what had happened to Hatchet, and he wasn't waiting around to find out. Beast swarmed the area like locusts, and Easy knew it wouldn't be long before they sealed off every street, crescent and avenue within a three-mile radius. The car park cleared as cars tore out. Police efforts to contain the situation were futile. Easy felt the wetness on his fingers. The piece of material was soaked through with blood where Storm's little bitch brother had virtually ripped his jaw open.

Easy climbed into the passenger side door as Slide opened the car with the central-locking system. He grimaced as his face seemed to boil and burn. He would get that redskin fucka for that. And his batty bwai brother.

Tek whey yu get till yuh get what yuh want.

He was so close to getting Ranks. A bullet-kiss away.

Slide turned the key in the ignition. Easy held the Colt.45 with his other hand. Michigan lit a cigarette. Slide pulled the vehicle out of the residential street. Turning around to say something to Michi, Easy noticed headlights behind them as a police car turned into the street as they left.

ZUKIE STARED AT the dark road ahead. They had been driving for about fifteen minutes, but Zukie hadn't noticed. Neither did he notice the stream of police vehicles screaming past them in the opposite direction. Nero drove steadily, careful not to draw attention to the stolen van. Zukie's mind was empty. It was as if someone had tipped him upside down and all thoughts and feelings had drained out of him like water.

Ranks wound down the van window on his side. Taking his mobile phone out of his jacket pocket he dialled a number and began to speak sternly.

"Yes. I want it done this night yah. Find him. What? I don't care where he ran off — get Easy — blood him up — wipe out de whole ah de Dodge Crew."

The wind from the open window touched Zukie's face gently like a cold hand. Shivering, thoughts raced back to him. Events past and present. A car, guns, rolling over and over, a phone conversation, Jigsy laughing — Easy staring. They were talking to his brother, Storm, on a mobile phone.

"Not one of dem must survive. One dead—" Ranks was cut off in mid-sentence, as Zukie snatched the mobile from his ear and flung it straight through the open window. It made a crunching noise as it shattered along the road. For a second or two Ranks was staggered.

"I don't believe what you just did. Nero stop the van."

"No, not now," Nero said calmly. Ranks stared ominously at Zukie. Zukie returned the cold glare.

"One of your man is dead," Zukie began unrepentantly, "you actin' like it never happened, like you don't give a shit about him."

"Look pretty bwai," Ranks retorted angrily. "I never fuckin' asked you to come wid us, y'know. I only saved your arse after all. I coulda just let Easy take you out right there and then." Zukie gave him no response.

Ranks kissed through his teeth savagely. Leaning forward, gripping the dashboard, Zukie suddenly clutched his stomach and groaned loudly. Ranks lifted his hands up and leant backwards, his face panic-stricken as he realised that Zukie was about to throw up his guts.

"PUT YOUR FOOT down Slide." Easy ordered.

Slide watched the police car in the rear mirror catching them up. Easy's fingers inched over his Colt.45 slowly. Slide looked askance at the gun in Easy's lap. He didn't want to serve life for killing no cop.

"I think we should stop. See what they want," Slide said.

"See what they wha-? Are you off yu fuckin' head or sumtin? There's two o' them. One of them might be on the radio checking out the number plates."

"And maybe they're just driving."

"Yeah right! Tagging three black men in a car."

Slide looked nervous, sweat on his forehead in beads. Suddenly the sound of a siren stabbed Easy's brain. The police car overtook them. Easy saw the face of a pasty cop looking at him sternly telling them to pull over. Slide pulled over. He tapped the steering wheel. Easy hid the gun down the front of his trousers. Michigan pulled on his cigarette and blew out smoke nonchalantly.

An officer leaned into the car and looked at the three boys. The other cop climbed out of the police vehicle. Walking towards the car, he used his radio to check the plates. Control told them they would be a while. They were dealing with a record amount of emergency calls.

"Where are you going to this time of night?" The cop asked.

"Have we done something wrong?" Easy asked, grinding his teeth. He hated the police.

"I'm asking the questions," the officer said.

"We're driving back to Derby." Slide said quickly.

"What brings you down here?"

Slide pinched his nostrils. "A dance in Chapletown. Big reggae superstar, yu know from Jamaica," he said smiling ingratiatingly. Ignoring Slide completely, the officer was studying Easy with interest. Slide could feel the agitation pouring from Easy.

"What happened to your face?" Easy was tempted to kiss his teeth. There was static over the police radio. Then it came across loud and clear for them to assist at The Club Planetarium.

The officer stared at the three boys, reluctant to leave.

Easy waited for the police car to drive away before he allowed himself to breathe a sigh of relief. But he was more angry than relieved. He was rabid-angry for revenge. He wanted Ranks, Storm, and his brother, Zukie even more now than ever.

NEROME DIDN'T KNOW what Candice was going to say or do with him turning up like that in the middle of the night, totally unannounced, with Zukie and Danny.

After they had dumped the van three miles away, Nerome let himself in to his baby-mother's home in Harrogate. Treading up the stairs carefully, Nero beckoned Zukie and Ranks in, pointing to the parlour room.

The landing light flicked on.

"Nerome?"

Candice stood at the top of the stairs, pulling the cord of her dressing gown tight around her waist. She was a fair-skinned beauty with natural long curly hair.

"Yeah it's me." Nero answered.

Zukie coughed. "Who's that with you?" She looked beyond Nero as Ranks and Zukie walked into the best room.

Candice was clearly apprehensive, rushing down the stairs into the room. Nerome walked in after her. Candice stood looking at

Ranks and Zukie. Zukie sat in her leather armchair, his head back, his eyes closed. Ranks stood, staring back at Candice arrogantly.

"Who the hell are they?" she caught sight of the blood on Zukie. "Oh my God, is that blood all over him? Is he bleeding? Nero, what's going on?"

Nerome tried vainly to reassure his woman that nothing was going on.

"You arrive at three in the morning with two people I don't know and tell me nothing's going on? Am I simple, Nerome is that it?"

"OK. OK. I'll explain."

Reaching behind to scratch an awkward itch at the base of his spine, Ranks accidentally knocked his gun out. It fell to the floor. Candice's eyes popped open.

"What the—! Get it out of my— get it out!"

Ranks picked the gun up casually.

"Control your bitch Nerome. She's gonna tell the whole damn world we're here."

Before Nerome could stop her Candice slapped Ranks' face viciously.

"Bitch? Bitch? Who you calling bitch you piece of low-life shit."

Ranks kept his face averted, still feeling the sting of her fingers on his cheeks. He'd allow her that, only because she was Nerome's woman. Nerome, on the other hand, offered no apology to Candice for Danny's behaviour. She'd dealt with him herself. He was only fearful of Danny's reaction. As long as he could remember no one had ever hit Ranks before. The situation was potent. Danny only smiled, staring at Candice. Zukie started to laugh. His laughter bubbled up until he calmed himself, building a spliff.

Candice was furious. "What the hell is going on here? Is this a lack of respect for me or is everyone here off their heads?"

"I'm sorry," Zukie said, pursing his lips. "I need a smoke." Candice saw his hands shaking, his foot bouncing uncontrollably as he sat, still building a spliff in her house without her permission. Candice gaped at her man questioningly.

"I can explain," he offered feebly. Candice looked on at Zukie who was now smoking, leaning back against the armchair with his eyes closed.

"I don't want no trouble at my door," Candice warned, her voice shaking with emotion. "D'y'hear me, Nerome?" She took a step backwards, her eyes interlocking with Danny's hatefully.

"There won't be."

"Make sure your facety friend takes that thing outta my house."

Candice continued to glare at Danny who stared back coldly. Nero sniffed.

"The kid needs to clean up." Nero indicated Zukie, who looked at Candice with wide tired eyes.

"There's hot water. Some spare linen in the cupboard. Anthony left some clothes here last week. You can sleep in the spare room with them. By tomorrow morning I want them and you out."

"Candice—"

Nerome was talking to her back as she walked away upstairs to her bedroom.

EXHAUSTED AND ANGRY, Easy let himself into his home. Slide had dropped him off and had gone on to his house with Michigan. Strong morning light was already pouring into the town house which overlooked the green vast space of Hulme Park.

Inside, he saw the devastation straightaway. Broken furniture, ornaments scattered across the living room. Framed photographs of himself and Chris completely shattered. If he didn't know better he would have said the police had raided him. Putting his keys on the side, Easy took the photographs, throwing them in the bin. He kissed through his teeth, sighing. More shit!

The house was silent. Easy walked into the dining room. It wasn't hard to work out that the table had been set for two. One candle stood upright, the other was on the wooden floor along with the remains of some plates and cutlery. All he could think of was that he needed time out from Chris's craziness. It wasn't what he needed right now, especially after last night's fiasco. What he needed was to conserve his energy and strength for Ranks. Sitting down at the large dining table he had bought with Ranks' money Easy put his hand to the dressing on his lower face. He sighed. The handwritten note was on the table.

"Gone back home. See you around. Chris."

Home. He thought home was here. She'd gone back home. To that cramped small flat in Levenshulme. And today he would have to deal with the fact that he had failed. He failed to get his main target. Well she wasn't the only one pissed off.

Using his forearm Easy swept the rest off the items off the table. A deep guttural roar bawled out of his mouth.

EASY FOUND IT hard to sleep. Hot and sweaty, his face throbbed with pain. He was anxious — wrought, fiery, mad that things had gone like shit in Leeds. The only satisfaction was that he'd outted one of them. Still agitated, after taking strong painkillers he at last fell into a deep, deep sleep.

He heard the vibrant laughter first, then his name called softly in a high-pitched echo that sounded far off.

Easy! Eaaaaaazzzzzzzeeee!

His eyes opened. Wide. He saw the wardrobe, open, empty of Chris's clothes, his own clothes on the floor, and the window with the curtains half-drawn.

He smelled the perfume. Strong. Recognised it as the bottle of Joop he had bought. He jumped up. Throat dry. Heart bouncing. And there she was at the end of the bed, smiling at him, holding something in her arms.

Easy tried to move but found that he couldn't. Dumb, couldn't speak.

Wait a minute. She's mothafuckin' dead!

She put the bundle under his face. A baby. A beautiful, small thing that stared up at him with curious brown eyes. She started to laugh loudly, hysterically, pointing a fat finger at him. The finger turned into a shotgun and the shots exploded loudly in his ears as she aimed at him over and over again. Bang, bang, bang!

The banging had woken him. Easy sprang to his feet, opening the French windows that led through to the balcony. Easy leaned over, heart still pounding, sweat on his face. Teeko's red jeep was parked up on New Stretford Road. Teeko's baldhead suddenly appeared. He looked up at Easy. Easy scraped the sleep from the corners of his eyes.

"Open up de door rudebwai!" Teeko bawled.

"Teeko! I thought you was gonna stay in London until next week?"

"Well I'm here now. Let me in nuh, star."

COLIN EDWARDS GOT the call around three fifteen am, disturbing his lawyer-wife Alicia from her sleep. The drive to Leeds had been quick, peppered with thoughts and questions along the way. But nothing could have prepared him for the tirade he received from the Chief Superintendent of Leeds Police, Michael John Carmey. Carmey, a tall, brooding, dark-haired man wanted to know why gun-toting criminals from Manchester chose his city to shoot out their differences like a scene from the OK Corral. He wanted to know why nothing had been done to apprehend these mad boys before this situation reached this outrageous level. Edwards tried to explain how difficult it was but Carmey wasn't interested in excuses.

The area surrounding the Club Planetarium was full of people. The ambulance, Edwards heard, had just taken away the body of one Wesley Matthew Anderson, alias Mr Mentian, aged twenty-five and six weeks away from his twenty-sixth birthday. Edwards had the dead boy's prints on file for GBH, and possession with intent to supply. He was a runner for a Cheetham Hill, North side, gang three years ago but had moved to Rusholme, Central Manchester where he was soon promoted in Ranks' gang after beating up another member to within an inch of his life.

Edwards saw forensics checking a burned out van. The Special Arms unit were retrieving spent cartridges for the ballistic experts. Soon Edwards' eyes encountered his most loathed people, second only to hard-faced selfish criminals. The press. Asking awkward questions, making insinuations. It angered Edwards.

A few gun-toting nutters were responsible for Manchester's reputation. But then again, that's all it took. A few. Edwards was furious. What did people expect? That there would be this magic wand able to make all the bad guys disappear? No chance, and it didn't help matters when Edwards tried to speak to the club's bar and security staff. He got nowhere fast, like a car's wheels spinning in mud. People evaded his questions like clever mice jumping over traps. All Edwards got was that one of the suspects had been slashed across his face with a bottle after he had got into an argument with a fair-skinned dreadlocks boy. After that it all went wild.

There was no security video footage. Disappeared, mysteriously. Edwards suspected the club owner feared retribution from the criminals. No witnesses came forward. There was one man dead and one man held in custody. Edwards didn't expect to get anything from the detainee: Ravel Palmer, aka Hatchet.

But at least Edwards had the description of three suspicious yout's in a car nearby the club. One of the suspects in the vehicle matched the description of Easy-Love Brown. Tall, dark, long funki-dreadlocks style hair. The car's registration had turned up; it was a hired Manchester vehicle. Edwards would check out the rental company later on.

Thanks to the vigilance of two patrol cops, things were looking good

SMALL HANDS POKED at his eyes. Storm jumped up from his

troubled sleep feeling for the gun under his back. He snapped it out and pointed it straight at the wide-eyed child staring at him with frightened eyes. Paradise pulled her away quickly.

"Shit!" Storm cursed, putting the gun away and putting his head in his hands, forgetting he had spent the rest of the night at Paradise's place, both of them talking in the early hours of the morning. "Shit! Paradise I'm so sorry. What the hell am I doing? My head's all over the place." Storm felt his body quivering, his heart swelling, his eyes burning. Tears fell from his eyes. "This is all my fault. I shoulda been honest with him in the first place. It wouldn't'a come to this." He heard Paradise tell Kyesha to go upstairs and draw. Storm recovered. Paradise put her arms around him and held him tightly, telling him everything was going to be OK. How could it be? Things would never be the same, now Zukie knew the truth.

DANNY SAT UPRIGHT. Smoking. Thinking. Listening. For the last hour he had been listening to the fall and rise of Zukie's breath next to him.

The truth was, Danny didn't want to sleep, to see Mentian's dead face, Celia crying and begging him to give up the bad life. Or Theo laughing and Easy brandishing a gun at him. A second, that was all that was needed for these people to invade his mind.

Danny sighed. Zukie was wrong. He cared about Mentian. Could have been in Mentian's place. Easily. Dead. Lying bloody on that wet dance-hall floor. Danny swallowed. Thinking about death for the first time in his life. Cold, heartless death. But at least Mentian died doing a good job.

Yes he did, didn't he?

Danny was going to make sure Mentian got a decent send off. Zukie stirred again. Danny looked across at him. Zukie tossed around in the bed, knocking the duvet off. Danny leaned over Zukie, retrieved the duvet and covered Zukie and himself. The boy's face was filled with anxiety — even in sleep. Danny pulled onto the cigarette deeply.

"It's OK," Danny whispered. "Don't fret. Easy *will* get popped."

Danny realised his own breathing was measured. The voices of Nero and Candice talking next door got louder.

"WHAT KIND OF shit are you in?" Candice asked quietly, her voice breaking, her eyes tearful. Nero swallowed deeply. Five minutes ago he had kissed his sleeping son on the cheek in the room where he slept with his half brothers, Taylor and Morgan. Braving her anger, he decided to step into her bedroom. And despite her harsh words earlier of not wanting him near her, she said nothing as he undressed and got into the bed with her. Nero sat up in the bed. Smoking his fifth cigarette. She had asked him the dreaded question. The question he knew one day she might ask. He couldn't even look at her.

The room was silent except for the sound of Nero's heartbeat echoing around the walls.

"OK," Nero paused. "OK. I'll level with you." He drew in his breath. "I'm a bodyguard for a drug dealer," he said slowly.

"You said you do security work for a firm."

"Yeah. That's what I do."

He looked at her. He felt the hurt and humiliation seep out of her into him.

"A drug dealer, baby, a gang? That changes everything."

"What did you want me to do? I couldn't get a job. I was an ex-soldier, black, I get depression. You needed money to look after Jake and the kids. My kid has to eat."

Candice half-laughed with disbelief.

"And you would lay down your life for him — that dirty, foul-mouthed, sexist piece of shit. Is that what happened tonight? Did something happen? Did some shooting go down? No, don't tell me — I don't want to know. I just can't believe you get paid to protect a cocky bastard like him."

"Danny's OK. He's not like you think. He's been through things when he was a kid."

"Like what?"

"Stuff. He asked me not to tell anybody. Anyway, it's a bit more than me protectin' him. I'm close to Dan. Feels like my kid brother."

"Will you listen to yourself? What about us? Don't you know you are going to get killed Nero — doing this?"

"I'm a trained soldier. Remember?"

"Still didn't stop Aston getting killed, did it? Look I love you, I don't want to lose you." She became silent. Nero scratched his ear. "Are you taking drugs?"

"Shiiiihhitt!! What do you think I am Candice?"

Candice was exasperated.

"Honey, I don't know. I really don't."

"I'm still Nerome Campbell."

"You're not the Nerome Campbell I know. You let us down. Your son. Me and Jake. We were the last people you were thinking of."

With that she turned her back to him. Nerome looked up at the ceiling as if it could provide him with the strength he needed right now. His loyalties, his priorities were laid out bare. Danny or Candice and Jake? Yet Danny needed him now more than ever. In lots of ways he was still a soldier and he could never desert Danny, could he?

IF COLIN EDWARDS was waiting for Easy-Love Brown to walk into his trap, or to suddenly fall into his arms like he did on the night of Jigsy's killing, Edwards was wrong. The hired car noted in Leeds by the patrol cops was due to be returned at twelve-thirty today. A visit to the rental depot had revealed some interesting information. The driving licence used to hire the vehicle was faked. The domestic household bills used as identification had come from an address in Levenshulme and the driving licence produced matched both name and address. The name was a Mr Chris McDermid.

The car rental company was small time, with only two offices based in the North. It was chosen specifically for the purpose of being duped. Easy's gang would have known this company wouldn't have made checks with the DVLA, nor would they have bothered too much about anything else but proof of residence. And cash. Oh yes cash. They paid the two-day's rental fee, deposit and insurance, cash. The depot had a video camera that captured images in stills but guess what, it wasn't working. As it was, the hire-assistant's recollection was vague. Either way, she wasn't bothered by the outcome. The car was insured against theft.

The manager was more concerned about the police presence around his premises. In particular, the armed police trying to hide out of view. Everything had to appear normal so as not to draw unnecessary attention to the gangsters. Edwards lay in wait for the boys to show. It was a big operation, costing the department thousands. Edwards was confident he was going to end Easy's reign. It made his blood tingle with exhilaration.

An hour later they were still waiting.

Two hours later a call came through on the radio to say the car had been found burned out in Moss Side on the estate.

Edwards was disappointed.

ZUKIE LOOKED AT his bloodied denim suit for a long time before stuffing it into a plastic bag. Mentian's blood.

Gonna burn these clothes when I get home. Home? Where the

hell's that?

Nerome had made them breakfast but Zukie had no stomach for it. His head was hot and heavy. Danny, on the other hand, ate the food like the world was going to end in two minutes, preoccupied with Candice and Nero while he ate. Zukie was sure Danny looked apprehensive. Nerome and his woman weren't talking. They avoided eye contact, taking pains not to cross each other's paths.

The dining room led into a huge conservatory that backed onto an immense garden. Nero, head wrapped in a red bandanna, played football with his son in the garden. Candice gathered the breakfast plates from the table noisily.

"It's OK. I'll do it. I'll wash them," Zukie said. Candice looked at him.

"I've got a dishwasher."

"Well, I'll load it. I want to help. It's the leasf I can do for putting on you." She looked at him, her eyes searching his face. Finally, smiling cautiously, she relented. Zukie took the dishes and went into the kitchen. Bending over, he loaded them into the machine.

Zukie heard the sound of Jake's laughter. Heard Nero talking to his son, pretending to be Manchester United's goal hero, Rio Ferdinand. The little boy was laughing. His laughter reminded him of Kyesha. He missed his newfound little girl.

Zukie felt like he had suddenly lost direction.

All he knew now was that there was no going back.

Whatsoever.

DANNY WAITED FOR Zukie to disappear out of earshot, and like a good boy scout doing his good deed for the week, tried making friends with Nero's bitch girlfriend. Candice was busying herself with some clothes, sorting them out for ironing, pretending Danny didn't exist. Danny looked around the house, a large four-bedroom semi, large gardens front and rear. The furniture was high quality, the floors polished wood. The boys had designer clothes, toys, accessories, and computers. A Mercedes Benz was parked in the driveway. Candice was living large. He cleared his throat, taking out a pre-rolled spliff from his shirt pocket.

"Mind if I smoke?" She looked at him with that now famous scowl, which enhanced her exotic beauty. Nero had taste. She looked like a model, brown skinned, almond-shaped eyes, long hair, pretty lips, and a good figure. Her bad temper was making him hard.

"Why you asking me? You're still going to light it aren't you?" she asked, vexed.

Danny leaned back in his chair. He'd play her. There wasn't one gyal who could weaken him.

"Not if you don't want me to," Danny said.

"I don't want you to. I don't want my boys thinking it's acceptable." Danny kept his eyes on Candice steadily.

"I was out of order last night. I had no right to talk to you and disrespect you like that. I'm sorry."

He caught her by surprise. Her jaw dropped slightly. "Also wanna thank you for letting us stay."

"Thank Nerome. Not me," she said tersely, wrapping clothes.

"Don't be too hard on him, Candice. He was only doing what I pay him for."

"Look, I don't know your name," she said offhandedly.

"Danny—"

"Danny, don"t tell me what to do or feel. I have three boys. They're my priority. It isn't about hardness. It's about options, the decisions people make that ultimately affect the lives of other people, whether overt or inadvertently."

"I see. So you're forcing a decision on my man Nero, right? What you're sayin' is, if he goes back to Manchester to do what you know he does, he'll never see his kid again?"

"Has he discussed our private business with you?"

"No. But I know what's going on. Nero can't hide nothing from me. His business is my business. Now, I'm gonna tell you something — you force him to make that decision to stay here with you, and you'll be living in misery. How do you think you'll maintain this fancy life style? Kids in private school, top house, good car. You used to live on an estate, yeah? You'll go back to that, I tell ya. Nerome took ya outta that, dint he? OK what he's doing ain't right to you, but he saved Jake from a life like mine. You think about that."

Candice stared at him frostily.

"And if Nerome leaves here today without your blessing it will always be on his mind. He won't concentrate on his task properly. It could be that his concentration slips and he takes the bullet for me when he shoulda been looking out — you might not see him again because his mind's on things he should leave well at home, d'y'get me? Get over it, get your man, get everything."

The doorbell rang. Candice stared at Danny fixedly.

"That'll probably be my man dem, Pipes and Fila."

Candice rose stiltedly, looking at Danny like a fox caught by hounds.

That's right, Danny thought sarcastically, me run tings, tings nuh run me.

TEEKO SCRATCHED HIS shiny shaved head watching Easy, as Easy built a spliff. A gun lay casually on the sofa, not far from an opened package of fresh cannabis. Teeko looked around the house. Chris and Easy looked as if they'd had a break in.

"What happened?"

"Bitch went off on one, didn't she?" Easy lit the spliff and inhaled. He picked up the Colt .45, and played with it. "She'll cool off. Give her a coupla days. Buy her flowers. Crap like that."

"I heard about Leeds. Drove back straight away. So? Gimme the low-down, nuh?"

Easy kissed his teeth casually.

"Hatchet's in custody. He called his woman. I didn't know Ranks got crews and breezes behind him all over the place, like a bad smell."

Easy lifted the .45 towards the window and closed one eye, pretending to take aim, leisurely.

"Now you know the meaning of The Worlders Crew." Teeko said. They became silent.

"No. It was more than that," Easy stated. "He was prepared. Somebody tipped him off." Easy swung his arm around so that the gun faced Teeko.

"Point that thing elsewhere Easy."

Easy dropped his arm.

"It ain't loaded," Easy said. Teeko said nothing.

"At least I took out one of his man. A life for a life."

"Who?"

"Mentian. The bodyguard."

"Mentian? Shit!" Teeko swallowed. He had been close to Mentian himself. Easy leaned back in his leather sofa, placing the gun back down. He closed his eyes savouring the taste of the cannabis.

"As my Grandma always says, Teeko. You gotta allow one jackass to bray one at a time."

"ZUKIE? ZUKIE?" STORM rushed upstairs, checking to see if Zukie had reached home since Leeds. He was frantic, checking Zukie's wardrobes and chest of drawers. His clothes were still there. At least he hadn't returned and taken off again without hearing Storm out about what happened to Chico. Storm checked the answering machine. No messages. He had not seen or heard from Zukie. Storm had constantly phoned Ranks, but the voicemail service kicked in. Zukie's phone was with Paradise. Storm phoned the shop and was told that Zukie hadn't been in nor had he called. No, Zukie had not been in or called. Storm felt lost. Empty. Afraid.

RANKS' CAR PULLED UP sharply outside Storm's record shop. The sun had set. The afternoon was slightly overcast. Humid. The drive from Leeds had taken them three-quarters of an hour; Nero took the fast lane all the way.

Cutting the engine, Nero looked back at Zukie who was seated alongside Fila and Pipes.

"Ya sure you want to do this?" Nero asked Zukie. Sniffing, Zukie looked at Ranks, saying nothing. Leaning forward he looked out at the shop. It was all a lie. Everything built on lies.

"Hurry up, star. I got things to do and arrange," Danny said impatiently, lighting a cigarette. Zukie stared at Ranks. Ranks dropped his eyes. Zukie summoned all his strength. His anger had been sapped. All that was left was a serene sort of bewilderment. Zukie pressed himself to get out of the car. But before he got out, Storm was already out of the shop. He stopped as Zukie stepped onto the pavement, reading Zukie's frosty expression.

"Zukie, where did you get to last night? I was worried about—."
Zukie walked straight past him into the shop. Storm followed.

The shop was full. Tariq was by the cash register watching cautiously. Zukie acknowledged him with a quick nod. Tariq swallowed.

"Zukie?"

"I just stopped to get my things."

"Zukie don't do this."

Zukie's heart sank. He looked around him. He had loved this place. Here he had felt safe and secure. Here was where he had put all his trust and hopes.

"Cliff, I'm not going to stay another minute around you. I just want my CD player, my CD's, my keyboards — you know my things. Things I bought with my money and not *your* blood money. Yeah, I know what you are." Hurrying forward Zukie stepped towards the counter, towards the back.

"Hole up — lemme talk to you a minute — please stop."

Blanking him Zukie grabbed what he could carry with two full arms. Nero had come into the shop and into the back. He stood behind Storm.

"Look at me — Zukie – talk to me."

Zukie didn't want to look at Storm's face.

"I don't got nuttin to say to you, you're a bullshitter Cliff. I trusted you. All those things you said about Chico and Oil — it was all shit. You're everything you tried to make out you wasn't. Because of you my best friends are dead. You killed them. I hate your guts. I wish you wasn't my blood."

"Zukie, don't say that. Please. It wasn't like that. I know I was an idiot. I only did what I thought, back then, was right. Zukie, don't do this. Things have changed. I've moved on. You can move on, too, with me. Put it all behind us." Storm tried to snatch Zukie's arm as he passed. Zukie pulled away, shrieking as if Storm had burned him with scalding water.

"Get off me! Don't you get the picture? Me and you are done! We're finished. I don't want nuttin to do with you, I don't wanna see you or breathe the same air as you. You're as dead to me as Chico and Hair Oil!" He was near hysterical.

"Zukie, just tell me where you're staying. Where are you staying?"

"None o' yu business."

"At least tell Paradise. She's worried about you." Zukie forced himself to look at his brother, frowning deeply. Even the mention of her name hurt.

"Why should I tell her anything? She's in with you, in't she?"

"And Kyesha, who's she in with?" Now that Storm had seized his brother's attention he held on. But the moment was brief. Zukie looked at him resentfully before barging past.

"Zukie!"

Zukie was walking fast, heart knocking like a conker duel, out of the studio. He could hear the tears in Storm's voice. He didn't want to see them. He wanted Storm to hurt, to die, to feel cut up like he was feeling now.

"He'll be OK with us, Storm," Nero assured.

Storm screamed at Nero, his eyes wild and spiked with red veins and anger. "He won't be safe with any of you. Easy-Love's gonna wipe you all out. I don't want my brother involved." Storm ran after Zukie. "Why are you doing this-Zukie? Why are you going with them?"

Nero took Zukie's things and put them in the boot of the car, embarrassed by Storm's high emotions. Zukie got into the car, slamming the door. Tariq came out of the shop. Zukie climbed into the back seat, next to Fila and Pipes. Everyone avoided looking at

Storm who was striding towards the car as the engine started up.

"Zukie!"

He was banging on the car window, trying to open the door. Zukie held the door.

"Central-lock it!" Zukie ordered. Nero did as he was told. Danny sighed, shaking his head at Storm solemnly.

"Zukie!"

The car screeched away. Nero watched Storm in the rear-view window running in the road after the car, screaming his brother's name. Tariq ran up to him, caught him up and held onto him.

Zukie sat silently, keeping his head low. Ranks looked out of the window.

THERE WOULD BE no need for a warrant. According to the report, a Miss Christine McDermid had reported a handbag stolen a month ago. Inside the bag was a mobile phone, a purse containing eighty pounds in cash, a watch, and a couple of bills she was about to pay. And of course her driving license. The report was handled by a young WPC from Saddler Street in Levenshulme, a local police unit. Edwards found WPC Blake pleasant and meticulous. They went for a bite to eat at a local café on Stockport Road in Longsight, an area bustling with Blacks and Asians, as well as various businesses that sold colourful wares or tasty dishes. Over coffee Edwards asked WPC Blake if she had any thoughts on the handbag theft. Blake said.

"Yes, I got the impression that she didn't look like the type of young lady who would walk on the street with a handbag." Blake had large green eyes, several moles on her face, blonde hair and thin lips which she licked from time to time.

"Why's that?" Edwards asked.

Blake said: "Well, when I went to speak to her about the mugging in her home. I noticed she had awards for kick-boxing and other types of martial arts."

Edwards had frowned.

"So?"

Blake helped him out.

"She said she was mugged in the street by two yout's, one mixed-race the other white. She may be small but she looks like a tough cookie, Inspector. A girl that would eat you alive if you so much as looked at her wrongly. The image of her with a handbag. No. I couldn't see it. Didn't quite gel."

A FIRE ESCAPE. A wheelie bin overflowing next to three bags of rubbish. An abandoned child's pushchair. Davidson rejoined his colleague Edwards at the entrance to the flats. Again they rang the doorbell to the flat upstairs, the address of Christine Bernadette McDermid. And waited. There was no response. Edwards rang once more, keeping his hand on the buzzer, looking about him on the busy street. A couple of kids, one blonde, one ginger, rode by on BMX bikes, eyeing the unmarked car. Broom Lane. A busy residential road in South Levenshulme, its buildings a mixture of terraced houses, semis, sheltered accommodation and flats. Sighing Davidson looked at his watch. Twelve thirty.

The two kids on bikes rode past again. One of them spat. The spit landed an inch away from Davidson's polished Italian shoe.

Laughing, they tore off up Broom Lane towards Mount Road, leading to West Gorton. Edwards looked up. Rain, maybe later.

"The curtains are drawn at the back. She could be in. Sleeping."

"What? On a day like this?"

"Could be a vampire."

Turning to leave they saw a woman in her thirties, nose stud, bright orange hair, walking towards the flats' entrance, searching in her duffle handbag.

"Christine McDermid?"

She looked at them, puzzled. "No. I'm Josie. Her neighbour. Chris isn't in."

"Oh? Do you know where she is?"

"Couldn't say. She comes and goes. Who are you?"

"Friends."

"Didn't know Chris had cops for friends." Josie said, straight-faced. "Is she in trouble?"

"No. We just wanted to talk to her about a mugging she reported."

"Maybe you'll catch her in next time?"

"Yeah." Edwards said, walking towards the car. "Maybe next time."

"WHEN I'M ON a downer I eat ice-cream," Danny said to Zukie, knowing Zukie wasn't exactly elated to be staying at Danny's and was there only because he had nowhere else to go. Zukie had thrown his things down despondently onto the floor, unpacked. They were alone. Nero had gone to Mentian's sister's home to offer condolences. Pipes and Fila had left to arrange a meeting with Kadeem for Danny.

Zukie swallowed, looking up at Danny through a greyish mist of spliff smoke.

"When I'm down I smoke," Zukie said flatly.

"Nah. Ice cream's way better," Danny said, walking into the living room with two small bowls, a box of ice cream and two spoons. He sat close to Zukie, opening the lid of a box of Carte D'or and scraping at the contents with a spoon.

"What have you got to be down about? You don't give a fuck about anything nor nobody," Zukie said bitterly. "Or do you think a spoonful of ice cream's gonna make me forget last night or about what my brother did to my friends?"

"No. I know you won't forget," Ranks paused. He sighed. He took all of Zukie in. Opening his mouth the words that were bothering him all day poured out. "My mother's getting buried today," Ranks said quietly, head low. Zukie turned and looked at Ranks slowly scraping ice cream.

"JAMAICAN RUM WITH ice cream is even better," Ranks said, rolling the bass in his voice for emphasis. Zukie squinted at Danny. Danny smiled, rubbing his hand over Zukie's dreadlocks playfully. He went into the kitchen/diner and returned with a bottle of white rum.

Ranks poured the rum into two glasses, a spliff in his mouth. He handed a glass to Zukie. Zukie took it and looked at it. Danny raised his glass.

"To absent friends. Mr Mentian."

"Chico. Hair Oil."

"My mother who was my enemy."

"Cheers!"

They knocked glasses, downing their drinks quickly. Zukie choked and shuddered, shaking his long sandy-brown dreadlocks like a lion's mane. Danny laughed.

"Want another?"

"Fill it up, star!" Zukie said hoarsely, his eyes springing water. Danny laughed again.

"ZUKIE YOU GOT ice cream all over your face." Zukie got up waveringly, reached over to the ice cream, and scooped some out with his bare hand. He pushed it into Danny's face, laughing.

Scooping out some more ice-cram Danny aimed a swipe and

missed. Zukie reacted, missed his target, and fell against Danny. The two fell, rolling about, grappling with each other, laughing, and cursing.

"What's going on?" A voice asked. Zukie couldn't get up. But even upside down he recognised the miserable face of the boy he had met not so long ago in Danny's apartment. Kurtis. He looked so serious. So displeased.

Zukie carried on laughing.

"KEJ MEET ZUKIE," Ranks said, laughing. Ranks wasn't drunk, tipsy maybe, but Danny could hold a drink. He sat on the sofa. Kurtis looked around. Melted ice-cream everywhere. Danny helped Zukie to his feet. Ranks had never sat with him to share a spliff, drink, chill out and have fun like he was doing now with this Zukie guy. The same guy who had caused problems for him before with Ranks. Kurtis suddenly felt low.

"I know. We already met, remember?"

"Zukie's staying with us. He's having the room you're sleeping in."

Kurtis was stunned. Ranks couldn't see.

"It's. It's my room, you said."

"It's my yard. What I say goes. You're still stayin' here in't you? Come Kurtis don't start whining like a gyal."

Kurtis was practically whimpering. "I don"t understand, why does he have to stay? He could be like a bad omen."

"A bad fuckin' what? Don't go dissin' my homeboy, Kurtis. He's my homeboy now. The only bad omen I know is your twat-brother Easy-Love."

"Easy-Love? Your brother?" Zukie asked, his face twisted with confusion. Kurtis looked down at his feet.

"Haven't you seen Easy yet?" Ranks asked casually. "Zukie glassed him. Gonna have a phat scar on his face. Mentian's dead. Easy took him out." Kurtis said nothing. Felt nothing. "You want some rock?"

Kurtis shook his head, keeping his eyes on Zukie as he spoke. "I'd better clear out my things and move them in here."

"It's already been done. Never know you have so much gyal staying over. Look like dem leave all dem underwear and frock every time."

Kurtis stared ahead blankly.

"HI. I'M CELIA. Veniesha's sister." Celia first noticed the tall, rough-looking boy, a huge scar on his left ear and over one eye, at her sister's burial, standing alone. He threw a single red rose onto Veniesha's coffin tearfully bidding her "Good night."

Now at the funeral reception held at the Manley Park Centre in Whalley Range, she saw him again. Still alone. Not eating or drinking. Sat with his head down. Taking a plate of food, Celia walked over to him.

He looked up at her. His eyes were hollow, distant, and red from crying. He sniffed.

"She told me about you. You're the eldest, right?" Celia nodded and sat down next to him. There was chatter around them. Veniesha's favourite songs blasted through some speakers on the hall's stage. Kids ran around on the stage as if it was a huge playground.

Celia had delayed things for as long as she could, waiting for Danny to show up for his mother's funeral. Throughout the service she looked out for him. At Southern Cemetery she searched for his caramel-skinned face in the crowd, but he didn't show. Family and friends came from as far as Bristol, Gloucester, and London. Every one now knew how Veniesha died. Celia had ignored the gossip and insincere sympathy. Celia ignored the presence of the black detective and his colleague mingling with the funeral guests. But the main thing was that Veniesha had received the best send off money could buy.

"I brought you some food."

"Nah thanks. Can't eat."

"Try. Veniesha hated to see good food go to waste you know."

The boy's shoulders shook. He laughed.

"Yeah. Yeah she did. I'm Terrence — known as Trench." Trench reached for a sandwich. He took a bite.

"She looked after you well, didn't she?"

"She was the best. The absolute best, yu know," he said solemnly.

"Where are the others?"

"They wouldn't chance it with the police. But they cared for her. They really did."

"So how come she died?"

"Only one person knows the answer to that."

"Who?"

"The one who killed her."

"It wasn't Danny Ranks," Celia said.

Trench looked at her frowning. Completely astonished.

"How do you — did she tell you about it?"

"I never knew about my sister's lifestyle until — anyway, it's just that. Veniesha had a son — she gave him to me as a baby — she went back to Jamaica, got married, divorced and got married again. Anyway, the son she had, that I raised, was Danny."

"Danny?"

Trench almost choked on his saliva. He burst out laughing. Laughed hard and loud until everyone in the hall was looking at them. Trench stopped laughing as abruptly as he had started.

"Ranks is Miss Small's son? Did he know?" Celia shook her head quickly. "Wait, did *she* know?" Celia nodded. Trench frowned.

Celia told him about the rendezvous at the park. "See? He couldn't have planned it," she added.

Trench looked as if someone had thrown a brick at him. He sat frowning. But Celia had another shock for him.

"Trench," she began gently. "Veniesha was pregnant."

"What?"

"Was it yours?" Celia noticed that Trench was staring ahead. "Trench?" She followed his eyes across the room. The black detective was looking over. He whispered something into the ear of his white colleague, who nodded. Trench stood up.

"Gotta go," he announced.

Before Celia could say anything, the exit doors slammed shut. Trench had gone.

Putting their food down the two detectives rushed out.

COPS COULDN'T KEEP Hatchet, couldn't put anything on him without evidence and witnesses. Transferred to Manchester from Leeds, questioned about other shootings in Manchester, they released Ravel Palmer alias Hatchet. He walked out into a burning midday sun confidently, smoking a cigarette. He was picked up by his brother Michigan and best friend Slide in a dark blue Honda Prelude. The Honda tore away like a rocket, down Dickenson Road in Longsight heading towards Rusholme and the curry mile of Wilmslow Road, up Great Western Street towards Moss Side.

"HOLE UP A minute. I need a haircut." Fila said to Pipes as they drove past Craig's Cuttin' Crew, a local respected barber's on the top of Yarburgh Street in the heart of Moss Side.

After last night's events in Leeds Pipes was rightfully cautious.

"Danny said not to hang about."

"Won't take five minutes. Look, Craig's is empty." Fila said, passing his hand through his lengthening blonde locks. He looked at Pipes with earnest blue eyes. Pipes lit a cigarette. It was warm. He needed a bath. Hadn't slept too well since last night. Since Mentian died right in front of his fucking eyes. The barber's shop was nearly empty. There was a woman who sat waiting patiently for her little boy's hair to be cut. Pipes saw them clearly through the large glass window.

Pipes judged it OK. Maybe he was being overcautious. What was five or ten more minutes?

THE DARK BLUE Honda Prelude cruised along Great Western Street, turning left at the lights into Upper Lloyd Street, and then right at the lights next to the Somalian takeaway where the teenage offspring of Somalian refugees stood in groups on the corner, chatting and laughing. A dog scavenged for food from a carelessly discarded bin bag.

The car was full of crack smoke. Music blasted through the high quality speaker system, filling the car with bone-drilling bass.

Michigan turned down the bass. "We needed more man, last night," Michigan said gruffly, a raw edge to his voice, which accentuated his agitation. "We was up against the world. Coulda been like mass fuckin' suicide to rahs."

"Yeah but we still got one of dem. We hold dem out. We nuh have no casualties."

"Mentian weren't the one we wanted, tho'. I wanted to see Ranks drop. I wanted to see the blood run from his body like a red swimming pool — for what he did to Miss Small."

"Yeah, for real."

"Legal!"

"Where was Trench? He shoulda bin there. Him and Teeko." They all agreed.

"If Ranger's woman wasn't havin' the kid, things woulda wrap up. We need to take out some of his main man, make the Worlders crew small — small, get what I'm sayin'?" There were nods all around.

Michigan took the car full up, down Yarburgh Street. Hatchet was fuming until the smell of food entered the car, filling his nostrils. Anger got taken over by hunger. He saw the Caribbean takeaway shop at the end next to Craig's barbershop. Then suddenly, like a vision, he saw them. Fila and Pipes. Hatchet did a double take as he saw Fila and Pipes step out of a blue Lexus and head towards Craig's. It was a million-to-one chance.

"Michi — circle the car." Hatchet said.

"What is it?" Slide asked.

"Two dead man juss step inna one barber shop, dread." Hatchet said coldly.

FILA STEPPED INTO the barber's leather, swivel chair, placing his head in position, making himself comfortable.

"How you want it Slim Shady?" Craig asked the good-looking, blonde haired white kid.

"Number two," Fila said, admiring his face in the mirror. "And another thing, I in't Eminem." The barber set about his task, smiling at his own little joke about the white American rap star. The mother with the little boy was paying for his haircut at the cash register where an older yout' sat reading a Hip-Hop magazine. The child was pestering his mother for money. She rebuked him with an unnecessary slap to the back of neck. The child started bawling. Fila smiled.

Pipes sat idling. They were wasting time. Danny wanted to know where he was meeting Kadeem. Scratching his finely china-bumped head, Pipes gazed absently through the window.

He saw the Honda Prelude drive up.

He saw the three yout's step from the vehicle, looking around guardedly, slamming the car's doors. Pipes recognised them directly.

Mr Slide, Mr Hatchet and Mr Michigan.

Dodge bad bwai.

His heart raced for a second as he realised they were striding towards the shop. Then his heart slowed.

They were carrying guns.

Pipes sprang to his feet and shouted.

"Fila!"

BULLETS SHATTERED THE window of Craig's Cuttin' Crew into tiny fragments. The woman with the child managed to grab him and run behind the counter, followed by Craig. Pipes snatched Fila from his seat and dragged him to the safety of the counter. Fila cursed. Breathing hard, Pipes took out his gun. The woman started screaming hysterically. The gunfire stopped. Pipes barked at the woman to shut up. She sat, clutching her child, shaking and sobbing. Pipes and Fila leapt from behind the counter, their feet crunching over shattered glass. Pipes ran straight through the hole where the window was, standing in the road aiming his gun at the screeching retreating car. Pipes spat on the cracked ground. He and Fila got into the Lexus and drove off.

Part way to their destination, Fila realised that only half of his hair was cut.

"**E**XCUSE ME! WAIT!" Trench tried vainly to ignore the stern authoritative voice behind him. The two fucking cops he'd spied at Vee's funeral reception, one black the other white like the two cops in Miami Vice repeats on satellite TV. Trench swiftly approached his green Golf GTI, parked on Withington Road outside the Manley Park Centre.

"CID. Stop. We'd like a word."

Trench's hand was on the handle of his vehicle. The black detective's hand covered it. Trench looked straight into a pair of serious brown irises.

"I'm in a rush," Trench said tersely, glaring at the cop's hand. The Detective moved his hand.

"It won't take a minute Trench. It *is* Trench isn't it?"

Trench took in Colin Edwards' handsome, dark features.

He knew the cop had questions.

Trench had one or two answers.

But none the ones these cops might be looking for.

"WHAT DO YOU want?" Trench asked warily. The white cop was leaning against a car, studying Trench.

"I'm DI Colin Edwards and this is my colleague."

"Me seh is wheh yu want?"

"Two people have been killed in the last couple of weeks, Trench; I understand one of them, Veniesha Michelle Brooks, was very close to you."

"So?"

"She died trying to call you Trench, doesn't that say or mean something to you?" Trench felt the hurt inside him resurface.

"How do you know she was calling *me*?"

"I didn't. I just guessed."

"You guess wrong den innit?" Trench said, unlocking his car door.

"Her killer showed no mercy. We want to get her killer, just like you."

Trench laughed.

"You'll never get her killer. He's too smart."

"Why not? Easy-Love Brown is bound to trip up one day."

Trench's heart flipped. He swallowed a huge ball of empty air staring at Colin Edwards.

Did he hear right?

EDWARDS WAS PLAYING his cards, noting the shocked expression etched on Trench's face after disclosing his revelation about Easy-Love's involvement in the shooting of his former gang leader. Edwards realised he'd got an ace. "Yeah, we know about him setting up Fluxy's killing four years ago." Trench was silent for a second. The cloudiness in his eyes cleared. His eyes passed from Davidson to Edwards.

"So it is true, he *did* kill Fluxy," Trench whispered quickly, his chest rising.

"He instigated it." Edwards said. "Got off because his co-assassinator was too afraid to give a statement despite our offer of protection."

"Protection? Yu mad? Dem tings is for The Bill on TV," Trench said scornfully. "Protection!" He shook his head mockingly. Edwards realised he was in grave danger of losing Trench's confidence.

"We know Easy was beaten up shortly after being released from prison and we suspect that you and Small did it. Easy knew what he was doing." Trench shook his head. Edwards sighed, watching Trench look away into the distance. "Easy was close to her wasn't he? Yet she tried to call you, Trench. You." Trench swallowed, his Adam's apple dipped.

Trench felt for a cigarette, looking around apprehensively. He looked at Edwards.

Nothing goes past this guy.

Sighing, Trench lit his cigarette inhaled then exhaled deeply. "Look, I can't be seen talking on the street in the middle of Whalley Range to two beast bwai."

"Maybe we could go to yours?"

"Nah. No way."

"What about the pub at Brooks' bar?"

Trench looked unsure.

"Just talk to me, Trench. Let's stop him."

Trench sighed heavily.

"I-I don't know."

Suddenly, Edwards' mobile began to ring, cutting into the atmosphere. Keeping his gaze on Trench, Colin answered his mobile. It was Headquarters informing him of a shooting on Yarburgh Street, a five minute drive from there. Without saying anything, Edwards glanced at Davidson and nodded slightly.

Edwards hung up. "Sounds like your mob have been making their presence felt again."

Trench blinked hard, as if someone had suddenly turned on a bright light, waking him up.

"Nah. I in't doing it. Easy's gonna get his. Believe. It's just a matter of time. But I in't betraying my crew to talk to no beast about business we gonna deal wid ourself."

With that Trench stepped into his car.

PARADISE SAT BY the phone. Waiting. But it didn't ring. If only Zukie would call, let her know everything was OK. Tears fell from her eyes. Kyesha walked into the room and saw her mummy crying. She touched Paradise's tears. Smiling, Paradise grabbed her daughter to her, holding her tightly.

Where was her other baby?

What was he doing now?

Was he safe?

Was he thinking of her?

Moreover, did he still love her?

TRENCH PARKED AND stepped out of his car, thinking about Edwards' subtle proposition to grass up Easy. Half of him wanted to reconsider, but the other half warned him that he was no informer and that no matter what he could never collaborate with no cop.

It had been a long day with lots of shocks: Danny being Miss Small's son; Miss Small's secret pregnancy; the funeral; and the cop's proposition.

His baggy black suit flapped around him as a cool breeze whipped up, cooling him down. He felt shaky. Sick with anger and frustration. The weather didn't help his mood, adding to the heat swarming his body. Jiggling his keys, Trench walked down the garden path leading to his basement flat. It was part of a huge detached Victorian house, on Demesne Road overlooking Alexandra Park and surrounded by gigantic leafy trees. Trench was only a couple of steps away from his front door when he heard the gravel on the path crunch behind him. He stopped instantly as he heard a deep voice exclaim.

"Hello Trench. Long time no see."

The sweat on his forehead turned cold.

Trench turned around slowly.

EASY STOOD UNANNOUNCED on Trench's garden path. He was dressed casually. His funki-dreds tied up on top like rap MC Busta Rhymes, he smiled wryly.

"Long time no see." Easy said cooly.

He looked over his shoulder then back again at Trench.

"Wassamatter?" Easy asked.

"Nuttin'." Trench said, clearing his throat.

"In't yu gonna 'vite me in. Share a smokes?"

"Look Easy, I in't in the mood for no small talk, nor smoke yeah? No disrespect, but yu see it's been a long day — with Miss Small's burial an' everythin'."

"Yeah," Easy said sorrowfully. "I couldn't make it. Did you see my wreath?"

"Your face woulda been better, after all she was your woman."

"You know the reasons why I couldn't show, Trench. You know the police have those tiny digital cameras. Click, and then they check their files. Not safe."

Trench turned on his heel, hearing the gravel crack beneath his feet. He swallowed again, struggling to keep his breathing controlled. He put his key in the door and felt Easy close behind him. Trench was trying to think, trying to remember where he had last put his gun. In the turmoil of the last week Trench had let his guard slip. Truly he hadn't banked on Easy showing his face around here. Trench knew Easy had come around for a reason. And that reason was to annihilate him.

Once inside Easy continued to study Trench, cockily placing his feet on Trench's glass coffee table.

"So. Trench, how goes it, rudebwai? We missed in you Leeds an' that."

"What happen to yu face? Knife, machete, or bullet?" Trench asked impassively, drinking from an open carton of fresh orange, leaving the fridge door open. The cool refrigerated drink only touched the fringes of his burning thirst. Easy laughed.

"If you was there you woulda known," Easy said, scratching his nose. The wound was healing. Sore but healing. "My granma has a saying for people like you. Silent river runs deep."

"Yeah, yeah," Trench said, wiping the corners of his mouth. "Whatever."

"So talk to me Trench. Tell me why we in't seen yu around for a while."

"Busy."

"Doing what?"

"Figuring things out."

"So what yu figurin' out?"

"How Miss Small got killed."

"But yu already know that. Ranks killed her."

It was Trench's turn to laugh.

"Huh… huhhn-huhhn. Yu see, Easy, Ranks is Veniesha's son."

"Bullshit," Easy uttered derisively.

Trench continued, his voice rising to an excitable peak. "Her kid, seventeen years old, yu heard her always talking about her kid — the kid she never really knew — well it turns out. He's Ranks. The day she got outted, I heard he was meeting her for the first time."

"Who tell yu dat?"

"Veniesha's sister, Celia told me today at the funeral," Easy frowned. His heart pounded.

"Danny is — Small's son?"

"Yep. And she knew all the time. He didn't. Nobody knew where she was going that day, apart from you."

"So? So did fucking Ranks. He coulda seen her and shot her before he knew it was his mother."

"So he came prepared, dressed in black on a mountain bike like the newspapers said? Is that how he went to meet a mother he didn't know? You have to come better than that Easy." Easy stared at Trench. "And another thing, Miss Small was pregnant. Did you know that? She was carrying a child. It wasn't mine so at a guess I'd say it was yours." Easy tried to hide his shock, remembering his dream. The cold shiver passed through him like an ice-cold stream.

"Pregnant?"

"Yeah-wassamatter? You look like yu seen a duppy."

"I DIDN'T KNOW Veniesha was expectin'." Easy said calmly. Although he was shocked he seemed to hold it well.

"Clearly." Trench muttered, walking around in his kitchen trying to remember where he had put his gun. So much had been going on recently he had lost his head. He put the gun somewhere safe in the kitchen, but he couldn't remember where. The cupboards? Behind the drainage system? Under the floorboards? Where? Trench was searching frantically. Easy walked into the kitchen.

Trench looked sideways at the counter for a suitable weapon.

"What was you talking to those two cops about?"

The large kitchen knife protruded out of the cutlery rack.

"What cops? When?"

"I was drivin' along Withington Road, weren't I? Thought I'd roll my car past the funeral reception and there you was, talking to two beast bwai." Trench was breathing hard. "What was they sayin"?" Easy asked.

Trench stared directly at Easy. He was angry and could barely contain himself. Veniesha was dead and buried with Easy's unborn child and this guy was so cold and casual about it. "They think you killed her like you did Fluxy."

Easy laughed. That black detective had never given up on him for Fluxy's death. He couldn't prove shit then nor now. Easy took the gun out from his waist. And smiled.

Trench was silent. He focussed on the knife handle. One jerk and then clean into Easy's stomach. Out him light. Looking up quickly he saw that Easy's eyes were also on the knife handle.

"In the second it takes you to pull out that jooker I'll empty every single bullet into you." Trench's eyes focused on Easy's gun, aimed at his torso. He was so angry he wanted to scream. "Now tell me what did you tell those cops?"

"Yeah. I told them. I told them I think you killed her too," Trench said, gritting his teeth. "They in't daft. They know Danny had nuttin to do with it."

"Well, as long as Michigan, Hatchet, Ranger and Slide think that Ranks killed her, that's OK. It in't gonna matter what you think you know or what those retarded beast bwai believe is it? They don't give a fuck what happens to you. So you told them what they think they know all ready? Big fuckin' deal.

"There in't no room in this crew for two chiefs. As my Gran'ma says two bull can't rule in the same pen."

"WHAT THE FUCK'S goin' on?" Ranks spat bitterly as Pipes and Fila burst into his living room angrily, cussing violently. Pipes was bleeding from a cut on his head. Fila's hair was half-shaved. Fila and Pipes had disturbed Zukie and Ranks from their PlayStation game.

Zukie had sobered up a little. He relit a zook and leaned back into the chair leisurely. Pipes was breathless. He sat down. Ranks stared at him.

"Yu see Kadeem?"

"Yeah."

"So what happen to unuh?"

Kurtis walked into the living room frowning. Pipes told them about the shooting at the barber's angrily, sitting down exasperatingly.

"Right. If it's a war Easy wants. Easy gonna get it. Tonight we avenge Mentian's death. Tomorrow one less Dodge bwai gonna walk the streets of Manchester," Ranks said forcefully, ignoring Zukie's penetrative grey eyes.

ZUKIE SAT WITH his feet beneath him, building yet another spliff. He was well aware of his surroundings and whose company he was in. Bad bwai company. He sat surveying Ranks' wealthy flat. Ranks' dog, Zel, rested near Zukie's feet. Easy's words in Leeds entered his head mockingly.

"Ya fuckin' brotha's a murderer! Knew you was in the car with yu friends an' all he still went ahead with the hit."

Zukie shook his head concentrating on what was happening now. Ranks was plotting with his crew to avenge Mentian's death. Already he'd gone to pick up Stukky and Sizzla. Zukie closed his eyes.

Slowly he became aware of a presence studying him. He forced his eyes open. Kurtis was standing in front of Zukie, watching him. Like a zombie. Zukie felt cold. This was Easy-Love's brother.

"Want a game on the PlayStation?" Kurtis asked timidly.

"What yu playing?"

"Dunno. Anyt'ing," Kurtis sat next to Zukie. He picked up the dual-shock controller.

"I want yu to know my half-brother's fuckall to do with me. He's hurt a lot of people — me included — and he's gonna pay."

Zukie noticed Kurtis's hands shaking.

STORM SAT IN his shop. Quiet, hardly any bookings. It wasn't hard to see that, without Zukie, they were losing business. When it came to recording music, people simply didn't want second best. Even their most regular customer, Alphonso Beppo Dread, was taking his business across town, to Cappella's in Hulme. Storm was trying to be brave. Trying to fight off the soldiers of despair marching in his gut.

But Ranks' semi-prophetic words kept coming back to haunt him.

"You go right ahead and have that heart-to-heart with your little bredrin. He's just going to appreciate it, in't he, when you tell him how you fucked up his life. How your stupid little payback killed his best friend. And then you won't have no business, no sound engineer, no partner, and no brother. I personally guarantee you that."

And those boys Zukie was mixing with were bad boys.

Real bad boys.

In fact Storm thought they made his former gang, the Grange, look like saints.

THE TWO SLEEK dark vehicles pulled up on the fringes of the Bankside Estate in Longsight, a huge development that bordered on the area of Ardwick, near the famous Apollo theatre and Manchester City football club's old ground. The nights were falling more quickly now and at eleven o' clock, darkness lay like a smooth velvet quilt. The long six-week school holidays were ending and there were a few children playing on the estate's streets and cul de sacs. A group of early teens were playing five-a-side football. They stopped as they saw a yout' in a black bandanna exit the passenger side of a vehicle. With a rough voice, he called a boy of thirteen over. The boy, brown-skinned, with dreadlocks on top and cropped sides walked with attitude towards the car.

"Yo Springy," Danny said. The boy smiled. "How's tings?"

"Smooth," The boy answered, grinning toothily. "What ya sayin' Ranks?"

"I'm looking for somebody. He lives on this estate. Drives a blue Prelude. Runs by the name of Hatchet."

Lighting a spliff Ranks watched the boy's indifferent face. Danny gave him a twenty-pound note.

"Got any weed?"

Ranks reached into his pocket and gave the boy a small bag of draw. The boy put it to his nose and smelled the flavour. He smiled appreciatively.

"Lives on Inca avenue. Next to the garages," the boy said walking away, stuffing the twenty-pound note in his pocket and hurrying towards the football game which had restarted without him. Springy's team scored. A roar went up as the boy ran to congratulate his teammates. Danny stepped back into the car. The two vehicles drove away. No one gave them a second glance.

HATCHET FLICKED TO the Discovery Channel, as he drank an ice cool beer. He watched, fascinated, as an eagle tore apart some kind of small bird. Hatchet heard the bird's vain screams and observed the wild savagery of the eagle as it killed its prey. Blood and feathers scattered everywhere.

Hatchet took another sip and turned up the volume.

THWACK! THE NOISE at the back door pulled him from his wildlife programme. Putting his drink down Hatchet slowly got up and walked towards his kitchen. Turning on his light he peered into the darkness of his council back yard. Something was wrong. Hatchet's Doberman Pincher dog Noble was unusually silent. Hatchet strained to see. Realising he would see better if the light was off, Hatchet killed it. Looked, listened. Couldn't see or hear his beloved dog.

For some reason Hatchet's heart was lurching and he didn't know why. As he turned Hatchet heard the sound again. Thwack! Somebody was there! Hatchet pulled his gun from the kitchen drawer. The key was in the back door. Hatchet turned it and pulled the door open. He tugged it wide, pointing his gun. The sight that greeted him stunned him completely. Two garbage wheelie bins blocked the back exit.

"What the—?"

He tried to move them but they were too heavy. Somebody had barricaded him in. Some shit was going down. Suddenly he saw a bright orange-yellow light roaring towards him from the kitchen window. If Hatchet had believed in angels he would have said he was seeing one now. The brightness was terrific, golden, absorbing. Suddenly the kitchen window exploded, scattering tiny fragments of glass over the kitchen floor. Instinctively Hatchet cowered, screwing his eyes shut. The smell of petrol invaded his nostrils, climbing into his lungs.

Opening his eyes quickly, Hatchet saw the liquid flames spreading quickly across the floor, towards him. Hatchet jumped onto the kitchen worktop. The flames danced beneath his dangling feet. Dropping his weapon, Hatchet reached for the washing up bowl which, unluckily, was full of water. This made the fire worse. The flames rose high and hissed at him. Summoning all his courage, Hatchet ran through the flames towards his living room. He picked up his house telephone and dialled 999. A dead dial tone made him realise quickly that the line had been cut.

The Worlders Crew weren't romping at all.

If he didn't act quickly tonight was the night 29 Inca Avenue became his tomb.

HATCHET'S CURSE CAME out like a whimper as he heard another muted explosion. This time the firebomb had gone through his front room window. The petrol bomb had hit the settee and set the curtains alight, the flames spreading rapidly.

Hatchet stood staring, his marble-brown eyes wide and fearful. He swallowed. Ran towards the front door. Flames already licking the ceiling. Smoke alarm screaming.

Hatchet opened his front door. He came face-to-face with a wheelie bin, which had another piled on top of it, and behind them Hatch could dimly make out three others. Panic blanked his mind. Hatchet forced himself to think as he choked and spluttered and his furniture crackled and burned like dry trees in a forest fire. The emergency services. He had to call them. Why didn't he think of his mobile phone? Hatchet searched his body frantically. He felt the solid slim shape of his Ericsson mobile in his back jeans pocket. Taking it out Hatchet dialled, breathlessly retreating upstairs, choking flames racing after him.

Hatchet heard the operator ask which service he required.

Smoke invaded his lungs.

The heat, they say, always rises to the top.

Hatchet felt himself baking, as the flesh on his forearms began to melt, his clothes and skin becoming one.

When the darkness came, Hatchet was glad for its peacefulness and the relief from the pain covering his body.

"DRIVE." EASY ORDERED. "And don't try no fuckeries."

Swallowing deeply Trench put Easy's BMW, formerly owned by Miss Small, into gear. It was getting dark and cooler. Trench looked around; praying someone would notice him, stop him. That maybe Slide or Michi would turn up. But the tree-lined street was dark and empty.

"Where we going?"

"Take the car onto Princess parkway. Then head for Cheadle."

Trench's foot shook uncontrollably as he pushed the accelerator. His mouth felt like dry grit. All he could think of was the gun aiming at his stomach. One wrong move and he knew Easy wouldn't hesitate.

"Remember when you beat me, you fucka?" Easy spat. "Rememba? Not even five minutes outta prison and yu and that fat bitch drag me off the streets and beat me." Trench had nowhere to run. On either side of him, deep in the Cheshire countryside, were dark fields. In the distance the lights of a farmhouse burned brightly. The night was clear and moonlit. Easy frog-marched Trench to the edges where there were overgrown bushes and hedges, sticking the gun into the base of Trench's spine savagely.

"Beating you had nuttin to do with Vee. It was my decision. I thought you was a danger to us. And I was right," Trench said.

"I never touched Small. I told you."

"Yeah — like the same way yu never touched Fluxy?" Trench asked sneeringly.

"No one can say I did nuttin' for sure. Either way, yu think I cared about that fat bitch? Going with her made me wanna spew. And knowing that my kid was going to be a half-brother or sister to Danny — well, as Grandma always says God moves in mysterious ways," Easy said, the disgust evident in his voice.

Something in Trench snapped. Easy's words were heartless. Turning quickly he caught Easy off-guard, throwing a kick into his groin area. Without hesitating, Trench started to run towards where he thought the road was. Guided by the sound of a car roaring close by, Trench ran, ignoring Easy screaming at him and calling his name. Trench heard the sound of gunshots behind him; he even felt them whisper close to his ears. Still he didn't stop. He was getting used to the darkness, and the moon was climbing high out of the clouds.

The road was within inches.

All he had to do was get there, flag a car down and he would be free.

Free from Easy.

TRENCH COULD HEAR the sound of a heavy vehicle approaching. He made it to the road. His heart whomped in his chest. His legs were shaking. Without thinking Trench threw himself into the road, stepping into large headlights, waving desperately for the truck to stop. In his panic, Trench had underestimated the speed of the fast truck as it made its way along the quiet country road.

Easy stepped out in time to see the truck's brakes screech an ear-splitting protest, as the driver slammed his pedal to the floor. Easy held out his hand futilely. He could only look on as the heavy vehicle sucked Trench under its wheels. Licking his lips, Easy watched as the driver jumped from his cab. Poor Trench.

You cannot sit on the back of the cow and curse the skin of the cow.

Easy backed into the bushes behind him. Any second now the man might turn and see him. Easy couldn't afford him that pleasure.

He retreated further.

The dark bushes swallowed him completely.

SOMETHING WASN'T RIGHT. Teeko Martial could feel it as he sat in the living room of his new home on Salisbury Street .

Easy's words played in his mind. He'd heard them in his head, repeatedly.

"No. It was more than that. He was prepared. Somebody tipped him off."

What the rahs did Easy mean, somebody had tipped him off to Danny in Leeds? Then Easy had swung his arm around and pointed a fucking piece at Teeko. That totally ripped Teeko up. Wasn't it enough that Teeko had left Ranks' crew to join Easy? Well, it was too late to go back to Ranks. Teeko didn't like the way Easy was operating. Totally reckless. Teeko could feel evil around him. The way things were happening. Miss Small's death because of Easy's haste. Then Mr Mentian, who Teeko had sparred with when he ran with Danny's crew. And last night Hatchet. Burned out. Who next?

When Michi phoned Teeko with the bad news, desperately trying to track Easy down, Teeko had felt peculiar. Easy wasn't answering his mobile or his phone at home. When he, Slide, Ranger and Michigan called around, they found Easy's house in darkness. One of his boys had almost been burnt to death and no one knew where Easy was. Teeko knew it was Ranks' work. Yes, he, of all people, should know.

Maybe it was time that he went freelance and held his own.

Maybe it was time for him to move on to somewhere, start afresh where no one knew him.

At least that way he might stay alive.

"COME ON STEPHEN!" Edwards watched proudly as his son tore up the left flank, dribbling the ball past two defenders. Stephen was tall for his thirteen years. Academically he was excelling. Along with his sports achievements he was a top pupil at Excelsior High Private School. They were playing a Sunday morning friendly against another of the area's private schools.

Edwards was aware that his two sons were only two of four black pupils at the exclusive school. Although other black people might consider him a sell out, separating his children from their black roots, Edwards felt that a first rate education would make his sons into powerful black men.

Rain began to fall. Edwards glanced at the sea of excited parents gathered on the fringes of the football pitch.

His phone buzzed in his pocket.

The news wasn't good.

A suspected gangster burned out of his home in Longsight.

He left without seeing his son score.

"WHAT DO *YOU* want?" Storm asked irreverently, rubbing his square chin, placing a box of imported reggae CD's on the counter and leaning casually on it. Ranks walked in, keeping his cool hazel eyes on Storm. He was dressed in baggy black jeans, a tight-fitting black vest that showed off his moulded form, and a black shirt opened down the front. The shop had two customers. One of them was surfing on the Internet. The other was browsing the CDs, tuned into a Sony Discman.

Outside he could see the sun shining brightly. Another day in the ghetto. But it didn't matter how hot it was, Danny Ranks always looked cool.

"Surprised you let me in," Ranks said steadily. His eyes took in Storm's jewellery, gold chains and signet rings.

Storm shook his head negatively, scowling.

"Yu know Danny, yu either brave or just plain stupid."

Danny began to brew. "Why do you hate me so much Storm? I saved your brother's arse in Leeds the other night remember? Even after Easy told Zukie everything? I mean, it wasn't me, was it? Man, you should be on yu knees thanking me. I told you to duss that nigga good-style before he fucked things up for you."

"This gang business is just a big kid's game to you, innit Danny? Runnin' around with guns and shootin' up the place like the Wild West. In't yu learnt nothing from Mentian's death? And don't come wid this nigga shit. Have respect for your fellow black man and leave the skin-insult to ignorant people."

"I'm so sorry. Never knew you was so sensitive." Danny rasped sarcastically.

"Nothing's changed between me and you, Danny. You still play on my nerves. And I still wanna bruk you up."

"You need me," Ranks said wryly, scratching his nose.

Storm laughed.

Ranks looked around self-consciously.

"You? Why the fuck would I need a fucka like you?"

"Two reasons. I'm the thing stoppin' your brotha from going completely over the edge."

Storm sighed.

"Is he OK?"

"How do you expect him to be? He's been through a lot of shit. His head's so fucked up he can't even sleep on his own." Ranks lit a cigarette. "He trusted you — I told you this would happen."

"Is this why yu came round? To gloat?"

"No. I came to warn you."

"Warn me?" Danny turned to walk towards the door. Storm held his breath momentarily.

"Yeah. Easy-Love is coming for you Storm. He's coming to get his share of your business. He's already back in your life, turning and twisting things for you. He's coming for you Storm."

"I'll be waitin' for him," Storm answered threateningly. Ranks turned around and looked at Storm.

"Ahh that's the Storm I know. Need any men?" Storm's brown eyes rolled all over Danny's lean, tall, athletic body unemotionally.

"I got my own man."

Ranks feigned surprise.

"I thought you turned your back on all that gangsta shit?" Storm's expression was unreadable. There was only a flicker of annoyance in his almond-shaped brown eyes. The look was enough to convince Ranks that he was stepping into dangerous territory. Ranks decided to leave while the going was good. Sighing, he opened the shop door wearily.

"Ranks?"

"Yeah?"

"Don't ever leave Zukie by himself, you know with his state of mind."

Ranks stared at Storm, his expression totally blank.

"Your kid brother's safe with me, Storm. Nuttin's going to happen to him while he's around me. I'll watch him twenty-four seven. You have my word."

Ranks closed the door.

EASY RANSACKED MISS SMALL'S, searching for bank books, land titles in Jamaica, property deeds, anything that would make him rich overnight. Instead he found a collection of letters, letters from her to Danny and vice versa, and inside them he found an ante natal appointment letter for the beginning of last month. Two days before she died. Easy sat on the bed, totally subdued.

His dream of her and a baby came rushing back.

So Trench was right about Danny and the baby.

Well serve the bastard right. Had a big mouth and didn't know how to stop running it off. Tried to torment Easy with his revelations. And ended tormenting his own self to death. So what if she hid her money from Easy? There were other ways of making money. Fuckin' smart fat bitch.

Tonight, Easy was gonna have a drink on Trench and Miss Small for their wisdom, foresight and ultimate bravado.

EDWARDS KNEW A chip pan fire wasn't the reason why Ravel Phoenix Palmer, alias Hatchet, was strapped to a hospital ventilator, with wires sticking out of his chest to monitor his breathing. As he sat alone in the hospital guest room, drinking vending machine coffee, waiting for Davidson to pick him up, Edwards released a long despondent, frustrating sigh. The fire service said that the fire which had partly destroyed Hatchet's home, had been started deliberately. Petrol bombers had targeted Ravel. They were callous, blocking all exits and strangling his dog. Obviously, nobody was banking on Hatchet escaping from an intense inferno like that alive. Edwards knew it was a direct retaliation for Mentian's killing in Leeds and the shootings of opposing gang members yesterday afternoon.

To make matters worse for the investigation, earlier that morning Edwards had been summoned to see the Chief Superintendent. He had shown Edwards an article in a national newspaper penned by an ex-Chief Constable who said that organised crime gangs were overrunning the streets of England. He stated that Yardie criminals were infiltrating and influencing gangs in Manchester and Liverpool. Edwards was furious. This was making life harder for him. Now the race to stop Easy-Love and Danny Ranks was desperate. They had to be halted before more innocent people got hurt.

The trouble was, who to concentrate on?

Who represented the baddest threat?

Easy or Danny?

"I NEED TO TALK to you," Easy whispered to his brother Kurtis. Grandma was sleeping peacefully. They sat on either side of her in her room in Oakwood private nursing home. Kurtis hoped that Easy wouldn't notice that he was agitated. That he badly needed a hit. Kurtis avoided Easy's stare.

"Are you lissening Kurtis? You look far away. I need you to lissen to me good."

"What?"

"If anybody asks you where I was two nights ago, I was with you."

"Who's gonna ask?"

"Juss lissen. This is important. You and me stayed at Gran's. We watched Rush Hour on video. We played cards until three in the morning. We went to bed. OK?"

"OK." Kurtis wondered what his brother had been up to.

Kissing goodbye to Grandma, Easy and Kurtis walked through the nursing home's double swing doors into the outside world. Traffic and people streamed by.

"What's this all about?' Kurtis asked. Pinching his nostrils, Easy looked at his younger brother. He could trust him.

'Trench got killed. I was there when it happened. He thought I had something to do with Miss Small's death."

Kurtis stopped in his tracks. His heart rocked like a boat in stormy waters. He stared hard at his brother.

"Did you?"

"I mean, you said you wanted to work with me? Well, we got to shift people so that me and yu are running things. Tight."

"You — you killed Miss Small?"

"People like she and Fluxy had to move on, let other people get a cut of the big cake."

"Fluxy? In't that the leader of the crew you use to run wid?"

"Kurtis, you should never have give up college. You're bright. You'll go far. When things cool down, me and you going to take a holiday — Florida, Jamaica. Just me and you. Yeah, I masterminded their outings." Easy laughed. "I let Bow-Bow take out Fluxy. That way people thought it was Storm and so Jigsy was out for Storm. And Miss Small. She got killed for love." Easy strode ahead, totally unaffected by the burden of revelation he had flung casually at his younger brother. Kurtis stood rooted to the grounds of the nursing home car park. He couldn't move forward or backward.

His thirst for cocaine was temporarily dampened.

"HEY MISTER! YOU the police?" A caramel-skinned kid aged about five eyed him up and down, squinting because Edwards stood tall in the sunlight. The place was blighted by mindless vandalism. A few houses stood boarded up, awaiting renovation. Although forensics had been through everything, Edwards thought there was something they might have missed about Hatchet's arson attack.

"Yes."

"A drug dealer lived there," The kid announced gleefully. "I watched him. I wanna be a policeman when I grow up so I can cuff bad people."

"That's a good choice of career, son." The words sounded strange coming from him. Like something his father, an ex-Barbadian police sergeant had said to him, a long time ago.

"Mummy sez police are shit and they lock black people up and kill 'em in prison." Edwards closed his eyes to stop himself from cringing. The boy's squeaky tone dropped to a low pitch. "They killed his dog." Edwards tried to hide his excitement. He bent down until his was eye-level with the brown-eyed boy. "They was wearing masks. They killed the dog." Colin could see that this upset the child. "Mummy told me to go to bed but I watched through my window. They made the fire fly through the air into his house. Like magic."

"What's your name?"

"Josh."

"Where"s your bedroom Josh?" The boy pointed to a house directly opposite Hatchet's. Edwards could barely contain his excitement. This was the best breakthrough he'd had in a while.

"Why did they kill his dog?" Josh asked despondently.

Edwards was going to give the boy the subtlest answer he could find when suddenly the boy's mother came rushing up the cordoned off avenue, snatching the boy ferociously towards her. She shook him until he started to cry.

"Din't I tell you not to talk to no strangers?"

"It's all right. I'm a…" He didn't even get time to take out his ID. Her black eyes bored into him coldly. "You stay away from my kid-y'hear. He's got nothing to say to no beast." She dragged the little boy screaming up the avenue. Over his whimpers he heard her still reprimanding him.

"Joshua you must be mad. You want dem bad boys to come burn down our house too, one night when we're sleepin' in bed?"

ZUKIE WOKE UP, hot, hearing voices. For a second he had forgotten where he was, like he did the other morning. The first night he'd awakened to find the flat completely empty. Then he remembered. They were out avenging Mentian's death. Zukie's head throbbed. Too much drink. His mouth longed for a spliff. Rubbing his head, he lay back. Don't remember falling asleep in here. He was in Danny's room again, in stretch boxer shorts. The voices from the main room were getting louder. Zukie sat up again.

The door flung open. Zukie stared at Danny as he walked in, bare-chested and Nike jogging pants.

"Light-Finger, you hungry?" Sighing, Zukie nodded, retrieving his jeans from the floor and searching in the pockets for his small bag of weed. He noticed his supply was going down as he licked some Rizla papers together.

"Nero's rustled up some ackee, salt-fish and dumplings. Come through and get some before they eat it all." Zukie smiled.

"You won't let them do that to me."

"Why, Light-Finger?"

"Cos if I waste away from starvation that'll be on your conscience."

"I in't got no conscience, star," Danny said seriously. He altered his voice to a low demonic tone. "When I was born my soul got sucked out by the devil. In its place is a cruel, uncaring, savage creature." Danny crossed his eyes, pulled a grimace and started to walk with his hands outstretched towards Zukie in his best impersonation of a friend.

Zukie laughed, shaking his head. His laughter built up as Danny began to near him. Zukie threw one pillow then another but Ranks kept coming. Zukie abandoned building his spliff as Danny threw himself on Zukie. The two play-fought, wrestling until Zukie, breathless, was forced to submit. They both sat up and Ranks put an arm around Zukie loosely, giving him a tight, small hug. He lifted his fist for Zukie to touch. Zukie touched it. Ranks smiled reassuringly.

Nerome barged into the room.

"Quick. There's something on the news." Leaning over, Danny found the remote for the portable on the floor. He switched the TV on. Nerome sat on the bed. Zukie stared at the small screen. A scene began to unfold. A field. A country road. Police searching the field.

"Terrence Michael Garvey, aged 21, from the Whalley Range area of Manchester."

"Shit, look at that — Trench is dead." Ranks said, genuinely taken aback. "I liked that roughneck gangster boy. He taught me a trick or two." A photograph of Trench flashed on the TV. "Phew what a waste. Still, what goes around comes around. Mentian is avenged."

Zukie frowned.

"I know him." Zukie said, swallowing. Ranks and Nero looked at him questioningly. Zukie leaned forward, gripping his knees. He suddenly felt cold.

"He called by the shop. Said he wanted to talk to my brother. Storm — Clifton was raw wid him. He looked like shit. He looked scared." Danny was frowning. "He mentioned Blueboy — Fluxy."

Danny stared at Zukie. Feeling awkward, Zukie climbed out of the bed.

"Where you going? You in't finish talkin'."

"My head's light. I need some food."

The room was moving a little. Zukie felt slightly unsteady on his feet.

As he walked out he could feel Danny watching his back curiously.

People were dying as if death was in vogue.

And he had to, had to see the one joy in his life.

For one last time.

STORM HAD SHUT the shop early to spend the afternoon with his children Lee and Tia at Stockport's luxurious leisure complex. They'd been in the fun pool, swirling down tubes and slides, and for an hour or so Storm could forget about the last week. Almost.

On the way home Tia chatted non stop in her little high-tone voice. Her carefree chitchat scuttled over his head. The windows of the jeep were open. The swim had done little to cool him. The kids asked for ice-lollies. Storm pulled over, outside a shop on the A6.

While the kids laughed and grabbed sweets, crisps, chocolate and ice-lollies, Storm's attention was seized by two chilling incidents on the front page of The Manchester Evening News, which was piled on top of the shop counter. It covered the story of Hatchet's arson attack. But it was the photograph of Trench staring at him that gripped his attention.

Grabbing a copy of the paper, Storm read it. Trench was dead. Killed by a truck on a country road in Cheshire. A tingling coolness forced its way through his body, numbing the base of his skull. Storm remembered the last time he saw Trench; he stopped by the shop begging for help. He remembered Trench's fearful, deadly premonition.

"You won't see me again. You're looking at a dead man. Then you'll know. That's the only way you're gonna know."

Tia pulled his arm and called him, dragged him from his uneasy thoughts. Storm paid for the goods and bought a copy of the newspaper. Folding it under his arm, he ushered the kids out of the shop and into the jeep. Ice cold sweat on his body.

Straightaway, Storm knew he had to phone Bluebwai.

Blue's mobile rang.

And rang.

ALICIA EDWARDS WAS trying to be supportive, but in reality had no idea how much things were affecting her husband. She bought him black coffee, expertly massaging his shoulders as he stayed up late in his study.

Trench was dead. He was talking to the kid a couple of days ago and now he was dead. It could have been simply a freak accident, but the driver had said Trench had run from the fields straight into his path. What was Trench doing there so far from home? How did he get there? Who was with him? The circumstances surrounding Trench's death were indeed suspicious, but without much evidence, it was certain there was no case.

Edwards was feeling the strain. He felt, somehow, that he had let Trench down. Like Josh's mother who felt that he had let the race down because he was a police officer, as if somehow it made him tarnished. He was used to black folks reviling him for his choice of profession. Yet he felt that people like Josh's mother could make a difference. Instead they let their lives be ruled by fear and ignorance. Then again he could understand their lack of trust in the police. Especially when he thought of eighteen-year-old Stephen Lawrence, killed by a group of white racists. And Christopher Alder, who died on the cold wet floor of a police station, gasping for breath, while police officers walked past him about their business.

Yet he had to concentrate on one element in all of this or he was going to lose it.

Colin poured some gin from a bottle, staring into his dark garden. He couldn't afford to lose it.

"ZUKIE! I WASN'T expecting you to want to see me again. Baby, what made you change your mind?"

Paradise Browne's face was a canvas painted with joy as she saw her beloved Zukie on her doorstep, unexpected. Zukie had a strange look in his eye as he walked into her living room. Playful. There was just a hint of a smile on his lips.

"Kyesha's asleep. Why didn't you call? I've been so worried about you since Leeds, I—" He put a finger to her lips. At least he wasn't bitter. Zukie smiled. He looked like he'd been smoking weed. Taking her by the hand, he pulled her towards the wooden circular stairwell.

Closing the bedroom door, Zukie pulled her into his arms and held her tightly, moving his hips slowly against her.

"Zukie let me just explain about why I kept it from you."

He put his finger to his mouth, frowning.

"Sssshhh!"

Keeping his eyes on her, he started to strip, laughing, until he stood in front of her buck-naked. Zukie turned and walked to the bed.

Their lovemaking started slow with him dominating every movement, savouring every touch, lick, bite or caress, ordering her to do things to him. He kissed her lovingly. She told him she loved him. He didn't respond. He kept his eyes open, staring deeply into hers. Paradise had never seen him this way before, making love so seriously. He didn't stop for a second, taking her from every position energetically, as if he had all night. Soon, she felt the tiredness of the day overcome her. She had given all she could to Zukie, physically, emotionally and yet he craved more. He pounded her until they were both soaking wet. When she cried for him to take his time, he moved faster and harder inside her. She grabbed his long brown dreadlocks as if she was holding onto her life. Then he came, it seemed to surprise him. His breathing increased. Closed his eyes. Buried his face in her neck. He allowed her to cradle him for a second before withdrawing from her, then turning onto his side, his back to her.

There was a tattoo of a roaring lion over his right shoulder. She had never seen it before.

She carried on touching his skin, kissing his back. Her dark, long fingers contrasted with his peanut-coloured skin.

KURTIS WATCHED THE crystals burn and crackle magically in the darkness, like bright stars against a dark sky. His eyes widened and his left leg jumped as the hard drug began to kick in. Soon he was high, sliding against Ranks' bed, wearing only a tight, lacy pair of women's briefs, touching himself, smoking, laughing as the voices entered his head. It sounded like Gran scolding him. Little did she know her favourite grandson was a sly killer. But this Kurtis would keep to himself. Could never tell this to Ranks. Not yet anyway. For now he was enjoying the ride. Shit, Danny's crack was the best yet.

"FIRST SMALL, THEN Hatchet now Trench." Michigan screeched hoarsely, punching his fist into Easy's wooden door, swearing to avenge his brother. Easy sighed. "Every fuckin' one of Danny's crew is gonna die. I swear." Michigan was enraged, crying bitter tears. Easy sat silently on his sofa building a spliff. Ranger looked down at the floor dismally. Slide looked vacantly out of the window.

"They mussta burned Hatchet out before they picked me and Trench up and brought us out to Cheshire." Easy declared solemnly. The room was dark. The atmosphere was sombre. They'd just heard how Ranks and his crew had kidnapped Easy and Trench, taking them to Cheshire where Trench got killed trying to escape and Easy managed to evade their captors.

"Poor Trench. Shit. I don't wanna think about it."

"So that's why we couldn't contact you all night," Michigan said.

"Yeah. I hid out there most of the night. Walking to the nearest village. Didn't know where the fuck I was. I found a train station and took a train to Macclesfield. Then one to Stretford. I just knew they had killed Trench," Easy said. He sniffed. "He fuckin' didn"t deserve to die like that. And what they did to Hatchet."

"Ranks is bang out of order. We're going to bleed every last drop of blood outta him body for what he's done to my brother and Trench," Michigan said.

"Don't worry bout that," Easy said, "my Grandma always says, every dog has his day, and every cat has his four o' clock."

Slide said nothing.

He stared out of the window, far into the dark Hulme night.

PARADISE WAS SUDDENLY wide-awake. Her bedroom was bright: morning was here.

"Zukie?" Paradise felt for him in the bed. Instead she found a hand written sheet of paper, along with a pile of twenty-pound notes. Sitting up quickly, she read the letter.

P,

I trusted you to help me and to be true to me. It's obvious that I have strong feelings for you, feelings that guided me back to you, but how can I trust you

after you and Storm did what you did? What I'm saying is, I can't even stay friends with you. Here's some money for Kyesha. I want to see her every weekend if that's OK with you. I don't think she should be the one to suffer through all of this. God knows I know what that kind of suffering is. I'll be in contact. Take care.
Zukie.

Paradise leapt from the bed.

CHRIS McDERMID WAS losing concentration, making silly mistakes so that the heavy bag bore into her. Easy hadn't bothered to contact her in weeks. No phone calls, text messages — nothing apart from a bunch of flowers, accompanied by a card professing his so-called apologies. Ten minutes ago he suddenly phoned to tell her he was coming over. Just like that.

To be truthful, Chris had missed Easy-Love, as manipulative and as selfish as he was. She'd left the main entrance and the front door open because she had changed the front door lock to prevent him from simply walking back in on her. Chris had something to say to Easy. Depending on some other news, it might make all the difference.

Chris unwrapped her hands. Breathless, covered in sweat she headed for the bathroom for a shower. She put a towel around her neck, remembering that she had left the pregnancy testing kit in the living room.

The stranger was casually standing in her living room. A tall dark official-looking black man wearing a suit, tie. Christine was stunned almost into a paralysed state.

"Sorry to startle you. The door was open. We called but got no answer. We've called around several times to see you. Miss McDermid, I'm DI Colin Edwards of the Manchester Serious Crime Division and my colleague behind the door is DC Steve Davidson." He flashed his ID. Chris's mousy brown hair stuck to the sweat on her forehead. Her throat suddenly felt dry.

"What do you want?" she asked firmly, striving to hide her irritation.

"Just a few questions."

The other cop came in. White, not bad-looking, tall, blonde hair, dreamy blue eyes. He sat down without being asked.

"You reported a street mugging some months ago."

"Look, can't you call back later? I've just done a workout. I need a shower." Chris's eyes were on the front door. Any second now Easy could show.

"This won't take long. I promise." Edwards' eyes were on the pregnancy kit.

"You expecting some good news?" He smiled warmly.

"Maybe." Chris said. Any second now Easy could show.

The white cop got up. Started walking around looking at her kickboxing trophies and awards. He was making Chris sick inside. *Any second now Easy could show*.

"Have they found the muggers?"

"No."

"Well, what is this all about?"

"Amongst the things that you listed in your bag were some bills and a driving licence, right?"

Lighting a cigarette Chris sat down on the armchair next to the large TV opposite the police.

"Do you mind not walking up and down in my flat?" Davidson gave Chris a surprised look then sat down. "Yeah, that's right."

"Can you describe the guys who snatched your bag?"

"Can't you look it up on a computer somewhere?"

"Miss McDermid, we have no other witnesses of the incident. We're trying to find the link between documents you used to hire a car seen at the scene of a very serious crime in Leeds. A young man was shot dead and two others were injured."

Christine exhaled.

"Somebody stole my handbag, used my documents. I can't help you."

"Christine, do you know a yout' by the name of Barrington Evander Brown, otherwise known as Easy-Love or Easy?" Any second now Easy could show.

Christine breathed slowly. Holding her cigarette she stared steadily at Edwards. Blue eyes interlocked with dark brown irises. For a moment. Chris looked away.

"No. Should I? Did he steal my bag or something?"

"We think he did. We think he got lucky when he got your driving licence." Davidson stood up.

"Think? You're not sure? He might've stolen my bag. I had photos of my dead baby daughter in that bag! It shit me up. Yet you think only he might have. Why did you come 'round here?"

"Just thought you might have been able to give us a better a description of the muggers. Like you might have remembered something since then. Sorry to have bothered you. We'll be going."

They turned to leave. Chris took a deep drag on the cigarette, following them.

Davidson stopped. Chris's heart bumped viciously.

"You need to make sure you keep your door locked, Miss McDermid. There are some dangerous criminals around," he said.

"Yeah," Chris said slowly. "I'll remember that." She watched them heading towards the stairs, terrified that they would bump into her estranged lover. She watched as their well-suited backs disappeared around the corner down the stairs.

A second later, the lift doors opened.

Chris felt the blood rush to her head.

Easy-Love Brown strode casually out of the lift, holding a bunch of flowers.

Smiling.

"REAL FUCKIN' BAD play," Slide muttered to Ranger and Michigan. They were at the Royal Infirmary, by Hatchet's bedside, some time after meeting with their new gang-leader Easy-Love. Hatchet remained unconscious, unable to tell them anything, his burned arms swathed in bandages. His bed was surrounded by cards, fresh fruit, and flowers from well-wishers. A couple of days ago his room had been guarded by a police officer, keeping Slide and the others from visiting their friend and brother.

"Pure fuckin' bad play," Slide repeated, his skin the colour of smooth cornmeal in the light that poured from the window. He sat on a chair, his hands under his chin. He looked despondent. Michigan was standing by the bed looking down at his brother. He suddenly focussed his attention on Slide, frowning.

"What do you mean?"

"We're losing people quicker than we have ever lost people before," Slide said.

"So that's why we should take Danny and his crew out. Fast. Innit?" Michigan said flatly.

Slide tried not to raise his voice.

"What with? Michi, we in't got no crew."

"Easy's recruitin'. He's got his brother and Teeko."

"Tell me something Michi, you seen them lately? When was the last time yu seen Teeko? If you ask me Teeko don't give a fuck. That Kurtis looks like he's suckin' dicks for crack. And if you ask me I think Easy's a crazy dog, jackin' Ranks' money like that. Crazy shit, man."

"Wait a minute, we was all in this. We all agreed to take Ranks' money," Ranger said, his brown eyes staring wide.

"Not Trench. And Trench is the one who's dead. He warned Miss Small and she's dead. Trench never did like Easy."

"So what you sayin'?"

Slide sighed. "Miss Small got man in Yard, yeah? Robbie, Kite, Cangoose. I checked them and they in't happy about losin' their UK connection. They're talkin' about slippin' in and runnin' tings." What Slide was trying to say was, he wanted anybody but Easy running the crew but the other two didn't seem to be hearing him.

"You discussed this with Easy?" Ranger asked.

"No."

"We don't want no Yardies fuckin' up our runnings. Mess wid dem man deh and they just empty a whole clip of bullets in you an' put another round in just to mek sure. Anyway, I say we follow Easy and just out dem facety Worlders man," Ranger stressed.

"Yeah and in the meantime we all die. Hatchet, Ranger, me, you."

Michigan watched him. Thoughts crowded his head. He too was feeling doubts and suspicions. A gang had no room for such thoughts and emotions. Maybe that's why things were slowly falling apart.

And he had nearly lost his brother because of it.

"WHAT DID YOU make of Chris McDermid?" Edwards asked Davidson as they drove along Stockport Road towards the city centre. The streets were crowded with shoppers. Thankfully, the temperature had dropped and the forecast was rain for the rest of the week.

"A damn good liar," Davidson said sighing.

"I seen her face somewhere before too," Edwards said. "Just can't place where."

"She's calm."

"A façade." Edwards said. He had a degree in psychology. "She's under control. I'd say behind that lies a cunning person. She has that don't-fuck-with-me look, don't she? Did you notice the scars on her forearms?"

"Yeah." It started to rain.

"Self-harm, I reckon. I bet she's been admitted to hospital on quite a few occasions."

The windscreen wipers wished backwards and forwards, like pendulums measuring out time spent uselessly: they were running nowhere with their investigations.

STORM STOOD LOOKING at the empty wardrobe. Obviously, Zukie had been back for the rest of his stuff, while Storm was at the shop. He'd left his front door key on the bed in his bedroom.

Storm sat on the bed dejectedly, looking at the key. Another funeral. Mr Mentian's. He wasn't in the mood for any more darkness. He had darkness of his own. But if there was any chance that Zukie might be at Mentian's funeral it was a chance worth taking. He needed to speak to Zukie. And he couldn't forget the fact that Mentian had helped to save Zukie's life in Leeds.

The doorbell rang. Storm found himself rushing downstairs, thinking and hoping it was Zukie. Opening the door he found Paradise on the doorstep, clutching Zukie's letter in one hand and holding onto her daughter with her other hand. She was crying. Storm pulled her inside.

"WE'RE LOSING HIM." Paradise Browne dabbed her eyes with a wet handkerchief. She was angry more than upset. "Just keep quiet and everything will be OK you said." Storm shook his head. It was his turn to comfort, holding Paradise in his arms.

"Just look at this letter he wrote. I mean what the hell does it mean? I love him, Cliff. I don't wanna lose him again. Not this time. Not ever. It took me so long — take me to Danny's so I can try and talk to him."

"Paradise, I've already done that. It doesn't work. He won't listen. Look I'll see him at the funeral of the guy who got shot in Leeds, yeah? I'll try and talk to him then."

Storm's head was spinning. With everything going on this was more than he could take. His rekindled relationship with Jasmine was floundering already. She had even accused him of spending too much time with Paradise, insinuating that there was more than friendship going on. He felt guilty because he knew he wasn't being honest with Jasmine. He couldn't possibly tell her what was really happening, could he? He hadn't felt this lost in a long time.

EASY-LOVE TOOK Chris in his arms and held her. And was surprised when, suddenly, she pulled him inside the flat fiercely, slamming the front door and slapping his face, right on his healing jaw wound. Easy-Love dropped the flowers and held his stinging face.

"The police have just been here," Chris announced virulently.

Easy frowned.

"What — why?"

"The documents you used to hire some car." Easy-Love stared at her. "Why did you doctor my driving licence? Now they're sniffing around — and what happened to your face?"

Easy-Love ran a finger over the dressing on his lower face, feeling the anger for Storm's younger brother rekindle. Ignoring her he walked over to the apartment window, looking out on the street. He sighed with relief. There were no unmarked cars staking the place out. For now anyway.

"Where have you been all this time Easy? No phone calls nothing. I thought you cared about me? Don't you love me?"

Easy was severely agitated. Her words were floating invisibly over his head and evaporating.

"I think I might be pregnant," she said. Easy gritted his teeth. He was more interested in what the police were doing here, what they wanted, how much they knew, and what his neurotic girlfriend might have told them.

"SO ZUKIE, YOU want employment here?" Marshall, a bald-headed, R. Kelly look-a-like invited Zukie into his luxury office at Cappella Records Inc, giving Zukie's hand a firm shake. Zukie viewed the awards and discs covering the walls. Zukie was dressed in his best black suit for Mentian's funeral, his dreads pulled back off his face. Marshall asked Zukie to sit down.

Marshall slouched back in his high-back leather chair, and looked at the grey-eyed kid.

"You and your brother fallen out?

"No. Just wanna venture out on my own."

"Zukie, I want full commitment I don't appreciate people just walking in and out. I know how blood is thicker than water and your brother might--"

"You don't need to worry bout dat Marshall. I won't be working with my brother not now or the future. So, do we have a deal?"

"Yes, but you have to understand that I have to pay you the same money as a studio hand. Raymond won't like it if I start you on the same scale as him, seeing as he has years of experience and has been with Cappella records for a long time."

"That's cool." Zukie rose, smiling.

"Your left arm. How did you break it?" Zukie dropped his eyes down to the cast. He was left-handed but could also use his right hand. He couldn't actually tell Marshall the truth.

"I, er, got knocked over a couple of weeks ago. It's cool. It's coming off in a little while. I can still operate with my right arm."

"All right Zukie. I'll see you tomorrow. Early OK?"

"Sure, and thanks Marshall. You won't regret it."

Zukie left his new employer feeling positive and vibrant. It was the best feeling he'd had for ages. He knew the news would reach Storm. His brother was working for a rival.

But that was his intention.

He wanted to hurt his brother.

Like he had hurt him.

Badly.

MICHIGAN WAS PACKING TWO pieces, an Israeli 9 mm Uzi, and a .38 Special. His brother was badly burned and lying unconscious in a hospital bed. He drove across the city and waited outside Southern Cemetery's main huge gates, waiting for Mr Mentian's funeral cortege.

WHAT WAS HER favourite food? Did she really care for him? Had she loved the person who helped to create him? Did she like carrot cake like Aunt Celia? Did she listen to John Holt and sing along to "A Thousand Volts of Holt"while hoovering, swirling the vacuum cleaner around the house like a dance partner in the way Aunt Celia did?

Slowly Ranks' attention was brought back to Mentian's funeral by the sound of singing. *Rock of Ages cleft for me, let me put my trust in Thee.* Ranks sighed. Was her funeral like this?

The day was dark, and rain was threatening. Ranks felt Zukie's unease. Standing close to Ranks, Zukie looked remote, tense. He stood, wavering slightly, in a designer black suit, the laces of one of his Rockport boots undone. Couldn't tie them because of his injury. Ranks rested his hand on the back of Zukie's neck firmly but comfortingly. Zukie looked at him briefly. Across the black-clad crowd around the hole where Mentian was about to be lowered, Ranks noticed Storm watching him with Zukie. Ranks knew it hurt him to see him with Zukie. But that wasn't Ranks' intention. Secretly, deep down, he was wondering how this was all going to end.

The Worlders crew stayed together, some distance from Mentian's estranged family, who knew who they were but said nothing, they knew their son had chosen the gang-banging from an early age.

As the coffin was lowered Ranks and Nero paid their last respects to a good friend, throwing gold signet rings onto the coffin. The rest followed suit, Pipes, Fila, Sizzla and Stukky still hobbling on crutches. Nero took up a spade ready to help bury his friend. Zukie stood back awkwardly, his eyes sorrowful. Ranks bent down and tied Zukie's laces.

POP, POP, POP, POP!

The sound was like firecrackers. Panic and confusion. Screams. People ran, zigzagged amongst graves. Some dived down into the mud and earth, hid behind gravestones. The lone gunman fired recklessly. Pipes, Fila and Stukky ran for cover behind the two Shoguns parked in a lane nearby. Pulling Zukie down Danny dived onto him protectively; they fell to the ground breathing heavily. Bullets flew around them.

The gunfire stopped. Ranks heard crying. He heard a car screech past and someone shouting obscenities. Ranks leapt to his feet. Zukie rose to a kneeling position, shock carved into his soft features. Ranks cursed. The rest of the crew edged back to Mentian's graveside. Pipes, Stukky, Fila, Sizzla. No Nerome.

"Nerome?" Ranks looked around. He saw Nerome. Nerome's legs sprawled wide: he sat leaning against a gravestone, clutching his chest. Blood was pouring from him. He was breathing fast, blinking hard.

Ranks felt as if he was running towards Nero in slow motion, as if he had two broken feet. He stumbled, recovering quickly, his hand outstretched. He heard his own scream in his ears, muffled as if he was deep underwater, as he leapt on to Nero.

"Nawwww! Nawww! Nero! No."

Slowly people started to gather around. Ranks shook Nero violently but he was already closing his eyes. No one was prepared for this. You don't go to a funeral tooled up, wearing flaks. Ranks felt strong hands on his body trying to pull him off. Storm's voice.

"Forget it Danny! He's dead Danny. He's dead."

Kneeling, Danny was screaming, tears flowing from his eyes.

"No. No. I don"t — Nero get up."

"He's dead."

Ranks looked on desperately as Storm dragged Zukie in front of Nero's bloodied body by his neck.

"This is the crowd you're with now. This is the shit that happens."

With a grunt Zukie pulled away, walking quickly towards one of the Shoguns, locking himself inside. Covering his ears and eyes, he scrunched up in a ball, rocking backwards and forwards.

Pipes called an ambulance on his mobile, hands trembling. A young black woman appeared, pushing her way through the crowd.

"I'm a nurse," she said, her voice oscillating with emotion, bending down, pulling Ranks away gently. "Get me some material, anything. Quickly." The Worlders crew started shredding shirts, someone brought a towel from their car.

She ordered Storm, the nearest and the most calm, to stem Nero's blood. The woman leant over Nero, checking his breathing. Frowning, she put her mouth to his. She started her long resuscitation, perspiration on her forehead, beating Nero's chest until the emergency crew arrived to take over ten minutes later.

NEROME CAMPBELL WALKED stiltedly along the long train aisle. People looked at him, some whispering. Eventually Nero found a vacant seat occupied by a man reading a newspaper.

The stranger looked up from the paper. Nerome's eyes widened. It was Aston. The train was slowing down, approaching a station.

"This is where you get off, Nero." Aston said.

"What about you?" Nero asked his friend. "Aren't you coming?"

Aston smiled in that way that made Nero's heart ache, shaking his head. Nero's throat constricted. In a second Nero was off the train. He was staring at a clock on a wall. He felt pain. Nero closed his eyes and went back to sleep.

RAIN, LIGHTNING AND thunder broke up the sultry weather bringing a welcome cool breeze. Storm waited in the hospital corridor. Restless. Looking up he saw the signs indicating various hospital departments, including the morgue. Further down the corridor the Worlders Crew waited silently. Pipes, Fila, Stukky, Sizzla stood desolately. Zukie sat next to Ranks, who sat with his head in his hands, his clothes covered in dried blood. He'd had stitches put into a wound in his right hand. The hand was wrapped in bandages. Zukie's plastered left arm hung loosely over the younger boy's shoulder. They looked and acted like long time close friends. It both angered Storm, and made him resentful and jealous. Storm had tried to reason with Zukie earlier, but Zukie wouldn't talk to him. Storm understood why. Zukie's neck was purple and blue where Storm had gripped it. Storm was sorry for what he had done. But not as sorry as the way Ranks was feeling now.

The corridor was full of people coming and going. Storm hated hospitals. It reminded him of the Old Lady and Zukie. Who thought a funeral could end like this? Getting up Storm heard his designer shoes clicking on the tiled floor. He knew Ranks knew he was there, even without looking up. Storm looked at Zukie who kept his eyes focused at the wall straight ahead.

"Danny. I'm really sorry about Nero," Storm said. Ranks just grunted. "Anyone called his woman?"

"Just an answering machine," Ranks said solemnly. "I need a smoke."

"Is your hand OK?"

"Fine." Danny spoke sharply.

"Danny why don't you go home? There's nothing you can do here."

"I in't leavin' Nero."

"Look, why don't *you* go home? Zukie said. "In't yu got things to do?"

Storm sighed.

"I'm gonna get some coffee. Do you two want anything?"

"Yeah! I want you to fuck off and leave us alone!" Zukie said bitterly. Storm stared at his brother, who eyeballed him back coldly. Their conversation was interrupted by a stern voice.

"Daniel Raymond Patterson?"

Everyone looked up. A tall, dark black man, dressed in jeans and a hooded sweatshirt, was looking at Ranks.

Danny frowned.

"Who the fuck wants to know?" Danny asked.

CHRIS HAD JUST cooked a meal for herself and Easy. She had moved back into the house in Hulme, back with her beloved Easy. And it felt as if she had never left. She had forgiven him and was looking forward to a night with him. The dining room was dimly lit with candles. Easy had put her flowers in a vase. Red chrysanthemums. They were halfway through the four-course meal Chris had spent all day preparing when there was a heavy pounding on the front door. Chris looked at Easy. Easy looked back at her quizzically.

"We're not expecting company are we? Ignore it."

She knew Easy was thinking about the police visit, and feared they had found out his address.

Easy's expression was of pure anxiety.

PUTTING HIS FORK down, intimate dinner for two interrupted, Easy-Love rose out of his seat slowly. He didn't see Chris put her head in her hands despondently. Easy walked over to the window, over to the balcony and peeped over. He saw Ranger's red Corsa fuel injection car.

"It's my man dem," he said emphatically, half-sighing with relief. He was already walking towards the front door not realising Chris was angry and annoyed. Before she could protest Ranger and Slide had walked in casually. They gave her a quick nod of acknowledgement, staring at the table.

"Wassamatter?"

They both looked at each other before looking at Chris. Quick to interpret that discretion was needed Easy took them into the bedroom where Ranger promptly sat on the huge bed, building a spliff. Slide chose to stare through the bedroom window. It seemed like he was out there in the night. Easy looked at Ranger.

"Michi's banged up." Ranger said.

"What?"

"He went to Mentian's funeral-tooled up — shot up Ranks' crew. I heard the bodyguard got shot."

Pleasure was evident in Easy's voice. "He lick out the bodyguard? Shiii-hiiit! Anybody else?"

"No."

"Yu sure?"

"Mmmmm."

"Fool shoulda took out Danny."

"He wants you to bail him," Slide said.

"Bail him? Like walk into a police station and shit? No fucking way. He's on his own. I don't want no beast knockin' on my door, raidin' my gates. He didn't consult none of us, especially me when he went off. Just get it back to him, Ranger. He in't to call me or any of us. He betta tell dem beast bwai he's workin' on his jack. If he's got any sense he will."

STORM MICHAELS LOOKED beyond the not so unfamiliar face that had questioned Danny Ranks and saw two uniformed policemen.

"I'm Detective Inspector Edwards of the Serious Crime

Department and this is my colleague Detective Constable Steve Davidson." A white man emerged, wearing the same serious expression. There was a look of recognition in Edwards' eyes as he stared at Storm, then Zukie. Danny looked down to the floor again, rubbing his nose and sighing. There were curses of 'rahs claht' and the crew sucked through their teeth viciously. Storm kept his eyes on his brother who averted his. A nurse walked by.

"Daniel we need to speak to you about the events today. We also need to speak to you about several incidents that have occurred over the last few months, including the murder of Mrs Veniesha Brooks."

"She was my mother. I didn't kill her."

Storm was stunned. He looked around at Danny's crew who were equally flummoxed, looking at each other, puzzled. Edwards was already focussing his attention on Fila.

"You. What's your name?" Fila looked at the black cop.

"Me? Fila Warren — Warren Jamieson."

"Take off your bandanna." Sighing, Fila did as he was told, frowning at Danny.

"Is your hair naturally blonde?"

"Yeah, for as long as I can remember. Want to see my pubic hair? I believe I'm blonde there too."

This elicited a few sniggers and grins.

"Well you won't mind accompanying us to the station and giving us a few samples for forensics."

"Samples? What for? Yu tryin' to fit me up?"

"What's the problem Fila?" Davidson asked. "If you're a natural blonde you get to walk home tonight."

"Daniel, we also need to speak to you about an arson attack on Ravel Palmer."

"Am I under arrest?"

"No. You could be if you refuse to come to the station."

"Yu got nuttin' on me. I'm stayin' here wid Nero."

"In a few minutes these officers will search you all for any illegal substances and illegal weapons."

"Whatever," Ranks said. "Tell ya what. Go ahead. Search." Ranks stood up, held out his hands, spun around then turned his stomach against the corridor walls, spreading his legs apart. "Frisk me. Den take me down to the station and ask your stupid little fedz questions."

"MICHIGAN! YOU'RE ONE dead nigga I swear. When I get ya. For what you did today I'm gonna out ya bright fuckin' light! Ya hear me? Ya hear me Dodge twat?" In a strange play of circumstances they were moving Michigan between cells when Edwards and Davidson brought Ranks into the police station past the custody desk.

Michigan was smiling. Unrepentant, giving Danny the index finger and mouthing the words, "fuck you". There was confusion as Ranks leapt at Michigan, swearing and cursing. It took six police officers to hold Danny down as he screamed threats at Michigan. Michigan had been caught immediately after the shooting at the cemetery. He had lost control of the car he was driving and crashed straight into a hearse entering the cemetery.

They got Ranks settled in an interview room off the main corridor. He was still scowling, sitting opposite Edwards, arms crossed, fuming. Edwards pressed the play button on a tape recorder, informing him that he could leave at any time but it was in his best interests to stay.

"Did you orchestrate the death of Mrs Veniesha Brooks alias Miss Small?" Edwards asked. Ranks laughed.

"Orchestrate? In't that when you play music or sumtin?"

"A 31-year-old pregnant woman died. This isn't funny."

A pair of smouldering hazel eyes studied Edwards obtusely although Danny tried to hide the shock of her pregnancy from the two detectives. The tape was rolling,

"I know my rights. I don't have to say Jack."

"Just answer the question Daniel." Davidson said.

"No comment."

"Did you order Fila to kill Miss Small?"

"What the hell is this? Was her killer white? Is there something yu in't tellin' me?"

Edwards twisted his lips. They thought they were going to be doubly lucky when they spied the white boy with the black bandanna waiting with Danny and the rest. Excitement was quickly followed by apprehension when they realised he had blonde hair. Tests, an hour later, eliminated Fila from the Miss Small murder inquiry.

"Why are you questioning me about Small's killing when you obviously know he was a white guy? And that bastard Michigan, you got him for blasting my man Nero, why in't you askin' him questions?"

They ignored him. "Where were you last Thursday at around 9pm?"

"Wid my woman, Jamilia," Danny was getting pissed off and tired.

"Doing what?" Davidson asked.

"Sex. What else do you do wid a woman? Charades?"

"Where does this Jamilia live?"

"Three four five, Seymour Grove, Old Trafford."

Ranks sat back casually in his chair.

"Were you at the Club Planetarium in Leeds on the night your friend Wesley, also known as Mr Mention was shot?"

Ranks suddenly leaned forward. "His name was Mentian. Mr. Men — SHAN. Say it like a true-born nigga instead of some wanna be middle-class white man."

"Answer the question."

Danny smirked. "You don't know do you? Because if you did you wouldn't be askin' me would ya? Stupid questions, going round and round and gettin' nowhere."

"Answer the question please, Daniel."

"I was with my woman, Nadine. Ask her. She'll tell you. Making love all night."

The next question almost threw Danny.

"The light skin boy back at the hospital, dreadlocks, was he the one who glassed Barrington Brown aka. Easy in the face in Leeds, sparking the whole thing off?"

"Look, either charge me for whatever so I can call my lawyer or let me go back to Nero. I know my rights."

Danny stood up. Sighing angrily Edwards looked at Davidson who swallowed. Edwards put his finger on the stop button.

"Interview terminated at 11.30 p.m."

Danny looked down at Edwards still seated.

"You know, Nerome Campbell is extremely lucky. Three bullets passed through him Daniel, just missing vital organs and arteries. He has had five pints of blood and he managed to survive a five-hour operation. Just. Makes you think, doesn't it?"

"Let me tell you sumtin, crackajack. I din't start no war. OK? But I'm gonna done it. Today, tomorrow or next fuckin' year, yu hear me? I tell you, Michigan Palmer's lucky he ran into that hearse today because pretty soon he woulda been in one."

"We need an address so we can contact you should we need to ask you any more questions," Edwards said.

"Address? Sure. Twelve Rainer Avenue Moss Side," Danny said blasé.

They both knew Danny didn't live there.

"Do you have a driving licence? Some proof of residence?"

"No. One, I don't have nuttin like dat because I don't drive and two, seein' as I'm not under arrest there's nuttin for me to comply wid. I answered your questions. You waan reach me — reach me pon street."

"Don't worry." Edwards said. "We *will* find you again if we need to speak with you, we'll just follow the trail of bodies and bullets."

Danny half-grunted, looking at his Rolex watch. As he swaggered out towards the police car park where Pipes waited for him in the Lexus, he took out his mobile and called the hospital, pretending to be Nero's brother. The hospital told him that Nerome had been transferred out of intensive care to a private room, his condition critical but stable.

"PUT A CAR on him," Edwards told Davidson, watching Ranks leave, "I want him followed everywhere. One way or another we're gonna end this madness. I want to know where he lives, who he speaks to, what he eats and even who he's sleeping with."

"There's no guess where he's going now, then is it?"

"No. But I'm not taking any chances. I want him followed now."

DRUNK. THE DRUNKEN Liverpudlian in the cell next door sang a pitiful version of "Wind Beneath My Wings" at the top of his voice. Devanté Reece Palmer alias Michigan shuddered. They were charging Michigan with attempted murder, and two counts of possessing an illegal firearm. He was up for court tomorrow. They told him if he snitched on who he was working with they would maybe get him a shorter sentence. Michigan cursed himself for getting caught, for crashing his car into that hearse and failing to get away. He stood no chance. Not when the police found the guns in the car.

Michigan sighed. His stomach tingled strangely. At seventeen he knew he was heading for a young offenders institution. He had expected Easy to set up a brief for him or to send some word to see if he was OK. Michigan knew Easy had disowned him to save his skin. Miss Small would never have done that. He only hoped that Easy would be decent enough to save him a place in the crew when he came out. Yeah, he was confident, had faith in Easy. Easy would honour and respect him for his work in putting the bodyguard out of action.

Yeah, Nero nearly became a zero hero.

At least now, the way was open for Easy to get Danny now that the two bodyguards were off the scene.

"YOU SAID THIS wouldn't happen." Ushering her boys in, Candice Mitchell was stunned at the sight of Nerome in the hospital. Wires. Tubes. Monitors. She had driven non-stop from Leeds an hour after retuning Danny's call. Candice gasped, almost breaking down.

Danny, standing by the bedside looked up, his eyes staring wide. Jake ran to his father, horrified by the white bandages covering Nero's chest. He jumped on his father trying to hug him. His mother pulled him back gently. The little boy ran to his mother holding her tight, burying his face in her body. Candice stared at Ranks angrily.

Ranks shook his head slowly.

"I didn't make no promises, Candice."

"Jake go and sit down next to Taylor and Morgan."

Ranks swallowed. Candice walked over to her man, looked at him, and kissed his unconscious face.

"Baby, I'm here now. I love you. Jake loves you."

"Mummy, is daddy gonna die?" Jake asked.

Candice looked at Ranks. "Why don't you just go?"

"Look, Candice, I know how hard tings are going to be now," Ranks put his hand in an inside pocket inside his jacket and withdrew a thick wad of cash. "Here, there's about a grand here. It should see you through."

"I don't want your money!" Candice shrieked, slapping the notes from Ranks' hand. She pushed him. Ranks closed his eyes. "I don't want it. I don't want it OK? Now get out and leave us alone." Jake started to cry.

Angry tears poured from Candice's eyes. Backing away, Ranks kissed his teeth. He scooped up the money from the hospital floor, aware of the three boys watching him hatefully. Danny left the room and the hospital subdued, a picture forever engraved on his mind, Nerome's son's terrified face.

It would haunt him forever.

"Mummy, is daddy gonna die?"

FROM THE CORNER of his eyes Kurtis saw shadows in Ranks' bedroom. His attention soon focussed back on Zukie, sleeping drunkenly on the bed. Urgent angry voices in his head told Kurtis that Zukie was a threat to his friendship with Danny. He wondered what Easy would do if he knew where Ranks lived and that Storm's brother was here too. Another voice told him that was not the way to win Ranks over.

Zukie mumbled in his sleep, grunted, then turned on his back. Kurtis's throat and mouth suddenly went dry as if all the water in the world couldn't hydrate him. Kurtis waited for Zukie to breathe deeply again then he took red lipstick from his pocket. Leaning over the boy he carefully drew an upside down five-pointed star on Zukie's stomach as he slept soundly.

Marked for death.

Kurtis sniggered.

AS HE PASSED, Ranks saw the tramp wrapped in tatty blankets, huddled against a large industrial bin in the hospital car park. Danny stopped. Reaching inside his jacket he flung the bundle of money Candice had rejected to the tramp. The vagrant hesitated, his eyes staring unbelievingly, before snatching the money and thanking Ranks endlessly.

As Ranks turned he heard the sound of a sharp whistle. Looking around, Danny saw Storm's Shogun parked under a hospital car park light. Storm beckoned him. Ranks walked towards the jeep. The passenger window slid down automatically.

"Yu brought five-o with you. Plainclothes park up behind Pipes. They followed you from the cop house. Get in." Danny climbed inside the jeep, closing the passenger door firmly. Taking his mobile out, he phoned Pipes and told him what was going down, telling him to drive. Sure enough a dark Vauxhall Astra pulled out behind him. Storm and Ranks watched silently. Ending the call Ranks turned to look at Storm, who was studying him with a serious face.

"So? What now?" Ranks asked ineptly. Storm started his motor, put the vehicle into gear, and tore out of the car park, watching his rear-view mirror carefully for any signs of a trailer.

"Your crew looked like you didn't tell them shit about Miss Small being your relations. If you keep things from people who trust you it causes ripples."

"So what if she was related to me? I never fuckin' knew her. Stupid bitch give me to her sister when I was a baby and happily forgot about me. And when she started to find out who I was on the streets, she still decided to keep quiet. I'm glad she's dead. Fuckin' bitch. I hate her."

Storm said. "You don"t mean that."

"I fuckin' do."

"You know about my brother Bluebwai? How we were brothers in different crews? Think about what you're saying." Ranks shifted uncomfortably in his seat. "There's some weed in there." Ranks rummaged through Storm's glove compartment finding the small bag.

"Where we goin'?"

"Your crib."

Ranks sighed, staring out of the window at the passing houses. It was getting lighter. All he could think of was Nero lying on that hospital bed. His friend, more like a brother. The only person on earth Danny had allowed himself to get close to. Ranks shivered, his head swimming as his raw emotions surfaced temporarily.

"Mummy, is daddy gonna die?"

"Stop da fuckin' car. I need some air." Storm stopped the jeep. Ranks got out. Holding onto the Shogun he vomited by the side of the road. He felt Storm close by.

"You OK?"

Ranks retched again, throwing up his empty guts. Felt like he was going to piss himself.

Back in the jeep Ranks was silent for a long while. Pensive. Storm drove. The Shogun pulled into Ranks' private car park. Ranks pressed a code on the panel of a level-barrier gate. It rose automatically. Storm parked, cutting the engine. For a few seconds the silence was like no other Ranks had experienced in his life. Then Storm said something that made Ranks sit up in his seat.

"Yesterday, you forgot to meet Kadeem," Ranks frowned deeply.

"How the fuck do you—? Wait, you fuckin' work for him, don't ya?"

"No. I don't work for him. He works for me." Storm said, lighting a cigarette. "Don't worry about your lost meeting. I also know Kadeem's got a meeting with Easy who wants a cut of your action. I got things covered. Gonna do a little nixing up for Easy seeing as he's so keen to get in with the big boys."

Shaking his head slowly smiling in half-disbelief and admiration, Ranks felt something dig him in the ribs, like an invisible elbow. It suddenly occurred to him that Storm had never really left the life. His various businesses, shop and recording studio were only fronts.

"And you're gonna need some body armour, now Nero and Mentian ain't on the scene," Storm continued unabated. Ranks was quiet, building his spliff. "I can put three man on you."

"How you know I in't got man of my own?"

"Better skilled than Colours, Juice McKenzie, and Snow-dog?"

Ranks blinked and swallowed, mainly at the mention of hit-man Colours. Suddenly Ranks realised Storm was looking past him into the distance. Looking over his shoulder, following Storm's eyes, Ranks watched as Colours, Juice McKenzie and Snow-dog stepped from a high-powered car parked up on the street. All three were dressed in long black coats. Colours lit a cigarette casually and nodded at Storm. Colours and Frenchie were reputed to have killed Jigsy on Storm's orders. Colours was deadly, but Ranks heard he had retired from the big game, had gone independent and was shacking up with Easy's ex-woman Cassie. Easy would be livid.

Ranks smiled knowingly.

"You're not doing this solely for me are you? Yu cutting in Colours for Zukie's protection." Storm smiled at Ranks' perception, the reason why this seventeen-year-old kid was top dog.

"After today at the cemetery? And Leeds? What did you expect? I'd leave my brother open to the mercy of bad boys?"

"And do you think Zukie's gonna like it cos you put bad bwai Colours to mind him? Remember Chico and Hair Oil died cos of Colours and Peter French?"

"Zukie don't know that unless you tell him." Ranks was amazed at Storm's casual attitude. "Yo Colours!" Storm called Colours over. Colours strode across effortlessly. He was a huge guy, tawny-coloured, with cane-rowed reddish-brown hair and tinted specs. The other two followed.

"I want you to talk to Zukie. I want you to persuade him to come home by telling him that I didn't mean to hurt or kill him or his friends. I want you to let him know that Paradise is cut up over the way he's treating her. I want you to convince him that if he's going to stay around you that having Colours protecting him is for the best."

"And if I talk to him, does this mean me and you are working together?" Colours and the other two stepped into the back seat of the Shogun. Ranks nodded briefly as Colours acknowledged him. Colours smiled slyly. He had a row of gold teeth. Looking down Ranks saw the Mac 11, protruding from Colours' long coat.

"Let's just say, Ranks, I'm your temporary advisor." Storm said quietly.

TWITCHY. EASY-LOVE FELT himself getting twitchy. Didn't know why. Sleep avoided Easy, like the rain evaded a dry scorched wasteland. Beside him Chris slept peacefully. Maybe it was because Michigan had got himself banged up avenging Hatchet and Trench.

Maybe it was because Chris said she was pregnant. Maybe it was because he didn't know Miss Small had been carrying his child and the other child she had was, of all people, Danny Ranks.

Easy-Love wondered if what he had told Kurtis was safe. He wondered if he should have told him anything at all. He wondered at Kurtis's readiness for the gang-life. Easy shivered, running his hand over his head. He rose, showered and dressed as Chris murmured in her sleep. He had a meeting with Kadeem in an hour. But he still couldn't shake the feeling that, even though he thought he was winning the war with the Worlders Crew, something wasn't right.

ANSWERS. COLIN EDWARDS needed some answers. Badly. Especially following the shooting of yet another black male at a cemetery yesterday afternoon and after receiving absolutely no new leads from his interviews with neither Danny Patterson nor Devanté Reece Palmer. Edwards was in his office earlier than usual, 7. 30 am seated at his desk full of papers, drinking black sugarless coffee.

Before him lay the videotape from BBC News North that he had requested about Miss Small's shooting. He had watched it four times since it arrived. Maybe it would tell him something new this morning. Maybe it would tell him jack. Edwards put the tape into the special Sony combined TV and video adjacent to his desk. The images flickered into play. The news reporter relayed the incident while the camera roved over the crowd. Two shocked residents awkwardly described their horror at the attack. Suddenly the tape went blank.

Sighing Edwards rewound it, sipping his coffee.

Back to the interviewees, back to the camera panning the crowd. Then Edwards saw her. A young woman. Early twenties. She had cropped hair. She walked hurriedly, pushing a mixed-race baby in a pushchair. Edwards got a clear view of her profile. It was only a six, maybe eight-second shot. Edwards blinked and rewound the tape by ten frames and studied her.

Short cropped brown hair.

Boyish-looking.

Distinctively Christine McDermid.

"I seen her face somewhere before too. Just can't place where."

The cup of hot coffee slipped from Edwards' hand.

DAVIDSON TYPED CHRISTINE McDermid's name into the national police computer criminal database. The search came up with no matching entries. Like countless times before. Not even a parking fine.

Davidson revised the spelling. McDermaid instead of McDermid. Suddenly her file flashed up, but access was permitted to MI5 only.

"Mmmm." Davidson remarked. "Interesting."

Strapped in bullet proof vests, and armed with regulation handguns, Davidson briefed Edwards as they stepped into their unmarked police Astra. Edwards nodded to the Armed Response Vehicles behind him, looking at his watch. Edwards had the gift of doing many things at once, listening, driving, talking, eating. He listened as Davidson read from the computer print out, driving and navigating the roads travelling down side streets.

"Christine Bernadette McDermid is actually Bernadette Christina McDermaid, aged twenty-four. Daughter of Patrick 'Two-Toes' McDermaid who escaped from the Maze prison in 1995 and is still on the run today, suspected of the Trafford Park bomb in '96. One of five children, four boys, the only daughter. Mother and father split up when she was six, father got custody of the kids despite having a record for violence. Mother was an alcoholic. Check this: McDermaid used his daughter to carry explosives in her schoolbag whenever he went on a bombing expedition. She has form under the name of Christina for assault, affray, and shoplifting. She was sent to England to live with her reformed alcoholic mother when Patrick was imprisoned. Did time at Styal for possessing a firearm."

"What kind?"

"Nine mm PM Makarov. Obviously changed her name because there's no record of her from '98 onwards. I guess other people will want to talk to her."

It was getting dark.

"Well, if anyone else wants to talk to Miss McDermaid they're gonna have to wait their turn. I'm getting her first. I want to know what her link is with Small. And I intend to find out soon."

"HALF OF WHAT we agreed now and the rest when I sell," Easy said. Kadeem Hussein smiled at Easy's boldness, looking out of the deserted warehouse window. A train rumbled over a bridge nearby. There was the sound of children playing at a nearby school.

Standing confidently, Easy pushed the bag across the derelict floor with his foot. One of Kadeem's guards picked it up. Opening the bag Kadeem saw the bundles of money in used notes.

Kadeem laughed.

"You pay me in full. No credit."

Easy nodded. If Kadeem hadn't have been surrounded by so many men Easy would have taken Kadeem out with one bullet and run off with the product. Easy weighed up the situation. He could maybe take out three of them before the fourth realised what was going down. *Me run tings, tings nuh run me.* Still, another time. Kadeem clicked his fingers and one of his men brought across a black holdall. Bending down, he unzipped it on the floor. Kadeem beckoned Easy over. Stooping down, Easy saw the two large brown packets of cocaine. Easy's heart warmed.

Kadeem slit one bag at the top with a penknife. Easy licked a finger, dipped it in and tasted the cocaine.

"S'good," Easy said.

"The very best," Kadeem enthused. "OK Mr Easy we got a deal. You sell my drugs in four weeks and I replace Ranks with you."

Easy shook the hand extended to him.

It was the best thing Easy had heard in weeks, apart from Trench stepping permanently out of the picture.

WHO THE HELL did Storm think he was, sticking a bodyguard on him like that? Zukie was angry. Angry about Storm interfering in his life, angry about Nero's critical condition. But he had to put that behind him, because today was the first day of his new job at Cappella's. Colours had driven him over and sat studying Zukie as he walked into Cappella's. Marshall was waiting, arms folded, looking stern. Zukie knew he wasn't late. In fact he was ten minutes early.

"Hi." Marshall was looking at Zukie awkwardly. "Where do you want me? The studio or—"

"Zukie, look, I had a talk with your brother."

Zukie sighed angrily. His brother again! "Who phoned who? Did he phone you?"

Marshall ignored the question. "I wanted to know if there was some friction between you and him like I suspected. He told me you weren't well, Zukie, because of a bad car accident. That you have problems with your memory."

"Who phoned who I said?"

"Does it matter?"

"Yes. Yes it fuckin' does!!" Zukie screamed hoarsely and then wished he hadn't when he saw the alarm on Marshall's face. He realised he had blown it. Big time. He had been proven right. It felt like a jagged-edge knife was turning in his spine. The pain felt so real.

Zukie stormed past Marshall, even as Marshall called him back.

But Zukie was already out of Cappella's studio. Outside he saw Colours in the car waiting. Zukie turned as Colours looked up, surprised that Zukie was out so soon. Zukie started to run. He heard the car engine roar to life. The panic was eating him up. Anger. Making him blind. All he knew was that he had to get away. He didn't get far. The car screamed to a halt behind him so sharply Zukie smelt tyre smoke. He felt his jacket being pulled and his feet almost lifted up off the ground. In the next second Colours had thrown him against the car's hood.

"Don't fuckin' try that again. You may not like me but your brother asked me to watch your back 24-7. That's what I'm here for."

"I didn't ask you though did I?" Readjusting his clothes Zukie walked towards the car. Colours followed him ranting and raving as they both climbed in. The engine was still running.

"I owe Storm a favour. I know you don't like it cos of what happened with me shootin' Jigsy's car off the road with you and yu friend dem in it. I didn't know until it was too late." Zukie's heart banged like an empty vessel. His head seemed to toss around as if it wasn't attached to his body.

"What? It was *you*, and he asked *you* to mind me after what you did?" Zukie's stomach churned. Hot vomit rose to the tip of his throat. His brother had assigned his friends' killer to bodyguard him, after fucking up his career prospects as well as his life. Colours suddenly halted the car and killed the engine.

"Zukie, I never knew you didn't know. I thought Storm told you. Y'arright?" Zukie swallowed. He composed himself. He felt a steel-like calmness grip his body.

"Yeah-yeah. I'm OK. Just take me to Ranks."

Colours started the car.

The silence was like cold fury.

TERROR RIPPED THROUGH Danny Ranks' soul like a sword as he stared at the empty hospital bed where Nero should have been. Nero's private room was empty. The bed stripped. A nurse nearby looked at Ranks' desperate face.

"Nerome Campbell has been transferred to Leeds General."

"Why?"

"His fiancée wanted him nearer the family and as he had improved a lot since this morning the consultant said it was OK."

Ranks was crushed. He continued to frown at the nurse.

"They've only just left. Shall I see if the ambulance is still—"

Ranks shook his head dismally, raising a hand. Turning, the nurse made the bed, unaware of Ranks' turmoil. Candice. That jumped up bitch. Anyway, that didn't matter. All that mattered was Nerome was OK.

Ranks would catch up with his spar another time. Soon. Very soon.

WHY? IF SHE had known all this time who he was why didn't she stop things getting this far? Leaving the Infirmary Ranks was thinking about Miss Small, Snow-Dog and Juice McKenzie. Everything could have been avoided. Nero wouldn't be riddled with bullets. Mentian wouldn't be six foot under. Instead she chose to ignore the fact that he was her son, chose to work with a fucka like Easy-Love Brown.

That hurt Ranks.

It hurt him terribly.

DESPAIR. ZUKIE HAD felt nothing like it before in his life. The agony came in spasms, the savagery of the truth he had learned, cut deep like a power saw. He needed to talk to Ranks, but learned Danny had gone to visit Nero at the hospital. Fully clothed, Zukie slid down the shower wall, holding his stomach. The two jets sprayed water down on him, merging with the tears on his face.

"COME ON, LIGHT-FINGER. It's me, Danny. Open up the door, star." Zukie sat hunched up on the shower floor, wet, cold, shaking. Behind the bathroom door, he heard Colours and Ranks discussing him.

Ranks knocked on the locked bathroom door again.

"Light, open up the door please."

Zukie unlocked the door. Danny's concerned eyes roved over Zukie. Using his foot he back-kicked the bathroom door shut on the others, wrapping a towel around Zukie's body.

"It hurts I know but you gotta take that shit, take it like a man. OK? Storm made a mistake that night. A mistake any bad bwai could make." Danny looked at Zukie intensely. Zukie avoided his stare, nodding, wiping his face quickly, allowing Ranks to pull him out of the bathroom, past the curious, awkward eyes outside.

WORD ABOUT BAD shit gets around quickly. People purchasing wraps from the Dodge Crew got the shits, violent stomach cramps, dizziness, and vomiting. By the end of the day sales had stopped and it soon got back to Easy that no one was going to buy even two ounces of cola-cubes from his Crew. Easy's investment was worthless. He had been set up. Obviously, Kadeem was in league with people to fuck him up good style.

Obviously, there was a spy in the Dodge crew. Teeko Martial used to work for Danny.

How loyal was Teeko now?

"WHAT DO YOU call a Scottish sheep with no head and feet?" Storm asked. Jasmine shook her head, making her bobbed screw-curls bounce. Storm thought Jasmine looked ravishing seated across from him at the posh restaurant in town. Her eyes danced playfully. She was dressed in a beautiful blue dress, a pair of diamond earrings hung from her ears. She was perfect. Her skin glowed.

"I dunno," she said, tossing her head, playing with her salad. "What do you call a Scottish sheep with no head and feet?"

"Mac Cloud," Storm said. She was taking a sip of wine and almost choked.

"What? Aww, God, Cliff that's awful. Where did you hear that?"

"Our son told me today," Storm said. "When I picked him up from school." Storm looked at his watch again.

"Are we rushing to go somewhere?"

"No. What makes you think that, babes?"

She looked annoyed.

"You keep checking the time."

"I'm waiting for a phone call," Storm said, then wished he had lied.

"Oh yeah from who?"

Licking his lips Storm sighed. Just then his mobile rang. Colours' name flashed up. She glared at him.

"We're supposed to be having a meal. Just us. Celebrating our reunion. Don't answer the phone, Cliff."

"I'm expecting an update on Zukie. Please, I need to take the call." A few diners had turned their attention to their table. Storm took the call walking away from the table. Storm was crushed when Colours told him he had accidentally told Zukie about his order to kill. He was mad at Storm for not filling him in properly. Storm told Colours he would deal with it. Storm turned around to rejoin Jasmine at the table.

It was empty.

Jasmine had left the restaurant.

"SHE ASKED FOR you to have these." Ranks had questions he needed answering. Seated in Aunt Celia's front room, he looked down at the things Celia had just given him. An Anita Baker CD entitled The Songstress, a book of poetry by someone called Langston Hughes and a small red bankbook.

"Track 5 was her favourite." Ranks stared at the CD. Then he flipped through the pages of the poetry book nonplussed. Poetry wasn't his shit at all. At school he had hated English literature. Poems were for pussies. He sniffed then opened the red bankbook, gasping. The last entry was for three hundred and fifty pounds. Was she paying him back for the money she robbed?

"I don't want her money!" Ranks kissed through his teeth and sighed. "Show me the other things. The photographs and cuttings and stuff," He said, flinging the bankbook on the coffee table and placing the other items inside his jacket pocket.

Veniesha had known all along who Danny was. Aunt Celia showed him some photo albums he had never seen before, taking him through each photographic history. He listened intently, sighing, aware of Snow-dog and Juice McKenzie waiting for him in the car. He didn't realise how late it was until Aunt Celia yawned. It was midnight. His thoughts turned to Zukie. He was concerned for Zukie's state of mind, having spoken to him about the Colours situation and what really happened the night Chico died. Zukie had been subdued. He drank one bottle of beer after another, and smoked a whole bag of weed, before falling asleep on the Futon.

Aunt Celia yawned again.

"Danny, I know how you feel."

Ranks jumped up and suddenly screamed.

"No one knows how I feel. NO ONE." When he realised she was staring at him with sudden fearfulness, he felt ashamed. "I'm sorry. I'm just weary."

"Your old room is upstairs, still the same. You could—"

"No. No thanks." Ranks suddenly felt cold. It was a mistake to come back here. The painful memories were resurfacing. "Look, I'd better be headin' off." Bending down, he kissed her.

"Please, Dan, stay."

"I can't. I got some serious business to take care of."

"Please Danny. Yu haf to stop this. Nuff blood spill already!"

He didn't see her tears. He turned and walked away.

MOSCHINO, ARMANI, KLEIN, Versace, Rockport, Nike. Suits, shirts, shoes, jeans, jewellery, Teeko Martial was packing them all into two suitcases hurriedly when he heard a knock on his front door. Stepping quietly to the front bedroom window, Teeko peeped through and saw Easy-Love Brown below. Teeko swore vehemently under his breath. Right then, Easy looked up. Teeko shrank back, his heart bumping at twice its normal speed. He stayed there until he heard a car start. Chancing it, he saw the back end of Small's BMW disappear up Salisbury street. Teeko let out a breath of relief. Walking back he began to pack faster. He knew he had left it late to leave but he had a few loose ends to tie up. Those loose ends did not include saying goodbye to Easy-Love Brown.

Teeko had started on a third suitcase when he heard a thud downstairs. Teeko frowned. Did he lock the back door? Teeko couldn't remember. He got as far as the bedroom door before clocking Easy walking up the stairs towards him.

"The back door was unlocked," Easy said, the tone of his voice cold. Teeko walked back into the bedroom, sighing silently. Easy's eyes travelled all over the luggage on the bed. Teeko continued to pack.

"You going on a trip?"

"Spending some time wid my family, yu know."

"Mmmmm-how long exactly? A week, month, year?"

Reaching over Teeko closed one of his bulging suitcases.

"Couldn't say really. What can I do for you Easy?"

Easy laughed cynically, shaking his head. "What happened to our partnership Teeko?"

Fuck this, Teeko thought, who did Easy think he was? Turning towards Easy angrily Teeko said.

"You got a gun on you Easy? Yu come round here to shoot me because you think I've gone back to Ranks? Like I'm a snitch-switch? I know what you think. You made it perfectly clear after Mentian got dusted. Well, go on. Go ahead and do it. Take out the same gun yu put in my face a coupla weeks ago and come shoot me nuh?"

Easy smiled.

He took the gun from the small of his back and levelled it straight at Teeko's chest.

ZUKIE STIRRED awake, feeling cold then hot. Sniffing. Wouldn't surprise him if he was coming down with a chill after his unconventional shower. He heard the sound of the TV before his eyes focussed on the large screen TV. Zukie remembered. Clifton had assigned the angel of death to protect him, Mr Colours. Depression was invading his spirit. If he lived a lifetime he didn't think he would ever get over what happened. Zukie felt a presence. Bolting upright, he accidentally knocked over two empty Pils bottles. Kurtis. Easy's brother. On the armchair opposite, watching him. Kurtis smiled.

"You look mash up." He commented. The light from the TV glinted against something in Kurtis' hand. As he put the glass object to his mouth, Zukie could clearly see that Kurtis was sucking on a homemade crack pipe, closing his eyes as smoke streamed out of his flared nostrils. "You need some o' this," he said leaning back, groaning loudly.

"No thanks," Zukie said, looking around nervously. "Where's D?"

Kurtis was already buzzing, laid back in the armchair, legs sprawled wide. Zukie didn't see his face sour.

"Out."

"Where?"

"Dunno. Danny don't tell me nuttin."

"Colours?"

"Sleepin'," Kurtis sniffed. "Yu sure you don't want some of the good stuff?"

"Naw! I don't take shit."

"Yu ever tried it? It takes away your worries, Zukie, makes yu forget how fucked up things and people are. One pull won't hook you like they say. It's just like a spliff only ten times more uplifting. Here, make up your own mind." Kurtis passed the pipe to Zukie who took it hesitantly. "What yu scared of?"

"Nuttin." Zukie muttered, swallowing. He held the glass bottle in his hands trembling. Kurtis heated the glass with a lighter.

Zukie looked at the pipe for a long time it seemed. He glanced at Kurtis, hearing Kurtis's words. *It takes away your worries, makes yu forget how fucked up things and people are.* Kurtis smiled. Zukie put the long tube to his lips. His first attempt made him cough violently.

"Slowly," Kurtis urged. Zukie pulled in with his lungs. He felt his chest burning. He exhaled and saw Kurtis disappear behind a thick veil of smoke.

In a second Zukie felt the blood around his body tingle. His brain seemed to vibrate in his head. Zukie looked far across the room, letting out a deep breathy groan. The furniture was moving. The characters in a TV sit-com were talking to him like something out of the X-Files telling him that Storm was evil. Zukie laughed. He took another pull, not noticing that Kurtis had disappeared from the room.

Feeling sick, Zukie closed his eyes as his body shuddered, reacting to the intoxicating chemicals invading it. When he opened them he saw a beautiful woman standing in front of him. She was wearing a long red evening dress, with matching gloves and high-heel shoes. She had beautiful long light-brown hair. Her face was made up exquisitely. She spun around with an exaggerated grace. Surreal. Zukie's heartbeat was pounding louder and louder.

Suddenly there was a bright flash. Zukie didn't realise it was the halogen lamp being turned on bright because the crack was exacerbating sound, vision and movement. He didn't even hear Ranks holler hey what the fuck is going on? It was more like a long deep growl.

He saw Ranks race across the room, snatching the beautiful woman by her throat. Zukie was petrified and confused. Ranks pushed a gun into the woman's face. Turning around towards the door, Zukie saw Snow-dog and Juice McKenzie standing there open-mouthed. Ranks tore across to the coffee table where Kurtis had laid out his rocks. In a violent rage he swept them off. The woman shouted and dived on the floor under the coffee table, plucking her things from the floor and stuffing it down her chest. In the next second, Ranks grabbed her by her long hair.

Her hair came off in his hands.

Shocked, Zukie stood up, dropping the pipe, which shattered, against the wooden floor. The sound vibrating in his head was his own scream.

TEEKO MARTIAL STARED in disbelief as Easy pointed his gun at him. His old spar, partner, mentor was holding a gun on him. He had trusted Easy, but Easy had never trusted him.

In an instant Teeko brought his right foot up in a high jump-kick, aimed straight at the gun. The gun fired a shot, shattering the light bulb, rendering the bedroom pitch black. With Easy temporarily disarmed Teeko ran. He leapt downstairs two at a time; with each leap he heard and felt the sound of bullets searing past.

Teeko ran to the back door down the back alley, setting off the two Alsatians at the end house, sprinting as if his life depended on it. His life *did* depend on it. He didn't stop until he got to Claremont Road where a blues party was in full swing. Teeko ran into the cramped session, mingling with the late night revellers, his heart bumping almost as loud as the deafening thud coming from the huge speakers. Thankfully the crowd enveloped him securely. He would be safe there until he could get the rest of his things.

THE FEELING WAS coming back to Zukie's hands and feet. And mind. And suddenly he was petrified as he realised he had taken Kurtis' crack. It went against everything he had ever said about messing with hard drugs. He was a weak, hypocritical, idiot.

Drawn by the commotion, Pipes and Fila walked in. Ranks was completely enraged, spitting, snarling, kicking Kurtis in his ribs, then hitting him with the gun. Kurtis spat until his spit turned the colour of the red dress he was wearing. Snow-dog and Juice pulled Ranks off Kurtis. Colours, who had been sleeping in Nero's room, came in stunned at the scene.

Ranks was furious. "Why yu give him shit to take? In fact don't answer that juss fuckin' come outta mi house yu dutty chi-chi bwai."

Ranks kicked him again. Zukie turned away, feeling dizzy and nauseous.

"My clothes?"

"Yeah, dem women clothes? Guess what, freak, bonfire night come early this year."

Kurtis was bawling, make-up ruined, bleeding, dress ripped to reveal a muscled thigh. Ranks' face was filled with repugnance. Kurtis pulled himself up off the wooden floor.

"You're gonna be sorry yu done this to me," he mumbled.

"How?"

"Easy's gonna get you, just like he got Small, Trench and Fluxy."

Ranks pushed the .38 into Kurtis's cheek.

"Explain, freak! You better explain what yu juss said."

"He told me how he pulled everything off, how Jigsy thought Storm killed Fluxy and how Dodge think you stupid lot killed Trench and Small." Kurtis sniggered, then grunted from pain. "Didn't know Easy was an engineer did ya? Likes to engineer big cakes."

Ranks swallowed, blinking slowly, frowning. "You're talking pure shit!" He released the safety clip, shoving the gun further into Kurtis's cheek.

"Awww! Go on! Kill me! I don't care! I just wanna die!" Kurtis squealed like a baby, snot dripping from his nose.

"Tell me where Easy lives."

Kurtis was screaming hysterically. "Shoot me! Kill me I said! I wanna die."

"Let him go Ranks." Pipes urged. "Let the freak go. In't gonna tell yu shit." Ranks had a determined look on his face and Zukie wondered if Danny was seeing straight. Ranks breathed hard, in quick spasms, as if he had been holding his breath all this time. Suddenly, he replaced the clip, stuffing the gun into the back of his waist.

"Here, take yu fuckin' wig, too! Look like a fuckin' yeti!" Ranks said, picking it up with disgust, forefinger and thumb, flinging it after him. Kurtis took up the long light-brown wig. Keeping his head low he staggered out on his red high heels.

"Suppose he runs to Easy?" Fila asked.

"Let him. I'll be waitin'! My gun got questions to ask Mr Easy."

Zukie walked unsteadily into the kitchen, throwing cold water on his face, putting a trembling hand on the moving wall for support. The kitchen twisted and turned as if he was on a roller-coaster ride. Feeling his stomach pinch, he doubled up and vomited in a corner watched by Colours who shook his head slowly.

Fila, Pipes, Snow-dog and Juice McKenzie stood around looking at each other.

Ranks stared angrily at the wall opposite, clenching and

unclenching his fists.

"JASMINE, IT IN'T LIKE you think," Storm said as she let him into her home, after the abandoned reunion meal. She was already dressed in a silk night-robe.

"Oh." She said, walking into the living room. He followed. She poured herself some wine from a bottle. "What is it like then?"

"I'm just concerned about Zukie that's all."

Storm lit a cigarette. He could see she was pissed off.

"And you think the solution is to enlist the help of Colours?"

Storm sighed.

"And if I tell you yes, we're finished again, right?"

Jasmine put her hand through her hair as she virtually collapsed onto the leather sofa. Storm's mobile phone began to ring. Colours' name flashed up on the display. Storm glanced at Jasmine. She was twisting her lips, which meant she was severely annoyed. Storm ignored the phone. Colours could wait, or leave a voicemail or a text message. Storm stood up.

"Come here," he said, holding out his arms wide. Her arms stayed wide and empty. Jasmine remained on the sofa, looking away. "Don't ya trust me?" He knew it was unfair of him to ask her that question.

Jasmine looked at Storm questioningly.

"I've organised a dance," Storm began. "A healing dance. Tomorrow night. It's all over the pirate radios. Hopefully I can get all the gangs to come."

Jasmine was horrified.

"What for? So they can have a massive shoot out?" She scoffed.

"No. I intend to mediate. Call a truce between Easy and Danny."

Jasmine shook her head.

"That isn't going to happen, after all, Easy still has this grudge against you."

"That's all in the past."

"Anyway, why would you do that after all that's happened? With Zukie? Your Mum?"

"Like I said, it's in the past. And that's what the theme of the dance is going to be all about. Healing. Healing the past."

"Let's do some healing of our own." Jasmine offered, smiling naughtily. Storm opened the belt tying Jasmine's robe together. It opened, revealing her naked breasts, slightly round stomach and long brown legs. He caressed her breast, running his finger over her neck. Then he kissed her slowly, manoeuvring her towards the sofa. He lay her down, kissing and stripping himself at the same time.

His mobile beeped indicating that there was a text message.

Call me. It's urgent. Colours.

Storm continued to make love.

SHIT! THAT'S WHAT Kadeem Hussein had sold Easy. Easy looked at the pile of dust on his kitchen table. He'd known people to do this, grind down aspirin, laxative, Epson Salts mix it in with the cocaine. Sighing he kissed his teeth. It was a pile of A grade crap. Kadeem had cut from the top, which was cocaine, but the rest was a mixture of shit. Look like all along Teeko had been working with Danny to set him up with Kadeem. Why else was he packing his bags and running scared in the night?

Suddenly there was a knock at the back door, making Easy jump. Easy grabbed the gun on the table. Who the fuck could that be at this time of night? Teeko? The Police? Would da police knock though? Would Teeko? Easy quickly scooped his useless investment back into the brown bag, hiding it in the kitchen sink cupboard while the knocking continued. Moving quietly towards the kitchen window Easy peered through the blinds into the back garden. Caught a glimpse of a red dress. Frowning, Easy unbolted the back door, opening it slightly.

"Who is this?"

"It's me — me, Kurtis."

Pulling the back door wide open, Easy looked the woman up and down. He saw the high-heeled shoes, the torn red dress, the bruised face, the blood and the spoilt make-up. Keeping his face lowered, Kurtis pulled off the long light brown wig slowly with a shaking hand. "Kurtis?" Easy swallowed. "Kurtis? Jesus Christ! What the hell are you wearing?" Then Easy remembered that Kurtis was taking medication for his illness. He pulled Kurtis inside gently. Kurtis winced with pain. "What's happened?" Kurtis sat down at the kitchen table, clearly distressed, shaking his head. Running upstairs, Easy got a pair of jeans and sweatshirt, handing them to Kurtis.

"Here, get outta dem clothes."

"I WANNA KNOW what happened to you, Kurtis." Easy's eyes travelled anxiously over his younger brother Kurtis, now dressed normally. Kurtis shook his head, shaking badly. "Want a glass of water?"

Kurtis nodded, burying his face in his hands deeply. Filling a glass Easy handed it to Kurtis. In the space of two minutes Kurtis was drenched in sweat, as if he'd been through a car wash without a car. Easy watched Kurtis' hands, shaking violently, spilling water, as he took the glass and tried to put it to his mouth. Nearly all the water ended up on the floor. He almost dropped the glass. Easy caught it from his loose grasp, setting it down on the kitchen table. Kurtis cleared his throat, his eyes closing.

"Kej?" Kurtis snored loudly. "Kurtis?"

He jumped awake suddenly.

"Huuuhhhhhhnnn? I'm sorry Ranks."

"Ranks? Why the fuck are you callin' me Ranks?" Easy said with revulsion. Kurtis licked his lips and looked around the room searchingly, twitching and sniffing, his eyes locking into the distance.

"I'm tired."

Easy's heart jumped. His throat suddenly felt like grit. He knew the signs of someone on hard drugs. The profuse sweating. The uncontrollable twitching.

"Kej, look at me. Look at me." Kurtis looked at Easy but he didn't see Easy. "Where was you Kurtis, before you came here?"

"Danny's," Kurtis muttered carelessly, his eyes remote. "I'm tired." He suddenly looked at Easy wildly, desperately. "No! I need a smoke. Have you got some crack? I smoked all I had on the way here. You must have some rocks. Loan me some. I'll pay you back."

Easy stood up slowly. Felt the room circling around him. Felt his head balloon. He gaped at Kurtis in awe. Easy hit the table. For the first time in a long time, Easy felt tears welling up, spilling from his eyes.

"I can't believe this. Kurtis, why? You were the bright one, gonna go to university and shit. How long have you been on crack?"

"Please give me some crack, man. Please. I didn't meant to — I just wanted to make you hurt. Please give me somethin' to smoke — please I know you got some." Kurtis was crying, pulling on to Easy's body. Easy backed away as if Kurtis had contaminated him.

"It was you wasn't it? Carryin' my business to Danny!! All this time? Not Teeko!"

"Ranks said he'd see me right. Now he don't wanna know me cos I gave his precious Zukie some crack." Kurtis began to laugh. Easy struck him so hard he fell then rolled backwards.

"You stupid shit!" Then realising what he had done Easy bent down but he couldn't touch Kurtis. Kurtis sobbed, whining.

"I didn't mean to — I just needed."

"It's OK, Kej." They were quiet for a while. Then Easy asked gently. "Did Danny Ranks start you on crack-cocaine Kurtis?"

Kurtis' speech began to slur.

"I told him about Small — and Trench — and Fluxy. I didn't mean to. I'm sorry. I'm sorry." Easy got up and roared like a savage, turning the kitchen table over in rage. Kurtis cowered in a corner. Closing his eyes Easy inhaled sharply. Torn between love and hate, he didn't dare turn to look at Kurtis in case he took a gun to his own brother.

"You said you been at Ranks' Kurtis? Where does Ranks live?" Easy heard silence. "Kurtis?" Turning around Easy saw Kurtis curled up on the floor. A loud snore erupted from his lungs. "Kurtis!" Easy shook him.

There was no response.

Easy left Kurtis where he was.

Lying on the cold kitchen floor snoring his head off.

Next to the dirty kitchen bin.

Easy walked towards the stairs.

His legs felt as if there were not his own.

THE HUGE HEAVY-DUTY sledge hammer crashed against the door frame, splintering it. After three more blows, the frame succumbed and the door was in.

"Armed police!" Armed Response officers tore into Christine McDermaid's flat, guns at the ready. But their well-trained aims met emptiness. Room after room, vacant space. Edwards and Davidson rushed in behind the trained officers. Their disappointment was immeasurable. It looked like McDermaid had had a leaving party a couple of nights ago. There was nothing and nobody here. Edwards punched the wall next to him. Then he saw the letters piled up on the floor behind the forced door. Picking them up, one by one, he examined them. They were addressed to Bernadette McDermott, Christina McDermaid, variations of her real name obviously. Edwards opened one. It contained a cheque for thirty-three thousand pounds.

Thirty-three grand was a lot of money to be left lying in an empty house.

Wasn't it?

EDWARDS PUT HIS money on Christine or someone returning for that cheque. And he was right. They had surveyed the flat all morning, he and Davidson taking it in turns to look through the high-powered binoculars from the empty flat opposite. Steve spotted something through the lens.

"Colin?"

"What is it, Steve?"

"Remember the neighbour, Josie, when we called the first time? Look."

Edwards took the binoculars and looked. Orange-haired Josie was in the flat, walking around.

Edwards watched as Josie bent down out of view. They started to put on their jackets, which concealed their flak jackets and regulation handguns held in leather shoulder holsters. Then Davidson glanced through the window. Josie was walking hurriedly out of the building. A taxi was parked up.

"Come on. Let's move! Quick!"

STORM MICHAELS PUSHED the record shop and studio front door open, giving him ten seconds to disarm the alarm system. The morning was clear, crisp, autumn was fading out. Storm breathed hard. He missed Zukie.

Suddenly he heard a noise at the front door. Storm had left the door wide open. He spun around.

In the doorway stood a very familiar figure. For a second Storm did a double take. He had blonde-brown dreadlocks and a goatee beard. He could have passed for Zukie except for the goatee and wide blue eyes.

"IN'T YOU GOT nuttin to say to your other little brother?" Eugene Bluebwai Michaels stepped into Storm's shop. Storm and Bluebwai walked towards each other and embraced before stepping back to look at each other, punching, laughing, touching skin. Then Bluebwai looked around, his blue eyes stared hard.

"So. What's happened?"

Storm sighed.

"A lot of shit's being going on, Zukie knows everything."

Blue sighed.

"What about you? There's something you're not sure about isn't there? That's why you've been leaving those messages on my phone about Fluxy and Easy. Yeah?" Blue's voice dropped. He lowered his eyes, looking stressed.

"I want you to tell me again exactly what happened when Fluxy got shot."

Blue nodded.

Storm walked over and locked the front door, beckoning his brother to the office in the back.

THEY WERE ALL around him, seated quietly, Pipes, Fila, Stukky, Sizzla, Snow-dog, Juice McKenzie and Colours. Zukie was still in bed. Colours had cooked breakfast and all who had wanted to eat had done so. Danny had no stomach for food. His stomach burned like scotch bonnet peppers. He was back in the day, thinking about Fluxy picking him up from school in his BMW convertible, making his school mates envious. It wasn't long before he was outta school, working for Fluxy as a scout, sometimes catching up at Fluxy's yard. Fluxy gave him everything, gave him his first trade.

Was it true? Did Easy really prevent him from seeing the one person he had longed to see all his life? His mother? Did he out Fluxy to move on up?

Ranks looked at Colours, still eating his food, looking cool and unaffected, stuffing his mouth with balloon-like fried dumplings.

"Fuckin' surprised at you," Colours suddenly said through a mouthful of food. "Lettin' Easy-Love's crack-head brother inna yu life. If you ask me that was invitin' bad play."

"Yeah? And who the fuck asked you anyway?" Ranks spat back.

"Easy was laughing at you and Storm, suppose to be experts back then, da fuckin' Grange Crew. He fuckin' killed Fluxy right under ya nose and had you shootin' up each other."

Colours stopped eating. He was scowling.

"What we gonna do now?" Stukky asked, intervening before a fight started. Ranks kept his eyes on Colours steadily.

"Well we in"t gonna shoot and ask questions later. I need to know if is truth that freak was chattin'." Ranks sat back down. "I'm gonna have to consult my personal advisor. See what he wants to do about Easy's liberties."

EASY WALKED INTO the kitchen, feeling rough. Did last night really happen? Was his brother really an informer? A nasty transvestite junkie? He saw Kurtis over by the kitchen cupboard, eyes closed, slumped against one of the lower units. Kissing his teeth, Easy was repulsed by the sight.

Walking over to the sink Easy poured himself a glass of cold water, drinking it slowly. This morning he was going to get out of Kurtis where Ranks lived. Putting the cup back on the drainer, Easy turned to Kurtis on the floor.

"Kurtis! Get up. C'mon wake up. I wanna know where this piece of shit slime, lives. Tell me. Wake up!"

Then suddenly, Easy noticed.

Easy noticed the kitchen cupboard where he had hastily hidden Kadeem's crap cocaine.

Wide open.

Easy could see Kurtis's face quite clearly. White residue was near his nostrils, some on his clothes. He saw where Kurtis had vomited and now his body was convulsing. The scream raided Easy's head silently. He reached down and held Kurtis. What to do? Call an ambulance and then have the place crawling with police? Or leave Kurtis choking to death on his own vomit? Easy-Love dragged his brother outside, out into the park. It was raining and dark. Easy didn't even notice. Frantically, he dialled the emergency services on his mobile phone.

A man with a dog walked over. Soon there was a small crowd.

Someone covered Kurtis with a blanket. As soon as Easy heard the ambulance approaching he moved away.

Easy felt something cold and wet on his face.

He was crying.

"I CAN'T BELIEVE I'm back in Gunchester." Blue said, lighting the spliff Storm had given him. They sat in the back office. Storm thought Blue looked good, but he wasn't sure about the dreadlocks. It made him look too much like Zukie. The uncanny resemblance and the mannerisms the two younger half-brothers shared sent an icy trickle down Storm's spine. Storm sat on his desk opposite Blue. Blue leaned forward, taking a deep pull on the spliff.

"It was a bad thing that happened. And it took me a long time to get over it. But you don't get over shit like that do you? Thinking you're going to die in a car accident 'cos the driver's got a massive hole in his head where somebody blasted him. Learning that the person who ordered the hit is your own brother. I saw those bodies in the road. Chico and Jigsy." Blue stopped, his eyes became watery. He composed himself. "Shit like that stays with you." Storm sighed. He knew that too.

"London was like another world, for a while. Getting into

university. Starting my e-business with you. I never, ever wanted to come back here. Then you phoned and left those messages. I ignored your first call." Bluebwai took a deep breath. "Easy and Jigsy were the only ones to know where me and Fluxy was going the day Fluxy was gunned down. Now answer my question: has this got to do with Easy coming out and the shootings down here all summer?"

Storm nodded and told Blue about Trench's unexpected visit to the studio.

"He sat right there, where you are, Blue. Questioning me about Easy, his own gang leader. It was obvious he didn't trust him, especially after Small got wiped. The next thing he's wiped, like he said he would be." Storm saw his brother shiver slightly.

"Fluxy's shooting weren't no chance shooting. Somebody knew where Fluxy was gonna be and they waited. Easy was with Jigsy all day, but he could easily have set it up. And I'll never forget how the blame fell on you and then later when they found out we was related fuckin' Easy tried to make out I worked with you. It makes sense to me now."

"It doesn"t make any sense to me. Why would Easy have Fluxy outted?"

"Position in the crew?"

"Yeah but the leadership woulda gone straight to Jigsy, wouldn't it?"

"Yeah. But what if Jigsy was at war with you cos he thought you killed his brother. You woulda outted Jigsy, Easy was next in line to take over." He was looking at the floor, his left foot banging the floor nervously.

Blue had figured the game plan out long time.

THE SHOP'S BUZZER buzzed loudly, making Blue jump. He looked at Storm questioningly.

"It's OK. They'll see the sign on the door and know we in't open for business." The buzzer rang persistently. Storm got up and walked down the short corridor into the shop. Tariq would have used his key. Storm opened the front door. He was greeted by the Worlders Crew: Colours, Snow-dog, Juice McKenzie and last but not least Zukie, all wearing grim expressions. Storm was slightly staggered but ushered them all in. Zukie. He kept his eyes fixed on the wall opposite. Colours whistled loudly, holding a takeaway meal.

Ranks lit a cigarette, looking at Zukie. Zukie looked peaky, ill. Storm concentrated on Zukie.

"Ya — OK?"

Zukie sighed wearily, then barely nodded before walking past him into the corridor.

"We gotta talk," Ranks said urgently. Storm wondered what was going on. Ranks suddenly saw ex-Pipers man, Bluebwai. "Long time," Blue said. Danny nodded coolly. Blue saw Zukie just behind Danny. They embraced solidly. It warmed Storm to see Zukie give a rare smile but there were too many bodies in the small office. Storm suggested they move to the studio where he got more chairs. Soon spliffs were going back and forth.

Ranks was about to open his mouth when Colours began to speak. "Me text yu. Yu get it?"

Storm shook his head. In the light of certain events he had not even switched his phone on.

"Den you don't know den do you?" He started to eat his meal. "Got any salt?" Ranks was staring at Colours with deep hatred. "Can't eat food fresh at all."

"Who's in charge here?" Ranks bellowed.

"You couldn't rule a fucking ruler," Colours said swallowing some food and making terrible eating noises. Pipes cleared his throat. Stukky's eyes widened at the insult. "This stupid fucka here had Easy's crack-head brother."

Ranks stood up angrily. Storm calmed him back down into his seat.

"Kurtis living at his yard." Colours continued undeterred. Storm recollected seeing the strange teen at Ranks' apartment. Big eyes, wild hair, haunted-looking. "Had some big idea he could trade crack with Kurtis for information on Easy. Only, last night Kurtis decides to share some of his crack with Zukie."

"What?" Storm stared shocked at Ranks, who had assured him of his brother's safety. Ranks closed his eyes in grief, despair and anger at Colours' raw outspokenness.

"But that's not the best part — Ranks gives Kurtis a good kicking and in the middle of this," Colours swallowed some more food keeping Storm on edge, "in the middle of this Kurtis tells us his brother got rid of Trench and had Small and Fluxy steamed."

Storm closed his eyes. He didn't know what to take in first, Zukie's foray into hard drugs, Ranks' foolish oversight or the confirmation that Easy-Love was a traitor and a killer.

"Is this true?"

Ranks nodded, sighing wearily.

Storm felt as if he was falling down a deep, red hole.

EDWARDS FLASHED HIS ID at the taxi driver. Josie, McDermaid's neighbour, looked extremely uncomfortable in the back of the private hire taxi. He noticed her hand drop beneath the seat.

"Get out."

Josie was angry, clutching her handbag to her chest. Davidson was in and out of the taxi in a second, emerging with a pile of letters.

"Mmmm," Edwards said, looking at the envelope containing the cheque for thirty-three grand they had resealed. "Didn't know you worked for her majesty's mail." Josie lit a cigarette, putting a shaking hand through her bright orange hair.

"I take it you're going to deliver them personally?"

Josie nervously pulled long on her cigarette, blowing a thick stream of smoke into the air surrounding them.

"Where is she?" Edwards demanded.

"I know my rights." Josie snapped.

Davidson waved a small bag of cannabis in Josie's face.

"Guess what I also found in the back of the taxi?'

"Personal use. You can't fuck me with that."

"Well, I can see what else we've got on file on you. Maybe we'll get a search warrant on your flat and see if we can trace the origin of—"

"OK. OK. OK," Josie sighed and leaned against the car, fidgeting with the stud in her nose. "I'm meeting her in a café on New Birley Street in Hulme. I give her the letters, she gives me some weed."

"Good," Edwards said, waving the taxi driver on. "*We'll* give you a lift."

EVERYTHING WAS AS Teeko had left it. No sign of Easy-Love Brown lurking in some dark corner. Waiting. Teeko put his luggage in the jeep, then went back to the house to lock it. When he returned to the jeep he realised it was leaning slightly to one side. Walking around to the driver's side Teeko saw the slashed front tyre. He stared in awe, catching a glimpse of his horrified expression in the jeep's window. Easy mussta did it. He would have to change the tyre before he set out to London to join Shanieka. Teeko cursed. As he turned to walk towards the rear of the jeep to retrieve the spare wheel he saw him. Teeko squinted. He hadn't seen Blue in years but he would recognise him anywhere dreadlocks or no dreadlocks.

"Yo, Teeko. Wassup!" Teeko said nothing. A strange tingling

sensation seemed to spread over his shaved-bald head. He looked around wildly. What the hell was going on? Blue drew nearer.

"How how did you find me? I thought you was in London?"

"Your cousin Ricky. I told him I was coming to Manchester to see you. Shit, Teeko why you looking so stressed? You look terrible!"

Teeko swallowed.

"I in't seen you. Not since I heard you were Storm's brother."

"True. True."

"Heard you was working with him to kill Fluxy."

"Not true. Easy told you that didn't he? I only found out Storm was my brother later on. Way after Fluxy was shot."

Teeko started to unwrap the wheel. He believed Blue. But he didn't know if he trusted him.

"Whatdya want? What ya come ya for?"

"To tell you that Easy was the one who outted Fluxy, not Storm. It's all out in the open now. His own brother, Kurtis, told Ranks yesterday." Teeko dropped the wheel. Retrieving it he said,

"I gotta go."

"Why?" Turning around Teeko stared at Bluebwai who was looking at the luggage on the back seat of the wide soft-top.

"Last night Easy came for me, Blue. Put a gatt to me. I din' do him nuttin. I gotta leave. I don't know if he got the Dodge Crew looking for me. I don't understand what the fuck's going on. All I know is I gotta get outta here." Two vans pulled up as he was divulging his fear to Blue.

"I already bin up that road." Blue said. "You can't hide forever. Everybody knows what Easy did. The Worlders know. But his crew don't know. Dodge need to know."

"So?" Teeko looked up and saw Ranks, Colours, Stukky, Storm, Pipes, Fila and the others crossing towards him. "What the fuck has that got to do with me?"

"So, you got to talk to them. Tell them the bad shit going down." Ranks said.

Teeko stared coldly at Ranks.

"You fuckin' burned me out, you kidnapped Shanieka, held my kids."

Ranks sounded weary, his voice low. "You walked. You crossed over. You chatted my business! I did what I thought was right. You know that, but that's in the past. I'm prepared to forget that if you are. Anyway, what yu gonna do about Fluxy's honour — let that bow-cart get away with it? What about Small and Trench? Consider yourself lucky Teeko he never got you."

Teeko looked at the jeep. He looked up Salisbury road, which would lead onto Princess Parkway, the M56 and then freedom. Then he turned and looked at this posse of men and he remembered — Easy wasn't playing with him last night.

Teeko, Consider yourself lucky he never got you.

Easy-Love had meant to steam him.

EASY-LOVE BROWN TOUCHED his brother's bruised face in the Intensive Care Unit. If Kej hadn't have taken the pot-pourri cocaine he wouldn't be on life-support. Ranks had used his brother as an informer, a spy, like a puppet he controlled with crack. Kadeem Hussein, along with Ranks or somebody else, had decided to play games with him. Only he didn't intend to be a loser. Especially now that Kurtis was a victim of their crass chemist skills.

"Kej, I'm gonna finish this. I swear."

JUST WALK TOWARDS her like normal," Edwards warned Josie. "No hand signals. Keep your arms low. Do this and you'll walk away from any charges."

"You two are two pricks, you know that?"

Through the window they saw her. Christine McDermaid. Looking at her watch, stirring her cup of coffee in the large, almost empty restaurant. They watched as Josie sat down and handed over the mail. Edwards did not know how dangerous McDermaid was, if she had a gun, or if she was working with gangster Easy-Love Brown. All he had was instinct, a gut feeling that the three people — Miss Small, Easy and Christine — were somehow linked.

Shouting a warning, Edwards pulled out his handgun and aimed it at her. Christine McDermaid's face was filled with absolute shock and confusion. Edwards and Davidson edged towards her slowly.

"Take your hands away from the table and put them on your head."

Josie was shaking with terror. Edwards yanked Christine from the chair, threw her onto the restaurant floor roughly, where he handcuffed her despite her screams that she was pregnant.

Then he read her her rights.

THE DOORBELL RANG. Slide was eating a slice of a Super Meat Feast Pizza round at Ranger's house in Newall Green, Wythenshawe.

Ranger looked at Slide cautiously. They weren't expecting anybody. Their gang, what was left of it, seemed to have lost direction. Miss Small was dead, Trench was dead, Hatchet was in the burns unit at Withington Hospital, and Michigan was up in court later. They had not seen nor heard from Easy for days. But all that might change now, with the knock on the door. Slide opened the door to find Teeko Martial on the doorstep. Here too, was another long-lost stranger.

"Yo! Can I come in?"

"Wazzup, man. Yu seen Easy?"

Teeko sighed with relief, at least the crew weren't against him like he had feared. Ranger had joined Slide in the passageway.

"That's what I'm here about," Teeko said, pinching his nostrils. "And it ain't good."

Curious, Slide closed Ranger's front door. The place was a tip. Empty beer cans, takeaway cartons, clothes, car magazines, computer games, DVDs. Teeko sat down on the messy settee. Slide waited.

"I need something strong to drink. Got any beer?" Slide got some bottles of Budweiser from the fridge and opened one for Teeko. Passing another to Ranger he kept one for himself. Teeko took two long gulps of the cool beer, then he told them. He told them everything he'd heard while they sat silently listening, uninterrupting. Then Ranger suddenly jumped up.

"Fuckin' loada bullshit! Why would Easy come after you, his own man, believe you was toutin' on him or arrange to have Miss Small killed. Trench got killed in an accident. This is just a trick, innit?"

"Think about it though," Slide said sighing. "Easy was close to Miss Small. Only he woulda known where she was gonna be. He killed his own gang leader, Fluxy. You know Trench didn't like Easy right from the start. And how comes he just happened to be with Trench when Ranks kidnapped him and took them to Cheshire. How comes he escaped?

"Anyway Ranks wasn't there cos he was busy burning down Hatchet's house not unless we got two Ranks, able to be in two places at once."

"Yeaaahhh and that's another thing. If you think I'm gonna work with Ranks to get Easy after he bun out Hatchet you can think again," Ranger drank his beer quickly.

Teeko looked at Slide. Slide exhaled again.

"*I* will. *I'll* work with him."

Slide knew Ranger would respect his decision.

"OK," Ranger said after a long pensive silence. "Where do we meet Ranks?"

"He's right outside." Teeko said.

"THAT'S YOU ISN'T it?" Edwards showed McDermaid the video recording of the news report. "For the benefit of the tape I am showing Miss McDermaid a news film clip containing the account of the death of Mrs. Veniesha Michelle Brooks." McDermaid shrugged her shoulders casually.

"Might be," she said flippantly.

"Is it or isn't it, Christine?" She was playing hard to get, casually smoking a cigarette. Freud believed that anxiety arose when a person's aggressive or sexual drives — which he believed were instinctual — made them behave unacceptably, and that the anxiety acted as a trigger for defensive action to repress or redirect these drives. When the unconscious defensive manoeuvres were unsuccessful, a neurotic anxiety reaction occurred.

Edwards studied McDermaid carefully. Her voice was calm but her body reactions to the questions betrayed her. She passed her hand through her short brunette hair several times. She had waived her rights to a lawyer as Edwards and Davidson questioned her, claiming she had nothing to hide.

"Look at the video Miss McDermaid. At this moment we are obtaining a warrant to search your house for the clothing in that video."

"Yes. It's me. I went to the park with my baby. OK? Is that a crime?" she said quickly through clenched teeth. Her blue eyes flashed angrily.

"No but the murder of a pregnant woman in broad daylight is. What can you tell me about that Christine?"

Christine shrugged her shoulders.

"For benefit of the tape Miss McDermaid has shrugged her shoulders." Christine bit her index finger, started to tap her feet. Then she began to claw at the old self-inflicted scars on her forearms.

"What can you tell me about Easy-Love Brown?"

"Don't know him. Never met him in my life."

"One of your neighbours said that a man fitting Easy-Love's description came and went to your flat on several occasions." Edwards threw that in, hoping to get a result. The result was Christine McDermaid flying into an unexpected violent rage, punching Edwards so hard he fell backwards.

"It was that bitch wasn't it? Fucking Josie? That stupid bitch who brought you lot to me!" She started to spit, snarl and lash out.

Edwards touched his burning nose and was stunned at the blood on his fingers. "I'm gonna kill her. I'm gonna kill the bitch." It took seven police officers to hold her down as she screamed, swore and spat.

And in a way Edwards was glad McDermaid had attacked him. It meant she wouldn't be going anywhere today.

"WHY DID YOU do it, Christine?" This time there was more than one female officer in the room. Christine McDermaid knew she was in deep shit. She had assaulted a senior police officer and incriminating items were found at her house in Hulme. It was late. She sat back, smoking a cigarette desperately and occasionally staring into space. She had no legal representation.

"Do what?"

Edwards resisted the urge to roll his eyes. He exchanged glances with Davidson, who glanced at his watch. Time was running out.

"Why did you kill Mrs. Veniesha Brooks?" Christine pulled a face, as if she had just seen dog dirt on the table.

"I don't know what you're talking about."

"Christine, the hair found in the hat worn by the killer matches your type. DNA results later will confirm it."

She said nothing, smoking hard.

"Did Easy-Love Brown ask you to?" Edwards' bruised nose throbbed painfully.

She still said nothing.

"Veniesha Brooks was four months gone. Did you know that?" Christine remained quiet but stared at Edwards coldly. "You're pregnant aren't you? Don't tell me you have no feelings about killing Easy's unborn child?"

"It wasn't his," she said quickly. Her Irish accent was strong.

"How do you know that?" Christine looked away. "I can't understand why you are protecting him. We know he must know about the raid. We know he must know you're in custody. He knows you're here. For Chrissakes Christine, you're mistaken if you think he cares for you."

"He does. He loves me. I know. He loves me."

"Even after he spent nights with her, lied to you, got her pregnant. Loves you? I don't think so. Easy-Love Brown loves himself and right now — you're the last person on his mind. He's probably planning on doing a runner and you look like you'll be having his baby in jail. For all you and I know Easy-Love Brown could be sunning it up in Jamaica, with a new identity and new woman right now, Christine.

Then later, when things have cooled, he'll sneak back into this country and you know what — you're history."

EDWARDS EXPECTED CHRISTINE McDermaid to fly into that deep dark rage again, but then she looked at him like a little girl lost and he knew that he had broken her. It finally sunk in that maybe she had been used and maybe her so-called man was leaving her well and truly in the shit. Her eyes filled up.

Knowing that her resolve had withered away, he asked again, softly this time, watching the tapes in the machine turn — like the hands of time.

"Why did you kill her?" She was quiet for a few seconds, then sobbed, recovering quickly, knocking ash from her cigarette into an ashtray.

"She was getting in the way of me and Easy. But I didn't kill her."

"How did you find out about her?" Davidson asked. She pulled hard on the cigarette.

"One night when Easy was sleeping his mobile rang. I answered it and it was her. She didn't seem surprised to hear me on the other end of Easy's phone — said she knew all about me." She paused and swallowed. "I told her to stay away from my man and she just laughed. I battered Easy awake and asked him about her. Easy said she was just some fat crank bitch who wouldn't leave him alone. Said she was carrying somebody else's kid and was tryin' to pass it off as his. After that she called all the time. Called my house and laughed all the time, never said anything just laughed. I asked Easy about her again and he told me a bit more about her how she had helped him set himself up again. Told me it was nothing more than a business arrangement. She was only a friend and that she had got the wrong idea about him and her. Anyway, he said he felt sorry for her and had spoke with her about things in her life that were making her unhappy."

"Like what?"

"The fact that she had a son that she had given up as a baby and had never met him since." Edwards found himself sighing. "Easy said he persuaded her to meet with her son and try to re-establish their relationship. She was glad of his advice."

"Veniesha told him where she was meeting the boy?" Edwards interjected. She nodded. "And he told you?" She nodded again.

"Did you ask him, or did he just happen to tell you where she was meeting the boy?" Davidson asked.

She was struggling with her words, her voice breaking with emotion as she sobbed uncontrollably.

"He — was — just — chatting you know. He didn't know I was going to do it. I didn't know myself. I was just angry that she was getting close to my man. Who did she think she was, confiding in him? She was trying to steal him away from me. And she was having the one thing I couldn't and still can't give Easy. A child."

"You mean you're — you're not pregnant?" She shook her head slowly, crying.

"I loved him. I'd do anything for him, cheat, lie, steal. Whatever it takes to keep him. I just wanted to warn her to stay away, frighten her, I didn't shoot her. I just wanted to frighten her. OK. I dressed in the gear. I had a gun but I didn't kill her. I couldn't do it. I dumped the bike, the clothes and picked up Tyrone from a woman in the park who was watching him."

"And you expect us to believe that crock of shit?"

"No. No I don't."

She calmed herself down. "But it's the truth." Edwards wanted to scream at her. He was using you like he used Bow-Bow Watkins, cleverly playing on your insecurity.

"I feel faint," Christine whispered, clearing her throat. "May I have some water please?" Five minutes later one of the female uniforms returned with a glass of water from the canteen. "Thank you." Christine drank the water eagerly.

Edwards turned away for a second.

A second, that's all it took for Christine McDermaid to smash the tumbler against the interview table and thrust the jagged glass into her jugular vein. Blood squirted out of her, covering the female officer nearest to her, sending her into hysterics, Edwards stood shocked. Davidson acted quickly along with the other police officer, trying to stem the copious flow of blood as Christine McDermaid collapsed to the floor. Two minutes later she was writhing as other officers ran into Interview Room Two. Thirty seconds later Christine McDermaid rolled the whites of her eyes while her body jerked viciously. Two seconds later she was dead.

Edwards had thought two police officers were enough to contain her rage.

He had not thought to handcuff her.

He had not thought of her harming herself this way.

Christine McDermaid was lying on the floor of Interview Room Two with her unseeing eyes looking at him.

Dead.

"I'M SUPPOSED TO JUST FORGIVE you, am I? Tell you I was sorry I doubted you and we hug and make up and everything's all right and shit?" Zukie said to Storm. Storm stared at Zukie — all he wanted to do was hold his brother. The three of them were alone. Storm, Blue and Zukie. Zukie turned towards Blue.

"And *you*? You went along with him to keep the truth from me."

"I'm sorry. We just wanted to protect you."

"Fuck protection. I had the right to know what happened and why it happened. You both lied to me. And ya got everyone in on it." Zukie was almost screaming. "No. Storm. Don't expect me to just pack my bags and go back home. Huhhn, that's history. I'm staying with Ranks until I can get a place of my own."

Zukie was shaking.

"OK. But promise me you won't mess with crack."

"That was a stupid one off," Zukie mumbled, embarrassed.

"You don't look so good, Zukie," Blue said.

"I in't hooked if that's what you think. I'm OK." He left Storm staring dismally at Blue. Bluebwai shrugged his shoulders in defeat.

POLICE SURROUNDED THE new private housing complex on New Stretford Road. Entry was forced. Inside they found arms. An Uzi, Mac 11, a pump-action and .38 special. In a kitchen cupboard they found half a ki of what looked like cocaine powder. They also found clothes and documents belonging to a one Barrington Evander Brown which confirmed the link between Easy-Love and Christine McDermaid. Fingerprints around the house also matched those on file for Easy and Chris. It was the breakthrough Edwards had prayed night and day for. But he reserved celebrations until he had Easy back behind bars.

And that, Colin Edwards thought, was surely, only a matter of time.

FROM THE TOP of New Stretford Road Easy-Love could clearly see police activity as he headed home from seeing Kurtis at the Royal Infirmary. The road itself was blocked off by police. Easy had never seen so many beast bwai in his life. There were vans, cars, CID and an Armed Response Unit vehicle. Easy noticed the crowd of people. Gathering. Parking up, he walked towards the crowd, tapping a young black man in the crowd with short dreadlocks sticking out of a red, gold and green tam.

"What a gowan, bro?"

"They raided a house near the park. Fine nuff tings. Drugs, firepower. I hear seh dem arrest the white gyal what live there. Dem a look for one dread."

Easy raised his eyebrows.

"Sure wouldn't like to be him," he said.

"Yeah, life ah go rough fe dem bwai deh, shootin' up de community. Here." He handed Easy a leaflet. Easy was about to stuff it ino his pocket, but the name Storm caught his attention.

Easy read the leaflet.

Storm Productions present,
A Night of Healing,
A Dance of Peace and Love
To be held at the Matrix Club.
Tonight.

"It's a good idea," the Rasta yout' said. "We need to heal the streets. Dat bwai Storm use to be one of dem but now, now he see Jah light."

By the time the dread turned around and looked Easy was gone.

HATCHET COULDN'T BELIEVE it as Slide, Ranger and Teeko gave him the low down. Released from hospital earlier that afternoon, he was recovering from his burns at his brother Michigan's flat, listening in silence and dismay to the story of Easy's betrayal.

Easy had committed the most dangerous sin of all.

You never fucked your own.

And they all knew Easy-Love Brown was going to pay the ultimate price for his betrayal.

The plan was simple.

Retribution.

Which equalled death.

"SO? HOW YOU WANT it?" The young barber asked Easy as he sat down in the chair. Easy looked at the kid through the mirror.

"I want it off. All of it. Face hair too. I wanna look completely different."

"OK," the kid said chirpily. "I bet it's for some gyal or you're hiding from someone."

"You got a wild imagination. No, I'm just a born-again Christian," Easy said. "I'm about to be baptised tomorrow morning. Cut it good and I'll leave you a good tip, ye-ahh?" The kid picked up his scissors eagerly, getting dizzy at the thought of chopping Easy's dreads off and replacing them with a smooth close-to-the-scalp cut.

EASY-LOVE BROWN, rubbing a hand over his new smooth head, parked his car outside Ranger's house. It was on a small private housing estate in Newall Green, Wythenshawe. The night was dark. Slide saw him as he walked towards Ranger's home. Unused to seeing Easy with short hair at first Slide didn't recognise him, but soon realised it was the sly mothafucka, all right. Deep in thought, Easy didn't notice Slide studying him.

"Fuck! He's here. Sportin' some clean-face-hair look, like some choirbwai. Remember, act like nuttin' don't happen." Slide knew that was going to be a damned hard task. The doorbell rang. Slide was the first to get up.

"W'happen?" Slide said. straining to be nice. Easy-Love followed him into Ranger's messy living room. "Yu hair's different."

"Yeah. It's cool innit?

Easy smiled. Then he must have noticed the silence in the room and the fact that the other two were staring at him peculiarly.

"Wassup wid you all? Is it cos I cut my hair? Yu all look like—"

"Nuttin's up with us. We're cool. Want a beer?" Slide uttered quickly.

"No," Easy said bluntly. "We got some tough shit to do tonight. Getting rid of Ranks, Storm. Tonight." Easy sat down and opened the holdall full of guns. He took out a pump-action and snapped it back. Then he looked at the Dodge Crew looking at each other.

"Unuh nuh ready fe action?"

"Where's Teeko?" Slide asked.

"How the fuck should I know? He's his own man, in't he? Wassup with you lot anyway?"

"We heard Storm is working with Ranks and Ranks got man like Colours and Snow-dog guarding him."

Easy frowned.

"What? Colours? That piece of shit."

Slide continued now that he had gained Easy's full attention. They were not bargaining for Easy to be full of guns. This wasn't part of the plan. They couldn't just surround him now. Couldn't ask him to be a nice boy and put the guns away. If Slide had his own way he woulda dussed Easy the minute he saw that traitor fucka walking towards Ranger's door, but Storm had insisted he held off.

"I think we should go for Storm. Wipe out his shop. Then go for Danny."

Easy smiled.

"Yeah — fucking hell. Slide — I like that — you're a fuckin' genius — apart from me that is." He laughed.

Slide laughed and kicked Ranger who laughed too.

Not for one second did Easy think they were laughing at him.

EDWARDS HAD BEEN here before. Driving around Hulme, Moss Side, checking Pubs and clubs, looking for Easy-Love Brown. He had been to Easy's grandmother's address but the house was in darkness. Surveillance reported no visitors at the house in Hulme. Nobody fitting Easy's description had been seen at Manchester or Liverpool airports boarding flights. Davidson was driving them around the area, going from pub to pub. And all the time Edwards was thinking of the horrible way Christine McDermaid took her own life. Edwards' mobile rang. He answered.

"Edwards."

"Detective Colin Edwards?" Edwards frowned.

"Who is this?"

"Am I speaking to Detective Colin Edwards?"

"Who is this?" Edwards frantically motioned Davidson to pull over. Davidson killed the engine and put his ear as near to Edwards' phone as he could. "How did you get my number?"

"A friend of a friend who works at the force." By the tone of his voice Edwards' knew he was talking to another black male. "I understand at the moment you're after someone by the name of Easy-Love Brown?"

"That's true."

"I can deliver him to you."

"Can I have your name and address please?"

The caller laughed ironically.

"Look like you want Easy to dead on the streets."

"No. No. No," said Edwards. Bring him to me. And what do you get from this deal?"

"I get the satisfaction of knowing he's rotting away inside. Killing him would be too easy. He needs to have time to think — and think. I also get to know that certain license applications for two forthcoming clubs will be approved and also zero harassment at those clubs." Edwards knew who he was dealing with now.

"Sure. I promise. When can you deliver him?"

"Soon."

"How soon?"

"A couple of hours. At the most. I'll phone you to tell you where the drop off is."

The caller hung up.

Edwards knew he couldn't phone back.

The number had been withheld.

All he could do now was sit tight.

And wait.

And try to get Christine McDermaid's hollow dead eyes out of his mind.

EASY SENSED A deep uneasiness in his car as they drove down the M56 towards Storm's record shop and studio on Princess Road. He knew the task at hand was going to be relatively straightforward. Slide had told him that Storm did the accounts late on Thursday nights. Easy smiled to himself. Tonight he would take care of Storm, then Danny.

It was raining. No one was talking.

"Stop da fucking car!" Easy bellowed. Ranger pulled over. Easy stared at them all.

"Is someone going to tell me what the fuck is really going on?"

STORM GLANCED AT his watch. They were meant to be here fifteen minutes ago. Colours and Snow-dog were waiting in the back for his signal. Where the hell were they?

"OK. OK." Slide said. "Don't get so edgy, Easy. This is what we didn't want." He stared directly at Easy. Easy stared back.

"Want what? Are you lot fucking me over?"

"What?" Ranger screamed. "Don't ya trust us or sometin' is dat what yu sayin'?" Mentally Slide urged Ranger to calm down before he blew everything. "I mean trust. This is what we're all about in't we? Right?" Easy nodded.

"We found out today Storm and Kadeem mixed up that bad batch and sold it us," Slide said.

Easy took the bait. Remembering Kurtis.

"What?"

Slide started the car.

"We lost a lot of money. I reckon he owes us. Big time. So let's go and clean him out good style."

SLIDE LED THE WAY. Easy and Ranger followed a short distance behind. It felt cold enough to snow.

Taking out his .45 Easy grinned. Slide walked towards the door. Easy, and Ranger leant against the shop window. Slide pressed the buzzer. Through the two-way intercom, Storm could be heard asking who it was.

"I want to book a late night studio session. I know yu in't open, two grand upfront, whah yu seh?"

The door buzzed open.

"He always was a greedy bastard. Wanted the streets for himself and his crew," Easy muttered.

They walked in and Easy aimed the gun at Storm's chest and squeezed the trigger. Storm dropped behind the counter, and stayed down on the floor. Slide and Ranger stared at each other, totally shocked. Clearly, this wasn't what they had planned at all.

"What the fuck yu waitin' for, because of him my brother Kurtis is in a coma, clean the fucka out. Go in the back take all his money."

THE MOBILE RANG. Edwards snatched it up immediately. It was a colleague, DI Janet Wood.

"Colin! We've been trying to get you on the radio." The radio was deliberately turned off. "Chief Super wants to see you about the death in custody."

"I can't. I'm busy right now."

"Colin, he wants to see you right now. He's red hot, delirious. She had IRA connections. You and Davidson just took off like that. You've done it now, going over his head to organise surveillances here there and everywhere. You know no authorisation came from him for you to do this shit. You're in deep Colin, way deep." Edwards didn't answer. "Colin. *Colin*?"

Edwards disconnected the call, avoiding Davidson's wide eyes.

He knew Davidson knew what he wanted.

And he wasn't going to settle for anything less.

KURTIS OPENED HIS eyes. He saw Sharon, smiling, looking down at him. She looked like an angel, like the photographs he had seen of his mother with her long straight brown hair and wearing her favourite red dress. For a few seconds Kurtis was confused, and then his mind cleared. He remembered. He coughed and it hurt.

"Sharon?"

"Don't try to talk, baby. Everything's going to be fine. I'm gonna take care of you and Grandma and everything's going to be fine. I'll help you get off drugs and help to heal your mind. I'll help you Kurtis, but you must let me. Do you want that?"

Kurtis nodded swallowing.

"I love you Kurtis. Grandma loves you. God loves you. Auntie Karina is coming down. We'll take care of you." He saw her crying before he fell into a deep comfortable sleep.

"I DON'T THINK they're just gonna hand him over. Specially after all the shit that's gone down lately," Davidson said irreverently, shaking his blonde head cheerlessly. It was cold in the car, the windows were steamed. They listened absently as the radio on Channel 2 broadcasted the things going down on the streets. A man stabbed through the skull with a screwdriver over an argument at a petrol pump. Dead. A fight between two women at a gym in Chorlton. Edwards said nothing waiting for his mobile to ring.

"I think they'll skin him and deliver a pile of bones to us." Davidson continued negatively, tapping the steering wheel.

ZUKIE LAY ON the bed in Danny's apartment, listening to the pirate radio station relay details of his brother's healing dance. Zukie wasn't sleeping yet he wasn't awake. The smell of cannabis was still in his nostrils. He was somewhere in between there and here, between two worlds. He had dreamt that he had seen Chico, and Chico was waving to him like he was going someplace. Zukie lay on his back thinking, wondering what was going to happen next, where life was going to take him. He had to decide if he really wanted to block out his brother, whether he wanted to move on. Zukie really wanted to forgive Storm but something was preventing him from doing so. All Storm wanted was for him to go to the healing dance but Zukie couldn't.

He wouldn't.

He had tried crack the other night.

What was happening to him and his brother?

Was it time to move on, now he knew what had really happened?

FIGHTING DIZZINESS, STORM'S shaking hand felt the slightly damaged material of his bullet-proof jacket, expecting to find blood. There was none. On the floor of his shop, hidden behind the counter, he heard Easy barking orders. Obviously Easy assumed he was dead. Without waiting for his cue, Colours' huge body burst through from the door from the back, quickly followed by the others. Storm jumped up behind the counter.

It was a beautiful sight. Colours, Juice McKenzie, Snow-dog, and Sizzla all pointing their guns at Easy-Love, completely surrounding him. Easy's surprised face quickly turned into a crease of indignation as he saw Storm smirking at him like the undead. But the counter-ambush was far from over. Ranks bolted through the front door with Teeko, Fila, Pipes and Stukky. Ranks smiled. Easy's face looked stricken. And despite being completely surrounded he still turned to Ranger and Slide for support. Instead he found that they too, were pointing their weapons at him.

Outplayed.

Easy let out a low, rumble of a laugh.

"Yeah — yeah," he said. "You got me."

"No. Not yet. We nuh get yu yet," Storm said sternly. Suddenly Easy turned to run. His actions were in vain, the reaction of a desperate, cornered rat. He was overpowered easily, but he still spat and struggled. They forced him to stand still.

Storm laughed adding sarcastically. "Nice hair cut." Easy reluctantly dropped his weapon, shrugging them off although they still clustered him. He turned towards Danny, winking at Teeko who was scowling at him.

"Small liked it up the ass is that how you like it, eh? Like mother like son. Storm jackin' up ya ass."

"Shut ya fuckin' face!" Danny snarled.

Easy continued. "She hated you, you know, fucking hated yu guts. She woulda killed yu herself if you wasn't from her womb."

"I said shut ya fuckin face before yu eat a bullet!" Ranks was becoming unstable. Agitated.

"Danny, we got plans for him, remember?"

Storm saw Danny swallow and blink slowly, one eye closing before the other. Easy twisted his lips, glaring at Slide and Ranger.

"So, so what now?" he asked rhetorically.

Ranks turned to walk away, then suddenly turned back and delivered a low hard punch to Easy's guts. Easy doubled up, gasping.

Storm grinned. He threw a set of car keys to Colours, enjoying the vision of Easy in pain, trying to look cool but sweating it. Storm lit a cigarette steadily, keeping Easy in suspense.

"You know that ride you took Trench on before you watched him die? Yu going to take a long ride like that. While yu taking that long journey to the end of yu life yu gonna be thinking about Miss Small and Jigsy and, oh yeah, Fluxy. And how yu let me take the rap for killing Fluxy. You nearly cost me my brothers and mother. Payback time, Easy. Payback time." Storm licked his lips and looked at Ranger and Slide. "I guess you two can have the delicious pleasure of binding this bow-cart with rope."

Easy glared at Storm coldly.

"See ya Easy."

"Not before I see you first," Easy said.

Storm laughed.

Easy struggled vainly as they dragged him towards the back of the shop, pausing only to allow Teeko to spit vehemently in his face.

"This ain't fuckin' over!" Easy screamed. "You watch and see!"

EDWARDS' MOBILE RANG, piercing the atmosphere. It was the same caller as before. Davidson put his ear to Edwards' Nokia, and listened as the caller spoke, confirming.

"An hour? Samson Avenue, Boat Lane Estate, Chorlton. No there'll be no police — just me and my colleague." The caller hung up, not before informing Edwards he'd be in touch about his nightclub deals very soon. In his desperation to catch a cunning criminal Edwards was not concerned about the illegitimate method used to detain Easy-Love Brown. He would deal with that and the Chief Super later.

All that mattered to him was that Easy-Love Brown was being delivered to him on a plate.

What more could he ask for?

ZUKIE HEARD THE front door of Ranks' apartment close loudly. He heard noisy, excitable voices. The crew had returned. Ranks walked into his dimly lit bedroom wearily. Without saying a word he virtually collapsed on the bed next to Zukie, throwing his hands over his face, breathing hard and slowly.

"It's over," he said. "Easy's finished. It's finished. Colours is gonna take care of him and this time the fucka ain't gonna mess up nobody's life. Make your peace with your brother and come to the dance wid me and the crew."

Zukie looked uncertainly at Ranks.

Was it over for real?

EASY-LOVE BROWN felt the car lurch from one side to the other as Colours made various twists and turns. He could not believe it had gotten to this. He had been in the car's boot for a long time. Felt like his bladder was bursting. Giddy and sick, hot and sweaty, he prayed for the journey to end. Behind his back his tightly bound hands burned. Easy tried to wriggle his toes but it was useless. His feet were dead. The boot was small and cramped. Easy tried to move his hands, desperately attempting to loosen the rope around his wrists. Suddenly Easy felt something sharp cut into his flesh. He gasped. Easy felt the blood trickle over his hand. Using his fingers, he traced the near edge of a very sharp instrument.

A knife.

"A TOAST. A TOAST to all bad things coming to an end." Storm burst open the bottle of champagne to the roar of cheers and poured its bubbling contents into the glasses on the surrounding tables. Storm raised his glass. Everyone, Small's gang, Ranks Crew, raised their glasses in the private room of the Matrix club. The heavy pounding of music could be clearly heard from the main dance hall where Paradise was to appear on stage shortly

Storm looked at his watch. In ten minutes time Easy would be keeping company with two very keen cops. Yeah, things were definitely looking up now that liberty-taking fucka was gone. And once Easy was inside, Storm intended to instigate plan B.

Storm had friends inside prison.

All of who owed him a favour or two.

And all would hear of Easy's treachery.

COLOURS' STOMACH BEGAN to groan. He saw the delicious West Indian takeaway food trailer parked up on Stretford Road in Hulme. Rocky's. The smell wafted into the car long before he pulled up. So what if he was gonna be another fifteen minutes? His stomach wasn't going to wait and Easy couldn't go anywhere could he? If he had had his way two seconds would have been all it took to get rid of Easy.

Right between the eyes, a bullet straight to the brain, but Storm had insisted on doing it this way.

"Yeah, one piece of breast, rice and yam please, Rocky."

Colours watched with a watery mouth as the hot piping food was served. The piece of breast looked brown and succulent. Eat this, Colours thought, do the deed, join my woman at the Matrix, then go home to a night of long slow lovemaking. Colours poured hot sauce, mustard and brown sauce over his meal. The steam rose high into the cold night. Taking his meal Colours walked leisurely back to the car to eat.

Fifteen minutes later Colours dashed the empty foil tray out the window, started the car's ignition and drove to his destination.

PARADISE SMILED LOVINGLY at Zukie as she sang to a rapturous crowd. Zukie stared back at her wondering how he could ever have contemplated giving up on such a beautiful woman. He was glad he came to Storm's Healing Dance. From now on, he was sure things would change, that's if she wanted him back. Zukie swallowed. The way she was looking at him convinced him that she had no need to reconsider. He was hers. She was his. Eternally. Slowly Zukie found himself walking closer to the stage, until he was inches from her. Paradise bent forward and kissed him. Yeah, Zukie thought, his chest beating hard. Things are going to be cool from this night onwards. Tonight he would heal things between Paradise and himself as well as his brothers.

"BLACK MAN TIME, this, is it?" Edwards asked cynically. "You"re nearly half an hour out." They reached the car as Colours got out, shaking his car keys. There were no introductions. Each person knew who the other was. Nearly five years of torment would be over. This time Easy-Love Brown would go down for a lot longer than five years. Edwards was panic-stricken, as he saw no signs of Easy in the car.

As if reading his mind Colours said flatly, lighting a cigarette.

"Fucka's in he boot! If I had my way he'd be alligator feed," Colours said opening the car's boot. The dismantled lock fell to the floor. All that was in the car boot was a pile of cut rope.

Colours cursed and kicked the car. He spun around helplessly. Edwards took up the rope and looked at it.

There was blood.

The rope had been sliced through.

EVEN AFTER TEN minutes, the pins and needles stayed in his feet, pricking and burning. But he was free. He had gained a weapon, a nine-inch kitchen blade left stupidly in the boot of Colours' car. Easy had accidentally slashed his wrist but pain wasn't important. Easy walked hurriedly along the dark streets, half-jogging. He reached Storm's club quickly. The so-called Healing Dance. What a fuckin' joke!

Easy didn't have a plan. But he prayed for some luck tonight. He heard music, laughter, jokes. Creeping behind some bushes in the main car park that led onto Barnhill Street, Easy saw Storm's flashy Shogun parked next to Danny's Lexus. Easy felt the anger burn in his chest. Then he heard the sweetest sounds he had ever heard in his life. Two voices he recognised. As the conversation became clearer he recognised the voices of Zukie and Ranks.

Ranks was teasing Zukie. Obviously tipsy, they started grappling and play fighting. Easy laughed inwardly, peeping through the bushes. He could hardly believe his luck at stumbling across the two prizes alone. His delight turned to sheer rapture as he realised Ranks was walking away to 'get more drink.' Look like they had some big tings to celebrate, Easy thought resentfully. Zukie lit a cigarette, looking at the sky, smiling happily.

Like a trained guerrilla soldier, Easy sprang from the bushes and in one second he snatched Zukie, pushing the blade at his throat, covering his mouth. Zukie grunted. Easy felt Zukie struggling against him as he dragged him out of the bright car park light towards the bushes.

Easy wanted to do it now, to slit the boy's neck like a butcher decapitating a hen, or slice his face like he did his in Leeds.

But he had to wait.

Had to wait for the other prize.

COLOURS FELT SO low it was like an ache in his balls. It was similar to the feeling he had had the that night he discovered Storm's brothers and friends were in the back of a car he had just shot off the road. Shit! What the hell was he going to tell Storm? How the hell did Easy escape? Colours smoked a quick cigarette before dialling Storm's number.

Storm's phone rang. Then stopped. His voicemail service kicked in. He tried the club office telephone. It rang twice before Juice McKenzie picked it up. There was laughter, and background noise. Urgently he barked for Storm. The casualness in Juice's voice faded quickly.

"Tell him Easy cut loose. Tell him to phone me. I'm on my way."

"STOP FUCKIN' STRUGGLING!" Not wanting to antagonise Easy further Zukie relaxed instantly. Easy heard Ranks approaching, calling Zukie. Through the bushes Easy saw him carrying two beer bottles, with a bandaged hand. Ranks frowned, puzzled by Zukie's unexplained disappearance.

"Call him!" Easy ordered.

"OK," Zukie said angrily. "OK."

DANNY TURNED TOWARDS the sound of Zukie's voice. Turning he saw Zukie standing near some bushes in the car park. Ranks stared at Zukie's face and read fear in his expression. Ranks' heart whopped in his chest.

"Zukie?"

Ranks saw something flash in the light near Zukie's shoulder. Then he saw Easy. Behind Zukie. Ranks inadvertently released the two beer bottles; beer spilled out on the ground as he saw the blade glint menacingly under the light. Ranks' heart continued to pound. His lips were dry.

"Waaaaaazzzzzuppppppp, mothafucka!!!! Déjà fucking vu," Easy bawled out, grinning. "Remember Leeds?" Ranks looked at Easy coldly. Then around him. But there was no one he could shout or call. Thinking Easy was safely incarcerated, security had lapsed. How did this happen? Where was Colours?

"Let him go, Easy. What has he ever done to you? It's me you want, innit? Take me."

"You got a gun?" Ranks nodded mutely, sighing. "Gimme it." Ranks removed the .38 handgun from the small of his back, placing it into Easy's shaking outstretched palm. Easy quickly dropped the knife to the ground. "Car keys? Gimme me 'em!" Ranks saw that Easy was bleeding; spots of blood dotted the ground.

"Let's go." Swallowing, watching Zukie's fearful expression Ranks nodded.

STORM WALKED TOWARDS the toilet. His mobile rang then stopped. Taking it from his pocket he realised his battery power was nil. There wasn't enough power to answer or make any calls. As he walked towards the toilets he met a couple of youth leaders congratulating him on his initiative in instigating a solution to the current gang problem in Manchester. Storm stood talking to them for twenty minutes. Then he made his excuses, leaving to go to the toilet.

"WHERE WE GOING?" Ranks asked. He drove slowly, keeping his eyes on Easy sitting in the back, his arm draped around Zukie loosely as if they were old friends. Easy was digging the nozzle of a loaded Magnum .38 Special into Zukie's ribs. Through the rear-view mirror Ranks saw Easy was in some pain from the cut wrist. Zukie looked abnormally calm. Ranks wondered what was going through his mind.

"Riverside. The Bluestone apartments. Know where that it is?" Ranks nodded quickly. He knew where it was. His apartment wasn't far from there. They arrived in five minutes. Ranks parked, unused to driving, he scraped his car against a parking stump. Easy cursed, handling Zukie roughly, yanking him out of the car. Zukie stumbled, fell on his knees, barely had time to recover before Easy dragged him up. Zukie swore. Ranks wanted to tear Easy apart but knew he had to keep cool. Easy jingled some keys, pulling Zukie towards the entrance. Ranks sighed, breathing hard, following, feeling stupid, angry, ineffectual and helpless. Easy opened the door to the huge semi-empty apartment. Dust. Ranks looked around. Straight across to the large window he saw a clear panoramic view of Salford Quays. Ranks almost gasped. His apartment was only across the way!

Holding the gun on Ranks, Easy ordered him to go into the kitchen and get some rope under the kitchen sink. Ranks did as he was told. Finding the rope quickly Ranks rejoined Easy and Zukie in the living room, all the time thinking. Easy pushed both boys into one of the bedrooms.

"Tie him up," Easy ordered Zukie. "And mek sure you do it tight or else I'll just kill you here and now."

Zukie bound Danny's hands and feet, behind his back, keeping his eyes on Ranks steadily. Down on the wooden floor, Ranks said nothing. Suddenly Easy lifted his foot and started to kick Danny repeatedly in the ribs. The pain was sharp, excruciating but he would not cry out, even though he distinctly heard two pops as ribs snapped. Zukie attempted to intervene but Easy flew at him with the handle of the gun, knocking him backwards violently.

STORM WALKED TOWARDS the office, thinking about calling Colours to check things. He was stopped by Paradise, wearing a beautiful smile on her pretty face. There was noise and people enjoying themselves all around him. Confident people, now the bad element was finally gone. Manchester's best sound system was playing its finest selection of hits.

"Zukie told me to meet him outside twenty minutes ago. But I can't see him anywhere. Is he in the office?" Paradise said.

"Dunno where he is. Look I'm sorry P. I got an important call to make."

"If you see Zukie —"

"Yeah — I'll tell him."

"By the way Juice was looking for you. Said it was urgent."

"OK. Thanks," Storm smiled. Paradise walked away, dragging on a cigarette, searching for Zukie's face. Storm pushed open the office door. Snow-dog jumped up quickly.

"Where the fuck have you been man?" Pulling back slightly Storm looked surprised.

"What?"

"Colours phoned. Easy's cut loose."

"What?"

The four walls of his office seemed to suck him in. Storm's eyes bulged. His ears ached as he heard the words echo in his head.

Colours phoned. Easy's cut loose.

"YOU KNOW WHERE we is?" Easy asked, lighting a spliff, watching Zukie's bruised face. Zukie sat on the wooden floor not far from Easy, watching him hatefully. Easy looked at Ranks. "Guess, rudebwai. Guess who lived here."

Again Ranks shrugged his shoulders. His ribs hurt. Whole body ached. His chest pained with each breath.

"A big fat bitch lived here. She was related to you. What was her name?"

Easy laughed, inhaling the spliff. Danny watched him re-bandage his left wrist.

"You're already dead," Ranks said between deep sharp breaths. Easy laughed again. His mobile phone rang. Easy answered.

"Yeah. Trainer, I know, ten more minutes. I'll be with ya. Just got one last thing to take care of."

Ranks watched as Easy opened a wall cupboard, retrieving a large packed holdall. He then took out some papers, a pile of money and what looked like a passport. "By the time they find you two sad dead bastards, I'll be long gone," he said, waving the passport and tickets at Ranks, spliff dangling in his mouth. "I got some good friends in Jamaica. Some people out there gonna link me up good style."

Easy threw back his head, revealing the nasty scar on his face, and laughed boomingly.

THERE WAS NO sign of Ranks. Nor Zukie. Anywhere. The Worlders and Dodge Crew had searched the whole nightclub. Danny wouldn't have chipped without notifying his crew first. Storm knew something was wrong. Just didn't feel right. Storm simply couldn't comprehend how it could have happened. But screaming at Colours for his negligence wasn't gonna change a damn thing.

Replacing the battery of his mobile phone, Storm dialled Zukie's number. It rang continuously until the answering service kicked in. Storm dialled Ranks' phone. The mobile was switched off.

Outside in the car park they found Danny's Lexus missing. A couple of broken beer bottles, beer on the ground. Storm stood puzzled. He rang Zukie's phone again. This time he became aware of a synchronized sound coming from the bushes. Colours walked towards the shrubbery where he found the ringing mobile and handed it to Storm. It was Zukie's Nokia with its distinctive red, gold and green fascia. As he walked back towards Storm, Colours saw the knife then the blood.

"This is my knife. I must have left it in the boot."

Storm walked over and looked.

Colours stared up at Storm, who was staring at the blood.

"WHERE HAS HE taken my brother?" Storm asked, full of anguish and frustration. He was thinking aloud, not expecting anyone to have any answers. "He can't go home. Cops are looking for him. Where the hell would he go – where?"

"Miss Small's," Teeko suggested. Storm's eyes widened.

"The police won't know about Small's place," Ranger said. "She rented it under a different name."

"Come on," Slide said, agreeing. "I'll take you there. I still have my key." Suddenly Paradise appeared from nowhere.

"I still can't find Zukie," she said. Storm dropped his eyes. He couldn't look at her. But she was quick to pick up. "What's going on? What's everybody doing out here? Where's Zukie?"

Storm sighed.

Paradise stared angrily.

"What the hell is going on?" The two crews piled into three separate vehicles.

He left her screaming at him hysterically as they drove out of the club car park.

EASY-LOVE BROWN reached inside his inner jacket pocket and pulled out a small brown bag. Ranks stared at him coldly.

"This is the stuff Storm and Kadeem had mixed up for me to fuck up my reputation." Ranks sighed loudly, looking at the gun resting casually next to Easy.

"Didn't just fuck up my reputation. It fucked up my brother, Kurtis when he decided to sample it. Remember Kurtis, my kid brother that you used for information and fed crack or coke or whatever shit you could find?"

Ranks stared at Easy icily. If only he could get free, get the gun, out Easy. But as it was Ranks could barely breathe. Easy shook the packet and looked at it.

"What is this shit? Kurtis can't tell me. He's in a coma." Easy picked up the gun and used it to beckon Zukie. "Oi you, prettiness, come here."

Zukie stayed where he was stubbornly, his grey eyes boring into Easy wildly. Easy leapt up, roaring crazily, and pistol-whipped Zukie. Zukie went down, holding his face. Easy grabbed Zukie's feet, swung him around, skilfully avoiding the kicks, and dragged Zukie by his jacket, forcing him into a kneeling position, Easy pointed the gun at his head.

"Snort it. All of it. Snort it now."

Zukie stared at the packet in front of his face. He shook his head. Putting the gun in his waist, Easy positioned himself behind Zukie yanking his head back by his dreads. Trapping Zukie between his legs and body, he took some cocaine from the packet, put it in his palm and pushed it in Zukie's nose, holding it there as Zukie fought and kicked vainly.

Zukie's eyes flicked over. Blood trickled from his nose. His body crumpled to the floor, jerking. Then he lay still.

"See I knew it! Wimpy little fucka can't take hard drugs," Easy announced triumphantly. Ranks swallowed emptily, staring stunned at Zukie lying motionless on the floor. "Where's yu mobile?"

Closing his eyes, Ranks felt Easy probing around roughly until he found Danny's phone inside an inner pocket. Smoking a spliff, he switched it on. "Storm's number's in here, right?" Danny nodded, subdued, watching Zukie lying still on the wooden floor, mentally urging him to get up. But Zukie stayed so still. Ranks closed his eyes tightly, hearing Easy dial Storm on his phone.

"Bling-bling Storm. Guess who?"

STORM HELD HIS mobile to his ear, stunned by the sound of Easy's sneering voice on Ranks' number, talking to him.

"Remember that shit you and Kadeem mixed up and sold me? Seem to have this adverse effect on Zukie. Adverse like dead, yu know what I mean?" Storm allowed himself to swallow as if it could hold down the panic swelling in his gut.

"What the fuck do you mean — ?" Storm heard a click. He tried to redial but Ranks' mobile was switched off. Storm slammed his mobile against the steering wheel.

"He said Zukie's dead!" Storm whispered stiltedly. Colours stared at Storm.

"He's blaggin'," Colours whispered. "I'll drive." Storm changed places with Colours. Bluebwai was holding his stomach. He let out a groan.

Colours put his foot down, listening as Slide directed him towards Miss Small's apartment.

After five minutes, the silence in the Shogun was deafening.

Impenetrable.

COLIN EDWARDS KNEW from his shaky phone conversation with Storm that things had gone drastic. Storm had taken a big risk, broken the sacred taboo by dealing with a cop. Maybe he had made his intentions to the other bad bwoys clear or maybe no one knew he was in league with a cop. Still, Edwards knew Storm warranted respect amongst most of the bad bwai in the ghetto. They would respect his decision but what Edwards knew he had to do now was to stop the situation from turning into massive bloodshed.

As Edwards and Davidson sped towards the direction of Salford Quays, where Storm told him to meet him, Edwards hoped and prayed that the night would not result in any more deaths.

"THERE — THERE'S DANNY'S wheels," Pipes said breathlessly. The car was parked jaggedly, a huge triangular dent in the driver's side. Storm's heart banged in time with the car doors shutting loudly. The lights of Small's top floor apartment could be seen. "He in't stupid he'll be expecting us," Slide advised. The other vehicles parked. Storm was already taking big strides. The crews tumbled out of both vehicles, eagerly running towards the entrance of the flats.

"WELL," EASY SAID, putting on his jacket, looking through the window. "I'd like to stay and enjoy the party but I have to go. Got a plane to catch." He lit a cigarette studying Ranks' scowling face. Easy laughed. "Yeah."

Easy disappeared into the kitchen, rummaging around until he found the large bottle of barbecue lighter fluid Miss Small kept for parties on the large balcony. Returning he looked at Ranks gloatingly, pouring the flammable liquid all over the room, concentrating on soft furnishings. Holding the lighted cigarette threateningly Easy studied Ranks' face for a reaction. "You got a thing about fire in't ya?" Ranks was smiling. Then he started to snigger. What the fuck was funny?

Something suddenly clicked.

The kid wasn't lying on the floor any more.

Zukie was missing.

As Easy swung around his face connected with a chair, which shattered his skull.

Easy saw bright colours.

Easy dropped the lighted cigarette.

A bright light flashed in the room.

ZUKIE SAW AND felt the flames around him. Somewhere he could hear Danny screaming but he couldn't find him. Coughing and smoking, Zukie quickly became disorientated, feeling tired and weak. It was getting dark. Danny was still screaming at him — about cutting the rope, but Zukie's limbs felt so heavy. His head was foggy. The whole room was going completely black. Then suddenly Zukie saw it. The eagle. It flew through the flames, straight at him. The last thing Zukie remembered was a strange lifting sensation. He smiled, feeling warm inside. The eagle was carrying him.

All this time he had been afraid of the eagle when it was his friend.

A SINGLE SHEET. A4 size. Colin Edwards studied the ballistics report on his desk. A bullet fired from a Magnum .38 Special had executed Miss Small. However, the Special found in the raid on Easy's house in Hulme was not the gun used to kill Miss Small. The Special had never been fired. Edwards leaned back in the chair, longing for a cigarette, even though he had given up years before.

The young child who had seen Miss Small's killer had come forward with his mother after all. The person he had seen was dressed in black. The person he had seen was not white but a tall huge fair-skinned black man, who stepped into a waiting car. The description didn't match Easy-Love nor Danny and definitely not Christine McDermaid.

"I couldn't do it. I dumped the bike, the clothes and picked up Tyrone from a woman in the park where I'd left him."

Edwards fidgeted with the piece of paper. The case was inconclusive. Was it possible that as Christine McDermaid rode off away on the mountain bike someone else had stepped in her place and shot Miss Small?

Who was that someone? Why did they shoot her? And were they possibly connected to Easy-Love? More importantly it looked as if that person was still at large.

COMPTON 'TRAINER' MCKINLEY stepped off the plane at Norman Manley airport in Kingston, squinting as the hot Jamaican sun blasted him. After three months in Manchester, England the tall slim Yardie gangster was glad to be back on home turf. His huge shoulders made him look like an American basketball player. Trainer fingered his doctored passport. He knew Anthon wouldn't be pleased with him returning without Easy but at least they had achieved their main mission.

Trainer had waited at Manchester's Ringway Airport for Easy to show and board the plane with him to JA. After a while Trainer figured Easy wasn't going to show. Something must have gone wrong. He knew he had to board the plane without the Manchester bad bwai. But the main thing was Easy had helped them track down Miss Small.

He had helped them to track down the fourteen-year-old who had robbed Anthon's ki of cocaine. Eighteen years it had taken them. They had suffered embarrassment, ruin and scorn at the hands of a fourteen-year-old gyal who seven years later, came back to out Tanga and One Foot Morris. Trainer had taken the flak because he had recommended the girl, his girl, who was expecting his child. Vaneshia's family had been trying for some time to get her to go to England because she was mixing with bad company. Unknown to her family in England, she was seven months pregnant by a seventeen-year-old gangsta from downtown Kingston. She was the opportunity they needed for someone to smuggle to their connection in London. Only she didn't arrive.

It took some convincing, trying to persuade Anthon he had nothing to do with his girlfriend's barefaced raid. Anthon had wanted to shoot him but Trainer persuaded the fiery gang leader he would track her down — no matter how long it took. All the time Trainer had thought Veniesha was nothing but a little country girl he could manipulate at will. She made him look like a fool.

Trainer thought about his kid, wondered where he was. He'd heard she'd had the baby in England. A man-child. He had a boy somewhere, now seventeen. She'd deprived him of that. He wondered what crap she'd told him. He wondered how she managed to run from place to place with a kid. The running was over now. Everything was sweet now. Trainer put on his sunglasses and passed through immigration. Sweet, sweet, sweet.

Anthon would be pleased.

He knew he was.

"SO WHAT'D'YA think?"

"I still don't think you shoulda taken your name out. I mean it's something we both worked hard at."

"It's all yours now. Nothing to do with me." Storm said. Zukie stood outside the revamped shop and read the sign. He laughed.

CHICO LIGHTFINGER RECORDS AND STUDIO.

"It's great." Zukie admitted, turning towards Chico and Hair Oil. But they weren't there. Danny and Slide were next to him. Ranks smiled warmly, touching Zukie's fist lightly. Storm had given Zukie total control of the shop and studio. Danny and Slide, now known as Fabian Nicholson, were Zukie's apprentices. Both had enrolled to do an HND in sound technology at North Trafford College, though Danny needed special help with his reading and writing.

The Palmer brothers had taken over the Worlders Crew. Bluebwai decided to stay in Manchester with Storm and Zukie. Teeko had gone to London to be with Shanieka and the twins. Fila and Pipes were still

selling wraps.
   And Easy?

GRANDMA ALWAYS SAYS, time has a way of catching up on you. For Easy-Love, the old woman's proverb was true. Easy was lying on his back on the hard prison bunk, hands crossed behind his head, looking up at the ceiling …